ENDURANCE

A BRITISH SPORTS ROMANCE NOVEL

AMY DAWS

Published by: Stars Hollow Publishing

ISBN: 978-1-944565-46-6

Editing: Stephanie Rose
Formatting: Champagne Formatting
Cover Design: Amy Daws

Dedicated to my London Lovers Fan Group.
You guys are the Tanner to my Belle.
Thank you for loving my crazy.

The Crazy Ones

TANNER

*T*HIS IS WHAT SHAGGING THE CRAZY ONES GETS ME.

Exhaling heavily, I shift my feet back and forth on the concrete as the cool October night air touches every inch of my body.

"The least she could do is turn the front step lights off," I murmur to myself, hunching over and adjusting my grip. "Kat!" I whisper scream at the closed door. All I'm greeted with is more arguing that's been going on for nearly five minutes now. "Open the bloody door! I'm out here with my fucking cock in my hands for Christ's sake. This is complete shit!"

The screaming stops. My eyes widen and I'm suddenly not so sure I want to see what's on the other side of the door. Maybe standing naked on a London street corner is a better option than facing the raging, fire-breathing dragon that is Kat.

With a high-pitched squeak, the door swings open and I'm met with eyes as dark as night, hair as wild as candy floss, and a lip with a curl that mimics a dog ready to attack.

"What exactly do you think is complete shit, Tanner?" She moves forward, forcing me backwards down the steps.

I look anywhere but her eyes because I'm quite certain they could turn me to stone. "Erm…nothing. I just…wondered if I might…nip

1

in and grab my clothes and then I'll be off."

"You'll be off all right. But if you think you're stepping one fucking foot back inside my flat, you're dead wrong. You called me by my sister's name!"

"Right, but you guys look alike—"

"That was *after* you told me she sucked cock better than me!"

"You misunderstood…" I stammer.

She slams her hands on the frame of the door like she's trying to stop herself from lunging at me. "Did I misunderstand your request for a threesome?"

I'm thankful my beard can hide the terrified quivering of my lips that's not happening because of the cool air. If she senses my fear, I'm a goner.

"I just thought after the mishap it might help to mend some fences. You seemed upset when you realised I'd slept with your sister, so…" My stammering voice trails off as I take in the psychotic look in her eyes.

"Tanner Harris?"

I wince.

"GET STUFFED!" she screams and slams the door in my face.

I deflate as all hope of obtaining my clothes, wallet, and mobile crumbles to the cold ground beneath my bare feet.

"Way to fucking go, Tanner," I mumble, releasing my grip to push my long hair back from my eyes and then returning my hands to cup my shrinking nutty buddies.

This is worse than last week when I had to jump from a second level balcony in West Yorkshire because the Spanish bird I met there didn't tell me she was engaged. How was I to know the Catalan word for fiancé is promès? My dad was not pleased when pictures of me running through a back alley started popping up on Twitter.

At least *she* tossed me my stuff.

It's brass monkeys out here and my boys need protection from the elements. I swerve my head around, looking for some form of shelter when a set of headlights begin to round the corner. I quickly scurry back up the stone steps to hide behind a pillar as I wait for the car to disappear. "How the fuck am I going to get out of this one?"

I spot a red phone box about twenty yards away and wonder if I can make a reverse call from it. Most phone boxes are ornamental these days—an iconic landmark for tourists to take pictures in front of. But it's worth a check considering I don't think either Kat or her sister is going to come to my aide any time soon. Plus, I really can't afford to knock on anybody's door around here. We lost a match at Tower Park today and I could be recognised since I'm near there.

My three brothers and I play professional football. My younger brother, Booker, and I play together for Bethnal Green F.C., which also happens to be the team our dad, Vaughn Harris, manages. So I know with absolute certainty that I'm in green and white country. *Christ, I can even see our stadium from here.*

On top of that, four months ago my twin brother, Camden, put the limelight on all of us even more when his love affair with his surgeon was plastered all over the papers. It was a media nightmare during the time he signed a huge contract with Arsenal. Leave it to Cam to still get the contract offer after a hugely inappropriate snog in a surgical theatre.

With all the recent publicity, the Harris Brothers have become a household name in the UK. My older brother, Gareth, was even asked to be on *Strictly Come Dancing* two weeks ago. So to go door-to-door right now and not have my shit blasted all over the Interweb is highly unlikely. I'm officially in the muck, and I have to figure a way out of this without making another headline or my dad will kill me.

After checking to see if the coast is clear, I jog down the darkened path to the box. I swing open the door, ready to rush inside for warmth, and nearly topple over when I step on something.

A deep, throaty voice croaks from beneath my foot, "Oi! I've got this box claimed so bugger off!"

"Fuck, mate. Sorry. I didn't see you there." I step back, holding the door open with one hand and struggling with my twig and berries in the other.

The scratchy voice resonates from under a mound of blankets. The man looks to be in his sixties, having a scraggly grey beard and big round eyes. He props his elbow on the large canvas bag that he was using as a pillow. His gaze falls to my hand. "Blimey, boy! You're buck naked. Did you know that?" He lumbers up to more of a sitting position and props the door open with his boot, freeing my hand to cover more of myself.

"I'm aware of my clothing status, thank you. I was hoping this box had a phone in it." My teeth begin to chatter from the cold.

"These don't have phones in them anymore. Everybody knows that," he harrumphs.

I purse my lips. "Right, well, as you can see, I'm a bit desperate. Just…forget you saw me." I turn to leave, giving him a proper shot of my arse as I go. *Time to knock on some doors.*

"If you need to make a call, why don't you just ask?"

I pause mid-step and quickly turn on my heel to look back at the man. He's waving a small flip phone in the air at me.

"You have a mobile?" I ask.

He shoots me a lopsided grin. "I may be homeless, but you should never be without a mobile, boy." When he holds it out to me, I note his dirty fingernails and calloused hands. Mine look practically feminine in comparison. Regardless, I grab the mobile and he mumbles, "Here, I'll give you some privacy."

"No, you don't have to get up," I argue, feeling like the biggest prat for uprooting this guy from his…home.

"Do I need to remind you that you're without trousers?" His voice is firm, but I swear I see mirth in his eyes.

I wince and nod, feeling completely emasculated by this homeless man as we switch places. As I close the door behind myself, I note that it smells like our stadium changing room after a horrid and muddy game.

I exhale. *All right, Tanner. Now, who do you call?*

I have a big family. Three brothers, one sister, and a dad who pretty much runs my career. But as the token family screw up, even this is a new sort of low for me. Normally, Camden is my go-to since he's my twin and we live together. Doing things for each other sort of comes with the territory, but he's travelling with his team this week. Since Booker still lives at home with our dad in Chigwell, I know it'd take him at least thirty minutes to get here. And big bro Gareth plays for Man U, so he's at his Manchester flat.

Christ, if I call my sister, Vi, about this, she'll have my balls on a skewer. She's eight months pregnant as it is, so I really can't get her riled up over something like this. Not only would she be raging pissed, but she would be disappointed, and that'd be worse than the humiliation of being cold and naked in public.

I don't know any of my teammates' numbers by heart, so that leaves only one more option. I punch in the last number I can recall.

"Hello?" a female voice answers.

"Who's this?" I ask when it's not the voice I was expecting.

"You called me. Who's this?" the female voice bites back.

A knowing doom creeps over me.

"This is Tanner. Is that you, Ryan?" Definitely not the doctor I was looking for.

"Tanner? Oh, how lovely." Her voice is flat and monotone. "Yes, you guessed right. Well done. Gold star!" Her forced patronising tone is unmistakable and has become quite natural in all of our exchanges.

"Why are you answering Indie's mobile?" I ask, doing nothing to hide the annoyance in my voice.

Indie is whom I was hoping to get a hold of. Indie is kind and good and decent. She also happens to be head over heels in love with Camden, so I know she'd have mercy on me. Her best friend and flatmate, Belle Ryan, on the other hand, will be less inclined to sympathise.

"Indie's in the bath. She told me to watch her mobile and only bring it in if Camden calls," she snaps. "You might share DNA with the man, but you're *nothing* like him."

A leer breaks across my face. "I don't even want to know what you mean by that because, knowing you, it's sure to be an insult."

"Another gold star, Harris."

"All right, can you just go get her," I huff. "It's an emergency."

"What's happened? Did you twist an ankle climbing out some girl's window again? Oh! Did her husband catch you this time and beat you to a bloody pulp like you deserve? Or did you call her by the wrong name while you were balls deep and she threw you through a closed window? Indie's your doctor for football, Tanner, not an STD clinic for whatever sideshow escapades you get into in your personal life."

I bite back a growl and reply, "I'm stuck and I need a ride before someone sees me and calls the paparazzi. It's…an urgent matter." I glance down at my birthday suit and can't help but feel that I've reached a new low with this one.

She huffs. "Give me the address. I'll tell her."

I give her the directions before we hang up without so much as a goodbye. I'm actually surprised she offered to give Indie the message. My relationship with Belle Ryan is difficult at best. In the early days of Cam and Indie getting together, Belle and I did some heavy flirting that I was certain would turn into heavy petting and eventually heavy shagging. The sexual chemistry between us was intense.

But all of that was before my brother decided to fall in love.

A few months ago, Cam and I were at a pub called Old George with Belle and Indie, and just when I was about to seal the deal with the crazy hot Dr. Ryan, I saw Camden dancing with Indie. And it wasn't the kind of dancing I'd seen him do a thousand times before with a thousand other birds at various clubs around London. It was the kind of dancing you feel ashamed to be watching because it was such an incredibly private moment. It was like they were Greek gods atop Mount Olympus and we were all watching from the lowly human plane. I couldn't bring myself to turn away, but what I saw between them made me horribly uncomfortable.

It was love.

My brother—the knicker-dropping, smirking sod that is Camden Bloody Harris—was in love.

A Harris Brother doesn't toss out that emotion freely either. We only have two loves in our lives. Our sister and the gorgeous game of football. Nothing more.

So, Indie Porter becoming a permanent fixture in my brother's life pretty much puts a NO ENTRY sign on Belle Ryan's sausage warmer. I'm a "shag 'em and bag 'em" type, and doing that with her would get my arse kicked by both my brother and Indie. My sister would be there at the end to finish the job.

But, bloody hell, it's not for lack of wanting. Belle Ryan is hot enough to resurrect adolescent wet dreams. She's tall and curvy in all the right places. Her body is the kind of shape that hourglasses are inspired by. As it is, I've never been one for the skinny birds. They just seem too frail. Too weak. Too breakable. Belle, on the other hand, looks like the type that could give it as good as she takes it. She has gorgeous muscled legs that I've fantasised wrapped around my face; a trim waist that accentuates the perfect swells of her arse; and tits that make me want to cry over the fact that I'll likely never see them. I'm a proper boob bloke, too, so it really is a shame because she's sporting a lot more than a handful. Top her off with long, nearly black hair and dark eyes to match, and Belle Ryan is a sexy, crazy-hot mystery that my body begs to uncover.

But I can't uncover her because, as soon as I did, I'd be done and that would hurt Indie. And I never want to hurt Indie. I've become close to her the last couple of months. Since the start of our season, she's been shadowing Bethnal Green F.C.'s team doctor. She used to be a surgeon with Belle at The Royal London Hospital, but after everything erupted in the media over her snog with Cam, she decided to leave there and shift her focus to sports medicine. She's good at it, too. The entire team loves her and not in the perverted way that Camden was worried sick over. He asked me to look after her and make sure the guys treat her with respect. Now I see her like a younger sister, and the aftermath of hurting her best friend is a place I intend to avoid.

So, after mine and Belle's flirty moment at the pub, I flipped the switch on her. I turned off the Harris charm and backed off. Since then, she's been hostile toward me. It's a bit of a nuisance because Indie is constantly with my brother, so Belle and I have been thrust together a lot. And it's not the horizontal thrusting that I excel at. She gives me a look like she wants to use my balls for a rousing game of Yahtzee.

The problem is that her acting like a raging bitch toward me every time we see each other doesn't ward me off of her. It only pours fuel on my fire. I've always liked the crazy ones, something my brothers give me a lot of shit about. It's that fire in their eyes that erupts when you least expect it. The unpredictability. You never fully know how they're going to react. It could be great, or it could be fatal. I guess I have a fetish for that sense of danger. On top of all of that, Belle's a surgeon so she's crazy smart along with all that hot anger.

I'm a striker with a wide open net.

Flesh 2 Sack

Belle

I SHOULD GO TELL INDIE.

    I should go tell Indie.

I should go tell Indie.

Bugger it.

I'd rather torture Tanner Harris.

Plus, Indie's exhausted from the match today. It was a miserable autumn day and she sat out on that pitch the entire time, tending to all those sweaty footballers' whiney needs. It's nearly eleven already; she's off the damn clock. And I'm quite certain Camden wouldn't want her going out at this time of night to help his git of a brother. I may be a tad overprotective, but Indie's my family and she's the one person I try to look out for. Between having her first real boyfriend and all the travelling she's been doing with the Bethnal team, she's a walking zombie these days. I never realised how late she stays up studying at night until she moved in with me a few months ago. I suppose changing professions like she did is what's prompted the extra work.

I've been pretty knackered, too, since I started my fellowship with Dr. Miller at Chelsea and Westminster Hospital. Operating on foetuses in-utero is fucking mind-blowing work. It's intense and

9

terrifying and heavy, but so bloody incredible. Nothing makes you feel closer to God than holding a developing baby's tiny hand while they remain inside the uterus, breathing in amniotic fluid and still attached by the umbilical cord. It's like waffling between two worlds, standing over a border, or going toward the white light. It's an adrenaline rush like no other.

But right now, my best friend is my concern and she has earned some time to herself. Yet somehow, Tanner Bloody Harris seems to find a way to put his needs above everyone else's. Him calling for her help tonight pisses me off. He doesn't deserve her generosity. Indie is wonderful. It's just my luck that she would fall for the twin brother of the one man I loathe with every fibre of my being. Tanner Harris is a knobhead spunk bubble who runs around like a dog with two dicks. And my hatred toward him is not because he's rejected me.

The real reason I detest Tanner Harris is because the minute he turned me down, he started his personal mission to shag the entire city of London, paparazzi be damned. I've lost count of the number of seedy pictures that have popped up in the papers and on social media. All of them include him and a football groupie flavour of the night. A few weeks ago, some paparazzi got a shot of Tanner naked from the waist down inside a limo with two women. Then last week he was running barefoot through Yorkshire, obviously on the run from someone, most likely a husband. He's a bloody pig, and he's turned into a paparazzi's dream come true with as many situations as he has got himself stuck in.

Yet he turned me down as if I was some kind of demotion for him. As if I didn't check all the appropriate boxes for him to shag. Oh, sorry Tanner, I do have a job. Oh, sorry Tanner, I don't need your bleeding money. Oh, sorry Tanner, I don't have a wide-set vagina like the kind of girls you're used to.

Maybe I'm still a bit cross.

But it wasn't like I asked to marry the sod. I wouldn't marry Tanner Harris if he was the last tosser on Earth, especially now that he's been sleeping around like he's got a terminal disease and he's trying to live out his last days permanently buried inside the Republic of Labia. I've got some indication from Indie that Tanner is on pretty thin ice with his dad because of all the horrid publicity he's causing for the team, but he just keeps going. It's ridiculous. I'm all about sowing wild oats, but not publicly. After everything I saw happen with Indie and Camden, I'm staying the hell away from that train wreck. My family and my career would not tolerate a scandal.

However, there's a dark, sick, masochistic part of my soul that wants to know what muck he's found himself in tonight. So for that reason, I grab my keys and the sticky note where I jotted down his instructions and head out. Let's see what kind of floozy he's pissed off tonight. He'll hate that it's me turning up and the thought brings a cheeky smile to my face.

I drive to the street corner he directed me to that's only minutes away from my flat. As I approach, I slow to a crawl in my white Mercedes to get a good look around for where Indie is supposed to be picking him up. He wasn't very specific so I turn in to park. I pull out my mobile to text back the number he called her from when, suddenly, flesh hits the hood of my car. Panic erupts as I worry about what kind of animal I've just ploughed in to or if we're finally being invaded by zombies like I've always suspected. The flesh sack falls off the other end of my hood and pops up again by my passenger side door. All I see are bare abs and a fist that begins rapping on the window like a psychopath.

"What the—" I start and quickly unlock my door.

The flesh sack yanks it open and folds himself inside. "Fucking hell, drive!" he shouts, making no move to cover himself as he swerves his head around to look behind us like a maniac on the run.

I am frozen. Completely gobsmacked as I take in the sight before me. Tanner Harris is sitting on my black leather seat, naked as the day he was born. And as much as I hate his every fibre, I can't help but admire the impressive human in front of me. It's loads of

11

stunningly inked, smooth skin covering mounds and mounds of tight, roped muscle. A half-sleeve decorates one arm and a full sleeve decorates the other. I've caught glimpses of his ink before, but nothing like this. His eight-pack is bunched and rippled as he twists in the seat and crouches down a bit. He looks enormous in my small car. All six foot three of him is evidently too large for my Mercedes A-Class.

My eyes are completely unapologetic as they glance down to his package. *What a package it is.* As far as penises go, it's impressive. For a beardy, long-haired, grizzly sort of fellow, you'd kind of expect the carpet to match the curtains.

It doesn't.

It's neat and tidy down there. Not bald, which I'm happy to see. Men shaving their cocks bald gives me the creeps. It makes me think of prepubescent boy penises and completely kills any attraction I have to them. A man should be as he is meant to be. Manly, hairy, and masculine. The overly groomed fellows flittering around east London these days just don't get my engine revving.

But Tanner's package is like a well-manicured garden, trimmed just enough and wreathing one of the most beautiful penises I've ever laid eyes on. It's not standing at full salute by any means, but you can see some seriously glorious potential. I swear I see it pulse right as—

"Stop staring at my trouser snake and drive!" Tanner shouts as I notice flashes going off from somewhere in the dark behind us.

"Bloody hell," I exclaim, looking over my shoulder for any oncoming traffic. "Tanner, if those are paparazzi and they get a shot of me, I'm fucking dead!"

"You're dead? I'm on strike two! If I get caught, I'm suspended from the team."

I begin pulling out of my parking stall and make my way away from the flashes, feeling a jolt as I gun the accelerator. "I can't believe you've put me in the middle of this."

"Well, I didn't ask *you* to come, did I?" he barks, resting his hand on the back of my seat to look behind us.

My jaw drops at his nervy comment and I flick my hand up to knock his arm away from me. "I'm saving your arse from the looks of it."

"Oh, remind me to send you a fucking thank-you card," he grumbles, looking out the window away from me.

I quickly slam my brakes and he lurches forward, bashing his head on the frame of the door. "You can get out right now!" I screech, the volume making my ears ring. My narrowed eyes go to the rearview mirror and I see the vultures begin running on foot toward us again.

"Ryan!" Tanner exclaims, turning toward me with a shocked expression and rubbing a spot by his eyebrow. "You're fucking nuts. I can't get out. Just drive!"

"No," I say through clenched teeth and narrow my eyes at him while pulling in an ounce of my control. "You don't get to squish around on my brand new leather seat with your filthy bare arse and then give me a tone. That's not how this works."

The flashes are getting closer as traffic whizzes by us with some rude honks. His steely blue eyes meet mine, narrowing to mirror my expression. I don't want to be photographed with him but, more than that, I don't want to be taken advantage of like this.

His voice is deep and authoritative when he replies, "This isn't a fucking joke, Ryan. This is my life we're talking about."

His shoulders rise and fall with intensity that swallows up the little bit of air we have left in the car. I'm breathing heavily, too, because no one gets up my shirt like Tanner Bloody Harris. We're staring at each other, both trying to eye-fuck the other into submission while the paparazzi get closer and closer.

His puckered lips purse with frustration and a dimple forms on his right cheek. "Belle Ryan, will you pretty, pretty please, with sugar and cherries on your tits, help me out right now and fucking drive?"

13

The corner of my mouth wants to lift into a victorious smile, but I hold back and turn my glare toward the road and floor it, leaving the flashing leeches well in our wake.

God, he gets me revved up. Almost as much as my car. Gunning my little Mercedes is quite fun, actually. I so rarely get a chance to drive her like this, mostly because I like to take the Tube just to piss off my father. He thinks the Ryans have an image to uphold and that requires us to have the best of everything. Even though I'm twenty-seven years old, he insists on buying me a new car every year. The last car he took back to the dealer only had four hundred fifty miles on it. The look on his face when he saw that was priceless. I can only imagine his face if he were to see me now. Maybe I'm dismissing a great opportunity by not enjoying the cars he gives me. Zipping around like this is thrilling. I don't think I'd be half bad at driving a getaway car should 007 ever stop me in the middle of the street to chase down a criminal.

Tanner exhales heavily once we've finally got a couple miles down the road. My gaze shifts over to him when he shoves his hands through his long, messy blonde hair that nearly touches his shoulders. He circles his palms around to scratch through his beard a few times, obviously deep in thought, and I have to will myself not to sneak a glimpse at his unit again. It's just sitting there staring at me like a one-eyed monster.

I've been driving around aimlessly for five minutes with no direction from him on where he wants me to drop him off. The longer the silence stretches, the weirder it begins to feel, so I say the first thing that comes to mind. "Whose wife did you screw this time?"

He scowls. "No one's." Discomfort radiates off of him as he drops his hands down to his package now that he has the mind to cover himself.

I roll my eyes and hold the wheel with one hand so I can peel off my black cardigan with the other. I hand it over without looking. I can feel his eyes on me, and I'm praying to God he can't see my nipples pebbling beneath my thin tank.

"No bra?" he asks.

I jerk the wheel just the slightest bit and swing him unexpectedly into the window frame again. His head makes a satisfying crack.

"You should buckle up."

He groans and rubs his head. "You should come with a warning label. Dangerous machinery, proceed with caution."

"Stop looking at my tits and you'll be a hell of a lot safer."

"Says the woman who was eyeing my tube steak like she hadn't eaten in days."

I bark out an incredulous laugh. "That is disgusting, even coming from you. Is that how you get all those footie slags in bed? Smooth words like *tube steak*?"

I glance over and catch his satisfied smirk. "No, they take far less effort than you." He leans closer to me and his voice is husky as he adds, "I bust out the big guns for you."

Biting my lip, I do my best to hide my grin, annoyed that he still has that bloody charm about him. It's not the standard charisma that most blokes spread on thick. It's like a charming Pee-wee Herman… without the kiddie porn charges.

He suddenly takes a sharp breath in and says, "At the risk of bashing this very tender moment we're having, we need to turn around and go back."

"To where?"

"To where you picked me up."

My eyes fly wide and I look over at him. He's situated my cardigan over his package and his face is all scrunched up as if he thinks I'm going to punch him. Or perhaps it's from the two goose eggs he has forming on his head, I can't tell.

"You want to go back? To that madness?" I ask, my jaw slack with disbelief.

He lifts his shoulders. "The paparazzi won't be there anymore and no one seems to be following us."

"Why the hell do we have to go back? I swear to Christ, Tanner, if you tell me it's for some bird, I'm going to send you through the windscreen this time."

"It's not for a girl, I promise. Will you please just do this for me, Ryan?"

I want to cringe at how he addresses me. Ever since he blew me off at Old George, he's refused to call me Belle, or even Dr. Ryan like he so flirtatiously referred to me as when we first met. It's maddening. He addresses me like he addresses a teammate.

He pierces me with wide, probing eyes, clearly desperate for my compliance. It's a look I don't think I've ever seen on him, so I can't help but agree out of sheer curiosity. "This better be good," I grumble and turn the car around to head back to the circus we just fled.

He directs me back down the streets we had just driven and eventually over to a red phone box near the corner.

"Pull right up to it. As close as you can."

Frowning the entire time, I do as he asks. When I stop, he rolls the window down and whisper shouts, "Sedgwick."

We're met with silence, so he increases his volume. "Sedgwick!"

I hear a rustling coming from inside the box before a head pops up from the ground. It's sheathed in a grey stocking cap, but I can only make out the face enough to see a beard. The red door swings open and an old man's head emerges.

"Tanner?"

"Sedg, get in."

"What?" I screech as I suss out that Tanner is offering up my car to a homeless man. "Tanner!"

Tanner turns to me with a pleading look of desperation. "Ryan, please. Just do this for me. Don't ask questions. I'll make it right with you one way or another. Anything you want. You have my word."

"Tanner, this isn't safe!" I look around his shoulder and see the man watching us with a curious expression on his face.

"I'll keep you safe." He reaches out and squeezes my forearm with his hand as an act of reassurance. It's the most serious look I've ever seen on Tanner. It's…disarming. And for some reason unbeknownst to me, I feel myself nodding.

Tanner turns back toward the window. "Sedgewick, hurry up and get in before they come back. Bring your stuff."

"I'd never pass up a tootle in a Mercedes," he says as he grabs his dirty canvas bag and stuffs some belongings into it. He tosses the bag over his shoulder and hustles over with a sneaky sort of walk, like he's committing some sort of crime.

"I'll…erm…open the boot," I mumble, pressing the button on my hatchback. Of all the things I thought I'd be doing tonight, popping the boot on my over-fucking-priced car for a homeless man never made the list.

"Would you look at that. A hatchback!" Sedgwick says as he dumps his bag in and closes the boot. He folds himself in behind Tanner and his eyes go wide as he takes in the lush interior. "This is some ride you have here, miss."

"Her name's Dr. Ryan," Tanner adds.

I'm momentarily shocked by Tanner's label for me, but my thoughts are interrupted by Sedgwick. "Oh! A doctor. What kind?"

Tanner frowns at me as if he just realised he has no idea.

"I'm a surgeon," I reply, turning around to look at Sedgwick.

"What's your specialty?" Sedgwick asks.

I smile at his question. "Well, I was doing emergency medicine before, but I've recently started on neonatal surgery."

"What's that?" Tanner asks, interrupting my focus.

"You operate on tiny babies before they're even born?" Sedgwick's face is full of awe.

My smile widens further. "I do."

17

Sedgwick has kind eyes. They're the kind of eyes that make me think he only sees the good in the world and none of the evil, which seems impossible considering he was sleeping in a phone box just seconds ago.

He shakes his head in amazement and sits back in his seat like he's getting comfortable. "What a night this has turned out to be."

Tanner asks me if I'd mind driving over to Grosvenor Square—a rather posh area in London—and then asks to use my mobile. I still have no clue what's going on, but I don't have a chance to ask because Sedgwick is keeping me busy, chatting about my job and some of the toughest cases I've worked. Tanner remains talking on my mobile the entire time. I assume he must be cancelling credit cards or something because I can't imagine what on earth could be so urgent that he'd leave me to tend to our rather interesting car guest. Regardless, Sedgwick and I come to find a lot in common when he tells me about his time selling medical equipment in the 90s. He actually seems quite knowledgeable about the medical field in general.

After Tanner hangs up, he instructs me through a couple turns. A few minutes later, we pull up to the valet line of the Grosvenor Hotel. A red carpet is stretched out below the warm bulbs of the awning. I'm completely confused as two men wearing formal suits come up to Tanner's window as if they were expecting him. Tanner holds up a finger and then turns around. Sedgwick looks as confused as I do.

"Sedg, I've booked you a room here," he says simply.

Sedgwick's eyes go wide. "Boy! No, I couldn't."

"I know the owner. It's all taken care of already," Tanner replies firmly. "It's nonrefundable."

"You should have asked. This is not the proper way—"

"Sedgwick, you showed me a kindness and I'm showing you one back. That's all this is. Repaying a favour."

"A favour? You only used my mobile. You wouldn't even take clothes from me." Sedgwick looks at me like he needs to argue his case. "I tried to give him some clothes, I really did. He wouldn't take them. Said he was getting what he deserved. I think the boy could do with some therapy, to be frank."

Tanner turns a flat face on me that has me pulling my lips between my teeth to hide my amusement.

"There's an incredible restaurant here. Order room service. Order laundry service. Go shopping in the stores. Put it all on the room bill. I mean it," Tanner says. "Please, Sedg. I want to do this for ya."

"I couldn't possibly." He shakes his head and folds his arms over his chest.

"You could!" I add with a smile and a nod. Sedgwick looks right at me as if he can't believe I'm buying all of this. His brow is furrowed so deeply, it's folding in on top of itself, so I add, "Do it. Tanner's a pain in the arse most days. You should definitely enjoy a night on him."

He harrumphs with a half-smile and eyes Tanner thoughtfully. "I suppose I could enjoy it for a night."

Tanner beams at Sedgwick and then at me. "That's the ticket. Now, I'd walk you in but as you can see, I'm a little skint on clothes."

"No, no, you stay put. I've seen enough of you for one lifetime, boy."

"Off you go then," Tanner says excitedly as I pop the boot for the man standing at the back of my car.

Sedgwick lumbers out of my car. After he closes the door, Tanner rolls down his window. "Oh, and I've booked your room for five nights, not one. I'll come by and visit while you're here."

Sedgwick's face falls and Tanner swats me lightly on the arm, silently telling me to drive away. I almost feel bad as Sedg comes walking out after us to argue. I roll my window down and give him a jovial wave with a double horn toot that elicits a chastising shake of his head.

I stare into my rearview mirror for as long as I can and am happy to see the valet's taking care of him. Tanner stares back longer as I pull out onto the road and head toward east London.

An aching in my stomach begins as I evaluate what just happened. Tanner Harris—the loathsome pig whom I've grown to detest—did something humane. Extraordinarily humane. I would have never in a million years expected that of him.

"Why didn't you take any clothes from him?" I ask, unsure why it's the one thing I have to know after everything that's just happened.

He sighs heavily. "They smelled like piss."

And it's the first time ever that I've laughed with Tanner Harris.

Owe You One

TANNER

"ALL RIGHT, SO WHERE AM I DROPPING YOU?" BELLE ASKS AS WE get closer to Bethnal Green.

Anxiety shivers over my skin. Or maybe it's just the cold air because I've left the window open. I roll it up and look over at Belle, bracing myself. "Look, Ryan, I erm…don't have my flat keys or my mobile."

"Or your clothes," she adds.

"Right, and well, you could run me out to my dad's in Chigwell, but I'm in the shit with him as it is. And on the off-chance that this night doesn't end with me being London's front-page news tomorrow, it'd be really spectacular if you'd maybe…"

"What, Tanner? Find the plot," she snaps.

"Can I stay at yours?" I force a toothy grin, hoping she will remember my moment of nobility with Sedgwick and not the mess I've found myself in.

Her dark eyes narrow and her black lashes are so thick I can only catch a sliver of glossiness through them. It's not easy to stay trained on her eyes right now, though. Her straight, dark hair is hanging down loose over her shoulders, which brings my eyes to her chest. Her black tank top is so thin that with the glow from the

21

dashboard, I can see the outline of her nipples almost perfectly. *Fuck,* I need to stay focused on her face. Focus on that one tiny freckle on the right arch of her lip. The one I noticed at Old George when I was so close to her that I could smell her strawberry lip gloss. That'll keep me busy. That little spot will keep my eyes up. But now I'm thinking about her lips, about kissing her lips, about where her lips could go, what her lips could wrap around, how deep she could take—

Christ, Tanner, stop your line of thinking or you'll get a stiffy under her cardigan. You know she'd never let you live that down.

"Tell me how you ended up like this and you have a deal," she says simply.

I exhale and turn to look out the window. Just when I thought I was making some ground with Belle, I'm about to get properly thrust back into the muck.

"It's probably one of the things you've already mentioned."

"Jilted husband?" she asks.

I shake my head.

"Boyfriend?"

I shake again.

"Fiancé again?"

"Again?" I scowl.

She half smiles. "I saw it on Twitter last week. You were trending with the hashtags 'Harris Hustle' and 'Tanner Tanks Again.'"

I drop my head back against the headrest. Of course I was. Knowing she won't let this go, I answer, "It was her sister."

Belle gasps. "Ew! Like incestuous sisters wanting it at the same time?"

"No!" I exclaim and look away.

"Well, I wouldn't put it past you. I don't think you have much of a standard for the women you pick."

"Like you would know," I scoff.

"Tanner, I'd have to be blind, deaf, and stupid to not know what kind of women you've been dipping your dingle in these past couple months. It's all over social media, the papers, the blogs."

"Oh, and you read all that rubbish?" I grind my teeth together with annoyance. "Don't believe everything you read, all right?"

"I used to read it and enjoy it. It was my guilty pleasure. But you seem to be taking slutty footballer to the next level, sucking all the pleasure out of it for me." She shakes her head and focuses back on the road, leaving me alone with my thoughts.

Silence stretches out and the longer it goes, the heavier the tension gets. I can tell she's mad. Her knuckles are white on the wheel, but it's not like I'm her problem. She's no picnic to tolerate either. Belle Ryan drives me fucking insane. She says whatever she wants, whenever she wants. She doesn't ever even consider holding back or biting her tongue. She's a fucking force of nature so sure about everything, she has no problem destroying anything in her path.

"So what happened then? You still haven't said," she utters.

I sigh heavily. "I was with a girl and her sister came home, and I'd been with her sister, too. I said some stupid things. Things I regret. Things I didn't mean."

"Like what?"

Of course she'd ask.

"Shit that I say when I'm being Tanner Harris, the footballer."

She puzzles over this comment. "What other kind of Tanner Harris is there?"

I clench my jaw in frustration. Of course she wouldn't know. How could she? I've never showed her any other side of me. "Don't worry about it, all right? Just know those crap papers don't know everything."

She pulls into the narrow parking stall in front of her building. I've been to Belle's flat a few times with Cam since Indie lives with her now. This past month, Cam and Indie seem to be making it their personal mission to make Belle and I be friendly with each other. I guess I can understand why. Belle is Indie's best friend. Cam is mine. But every time we're together, we bicker so much that I have to go for a run immediately after I leave her flat or I'd go mad with pent-up aggression.

Belle removes the keys from the ignition, and when I think she's moving to get out of the car, she turns to face me. "Tanner, there's obviously another side to you. A side that you showed with Sedgwick. I just can't, for the life of me, understand why you think hiding behind Tanner the Slutty Footballer is a better choice for your day-to-day life."

I instantly feel angry. I don't appreciate her acting like she knows me. I don't appreciate her acting like she can push me to be a different person. I don't need anyone else pushing me right now. I need to be left the hell alone.

"Ryan," I grind out, leaning over to her side of the car. "Just, don't. Don't try to be the hero in my story. Don't try to mother me, or push me, or see the best in me. I am what you see. I was shoved out of a flat naked because I told the girl I was fucking that her sister sucked cock better than she did."

Her dark eyes turn black with an icy glower. "You are a fucking pig." She throws herself out of the car and storms up the steps to her flat, leaving me alone with only her tiny cardigan to keep me warm.

"Here you go, Tanner," Indie smiles, handing me a pair of joggers through the downstairs bathroom door and awkwardly adjusting her glasses. "I thought Cam had a T-shirt here somewhere, but this is all I can find. Do you want one of mine?"

"This is fine. Cheers, Indie," I murmur as I close the door, reluctant to make eye contact with her when I'm in this state.

I slip into the soft material. It feels good against my balls and shaft. There was a time when walking around naked like Adam and Eve sounded fucking bad arse in my head, but the actual act of doing it is far less thrilling.

I glance at myself in the mirror. I look tired. Being a couple months into the season, I'm usually in bed hours before now. This is not how I treat my body during the season. Normally, my routine is training, team meetings, practicing, eating, sleeping, attending matches. Mix and repeat for months on end. In professional football, we get two months break if we haven't had a great season, but there are usually FA cup games and international friendly matches that keep us busy even in the off-season. Being a footballer is gruelling. Staying out late and partying after matches is not how I've been in past seasons. But without Cam on my team, everything feels different.

A knock on the door snaps me out of my fog. "Tanner, Camden's on the phone."

Speak of the devil. I drop my head to avoid eye contact with Indie as I open the door and take the mobile. "Hiya," I say with a sigh, pressing my back against the door. I don't need an audience for this conversation.

"Broseph, Indie just filled me in. What the fuck?"

"Don't have a go at me, all right? I'm fucking shattered as it is and I don't need to hear it right now, okay?"

"Fine, fine, I won't. But are you…okay?" he asks, his voice worrisome. The concern irritates me because I don't like being fussed over like I'm his child.

"I'm fine," I lie. "Just a dodgy case of *bird* flu." I force a laugh at my lame joke. "You know the kind. Or, erm…you used to."

"Right," Camden replies slowly. "Well, I've called Santino. He said he'd pop over to the bird's flat tomorrow morning by seven with some cash to see if he can get her to sign an NDA and get your stuff back. At least your keys and all that. I just need her address and I'll text it over to him."

Santino is our family lawyer and has been working overtime the last couple of months since I can't seem to stop landing myself in the shit. Without hesitation, I give Cam the address and feel a weight lifted from my shoulders thinking he might be able to get me out of this. Tomorrow I have a strategy meeting with the team at eight in the morning. Then Dad and Booker always come over and go through the footage from the previous match. It'd be nice to have my keys and mobile back before my dad figures things out. I'm just crossing my fingers that he won't try to call me before then. I can just hear Kat answering the call with something sweet like, "Tanner Harris gave me herpes."

"Did they get pictures?" Cam asks.

"I don't know. Maybe?"

He exhales heavily and I swear I feel the compression of my own lungs mirror his. Having a twin can be a nightmare sometimes. There's a connection between us that makes me feel like I'm never truly alone. Plus, the comparisons are endless. It's a huge reason I opted to leave my hair and beard long this season. I've also been adding more ink to my body just to give me a sense of individuality.

I don't consider myself a jealous person, especially when it comes to Cam, who's always there for me. But when he got injured last year, fell in love, and still ended up with the Premiership contract of a lifetime, I couldn't help but think, *What the fuck?*

Cam and I had been co-strikers for Bethnal Green for years. I was right side, he was left. We could sense each other's decisions on the pitch perfectly, often passing without looking because we instinctually knew the other was there. I've seen enough match footage to know that watching the Harris twins playing together was a beautiful thing.

Then he had the season of his life last year, scoring more goals than any player in the Championship and Premier League. It was a sight to behold. Everybody was talking about him, so of course he got a major offer. He'd earned it.

But since he fell for Indie and left our team all at the same time, things have been different. Cam's slot beside me as fellow striker was filled by Roan DeWalt—a South African transfer from Cape Town City—and it isn't the same. We're not in sync. I don't want to be a moaning sap, but I fucking miss my brother. You don't go from sharing a pitch and a flat with someone every day to seeing him briefly once a week, if our match schedules allow it, and not feel some sense of loss.

However, when shit hits the fan for me, he's always the first to call. And he never judges. He never makes me feel worse than I already do. He just…helps. So yeah, the good bits of having a twin far outweigh the bad.

"I'll let Santino know there may be pictures and see if he can do damage control to minimise any exposure," Camden says, using his business voice. I fucking hate his business voice.

"I'm the older brother here, not you."

He scoffs, "You're older by four minutes. I was heavier so that makes me more equipped to do the heavy lifting."

"You were heavier because you hogged all the food. You were a fat arse then and you're a fat arse now."

"Oink, oink, bro. I got this."

I nod. "Thanks for your help," I say simply, knowing anything more will make it awkward.

"What are brothers for?"

"To make it glaringly obvious that I'm the best looking Harris Brother."

"Oh, Tanner, your delusions never cease to amaze me. You better watch your tongue or I'll tell Vi on you."

"You wouldn't dare," I gasp with a genuine smile lightening my mood.

"I'll save it for when I'm there to witness the beating she'll give you."

We hang up and I'm grateful he didn't try to get deep with me about why I screwed up this time. I'm not ready to talk it out. Right now, I'm ready to pass out for as long as real life will permit.

I walk out of the loo and look around to see that I'm all alone. Belle's flat is an expansive two-level loft inside a former factory. One whole wall is completely covered with industrial windows from the first level to the second. It's got a cool, modern feel, but the dark wooden floors give it a rustic vibe. The colour scheme is completely white washed aside from the plastic chairs around her glass-top table. They are each a different solid colour and look like they belong in a nursery school, not at a grownup's dining table. She has an enormous grey sectional that takes up the entire living space with a red, barnwood coffee table centred in the middle. Her kitchen is walled off with a door and a large cutout that overlooks the connected living and dining areas. The only décor to speak of are multicoloured canvases anchored prominently on various walls.

"I see Indie found you some clothes."

I turn to see Belle standing at the base of the large wooden staircase with a blanket and pillow in her hands.

"Better than nothing," I reply with a shrug.

Belle's eyes move down my chest and linger on the trousers for a moment. This is the second time she's looked at me with such brazenness. Completely unapologetic. And I really wish I didn't like it.

When she's finished her perusal, her eyes snap back up to my face and narrow. "Blanket, pillow, sofa." She points to the sectional. "It's all I've got since Indie squats in the guestroom now."

"It's fine." She drops the stuff off on the coffee table and turns to head back upstairs. Before she's gone, I add, "Thanks again for helping me tonight."

She stops halfway and turns, gripping the railing tightly with her black tipped nails. "You owe me one, Harris. A big one." Her voice is back to the same punishing tone she's been using on me for weeks.

My brows lift. "Just say the word and I'm yours."

Her glower morphs into confusion and my nerves shoot up my

back over how that must have sounded.

"I didn't mean…I just meant…" I stammer.

She moves to jog up the rest of the stairs without another look back.

Late Night Obsession

Belle

"**N**IGHT," I CALL OUT TO INDIE AS I PASS HER DOOR AT THE TOP of the staircase and turn left to hurry off to my room.

"Wait!" Indie replies, leaping off her bed and bounding toward the door in all her cuteness. Her curly red hair's in a standard top-knot and she's sporting some fiercely wild zebra-print specs. "I didn't have a chance to say thanks."

I frown. "Whatever for?"

She bites down on the sweet in her mouth and then answers, "For getting Tanner. I could have done it. You didn't have to."

"It was nothing." *Even though Tanner Harris still has my blood boiling.* "It was actually somewhat amusing…at times."

She smiles. "Well, I really appreciate it. You're kind of an epic roommate, you know. Had I known, I would have stopped resisting ages ago."

I laugh at that comment. The only reason Indie finally broke down and moved in with me is because her gig with Bethnal Green doesn't pay very much and she refuses to accept any money from her disgustingly wealthy boyfriend. Camden's contract with Arsenal was monstrous. The papers reported it at one hundred fifty thousand pounds per week. But I'm not about to complain about her morals.

Indie is a genius and doesn't need to be kept by any man. I pay for my flat with my trust fund so it's really no bother.

Plus, I love having her here. We've been friends since the first day we met in med school, and she's as close to what I think a normal family should feel like. In fact, I wish we were family. She'd make a hell of a lot better sibling than my brother who's a barrister just like my father. If she needs somewhere to stay, she belongs with me.

Indie smiles once more and turns to go back into her room, but I shock her with a hardy smack on her arse. "I knew it was only a matter of time before you succumbed to your desperate love for me."

"Oh yes, I am your kept woman and proud of it," she says, wiggling her butt at me as I chortle and turn to walk away.

It takes all of my willpower not to look down over the railing to the lower level where Tanner's lying shirtless on my sofa. His stupid, nappy beard and half naked presence in my home is like a sweet calling me in the night when I'm on one of my ghastly diets.

Maybe just a quick peek.

Bugger, he was looking right at me.

My face heats with annoyance and I storm into my master suite, slamming the door behind me and flopping down onto my bed in utter frustration. I'm typically not one to run away from a fight, but Tanner is one person I do my best to stay far away from.

I stare up at the ceiling fan. It rotates slowly above me and, instead of cooling me down like it's meant to, it only stokes the thoughts of Tanner running wildly through my mind. What he did for Sedgwick tonight was extremely generous. Did he mean what he said about popping over to pay Sedg a visit? I can't envision Tanner Harris having tea with a homeless man. I just can't. I've never seen him do anything charitable before. If he had, I would have read about it somewhere, surely. Did he do it to save face in front of me? No, that can't be it. He hates me, and the feeling is mutual. Perhaps he was just extremely grateful. Perhaps I should remember that when I ask for payback.

I hop out of bed and pop into my attached loo to brush my teeth and get ready for bed. I am in serious need of sleep. Arguing with Tanner is more exhausting than a twelve-hour surgery at the hospital. Thank God I'm not on call tomorrow.

My face heats when I look at myself in the mirror and recall how Tanner looked in those joggers downstairs. Christ, they were riding so low, his V-line was on perfect display for me, pointing to the area I remember with absolute clarity. He probably did that on purpose, the cheeky bastard. But the damage is done. Tanner Harris' cock is burned into the penis vault of my mind, whether I like it or not. Why couldn't it have been crooked? Or bald? Or overflowing with so much pubic hair you couldn't see where his hair ended and his dick started? That seems like the kind of penis he should have been swinging. It enrages me that it had to look better than all the others I've had before.

And I've had plenty.

I'm not a whore, per se. I'm experienced. I'm twenty-seven years old, I'm unattached, I have a stressful job, and I like to have fun. Indie and I have our tradition called Tequila Sunrise that we started when we both first became doctors. It basically involves us going out and partying our arses off, and that level of commitment usually coincides with a good amount of blokes.

Tequila Sunrise began when we got a harsh dose of reality at the hospital one night. We thought life couldn't look any grimmer. It essentially became our version of carpe diem, which is survival to get through the bad days of being a doctor. We make it a priority to take advantage of all sorts of experiences life has to offer. As a result, this is the lifestyle I've chosen for myself: Single, ready to mingle, and happy to have a dingle on a regular and satisfactory basis.

I don't date seriously because I don't have the bloody time. My fellowship with Dr. Miller at Chelsea and Westminster Hospital is gruelling. Dr. Miller is so talented and smart that I'm constantly on my toes, trying to keep my head above water. She's devoted her life to saving babies before they're born, and I want to soak up everything I can while I have her. It's important to me to feel I've made an impact on this world and I can't think of a better way to do so.

As I slip into a pale blue, satin cami with matching shorts, I argue with myself that I'm not wearing these because of the fact that Tanner is here. Rather, I'm wearing them in spite of the fact that Tanner is here. I'm not going to change what I want to wear just because we have an unruly boy in the flat. No indeed.

By the time I snuggle into my bed and allow myself to drift off to sleep, I've forgotten all about the obnoxious man downstairs and am very much feeling completely secure with my place in this world.

But I don't sleep for long because, nearly every single night, I wake up out of nowhere and see three a.m. on my digital clock. My body has developed an annoying internal clock that thinks three a.m. is a great time for a snack. My great Aunt Doris was afflicted with the same syndrome. She used to say, "Oh, honey, I have the same trouble. It's those biscuits. They call to me in the night! Bloody well scream until I get up and eat them."

Except my biscuits come in the form of dark chocolate. I've been snacking in the middle of the night since I was twelve years old. My mother even had me see a sleep specialist to try to break me of the habit. I used to say I never remembered eating the snacks, so the doctor told her that I was sleep eating and not much could be done for it.

But that was a bald-faced lie. I knew exactly what I was doing when I sunk my teeth into the gorgeously bitter chocolate that exploded in my mouth with a riot of sweet, zingy comfort. My late night indulgence is a large reason why I have trouble with my weight. But my indulgence is louder than my vanity so chocolate always wins.

My nighttime snack is not an accident; it's a commitment.

"I deserve it." I say my three little magic words and toss off my duvet. I pad out the door of my bedroom and glance over the railing to see a sleeping Tanner still down on my sofa. The bluish security light from outside illuminates his bare chest enough for me to assess he's breathing heavily. He's just coming off of a match and with all his extracurricular activities last night, he has to be out cold.

I tiptoe down the stairs, doing my best to avoid all the creaky spots when I walk by Tanner's chiselled abs that are mercilessly taunting me. I make it past my dining room table and through the door into the kitchen without a peep. I open the cubby that hides my secret stash of Cadburys and begin nibbling on a dark chocolate bar. It tastes divine. It's smooth and creamy with fruity notes that makes my inner fat girl purr with satisfaction. I've never understood the women who prefer salty snacks like crisps. Get me a lump of chocolate any day and you have me begging like a sex addict in a strip club.

The only thing that could top off this treat is a dash of milk. I open the fridge and am rummaging around for the carton when a voice from behind me says, "Well, hello, hello. Mind if I have a bite?"

I jump straight up and knock my head into something hard and hear a groan of pain. I turn to find Tanner stumbling backwards, holding onto the refrigerator door for balance with one hand and clutching his chin with the other.

"Bollocks, my head," I moan and rub the spot beneath my topknot that whacked into him. "You scared me half to death, you arse!"

I prop myself against the counter next to the fridge, my hand over my chest as I try to slow my heart rate. It's racing partly because I didn't hear him, but mostly because my guilty conscience is waking up more fully and scolding me for sneaking chocolate at three in the morning.

"I just wanted a bit of whatever you're nibbling on," he says innocently while draping his forearm on the open door. The light from inside is blasting straight on him, casting extreme shadows over every single ridge of muscle.

I tear my eyes away from his body and reply through clenched teeth, "Did you have to drape yourself over the top of me to ask? God, you were practically mounting me!"

34

The corner of his mouth twitches. "Well, I was enjoying the view for a while, but then I started to feel a bit pervy staring at your arse hanging out of those tiny shorts. I figured I'd better make my presence known before I took a bite of the wrong treat." He winks.

My jaw drops as my hand moves to my backside. Standing upright, the hem barely reaches the bottom of my arse. *Bloody hell, he had quite the view indeed.*

Before I have a chance to think about what he's just said, his deep voice adds, "Though I will say the front view isn't half bad either."

I suck in a gasp of air as he closes the fridge and moves into my personal space to rest a hand on either side of the counter behind me. In the sudden darkness, my other senses kick into overdrive. He smells a bit like my car and a bit like the musky scent a man gets after a busy day. It's a touch of deodorant, faint remnants of soap, and then just...*man*. I can feel the hardness of my nipples drag along the satiny material of my cami as I take in big gulps of air. The sensation of the fabric makes everything inside of me hum. I'm on Tanner sensory overload, and I feel like a completely different person right now.

"What are you doing?" I ask, my voice raspier than I anticipated in response to Tanner's warm breath hitting the top of my head as he looms over me.

He's tall. I'm five nine and have an undying love for heels, so I'm used to dating men my height. But with both of us barefoot, my gaze barely meets his furry chin. He presses himself flush against me and I nearly moan as I feel the outline of his semi hard cock on my hip. At least I think it's a little hard. If that's Tanner Harris soft, I don't know what to think of how he'd feel if he was completely erect.

I should be pushing him away. I should be disgusted by his body touching mine, especially when Lord only knows what else it's touched in the last twenty-four hours. But in the night like this, I'm a slave to my hormones. And the truth is, there's a little dark place in my body that still aches to know what it would be like to fuck Tanner Harris. Just once.

I hate that part of me. I loathe and despise it. She's an adulterous cunt.

Suddenly, his warm breath in my ear sends a shiver down my neck as he fumbles for something behind me. He pulls back with a foiled chocolate in his hand.

"This will be the perfect starter." His eyebrows tweak lasciviously as he turns to walk away, calling over his shoulder, "You might need to find a new hiding place, Ryan."

Inverted Penis

TANNER

I WAKE THE NEXT MORNING TO INDIE FERVENTLY SHAKING ME.

"Tanner. Tanner, it's Camden on the phone."

"What?" I croak, my voice hoarse as I throw the blanket off of me and begin to sit up.

"It's Cam," she says, stepping back from me. Her cheeks turn pink and she quickly diverts her gaze to the window.

My brows lift as I look down to see I'm sporting a full stiffy beneath my joggers. "Sorry about that. Guess he's a morning person."

Indie shakes her head and blindly reaches back with her mobile in her hand.

"Did my girlfriend just see you pitching a tent?"

"I'm afraid she did, bro. Don't worry about it, though. She's seen worse in the changing room. Those ice baths don't pour themselves."

"Tanner!" Cam roars.

I wince but, despite my better judgement, don't relent. "I hope this doesn't create a complex between you two. You may have been bigger when we were born, but that's because all my muscle went to my cock."

I give myself a lazy but proud laugh at his harsh exhale.

"You're not going to be laughing any longer when you hear what

I'm calling about." My stomach drops and I throw my feet on the floor. "There aren't just pictures, Tanner. There's a whole spread in the paper this morning."

"What do you mean?" I ask. "What could they have to say about me other than stupid hashtags?"

"Belle," he answers.

"What?"

"Belle Ryan. Dr. Ryan. Indie's flatmate and best fucking friend."

"I know who she is. What does she have to do with it?" I snap, tension radiating in my temples. This is way too much stress for seven in the morning.

"They ran her plate. They know who she is."

I'm still not getting the picture.

"Tanner, do you not know who Belle is?"

"What do you mean? I just said I do!" My voice is really high-pitched. Why is my voice so high-pitched?

"I mean, do you not know who her family is?"

"Obviously not. Who the fuck are they? The Royal Family?"

"Bloody close," Camden answers. "Her dad's a Lord and a High Court judge, Tan. He's due to take a seat on the Supreme Court. Her family is a big fucking deal and this isn't the kind of scandal they'll be willing to tolerate."

I stand up and my morning stiffy is practically inverted right now. "Fuck."

"Fuck is right."

"So what's the paper say? Did they see everything?"

"No, it doesn't look like anybody got a shot of you completely naked. You're damn lucky Belle got there when she did. It looks like you might just be shirtless in her car. It still looks bad, though. The paper included shots of all the other women you've been seen with recently, and they are putting Belle into the mix of being just another one of many *casual conquests*, I think they called her."

"Christ," I groan. This isn't fair to her, and with who her father is,

38

I don't know what this will mean. "Does Dad know?"

A long pause.

"Camden, just tell me."

"Yes. Dad knows."

The way he says it so flatly, I know there's something he's not saying. "I'm suspended, aren't I?"

"Tan—"

"Fuck!" I shout and turn to kick the sofa as hard as I can, jamming my big toe in the process. "This is all fucked."

"Tanner, I know, but just calm down. We'll figure this out. You're not the only one to worry about right now. Belle's family is going to go mental. We have to figure out a way to make this better. To make this right. We'll just…"

He continues talking, but I don't hear a word from him anymore when I catch sight of Belle sitting at the bottom of the stairs, mobile clutched firmly in her hand. She's staring out the windows like a mannequin, completely immobile. Suddenly, everything I was worried about for myself has evaporated.

"Cam, I'll call you back," I state and hang up without another word.

I walk over to her. "Ryan, look, I'm so sorr—"

"No, no. Don't speak," she says quickly, her speech on some sort of weird hyper speed as she shakes her head back and forth like she has Tourette's.

I crouch down in front of her. Her dark eyes are glossy with unshed tears. Her hair is sleep tousled and in a messy bun on the side of her head. She's still in her silky pyjamas. The ones that I was thinking about when Indie woke me up this morning. I don't know what that was in her kitchen last night, flirting or something more, but I know it felt fucking fantastic to be pressed up against her. I liked her like that. She was quiet and soft, completely disarmed in the dark. She didn't have the hard shell of contempt that she usually does for me.

I try again. "No really, Ryan, I'll make this right. I have to—"

"Not another word," she snaps and stands up so we're eye-to-eye. "It's not bad enough you have to fuck up your own life, but now you're fucking up mine, too."

"Look, I can fix this. We'll find a way."

"You can't fix anything!" she shrieks. "This is out there already. I'm a 'Tanner Harris Casual Conquest.' It's unfixable. Unless you have a time machine, there's nothing you can do."

"Let me talk to my dad," I say. "We will figure something out."

"I don't need your help," she bites. "You said it yourself last night, Tanner. I did this to myself. I could have sent Indie. I could have called you a cab. I drove over there to get you and now I've exposed myself to the city of London. This is my mess and I'll figure out what to do from here."

"Exposed yourself?" I ask, thinking that's a strange choice of words considering I was the naked one. But I'm silenced again as she turns her mobile screen toward me.

It's a shot of us in her car. She's in a thin tank top, one strap slipped off her shoulder. My hand is on the back of her seat, and the way we're leaning into each other looks like we're about ready to fuck like animals.

She turns and makes her way back up the stairs.

"Belle, please," I beg.

She stops at the top and laughs. "Now you call me Belle. That's so ironic."

I jump as she slams the door to her bedroom, effectively punching me right in the nuts.

Dr. Black Sheep

Belle

SIX MISSED CALLS. SIX MISSED CALLS FROM MY FATHER THAT I'M terrified to answer. My father and I never talk on the phone. Ever. My mother always calls to relay whatever family information I need to be aware of and that's that. I haven't even told them about my new job yet. They wouldn't care. They never care.

The Ryan family comes from a long line of barristers. My grandfather was on the Supreme Court for years, earning the Ryans a courtesy title of Lord Ryan. My father is positioning to take the next open seat, so everything our family does has been calculated and orchestrated my entire life. Everything *I* do is judged, right down to the way I wear my hair to the colour of my shoes at a party.

Then, I had the audacity to become a doctor instead of a barrister like my older brother, and that basically secured my label as the permanent black sheep of the family. It's ridiculous to think a child who chooses to practice medicine instead of law is a lesser person, but my family sees medicine as a service job and beneath our station.

My older brother, Ronald, always did exactly as he was told. He went to the right schools, got the perfect grades, dated girls from appropriate families. He would never admit this but his marriage was practically arranged. I overheard my father talking to his fiancé's

41

father at their engagement party and the whole conversation made me sick.

Growing up, we lived in Kensington in a huge mansion with staff as if we were one position away from The Royal Family. It was ridiculous and I never knew what it was like to be comfortable in my own home. I was also constantly getting picked at by my mother. I was too transparent. I had too many feelings, too many expressions. I did too much sharing. I wasn't to speak until I was spoken to and I never could get the hang of that.

I've always had a voice. I lead my life by my emotions and my opinions. It's served me well in the field of medicine, helping me empathise with my patients and pour my passion into doing good work. I don't know how I could live any other way. That is why I went to med school instead of law school. If there was anything I could do to pull myself away from the cold lifestyle they thrust at me, I was in.

So I received my degree and accepted a job that kept me so busy I couldn't see straight most days. My work schedule was erratic and I was always on call or in the middle of surgery. It was exhausting, but it helped me escape that life because I wasn't able to attend society parties and functions.

Eventually my parents stopped forcing me to attend. They even quit requesting my presence at smaller family functions. They knew I hated it all. And I think part of them was relieved when they realised life could go on without me.

The circle my family runs in is full of political, narcissistic, holier-than-thou, rich arseholes. And up until now, I was all but forgotten. But, to my family, me being photographed semi-naked with a footballer who has a publicly loose reputation will be as devastating as the divorce of Prince Charles and Princess Diana.

In two words, I'm fucked.

A Family Affair Part One

TANNER

BOOKER PICKS ME UP FROM BELLE AND INDIE'S FLAT THIRTY minutes later. Belle never came out of her room again. I looked to Indie for clues as to what I should do, but she didn't have the faintest idea. She just silently handed me sherbet lemons to tamper my rage.

"You all right?" Booker asks, tossing me a bag as I slide into the truck that used to be mine but has since been commandeered by Booker. The parking situation at mine and Camden's flat is horrid, and since we're both on the road so much and Tower Park is so close to our place, I let Booker use it.

I open the bag and feel immediate relief when I see my keys, wallet, mobile, shoes, and clothes. Santino deserves a blow job for this one.

I throw my shirt on over my head and pull my trainers out of the bag. "I'm just peachy, Book. How are you?"

He exhales heavily, scratching his mop of dark hair like he's developed a nervous tick. "I'm all right. I'm sure I don't have to tell you that Dad's on the warpath."

I purse my lips together. "I figured."

"What the fuck, Tanner?" Booker's eyes pierce me from the driver's seat.

"What the fuck, Book?"

"This is fucked, even for you."

"I don't need to hear it, all right?"

"Well, someone needs to tell you. After the mess in Yorkshire, I thought you'd cool it. You've been having a shitty season as it is, so I don't even feel bad that you're suspended. You need to figure your shit out. You're so much better than this."

"Look, baby bro, don't come at me like you can impart some great wisdom at the ripe old age of twenty-four. You don't know what I'm going through."

"I lost Cam as a teammate, too. You weren't the only one!" he snaps back. "Now I'm losing you on top of it. This is complete crap and I'm sick of it. This isn't how our family functions."

"I'm sick of you," I retort immaturely. "Where are we going?" I ask as he passes the turn for Tower Park. "The stadium is that way."

Booker's jaw muscle ticks.

"Booker?" I urge again.

He remains silent so I wallop him on the shoulder.

"Fuck! We're going to Vi's, all right?"

My heart drops. "No. No, no, no! Not Vi's. Whose idea was it? Dad's?"

"It was Vi's. She said she wouldn't let me hold the baby when it's born if I didn't bring you there."

Booker has always been wrapped around our sister's finger. Not that we all aren't to an extent, but the two of them have a bond that's different than the rest of us. I think since he's the youngest, Vi's favoured him all these years and has been softer on him, more gentle. But that softness didn't affect his game. As the goal keeper for Bethnal Green, Booker is one of the smartest and bravest players on the pitch. You have to have balls of steel as the keeper. He needs to know everyone's role on the pitch and have complete confidence when he's stuck between those posts. His mental strength has always impressed me. The older he gets and the better he gets, the less he seems like the baby. Not that he looks like the baby anymore as it is. He's nearly the same height as me and I swear every time I see him, he's gained more weight. He trains harder than anyone on the team. I think the reason he hasn't moved out of Dad's house is because it is a great place to train and focus on nothing but football.

Bloody hell, what if Dad makes me move home?

"I think it's for your own protection." Booker's words release me from my panic. "She knows Dad won't skin you alive if she's there. He'd be too worried about sending her into early labour."

I nod, nervously chewing on my lower lip. I think I'd rather have Dad skin me than see Vi's look of disappointment.

"You've got to come up with a plan, Tanner," Booker adds. "You need to figure a way out of this. Make it go away."

"How? It's already out there for the bloody world to see!"

"Well, change how it looks. Make it not look so bad…Make up a story or something, I don't know."

I crouch over and rake my hand through my hair, catching it in all the tangles. Having my dad as my team manager sucks in this kind of scenario, but I know he'd give any other player the boot, too. It's just harder to take when it comes from your dad. *Fuck me, I feel like I've been through hell and back, and I haven't even seen the worst of it yet.*

Thinking of my own personal hell, a flash of inspiration strikes and I pull my mobile out of the bag only to see that it's dead. I'm hoping that's not a bad omen, so I ask Booker for his instead. "You have Santino's number saved?"

"Yeah, why?"

"I need to talk to him before he talks to Dad. I think I have an idea."

Having five children in a family, there's always some sort of argument someone is having with someone else. When Cam was single, we constantly squabbled over women. He'd try to nick the girls I was putting time in with at the clubs just because he could. Or he thought he could. So, a while back, we declared the Bacon Sandwich Rule.

As kids, Vi used to make us the best food. Swedish pancakes were her specialty, but there really wasn't a bad meal she cooked. As a result, my brothers and I—being the disgusting animals we were—used to lick the food to call dibs on it so no one else would eat it. I wouldn't even be hungry and I'd lick the shepherd's pie so none of my brothers could have it.

I'm not proud.

Eventually, we applied the Bacon Sandwich Rule to women. If I licked her first, she was mine. Again, no pride. Vi found out about our rule a year ago and was livid. She called us womanising whores with no morals and made us feel guilty because she thought she'd raised us better than that. She's only a year older than Cam and me, but she's always seemed decades more mature. She pretty much had to be the grownup after our mum passed away. So right now, I feel like a guilty child on my way to Mum's room to face the music and receive my punishment. Our little bacon sandwich quarrel seems trivial compared to this situation. This is like the worst walk of shame times a billion.

Vi's place is essentially the Harris High Court. It's where Camden and I always go to settle our arguments. She gives us a knock on our heads for a dose of reality. Then we have to accept the hand she deals and leave it all there when we leave.

So my goal right now, as I ride the eleven levels up to her penthouse flat, is to have a plan that will instantly calm her nerves and take away all the anxiety she's probably currently suffering.

She's got my niece in her after all.

When the lift doors open into Vi and Hayden's flat, Booker and I are greeted by the crotch-sniffing pervert that is Bruce. Bruce is an enormous Saint Bernard that Vi inherited from a neighbour a couple of years ago. He was our little insurance policy that she was safe when she moved out of Dad's house and into a flat all on her own. Now that she's engaged to Hayden, I'm far less worried about her.

"Hey, Tanner," Hayden says, striding over to the lift with Bruce's leash in hand. "Booker."

Hayden looks at me like I'm walking down death row.

"Is she raging?"

"Oh, she's raging, all right," he replies with a smirk playing on his lips. "But I think I calmed her down for you. She's out on the terrace with your dad and Santino."

"Bugger," I say with an exhale. "I was hoping we beat Dad here."

Hayden gives me a sympathetic smile and hooks the lead on Bruce to take him for a walk. I'd do anything to be that dog and go with him right now so that the only thing on my mind was sniffing butts and chasing birds.

Not all that dissimilar to my life now.

Knowing I need to face the music, I make my way out to the terrace. Vi is stretched out comfortably on one of the loungers, her hands on her pregnant belly while Dad and Santino stand near her, talking quietly.

"Tanner," Santino says with a jovial tone that does not fit the mood. "Good to see you, mate."

"We saw more than we ever needed to in those pictures," Dad adds. I eye him for a minute, trying to get a read on how angry he is. His normally broad, muscular frame seems hunched and curled in.

I lean over, dropping a kiss on Vi's head. "Hiya, Vi."

"Hey, whore."

I drop down in the lounger next to her. "I'm sorry."

She smiles, her blue eyes still holding some form of kindness toward me. "I know you are."

Booker maintains a safe distance at the doorway as Dad's voice booms next.

"You're always sorry, Tanner, but what are we going to do about it? You have a four-week suspension that I have to enforce or it will look like I'm playing favouritism." He rubs the top of his grey-haired head aggressively, pacing back and forth before continuing, "Four weeks! Your game has been off all season. You and DeWalt can't find a bloody rhythm and now this. You're the team captain for Christ's sake. You cannot afford this kind of a break, but here we are."

"Dad," Vi warns, throwing around her protective blonde-haired, blue-eyed power like a bad arse.

"I'm not shouting, am I?" he defends, the veins on his temples betraying him.

"No, but you're getting close." She squints up at him even though the London sky is completely overcast, mirroring my mood.

"Santino, did you talk to him yet?" I ask, looking at him hopefully.

"No," he replies, buttoning his blue waistcoat. "I was waiting for you."

Santino is part Italian and is a thirty-something, hotshot lawyer that's on retainer for Bethnal Green F.C. He's cool as hell and has even taken us all out for drinks on occasion just so we can help him score women. I think he's the only one who sympathises with my situation.

"Tanner called me on his way over. He thinks he has an idea to help shift the media's view on what they think they saw last night."

My dad shifts his focus from Santino to me.

I swallow hard, suddenly terrified that my idea will get me laughed at. "Well, the press are all over this story because they believe Dr. Ryan to be just another fling of mine, like all my other... indiscretions...have been. But what if she wasn't?"

"What do you mean?" Vi asks.

"What if Belle and I were dating?"

Vi's eyes fly wide with excitement. "You two are dating? Tanner, that's fantastic! Belle is perfect for you. She's sharp, she's funny, she's friends with Indie. It couldn't be more lovely—"

"No, Vi, we're not really dating. I'm saying, what if we date for sake of the media? What if I take my suspension and show the media that she isn't some fly-by-night woman? That I genuinely care about her. I'll be on my best behaviour to help her family save face, too, so it doesn't look like a casual hook up. It looks like two young people falling in...love." The words feel all wrong coming out of my mouth, but they all seem to be gobbling them up.

"Do you think the Ryans would go for it?" My dad directs his question at Santino.

"They already said yes." This shocks me. "They said if we can do a spread in a big magazine similar to what Arsenal lined up for Cam and Indie, they would agree to the terms."

"Wait a second," I argue, rising up from the lounger. "An interview? I never said anything about an interview."

Santino puts a hand on my shoulder. "Tanner, it'll be fine. We can rig it all, even the reporter. Just leave that to me, mate."

"Belle agreed to all of this?" I ask, still in shock that they are actually taking my plan seriously. Belle wouldn't even come out of her room for me before I left. I can't believe she's all for fake dating me in public now.

"Her family said she will so long as we all sign NDAs and it doesn't go outside the family," Santino answers casually. "The team can't find out this is all a ruse."

"No shit!" my dad snaps.

I groan realising this half-cracked idea I had might actually come to fruition. "Can I talk to Belle first? Before they strong-arm her into doing something she potentially doesn't want to do?"

"Tanner, I don't think we're in the position for her to say no. The team needs this to survive this scandal."

I frown at my dad's words, but I'm not surprised. The team saved his life. He was a shell of a man after my mum passed. It wasn't until he let football back into his life that he became halfway functional again. He's always putting Bethnal first.

"Just let me try to talk to her first. I think I can convince her without making her feel like she's being forced into prostitution."

"You've already done quite enough." My dad strides past me, making his way back inside. He looks over his shoulder and adds, "Just let Santino work out the particulars. I'll see you at Sunday dinner."

Without another word, he leaves me outside standing by the ledge, feeling a whole lot more exposed than I did naked on a street corner last night. I'm suspended from football for a month and I have to fake date Belle Ryan—the one woman I swore I'd stay away from. *What the hell was I thinking?*

A Family Affair Part Two

Belle

"**T**HIS IS FUCKING HORSESHIT! CRAPPY, SMELLY, RIDICULOUS, foul horseshit!" I scream, standing in the middle of my living room and looking out the window all the while feeling my father's glacial stare on my back.

"Nice to see your language has improved exponentially since the last time we spoke."

I turn around and stare Lord Jonathan Ryan right in the eyes, regretting the second I opened my door to him. Once upon a time, I couldn't make eye contact with my father. I'd cower in his presence. But once upon a time, I also cared what he thought of me. That is no longer the case.

He stands before me in all his pretentious glory, wearing a custom-cut, three-piece black suit and Gucci loafers that cost every bit of two thousand pounds. He's a tall, slender man with deep wrinkles from years of working long hours for his own firm before moving up to the High Court. His grey hair is short and trim from his weekly cut that he gets every Monday morning, and he still has that annoying habit of fiddling with his Cartier watch when he speaks.

"Well, I can't believe that you actually think me dating a slutty footballer *publicly* is going to improve your image. This makes absolutely no sense!"

He peers down his nose at me. "It makes more sense than you being photographed as a common whore."

I bark out a laugh. "Oh my God, you sound medieval. This is ridiculous. I won't do it." I cross my arms over my chest with determination.

"You will, Belle," he thunders. "This isn't up for discussion."

My jaw drops from the nerve of him thinking he can come in here and tell me what to do. I speak slowly this time. "Father, I am an adult. I am a doctor for Christ's sake! I no longer live in your world. I no longer attend your functions. I'm not in London Society anymore. I've disappeared just like you all wanted. I don't see how you think you can come in here and dictate what I do."

"Belle Ryan," he roars, his beady eyes twitching with the volume. "You are still a member of the Ryan family, and you will do what you must to ensure that I don't lose my spot on the Court. I know you only care about yourself, but this is much, much bigger than you and your petty needs. We haven't asked anything of you for many years, but this is what must be done. End of discussion."

He turns on his heel and marches out of my flat without a glance back over his shoulder. Of course he wouldn't look back. Looking back would show a sign of weakness. Looking back would mean he cares how I feel. It's then that I realise I'm heaving huge gulps of air. I glance up and spot Indie sitting at the top of the stairs with a terrified look in her eyes.

"Can you fucking believe him?" I exclaim. "He's outrageous!"

Her face contorts in sympathy as she stands and rushes down the steps toward me.

"That's not how you speak to another adult." I begin pacing in front of the window, my mind racing with the weight of years of resentment pushing down on my shoulders. "He can't snap orders at me as if I'm his property or his subordinate. Fuck! I can't stand him!"

Indie perches on the edge of the sofa, clutching a pillow to her chest and nodding silently in solidarity.

"Publicly date Tanner Harris?" A barking, angry sort of laugh explodes from a weird place in my belly. "This is the most preposterous thing I've ever heard of."

"It is." Indie's nodding her head up and down in complete agreement.

"Right! It completely is. Fake date Tanner? He's a pig. An animal. He needs to be caged up and vaccinated. Plus, I don't care about my family or about him, so why the hell would I do anything for any of them? I won't! I refuse."

"You should refuse," Indie adds.

"Exactly! I do great things, Indie! I save babies." I ball my hands into fists and curse the heavens for this madness. How is this real life? How do I do what I do all day long at work and come home to shit like this? "And then he throws the Supreme Court in my face and makes me feel small and inconsequential. For fuck's sake. Just last week I helped repair a blockage in the aortic valve of a twenty-four-week foetus. Why does that mean nothing to them?"

"It's sad."

"It is sad." I want to cry. But I won't. I refuse to do that as well. My family doesn't deserve my tears. I swallow down the sadness and turn it into anger. "This is all Tanner's fault."

"It is. It totally is…"

I look at her, suddenly feeling like she's been placating me this entire time. "Why do I think I hear a *but* coming?"

She cringes and reluctantly replies, "Well, would it be the worst thing in the world for you to do this, Belle? I mean, I'm in love with Tanner's brother. I love Tanner by association. He's a pig and he's horrid, but he's not the worst bloke you'd ever come across, despite what I know you believe."

"You've seen how he's been behaving recently, Indie. Don't tell me you turn a blind eye to it."

"All I see is a man trying to find his way without his brother by his side anymore."

"Oh stop," I groan. "He's not a child."

"No, listen. Camden and Tanner are twins. Their connection is strong. They shared a womb. They grew up together and now live together. They played football together up until very recently. He's just adjusting."

"Shagging half of London is how he adjusts to spending less time with his brother?"

She exhales. "The Harrises are a different type of family. They are very close. Codependent almost. You and I didn't grow up that way. Every day that I'm with Camden, I learn more and more how reliant he is on his family. Bloody hell, he can hardly wipe his arse without letting one of his siblings know."

My lip curls. "Gross."

"Very. But besides all of that, what about your contract at the hospital? This could be an issue for them. You haven't been there long and you said you've been struggling to keep up with Dr. Miller. What if they catch wind of this? You need good press as much as Tanner and your parents do."

"I hate you," I moan and drop down onto the sofa beside her, hunched over and pathetic. She's being reasonable. I hate reasonable. "I'd like to punch you, but your bloody face looks like an angel and I'm afraid it would secure my seat in hell."

She laughs and shuffles closer to me. "I'm going to say another thing that will make you want to punch me."

"What?" I side-eye the shit out of her.

"Doing this fake dating thing with Tanner seems like a very Tequila Sunrise sort of opportunity."

My jaw drops as I flop back to rest my head on the sofa. "Don't throw Tequila Sunrise in my face, Indie. That's our thing. Yours and mine. I thought it was sacred."

"It is sacred!" she exclaims and tucks up beside me, resting her head on my shoulder. "It was only a few months ago that you pushed me into Camden's arms claiming Tequila Sunrise propaganda. Remember?"

"And you screwed up everything by falling in love with him," I mumble, missing the friendship we had when we were both single. I'm happy for Indie. I am. But I can slightly sympathise with what Tanner the Slut is going through.

Indie smiles and I can practically feel the twinkle in her eyes. God, she's so damn happy all the time.

"I'm not telling you to fall in love with him. I'm just telling you to play the part, have some fun, and keep your bloody job."

I groan in submission, annoyed that I'm going to be helping my family and Testicle Tanner get ahead. I liked living in the dark and openly hating everyone so much better.

"And you know what else I think you should do?" Indie sits up and looks at me with a conspiratorial slant to her gaze. "Figure out a way to mess with Tanner until his balls feel like they're going to shrivel up and die."

My brows lift at my scarily vindictive friend, but it's not a bad idea. If I'm being forced to date London's sluttiest footballer—a man I loathe—then I'm going to make it my mission in life to torture him while I do.

Deep Talk

TANNER

I WANTED TO GO STRAIGHT BACK TO BELLE'S FLAT AFTER WE finished up at Vi's, but Indie said she was working and Santino said she had already discussed everything with her father. Dread washed over me at that realisation. Belle already hates me for reasons I probably deserve, but being forced to be seen with me for the next month…Now she'll want me dead, and it sounds like her family is the type to know exactly where to hide a body.

All because she tried to help me out. *God, I'm such a prat.*

So, instead of trying to smooth things over with Belle, I was forced to have brunch with Santino and brainstorm some of the events we can attend together. *Fucking brunch.* It's such a girl-ie-sounding meal but, bloody hell, it was the only decent thing that's happened to me in days.

While I ate and listened to Santino go on and on about how I should behave with her in public, I kept thinking about the fact that I wasn't at the team meeting with Dad and Booker. It was the first time I realised how different my day-to-day life will be for the next month while I'm suspended. It's going to be even more unusual since I'm required to have some semblance of a girlfriend the entire time.

I've never had a girlfriend in my life. Truthfully, the only woman

I've ever really cared for is my sister. Camden and I were three when our mum died from cancer, so Vi practically raised us. The only real memory I have of our mum is her lying in bed a lot. But Vi did everything she could to replace that loss, and I've put her on a pedestal for it. She's kind, compassionate, strong, and has an uncanny way of helping us find our own answers. No other woman I've ever met comes close to Vi's greatness.

Therefore, rather than having a girlfriend, I use women to fulfil my needs, content to live life as a bachelor. There's never been a woman whom I've wanted for more than one night, and I don't see that changing with Belle Ryan. I'll just have to find a way to make the most of our situation.

Santino drops me at my flat and says he'll email me the list of the sightings and events after he works out the particulars with the Ryan family.

I'm grateful Camden isn't back from his match in Liverpool yet because I can't stomach facing anymore disappointing looks today. Plus, I have to get ready to fulfil my first marching order.

I'm to take Belle out tonight so that last night doesn't look like a one-night stand. Santino secured us a reservation at The Barbary in Neal's Yard, Covent Garden and said there will be plenty of paparazzi there to get a photo of us together.

Together.

I've spent the last few months running from commitment, from women, and from the paparazzi. Now I'm dating a girl who hates me and am begging to have my picture taken with her. If I make it through all of this with my balls still intact, I'll be shocked.

I arrive at Belle and Indie's flat by seven like Santino instructed. I'll need to actually get Belle's mobile number if we're going to make this a regular thing for the next few weeks. But for now, I'm just grateful she agreed at all.

Indie answers the door all bright-eyed and bushy-tailed wearing a pair of teal glasses. "Tanner! Hey! I was hoping you were Cam. He's going to be here any minute."

"He's back already? He wasn't at our flat."

She looks down, red colouring her cheeks. "Yeah, he said he'd come straight here from the airport because he didn't want to miss you and Belle erm…heading out."

I roll my eyes. Of course my brother wants a front row seat for the show. The bastard. He's probably enjoying this spectacle.

"I think it's sweet," Indie stammers like she has to defend their actions. "You and Belle will have fun, I just know it."

Inhaling deeply, I reply, "I'm just looking forward to this all being over."

"Guess who brought their camera!" Cam's voice makes me jump as he emerges behind me and throws a matey arm over my shoulders. His tone goes up an octave as he speaks like a doting mummy. "Our little boy is going on his first date!"

"Cam!" Indie peals, ignoring his jabs at me and leaping into his free arm.

"I missed you, Specs." He moans his pet name to her and, by the looks of their embrace, you'd think he's returned home from war, not a few days away for a match.

In seconds, she's cupping his face and her lips are on his. I stare in horror as his free hand moves down to grab her arse. He's still holding onto me by the shoulders, reflexively tightening his grip ever so slightly.

"Unless this is a subtle way of asking me to join you for a threesome, maybe you can let me go before you start tongue raping your girlfriend," I groan, sliding out from under his heavy arm and shaking off the disgust coursing through my body over that peculiar encounter.

"I thought threesomes were right up your alley."

I look over to see Belle standing at the bottom of the staircase with one hand on the railing and the other perched on her hip.

"Not with that duo," I mumble, trying to erase the odd sensation of my brother's touch. "With you on the other hand..." I look Belle up and down, appreciating everything she has going on right now. She's wearing tight brown leather leggings with black pointy toe heels that make her legs go on for days. Her top is a cream flowy number that hides some of my favourite assets of hers. Regardless, she still looks fit as fuck. "...I could entertain the idea."

"Save the smooth talk. We have to have a real talk. Now." She eyes Camden and Indie, who have moved their make out session from the doorway to the dining room table. Raising her brows knowingly, she turns and makes her way up the stairs. "They look like they need a minute. Follow me."

I cock my head to the side and watch her curvy body take the stairs with a power that cannot be ignored. Her inky black ponytail bounces with every step, and I find myself picturing her spread out naked on those steps as I drive myself into her. Being invited up to her bedroom is quite a turn of events.

I take the stairs two at a time and catch up to her just as she enters her room. I cross my arms over my chest and prop myself against the doorframe, shooting her a lascivious smirk. "Maybe this arrangement won't be so bad after all. Let's get naked and talk about our fears."

The look she gives me reminds me of smelling a carton of rotten milk. "If you think I asked you up here to fuck, you're more delusional than I thought." Her tone is visceral and her dark eyes are alight with a touch of rage. "I brought you up here because I need to say something and I don't want Indie to hear."

Deflated, I step in and close the door. Her room smells like fruit and flowers and perfume and all things girlie. I have a strange desire to roll around in it and coat it all over me. And then I realise that I'm a bloke and having those thoughts is really unmanly.

I touch my balls.

"Look. You fucked me up the arse without lube with this mess we're in, Tanner Harris. So let's get a few things straight."

Her choice of words has me staring at her arse as she paces in front of her bed. The large window at the head of her bed has no curtains and I immediately wonder why the fuck she doesn't have blinds in her bedroom.

"I'm aware," I reply and she eyes me harshly. Like a dog being commanded, I sit down on the cream button-tufted chair beside her dresser.

"I hate this. I hate every bit of this arrangement. I barely speak to my father, let alone see him. Then today he was in my flat, barking orders at me like I'm one of his fucking secretaries." She stops pacing and stares me down. "No one tells me what to do."

"Then why did you agree to this?" I ask, my curiosity piqued.

"Because I have a job. A real fucking job. I don't just kick a ball around on a pitch. I need this fellowship to go well because this is the specialty I want to end up in. I cannot afford this scandal. So you need to make this look good, Tanner Harris. You need to make us look like the King and Queen themselves. If I go into work tomorrow and face my attending, who is a world-renowned surgeon, and she looks at me as if I'm a slut who sleeps around, I will find a way to drug you, shave your head, drag your body to a tattoo shop, and have them mark you for life with something so horrid, so ghastly, so incredibly humiliating, you won't be able to get your willy up for years!"

A gust of air flies out of my mouth. "How did you get that all said in one breath?" I'm panting with fear.

"Because, I'm Jesus," she states, her face revealing nothing but icy, dark, dangerous promise.

I swallow hard and give my balls a touch again. Thank fuck they are still there.

"Well, Messiah, I promise I won't let you down."

Belle

The cab ride is silent as Tanner and I ride toward Covent Garden. I glance over at him beside me as he stares out the window. He looks a bit like a whipped puppy. Don't get me wrong, he's a hot little hound dog. His blonde hair is tied up into a messy man bun, some strands falling out around his face. His beard looks a bit more trim than it did last night. I assume he cleaned it up since they lost their match yesterday and his superstition of never cutting his hair during a winning streak is no longer relevant.

My eyes trail down to the small hole on the right leg of his faded jeans. It's not an artfully designed hole either. It's the type of hole a careless teenager gets from hopping a fence. Seeing the blonde fuzz on his kneecap up close and personal makes him seem so much more human and…normal, rather than a famous footballer.

Then I remember there's nothing normal about Tanner Harris. He's a manwhore with no regard for other people's feelings. He probably got that hole in his jeans hopping a fence to flee from another Harris Ho's bedroom. He might be used to girls falling at his feet and taking whatever scraps he throws at them, but that won't be me. I made that mistake once; I won't make it again. This arrangement is strictly business.

Sure, I may have spent some extra time on my appearance, carefully lining my dark eyes to within an inch of their life. But my eyes are one of my best features. They're large and almond-shaped, and when made-up right, I feel unstoppable.

And let's face it, I liked Indie's idea of making Tanner miserable.

He rejected me once, so I crave the pleasure of returning the kindness.

We arrive at a restaurant called The Barbary. It's a brand new North African cuisine hot spot located in the alley of Neal's Yard. This area is packed full of trendy pubs, so it's always brimming with patrons. Crowds of people stand outside on the cobblestone alley with glasses of beer in hand, enjoying the mild autumn weather. Music pours out of several establishments as we make our way through the boisterous crowd.

Tanner puts a hesitant hand on the small of my back as he ushers me through the door and around a huge queue of people waiting to dine. This is one of those cosy, counter-dining type of restaurants. It has a large U-shaped bar that surrounds the open kitchen where the staff works. The chefs aren't putting on a show, though. They're just sending out gorgeously plated food, which is a show in and of itself. There's a lot of bare brick, neon signs, reclaimed floor tiles, and a big, coffered terracotta wall. Overall, it's got great energy, all the way down to the charcoal smoky air from the clay oven. There's something magical about being amongst Londoners lusting after the latest craze. Even the customers queuing seem to be happy.

The hostess smiles way too brightly at Tanner as she grabs menus and instructs us to follow her. We're seated immediately at the very end of the counter in front of the large storefront window. It's the best spot in the house, showcasing the energy of the restaurant inside and the buzz of excitement outside. Display lights from the alley stream in, casting our seats in a riot of colours. It's kind of awesome.

The hostess gives Tanner one final brazen look and leaves us at last.

"This isn't so bad," Tanner says, dropping down on the outside stool and turning to face me. He spreads his long legs out wide so he's practically straddling my seat.

I shift nervously, crossing my legs to make myself as small and closed off as possible. I sit up straight, though, not wanting to seem intimidated by all his…manliness near me.

"I know people who have been trying to get in here for weeks."

"Sometimes it pays to be a Harris." The side of his mouth curves up, which forces me to look away immediately.

Back when Tanner and I first met and we were in the friendly, flirting stage of our newfound friendship, I used to catch myself staring at his mouth. It always had a smirk to it that was an indescribably attractive contrast to the serious smoulder in his eyes. Tonight, that contrast annoys me.

"You've probably never eaten a proper meal with a girl, have you?"

I can feel his smile. "This would actually be a first. Aren't you lucky."

"Oh yes, I've hit the jackpot indeed," I murmur as I peruse the menu even though I'll let the waitress pick out my food.

"What do you like?" Tanner asks.

"I like most things."

I can feel his knowing, steely blue eyes on me as he interprets that in a blatantly sexual way.

"But not all," I add with a flat note to my voice, cutting my eyes at him in challenge.

He lets out a soft huff of a laugh. "You seem to enjoy chocolate a bit more than most."

"Sweets are different. I'm very particular about those. Dark chocolate is a religion."

He puts the menu down and eyes me with appreciation. "So you love dark chocolate. What else do you love, Ryan?"

I close my eyes and do my best to ignore the way he says Ryan. I don't know why it irks me that he refers to me by my last name. Perhaps it's because I can't stand my family and the bullshit title they like to flaunt with it. Or perhaps it's because it's Tanner and most things he does irk me.

The waitress stops at our end of the counter to take our drink order. I have her pick a glass of red for me and Tanner gets a beer.

As soon as the drinks are placed in front of us, I almost regret not ordering a bottle. He slips off his grey jacket and is wearing a simple T-shirt, his veiny, inked arms on full display now. I can practically feel the warmth of the blood in his veins. His scent and the smell of food are overwhelming all the parts of my body.

"So, Ryan, let's have some Tanner Harris Deep Talk right now. How do you foresee this going?" he asks as he closes his menu and takes a long drink of his dark beer.

"You tell me," I reply. "I'm curious to hear whose clever idea this was. My father didn't really have a chance to say."

He cringes. "It was mine, actually."

"Yours?" I shake my head in disbelief.

"That so hard to believe?"

"That you would come up with the idea to fake date me in order to help save our reputations? Yes, that's incredibly hard to believe, Tanner."

He looks offended. "Why is that?"

"Because you can't stand me!" I exclaim. Then I lower my voice and lean toward him a bit. "Because you make it your mission to annoy the shit out of me any chance you get. Because for the next four weeks you're going to have to keep your dick dry! What will your teammates say?"

His face falls. "Keep my dick dry? Why on earth would I do that?"

My mouth falls open. "Because you're supposed to be in a relationship with me. That's what's expected of us. That's what your lawyer told my father we were supposed to be doing."

"You said it yourself, though. It's a fake relationship. I don't see why I have to be faithful." He shrugs as if this is the most obvious thing in the world. But what we're seeing as obvious are two very different things.

"It's a fake relationship," I punctuate. "A fake *monogamous* relationship."

"But it's not real." He leans closer to me and I pull away. "So I don't see why we can't act on our urges."

"You are not getting between my legs, Tanner Harris!" I hiss.

"I didn't say I'd be fucking *you*, Ryan. It'd be a shame for my superior endurance to go to waste."

His cavalier expression is cutting. His half-smile now looks horrifying as I realise what he's implying. But instead of letting his words hurt, I turn my emotions into anger. I zero that anger in on him so hard that everything around his face blurs. I'm barely able to keep my scathing tone to a whisper.

"Look, Harris. This is *my* reputation at stake, too. I'm not going to be your fucking political *beard* while you continue whoring around London as if you're on some bloody holiday and I'm a pathetic wife stuck at home."

"You say beard like it's a bad thing." He rubs his chin, a dirty glint in his eyes. "Most women call this their thigh tickler."

I baulk. "You are disgusting. I don't care what most women call it. This is the situation we're faced with, and I won't let you jeopardise what we're doing and humiliate me because you can't keep your STD-infested cock in your trousers for a few short weeks."

"Look," he barks back at me and then looks around as he draws attention to us. He shifts to the edge of his seat, so close now that I can feel the heat between his legs and smell the alcohol on his breath. "I'm suspended from everything. Football practice, team meetings, matches. All of it. I can't attend, not even to sit on the bench. So you are not about to bench me at the one thing I can actually take pleasure in during this entire mess."

"This is a mess you created! Not me!" I insist.

He shakes his head and turns so he's facing the counter again. Taking another large gulp of his drink, his jaw muscle ticks with annoyance. "I'm not even sure my team will believe this anyhow. You and me together? It doesn't make sense. And it's certainly not worth being completely miserable the entire time."

The look of disdain he shoots me out of the corner of his eye sends me over the edge. Before I realise what I'm doing, I grab my glass of wine and chuck it in his face. "Surely they'll believe that."

I slam my glass down and shove myself off the stool, stomping through the crowd of people as fast as my stilettos will allow. I'm completely oblivious to the gawking eyes all around me. Tanner Harris will not get the upper hand on me again!

Fuck.

Him.

I burst through the doors of the restaurant and my vision blurs as flashes begin going off. There are at least three photographers with huge-lens cameras standing in the crowd of people. Everyone's eyes are on me as they try to figure out why all the attention is facing my way.

I hear Tanner yelling my name from inside, but it doesn't stop me. I make a quick left down the busy alley full of people, excusing myself as I bump into a group of men.

"Ryan, stop!" he shouts again.

Now, not only are there photographers furiously snapping photos, but people have their mobiles lifted and are recording the entire scene.

Tanner's voice sounds closer, so I look back and see him swerving around the crowd. His eyes are wide and desperate as he takes in all the mobiles pointed at him.

I try to increase my speed but it's no use. I'm in heels and he's in boots. A firm grip wraps around my bicep, stopping me in my tracks.

"Bloody hell, Belle, would you just stop?"

He twirls me around to face him, a pleading look in his eyes. Glancing around with annoyance ticking in his jaw, he pulls me over to a brick doorframe in the alley. It's not any farther away from the onlookers, but at least it's out of the street lights.

"I'm sorry, all right. I didn't mean what I said." He moves his other hand to my free arm so he can force me to face him. The red wine has been wiped off of his face, but I can still see flecks of moisture clinging to his beard.

"Of course you meant it!" I rip my arms out of his grasp, not giving a shit that I'm shouting. "I make you miserable. Your words were very clear. Feeling's mutual, arsehole."

I turn to walk away, but his rough hand gently cups my cheek, giving me pause. His other hand reaches up to embrace the other side of my face so he can force my gaze to his. His face is dangerously close to mine as he speaks. "It's not you that makes me miserable. It's this scenario. You can't be happy with this either."

"God, no!" I exclaim. "I don't want to be here anymore than you do, but here we are. You need to commit to this, Tanner."

The crowd feels as if they are slowly closing in around us. He swallows hard, looking like he wants to argue but knowing he needs to watch what he says so they don't overhear. It annoys me. His weakness burns the very fibre of my being.

"Be a man for once in your life!" I snap. "Take responsibility and own this. The very *least* you can do is be a fucking gentleman. I know it's a completely foreign concept to you and not one the Harris Hoes ever expect, but—"

Kiss.

He's kissing me.

He's pressing me up against the brick wall and he's kissing me as if his life depends on it.

Perhaps in this case, it does.

But it catches me off guard. My stony lips reflexively soften as he tilts his head and increases the pressure on the inside of my mouth... with his tongue.

His tongue!

The cheeky bastard is completely out of control, and I'm still so mad at him. My adrenaline is still high, my rage still so acute. So I decide to fight fire with fire.

I bite down.

He lets out an audible growl against my lips and his tongue retracts, giving me room to sink my teeth down onto his pouty, smouldering, annoying as fuck, lower lip. This elicits a different reaction than I expected. He releases my face and lowers his hands to my waist, pulling my hips into his. His body is rock hard against mine as he pushes us both further into the bricks.

Further into this madness.

My hands reach up and comb through the damp beard on his jaw, tugging softly and relishing in the coarse texture of it on my fingertips, lips, and chin. The messiness, the burn, the wild, beast-like feeling of him is intoxicating.

This foolishness has to stop.

I'm kissing Tanner Harris in a busy London alley with people snapping pictures all around us. And the way he rolls his hips into mine makes everything in my body quiver with need.

I need to get a hold of this situation.

Finally, I find myself again, no longer lost in his touch and his kiss. I pull back, breathing heavily on his lips. "What the fuck was that?" I pant.

The side of his mouth curls up. "Sorry, I've never been much of a gentleman."

TANNER

I grab Belle's hand and pull her through the crowd of people flocking around us. As we make our way back toward the restaurant, I'm praying like fuck that our seats haven't been filled yet. If they have, I'll wait. I'm starving and that starter I had of Belle's fucking lips did nothing to satisfy my appetite.

If anything, it made me hungrier.

What started as a simple solution—kiss her and make it look like a lover's quarrel—quickly ramped up into, *Holy shit, I need to be inside this woman right now. Sod all these prats watching us.*

This situation with Belle is going to get very complicated very fast. I haven't forgotten all the reasons I didn't kiss her three months ago. But the fact that we're being forced together for the next few weeks seems to overrule all those reasons.

Doesn't it?

Even if it doesn't, Belle certainly isn't too keen on turning this fake dating into a friends with benefits scenario, which would suit me a lot better. So if monogamy is what will be required of me, I'm going to become very well acquainted with my hand over the next month.

I find our seats waiting for us when we get back inside and do my best to ignore all the people gawking at us. Belle did just throw a glass of red wine in my face, so I'd probably be staring, too. I zip up my jacket to hide the evidence of her outburst on my T-shirt. Then, when the waitress comes over, I tell her to bring us a variety of whatever she recommends.

"I hope that's all right," I say, feeling tense and introspective and glancing awkwardly at Belle.

She nods woodenly, and I just now notice that her dark lipstick is smeared on her face.

"You, uh…" I gesture toward my lips and she immediately touches her mouth.

"Will you excuse me?"

I nod and she gets up and walks toward the toilets.

I take the moment of solitude to give myself a quick pep talk so I can get out of my head once and for all. I've been going about this situation all wrong. I've only been thinking about myself and haven't been listening to what she needs out of this. I need to quit being the Tanner Harris I've been for the last couple of months and start being the Tanner Harris that Vi would expect of me. This arrangement is important for Belle's job, too, and it's time I be considerate of that.

When she gets back, she barely sits down on her stool before I puke out the words that have been rolling around in my mouth. "I'm sorry, Belle. I said stupid things. Awful things. I was being a prat and only thinking of myself and you didn't deserve that. I'm also sorry for attacking you out there like that without any warning. I just…felt everybody surrounding us, and it was the only thing I could think of to salvage this evening. I am sorry."

"You called me Belle again," she replies, frowning.

After everything I said, her response is unexpected.

"Do you prefer I continue calling you Ryan?"

She adamantly shakes her head. "No, no, it's just something I've notice you do when you're not being the arrogant arse the papers all portray you to be."

I swallow a drink of my now slightly warm beer and mull over her observation. I guess I started calling her Ryan after that night at Old George when I realised we could never be anything more than acquaintances. Maybe it helped establish some boundaries for me. Boundaries seem rather irrelevant now.

She interrupts my thoughts. "I'm sorry, too, for erm…throwing my wine in your face."

I smile. I can't believe I'm smiling. A crazy chick tossed a drink in my face and I'm smiling at her like she couldn't possibly help herself. "It's okay."

She shakes her head. "It's not. It's awful. I have a hair-trigger temper and it gets me in trouble…a lot."

My brows climb. "What kind of trouble? Like at work?"

"No, actually. That's the one place I'm completely level-headed. I think the drama of the medical situations I'm faced with are so intense there's not really room for me to be irrational." The waitress sets fresh drinks down between us and we both take a necessary gulp. "My family life, on the other hand, is a whole other story."

70

"You said you and your dad aren't close?"

"No. I'm not close with any of my family. All of this"—she gestures to her face and body—"is just a bit much for their scene." She lets out a sad sort of self-deprecating laugh that bothers me.

I eye her objectively for a minute and can't find a single flaw. "What does that mean?"

Her dark eyes pin me with a look that tells me she thinks I'm clueless. "It means that if I would have tossed my wine on anybody in *their* social circle, I would be written out of the will." She pauses and frowns at me. "Why is it you seem to be so forgiving?"

"For you throwing wine on me in public?"

She nods.

I shrug. "I guess I can admire someone who's passionate about their convictions, even if it is at the expense of mine."

"Aren't you equally passionate?"

I shake my head. "No. I'm quite laid back for the most part. Growing up with four siblings and a father who cares more about football than he does about anything else sort of forces you to be."

"Then we're a match made in heaven, Tanner, because my *passion*, as you so kindly called it, usually sends men running for the hills." She looks at me for a few seconds. "Then again, I forgot the fact that you are not here by choice."

The chef behind the counter interrupts our quickly darkening conversation by serving us several small plates of food. It all looks and smells amazing. Plus, I think we both know that more eating and less talking is probably for the best.

We tuck into it all like it's our last meal. I don't know what the majority of the food is when the waitress tells us all about the various sauces and seasonings, but I don't have to understand what I'm eating to know it's incredible. Belle seems to be enjoying it just as much. I guess this would be a perk of monogamous dating. Restaurants, good food, good drinks, attractive company. I can see the appeal.

But nothing about the night tops the way Belle's eyes light up when she sees they have a dark chocolate ganache truffle dessert. She looks like a kid getting a puppy on Christmas morning. It's sweet and hilarious and innocent.

Watching her eat it, however, is the exact opposite description. Her large, touched-up lips wrap around the spoon of chocolate like she's devouring the most sensual thing on the planet. I suppose it is to her. To me, I'm envisioning something a bit more salty tasting.

My dick twitches as I recall her referring to dark chocolate as a religion before. I can't help but feel like I'm witnessing a religious experience. She offers me a bite on more than one occasion, but I refuse because I don't want to take a single bit away from the show I'm enjoying more than I care to admit. It's ten times better than any foreplay I've ever had.

When my dirty mind begins picturing her sucking chocolate off my cock, I have to excuse myself to go to the loo and get control of my faculties. Fuck me. How did this bird go from throwing her wine in my face to making me as hard as a rock within the space of an hour? She's a witch. A temptress. She's got me completely under her chocolatey, crazy chick spell and I'm entranced.

She's just finished off her coffee when I come out, so I quickly pay our bill and pull her behind me as we exit the busy restaurant. The photographers are all gone, which doesn't surprise me because I'm sure they won't use any of the shots of us laughing and talking like civilised adults. No, no. They'll use the one of me covered in wine and her screaming at me in the alley. The media are arseholes like that. Nobody cares to read about a happy story. They want dirt, they want drama, they want domestic disputes. They want something that will trend, and nothing gets people talking more than something completely unexpected.

As I hail down a cab, I glance at the time on my mobile and see it's not quite nine. "I kind of want to do one last thing. Think you're up for it?"

"What is it?" Belle asks, folding herself into the cab and sliding

72

across the bench to make room for me.

"I want to see how Sedgewick is doing."

She smiles. Genuinely smiles and nods. "I'd love to."

The Grosvenor Hotel is owned by one of my old schoolmates whom I grew up with in Chigwell. Duncan and I used to sneak girls into the private park behind my dad's mansion and get them to show us their boobies. Now, as grown men, we're still trying to get girls to show us their boobies, but they're out of their training bras and are wearing sexy lingerie as they spread out in posh hotel rooms. So life is good.

Duncan texts me Sedgwick's room number and lets me know that he was still there earlier in the evening. I was relieved to hear that because, after Sedgwick's resistance last night, I wasn't sure he would stay.

I barely recognise the man who opens the door.

"Tanner, old boy!" Sedgwick bellows with a jovial smile. "Lovely to see you. Come in, come in! Is that Dr. Ryan with you?"

"It is," I reply, glancing down at his bare feet sticking out from beneath the white terry cloth robe.

"Well, this is a treat. Please, come in. I'm not quite appropriate," he says, pulling the white towel off his mop of curly greyish-white hair. "But after all we saw of Mr. Harris here last night, I think we're past the point of proper decorum, don't you?"

Belle giggles behind me and I roll my eyes. "For a man so concerned about manners, you sure don't seem to miss a chance of having a go at me."

He laughs and steps back for us to enter. The room looks like it hasn't been slept in. The bed is made perfectly. The minibar still seems fully stocked. Even the telly is off.

"How are we this evening, Dr. Ryan? It's so nice to see you again.

I'm not sure I got a chance to properly thank you for the lift last night."

"Oh, it was my pleasure. Especially since you had the decency to wear clothes."

Sedgwick hoots with a laugh but then purses his lips when I eye them both harshly.

"Have you been sleeping in the bed?" I ask, walking over to the bed and noting the pillow mint still sitting there.

Sedg looks down and runs a hand through his damp hair. "I erm…I sat on it once. It wasn't my cup of tea. I have a bad back." He looks at Belle as he says the last part like she can understand better because she's a doctor or something.

"You probably have a bad back because you slept in a phone box, Sedgwick." My words are cutting, but I can't believe what I'm hearing. Even his canvas bag looks like it hasn't been touched, let alone laundered. I walk over to the mini-fridge and look inside only to see that not a single drink has been touched. "Sedgwick. I told you to order room service. Did you do that?"

"There was no need." He begins shifting nervously on his feet.

"No need?" I turn my accusing gaze on him.

"I went to the soup kitchen. It was fine."

I let out an exasperated sigh and rub my chin with frustration. "You don't need to go to the soup kitchen while you're staying here."

"Well, if I don't, people will worry about me."

This gives me pause. Of course this man has some semblance of a family that cares about him. Apart from the fact that I know he's homeless, he seems like the kind of bloke you couldn't stand losing.

"This isn't how it's supposed to be, Sedg. This should feel like a holiday. You should be living it up, relaxing, watching telly, having friends over—"

"Sedgwick," Belle interjects. "I'm really quite peckish. Would you mind if I use your phone?"

"By all means." He gestures toward the end table where the phone sits.

I frown at Belle as she sits down, opens the menu, and proceeds to order a plethora of food. How the hell can she still be hungry after the feast we've just eaten?

I walk over to Sedg and give him a pleading look. "Sedgwick, it would mean a lot to me if you would take advantage of some of the luxuries this hotel has to offer. It's why I brought you here specifically. Get yourself some new clothes, whatever you'd like. You really helped me out last night and I want to do this for ya."

He looks uncomfortable. "It's not that simple, Tanner."

"Well, let's make it simple."

"Oh! There's a marathon of Downton Abbey on right now!" Belle crows, interrupting our discussion again.

I look over to see she's kicked off her heels and pulled back the blankets on the bed to tuck her feet under the covers.

"Have you seen this show, Sedg?"

"I can't say I have," he says and moseys over to stare at the large telly. "I do like the odd historical documentary from time to time, though."

"This is basically the same thing," Belle says, popping one of the pillow mints in her mouth like she owns the joint. "Come. Sit. You'll love it."

I can't believe my eyes as I watch Sedgwick and Belle sidle up next to each other and watch the show. She mindlessly hands him one of the pillow mints and he takes it without a word. I drop down on the desk chair feeling a bit in the way and a lot out of sorts.

Later, there's a knock on the door.

"Can you get that, Tan?" Belle asks, barely looking at me as she shortens my name like she's a member of my family or something.

I shake my head and do as I'm told, opening the door to a hotel staff member with a rolling cart. It looks like Belle ordered enough food to feed a small family. I generously tip the man and bring the cart in. "Anywhere in particular, miss?"

She looks up at me and smiles, a mischievous glint in her eyes. "That looks like a good spot. You want to grab us some drinks, too, while you're up?"

I look at Sedgwick, whose eyes are still glued to the telly. I walk over and grab three fizzy drinks and set them on the cart. Belle gets up and comes over to me, pulling off all the tray lids and smiling like the cat that got the cream.

"How can you be hungry?" I ask her softly. "I'm not judging. I'm just incredibly impressed."

"I'm not." She smiles widely at me and then her face suddenly falls. "Oh, Tanner, I'm not feeling well." She rubs her forehead and places a hand on my chest for support. "I feel a bit queasy and faint."

Sedgwick peels his eyes from the show and looks over at us with concern. "Are you all right, love? Maybe you need to eat something."

She shakes her head. "I don't think that's it. My roommate came down with a sore throat a couple of days ago. I wonder if I'm getting that." She winks at me and I finally get the clue.

"Oh yeah, Indie was telling me how awful she felt." I nod with sympathy. "I better get you home."

She begins walking toward the door and casually calls over her shoulder, "Sedg, can you eat some of that food? It'd be a shame for it to go to waste."

He stands up from the bed, glancing down at the food. I swear I see him inhale deeply, relishing in the scent of greasy room service.

"I'm sure I can manage, love. You just take care."

I nod at him and move to help Belle out the door. "I'll stop by tomorrow and let you know how she's doing."

"That'd be nice, Tanner. Take good care of her. A nice steamy shower is good for a sore throat."

"You hear that, Belle? I get to give you a shower." I smile and give her waist a cheeky squeeze. She rolls her eyes and shoots me a secretive glare that goes unseen by Sedgwick.

When the door closes behind us, I can't help myself. I lean down and kiss Belle on the cheek. "You're a goddess."

She smiles back. "I know."

Tiny Patients

Belle

FOETAL SURGERY. IT'S NOT EVEN A SPECIFIC SPECIALTY YOU CAN focus on in med school or during your residency. Rather, it's something you come into after mastering obstetrics and paediatrics. There are few doctors who are skilled enough to operate in-utero, so the ones who are doing it are extremely busy, highly coveted, and geniuses in their own right. But the medical industry not only needs them to save these tiny babies that have yet to leave their mothers' wombs, they also need them to pass on their skills. Their knowledge. And not only in medical publications and research, but through hands-on, surgical training. They have to pass on their legacy.

So, to be twenty-seven and shadowing none other than Dr. Elizabeth Miller—who has more abbreviations in her title than I thought possible—is the stuff professional dreams are made of. I thought for sure I'd be booted out of the fellowship programme after week one. Now, here I am, two months in and still treading water.

Dressed in a pair of green scrubs, I stride into Dr. Miller's office, steeling myself to be calm, cool, and collected despite my imminent fear that she's asked me to come in here to discuss the events of the past two days. The photos that surfaced of me throwing my wine in Tanner's face last night were not ideal. No one got an action shot of the actual toss, thank God, but the images of us arguing were quite mortifying. Thankfully, the alley was too noisy for the videos to capture any credible audio of our fight, or I'd be a lot more scared than I am now. The only saving grace were the ones of us kissing. We looked quite…passionate.

Dr. Miller lifts one finger to tell me she'll be another minute and gestures for me to take a seat. She's been working in London for over ten years, but her American accent is clear as day as she soothes a worried patient over the phone.

Looking at her objectively, you'd never know she's the miracle maker the whole medical industry marvels over. She's got more of a cosy, cake baker look about her than a baby saving, surgical bad arse look. She's around sixty years old and wears trainers with a pencil skirt every single day. The only doctor-labeling characteristic about her is the white lab coat that pulls tightly around her thick arms.

Not only does she look sweet and cuddly, but she acts like it, too. I expected her to be harsh and demanding when I first started here, assuming she'd bark out requests only Einstein could accomplish. This industry doesn't have time for patience and she needs to pass the torch. But Dr. Miller has a soft, quiet way of empowering a person. She leads with her kindness and it's inspiring on many levels.

She hangs up the phone on her desk and her round blue eyes look softly at me. "Sorry, hun. I had to call that mother back. She's a worrier."

I smile. "Most of them are."

Her brows climb. "Rightfully so. Our tiny patients are completely dependent on their mothers. So, by relation, the mothers are our patients, and mothers are worriers." She laughs awkwardly and a strange pull begins around her mouth. Her smile turns to a frown and a garbled cry gushes from her throat. In seconds, she cups her face in her hands and launches into full on hysterics.

I quickly rush over to her side of the desk.

"What is it, Dr. Miller?" I place a gentle hand on her shoulder.

"What's happened?"

She sniffles and then clears her throat, sliding her hands off her face and smoothing them over her dark bob, stacked up short on the back of her head. "Nothing. Well, nothing yet. I erm…I have some happy news." She plasters a smile on her face and it looks off. "I'm going to be a grandma!"

My jaw drops and I force a similar off-putting smile, confused by the moisture in her eyes. "Well, that is happy news! Why the tears then?" I step back to give her some space, crossing my arms over my chest awkwardly.

In the two months I've worked here, I've never seen her break down like this, nor have I ever touched her in comfort. And that's even after losing one of our *tiny patients*, as she lovingly refers to them as.

"Sit down, please. We have to talk," she says, shaking her head and aimlessly shuffling some papers around.

I make my way over to the chair. By the time I look up at her face again, I see her resolve climbing back to the surface.

"There are two important matters to discuss. The first is that I want you to do a 4D ultrasound on my daughter."

"Okay," I say slowly, feeling like this is an odd request.

"I know we don't specialise in standard obstetrics anymore, but I need this." She swallows hard and rushes out, "She's pregnant with triplets and she's terrified."

"Triplets!" I exclaim with a gust of air rushing out of me. "Wow."

She turns away from me with closed eyes, almost as if my reaction pains her. She wrings her hands over and over as she adds, "She's eleven weeks along and has already had one scan. They saw no complications. However, since she was a preemie quad, we are decidedly uneasy and would like a high-level scan to ensure there are no abnormalities or early markers of any problems. You are the only fellow I trust with this."

My jaw drops. I've researched this woman. I've researched her like crazy. All I found was that she had one daughter, a deceased husband from many years ago, and was recently remarried. How the fuck could I have possibly missed the fact that she's a mother to quadruplets?

I open my mouth to speak but she cuts me off. "Reyna was the only survivor. I lost the other three in the NICU."

I pull my lips into my mouth and nod, unsure if I should give her sympathy or professionalism. I've witnessed immense sadness in the medical field, but seeing a doctor lose three of her own babies would be near the top of my list.

"I understand how important this is to you."

She looks at me and nods slowly, comforted by my response. In this moment, she's no longer the bad arse foetal surgeon the world knows her to be. She's a mother. A worried mother, whose daughter is venturing into a high-risk pregnancy.

"I will not be present for the scan. Reyna won't let me. So I need you to do this well, Dr. Ryan. It has to be thorough."

Her chin trembles and I want to reach across the desk and clutch her hand. Whatever history Dr. Miller has with her daughter must be heavy for her to deny her mother this. My relationship with my mother is extremely lacking, but would I refuse her this? I don't know.

"I will do my very best, Dr. Miller."

"Thank you. Now, on to other items." Her face turns back into the woman I'm more accustomed to seeing every day. "The PR department sent me some very interesting and very recent public photographs of you."

My heart drops. I knew it was coming. Hospital gossip is always strong, but there was a delusional part of me that hoped maybe I would get by unnoticed considering the world of football and the world of medicine are two very different places. No such luck.

"You are welcome to do whatever you'd like in your personal life, Dr. Ryan. I cannot stop you. But you did sign a morality clause in your contract. We operate here with a code of honour that we have to uphold. Our hospital has to maintain a good reputation. We have families that depend on us. When mothers and fathers walk in our doors, it's because they have exhausted all their other options and they are looking to us to perform a miracle. Those tiny patients of ours need us to be mature."

"I know and I am so sorry," I stammer, feeling utterly small. "The media twists things. They portray things in the worst way."

She nods with sympathy. "I can understand that and if I didn't see such great potential in you, I wouldn't care. However, when you are working in a professional career, the company you keep can affect all that you've worked for."

I look down, picking at a hangnail on my index finger and ruing the day I met Tanner Harris. I've been a doctor for many years and have made some questionable choices regarding the company I kept. It was how I let off steam. It was how Indie and I lived our Tequila Sunrise mantra. But never has it turned into something I was forced to discuss with my employer. This is mortifying.

Right when I'm about to come clean about everything to Dr. Miller, she begins speaking again. "The company you keep can also advance your career." Her eyes narrow with a conspiratorial glint. "Connections, networking, funding. It's all equally important in this field."

Frowning, I say, "I'm not sure I understand what you're getting at."

"I'm sure you're aware of our Foetal Surgery Foundation benefit coming up in two weeks." I nod. "This is the event that gets us money for research and training. The funding helps me hire fellows like you. It's what keeps this specialty growing so that we can continue to identify abnormalities and create minimally invasive procedures to correct them. To save babies, Dr. Ryan."

"Of course," I reply, my voice urgent with understanding.

"Finding donors gets harder and harder every year, but a contact in the world of professional football could be wonderful for opening doors. England loves their soccer!"

I smile politely as her unsubtle meaning becomes clear. It reminds me of exchanges I heard between my parents whenever a boujie family came into our lives.

"You'd like me to try to get some of Tanner's contacts to attend the event."

She purses her lips. "It would turn your lemons into lemonade, hon. And it would help the good work we're doing here."

I swallow once, feeling a heavy sense of foreboding wash over me. "I'm sure I can arrange something."

She beams. "Oh, Dr. Ryan, that would be wonderful! This year's event is sure to be the best one yet!" She gets up and twirls toward her filing cabinet. "Now, we'd better get a move on. You're scrubbing in on a urinary tract obstruction today."

Resistance is Futile

TANNER

"**S**O LET'S HEAR IT. HOW'D IT GO?" CAMDEN ASKS AS I STRIDE out of my bedroom, scratching my abs and beelining for the coffeepot.

"How'd what go?" I grumble, pushing the messy snarls of hair out of my face.

Having longer hair has made me far more sympathetic to women. It's high fucking maintenance, and it's not lost on me that I can no longer just roll out of bed and head out for the day. Now I have to tame the mane on a daily basis.

But at least I'm not identical to Cam anymore.

"How was the other night? I'm looking at the pictures right now."

I pour my coffee and exhale, shuffling over to his seat at the breakfast bar. Without asking, I snatch his mobile from his hands and flop my elbows down on the counter, lazily scrolling through the photos. Santino had sent me some links but I didn't want to click on them. Knowing my brother is trolling the net has me curious, though.

I'm relieved to see there are no shots of Belle chucking the wine in my face. And there are no shots of us going inside the hotel to visit Sedgwick. The photos also aren't a glowing review of our fake relationship. We are clearly in the midst of a quarrel, but the kiss that comes after the sequence of fighting shots looks somewhat redeeming. The best shot is one of us back in the restaurant when she's eating her dessert. I'm laughing at something and her eyes are practically twinkling with delight staring back at me. If there wasn't photographic proof, I'd hardly believe we looked at each other that way.

"Harryn?" I groan. "They came up with a couple name for us already? This is fucking ridiculous." I pause and try the word out a few more times in my head. "Harryn is the best they could do?"

"It's probably your beard," Cam says over a mouthful of cereal, like a twelve-year-old boy with it dribbling down his chin. "What did you expect? You've been whoring yourself around London like a champion stallion for the last few months and now you've been seen with the same woman two nights in a row. They see wedding bells in your future."

I scoff, "This arrangement is going to be the death of me."

"Why do you say that? Belle's not so bad. I thought you fancied her once upon a time."

"I did. I still do...a bit. But as a shag and bag type."

I hand his mobile back to him and hitch myself up on the counter, grabbing my coffee for comfort.

"I see." Camden stands up from his seat and stretches, a purple bruise colouring the inside of his bicep just below his ink—a result of his match yesterday, I'm sure.

"Congrats on your goal the other day."

He gives me a small smile. One that looks polite and slightly uncomfortable. "It's no big deal."

I frown, watching him walk around me to the sink and placing his bowl inside. "Of course it's a big deal. This is your first season with Arsenal. You're killin' it, broseph."

"Yeah, but still. It's just a game."

Just a game? What? Is he nuts?

"Why are you being weird right now?"

"I'm not being weird," he defends. "I just don't think we have to talk about football all the time."

"What the hell else would we talk about?" I honestly haven't a clue. We used to talk about women, but now that he's wifed up and I've got a ball and chain attached to my neck, that pretty much just leaves football for discussion.

"We could talk about how you're doing. Maybe...your...feelings." He looks like he regrets the words as soon as they spill out of his mouth. "Just forget it," he rushes.

I roar with laughter, my stomach tightening with each exhale. "There's no way I'm forgetting that. Did you just ask me to talk about my feelings?" I chuckle some more, completely disturbed by this entire exchange. I squint down at his groin. "Oh fuck, Cam! Your vagina is showing!"

He shoves me so hard I nearly fall backwards off the counter.

"My balls are right where they belong," he seethes. "And they were emptied last night. How about yours?"

My good humour is lost at his low blow. "Mine are blue and likely to shrivel up and die before this month is over."

Cam gives me a knowing nod, crossing his arms and leaning back against the wall. "I'm genuinely curious how you're going to handle this."

"I don't know. Fuck me, I wasn't ready for Deep Talk this early in the morning." I moan, tucking my hair behind one of my ears and taking a sip of hot coffee. "Santino emailed me the list of events we have to attend and the more I read, the more it felt like a bloody noose tightening around my neck."

"But you said you like Belle."

"I do, but not for anything long-term. So I can't go there. I won't hurt Indie like that."

He frowns. "What does Indie have to do with it?"

"She's your girlfriend. You're in fucking love from what I and the rest of the world can see. I'm not going to fuck over her best friend and make life complicated for everyone. I like Indie too much to do that."

He shakes his head. "Indie wouldn't give a toss! She's always moaning about how you two can't get along. Maybe this would fix that?"

"Well, it wouldn't be a long-term fix. Therein lies the problem."

He scoffs, "It sounds to me like you're searching for excuses. Belle's not some young, innocent bird you're taking advantage of. The first night I started things with Indie, I picked her up at a club and she left Belle there with some random bloke like it was a normal weekly occurrence."

I set down my coffee, trying to hide my level of shock. "Really?"

"Yeah, Indie says Belle isn't into commitment. I think she's a bit of a party girl, Tan." He moves back over to his stool near where my legs are dangling. "They're married to their careers. Indie was resistant to me at first, too, but it's partly why we work so well together. We both travel a lot. Our careers are important and we respect that about each other."

I'm not sure what to make of all of this. When I think back to the night Belle and I flirted so heavily at Old George, I will admit that's the vibe I got from her. I'm quite accustomed to sussing out the birds who see me as husband material and the ones who see me as shagging material. But I'm always wary of going back for seconds because women will say they want casual and then change their minds after a few shags. Their vaginas are directly wired to their hearts. My dick is directly wired to my dick, like an infinity sign with a constant revolving movement. *Shag and bag. Shag and bag.*

However, Belle is a doctor. She's crazy fucking smart and loads more mature than the women I'm used to. Maybe she is some female anomaly I've been mistakenly turning away from.

"Well, none of this matters," I reply. "She bloody well hates me. She's pretty clear, especially when she says those exact words to my face."

Camden laughs. "She's not overly subtle, is she? But can you blame her? You gave her the impression you didn't want a shag and then started fucking anything with legs."

I glower at him. "You were right there beside me not long ago."

He smiles and shakes his head, slapping a hand on my shoulder. "I know I was. But you'd be surprised how great regular sex with the same person is. It gives you a chance to...fine-tune things. Find brand new buttons." He winks and shoots me a dirty look that has me holding back the vomit climbing up my throat.

"You can't talk to me about Indie like that. Ever. She's...like a sister to me now. Just...no." He continues leering at me like a creep. "I'm not kidding. We can't talk girls anymore. Ever." I lean down and grab him by the shirt collar, hitching my voice to be wildly dramatic. "Promise me, Cam. Promise me right now!"

He laughs. "I promise you, drama queen. Just promise me you'll consider it. Maybe by the time I get back from my match this weekend you and Belle will have found a way to make some fun out of this arrangement."

It's the first time I've seen a tiny glimmer of hope since the dark storm of Belle clouded my life.

Belle

Typically, my showers after work are consumed by thoughts about the cases we have going on at the hospital. I use the quiet time in my bathroom to mentally decompress from the day's challenges. Right now, we're preparing for a mother who's coming in next week for selective laser ablation. It's a treatment used to treat twin-to-twin transfusion syndrome, or as Dr. Miller likes to affectionately call them, The Thief and The Giver. Essentially, one baby absorbs more blood than its sibling. With this technique, we go into the uterus using a tiny camera and are able to separate the blood flow between the two babies to help them both get an equal share. It's a fascinating procedure that I should be consumed by.

Instead, all I'm thinking about as I stand under the pounding water, aggressively rubbing shampoo in my hair, are the texts Tanner sent me this morning. A stupid smirk flicks across my face.

Tanner: Do you mind if I pop by tonight to discuss Santino's email?
Belle: Yes
Tanner: Yes you mind or yes I can come over?
Belle: Yes I mind. I just cleaned and I don't want you dragging in the clap.
Tanner: Hey, that's all cleared up now.
Belle: I'm going to be sick.
Tanner: Oh come on, take a joke.
Belle: STDs aren't funny. I'm a doctor. I would know. I'll show you pictures sometime.
Tanner: Seriously, I'll bring food. Whatever you want.
Belle: Fine but this doesn't count toward the massive favour you still owe me.
Tanner: Duly noted.

Fuck.

I hate Tanner. I really hate him. But mostly, I hate my attraction to him. That dumb, boyish smirk and the way he shakes his head from side to side to get his hair out of his face. And that stupid sweatband I've seen him wear around his forehead when he's on the pitch makes him look like a complete man-child.

But he did *not* look like a child when he was naked in my car the other night. And he did *not* feel like a child when he was pressed up against me in the alley two nights ago.

He certainly kisses like a man.

My thoughts darken to how much more we could have done if we would have been alone. So the thought of him coming over to my flat tonight while Indie is away evokes *ideas.*

Indie's suggestion to torture him while we go through this whole façade sounds like a fun sort of challenge. However, I can't seem to quiet the small voice in my head that feels insecure around him.

Tanner blatantly rejected me that night at Old George. Perhaps the chemistry I felt with him was all one-sided? Perhaps he doesn't even find me attractive? I'm certainly different than the women he's been banging more recently, that's for sure. Yes, he's a scruffy manwhore who you'd think would shag anything that walks, but he's also a famous footballer. They have stunning women throw themselves at them all the time.

"Bloody hell!" I exclaim, stepping out of the shower and towel drying myself off.

This sense of uneasiness reminds me of Sunday mornings as a child. My mother paraded my brother and me down the stairs for our father's inspection before we went off to church. Our outfits had to be just so, our hair had to be just right, and our mannerisms had to be completely devoid of anything resembling a human.

I *loathed* that feeling of being scrutinised and I refuse to let Tanner Harris put me back in that place. I need to know if he sees me that way or not. And if I get to torture him a bit in return, all the better.

It's time to take the power back.

Promises, Promises

TANNER

INDIE IS ON THE ROAD WITH BETHNAL GREEN F.C. HEADING TO God knows where, so I'm acutely aware that Belle and I will have her place to ourselves for the night. It gives me a bit of a thrill because I'm already imagining her naked on her bed, begging me to show her what I've been denying us for too long. I'm hopeful that Camden is right and that we can find a way to get through this month with better working conditions than stuffy, scheduled, photographed dates and dull events.

I ring her flat number and she buzzes me in, meeting me at her door wearing nothing but a long, black satin nightie.

"Jesus fuck," I mumble, nearly dropping the Chinese as I stumble on the last step.

"What?" She quirks a brow like she doesn't have a clue what my reaction could be about.

I grin. "This night just got a whole lot better, Ryan."

She bats her eyes and watches me thoughtfully for a few seconds, like she's trying to get a read on me or something. I thought I was usually a pretty obvious bloke.

"This is a business meeting, nothing more." She twirls on her heel and strides back into her flat. I have to hustle to catch the door before it closes. When I walk in, she's rummaging in the refrigerator.

The swells of her arse look positively edible beneath the smooth fabric of her nightie. Her dark hair hangs long and straight over her shoulder as she reaches into the lower drawer. Then she turns around with two brown bottles in her hands.

"Beer?" she asks, the bottles pressing against the tips of her breasts. My dick jolts with excitement as I place the food on the counter.

I reach out and take one from her, relishing in the sight of her firm nipple that the exchange of possession reveals. Fuck me, she's stunning. She grabs a bottle opener off the fridge and pries the top off of her beer and then steps into my space to do mine. She smells like eighty different kinds of girlie shit all rolled into one mouthwatering bouquet. My lips quiver with need to taste her.

"I'm liking this side of you, Ryan." I barely contain my crooked smile as I take a cooling drink from my bottle, wishing my lips were wrapping around something else.

"What side is that?" she asks, remaining so close to me I can feel her breath on my shoulder.

"The side that includes soft nighties."

I reach out and trail the backs of my fingers down her ribs. She sucks in a sharp breath like she didn't expect me to touch her. She doesn't move away, though. Instead, she stands firmly rooted in her spot. Her body squirms beneath the fabric, warmth radiating in the wake of my touch.

She clears her throat, a surprising blush colouring her cheeks. "Well, it's nearing my bedtime and I have to work tomorrow so I don't know what you expected."

She grabs the bags of food and waltzes out the kitchen door toward her dining room table. I watch her through the cutout opening, begging my dick to stand down. We haven't even eaten yet. *No need to embarrass yourself, Tanner.*

When I walk out and sit down in the chair near her, she looks like she is trying to work something out in her head.

"Everything all right?" I ask as she opens the cartons and swaps the chopsticks for real forks.

Her head snaps up to look at me. "Just fine."

She asks me which dish I want first. This is only the second meal I've eaten with Belle, but I've already noticed she doesn't seem to care what she eats.

"Most girls are picky eaters," I say, dunking a spring roll into a plastic cup of sweet and sour.

"Most girls don't look like me." She says it so matter-of-factly, I'm not sure I know what she means.

"Don't they?"

She stops eating and narrows her eyes at me. "Don't act like you don't notice."

"Notice what?" I ask around a mouthful of cabbage.

She scoffs.

"What?" I push.

"Tanner, I'm not a size eight. I'm a fourteen. And that's during the months that I haven't eaten my weight in chocolate. Stop skirting around it. It's insulting."

Her words stun me. Does she seriously think this way? I swallow. "What's insulting is how you see yourself. It's fucked up if you ask me."

"You are so full of crap," she snipes, stabbing the food in her carton like she's trying to envision it as my eyeballs instead of the delicious Kung Pao chicken it is.

"How am I full of crap?" I drop my fork loudly and sit back, crossing my arms over my chest, impatiently waiting for her reply.

She spears me with a glare. "I've seen the women you shag."

"What is that supposed to mean?"

"They are thin, Tanner!" She throws her head back. "I'm not. I'm the before picture for a weight loss challenge. I'm not ashamed of it, but I don't appreciate you acting as if this isn't reality."

I shove my food away, annoyance pulsing through my veins. Does she seriously think of herself like that? She can't. I won't believe it.

"That can't honestly be how you see yourself. If this is your way of fishing for a compliment—"

"Fishing for a compliment?" she screams and I swear I think she's going to lunge across the table at me. "Why the fuck would I care what *you* think? I don't care that I'm fat. And I sure as hell don't need your reassurances to feel good about myself. I know exactly what you think of me."

"And what's that?" I roar, nearly boiling over the fact that she used the word fat in reference to herself.

"That I'm good for a laugh but nothing more." Her face is stony serious as I sit before her, stunned into silence.

Belle comes across so confident. So sure-footed. She never missteps and if she does, she has a sharp tongue to bring it back to recover so she's in complete control. Couple that with the fact that she's drop-dead fucking gorgeous and you get stone cold fucking crazy bullshit, which is right where I've found myself.

"Are you mental?" I ask, finding my voice again. "No really, I want to know. Have your proper pyjamas run off with all your sanity and left you with a hole in your head and a skimpy nightie that's what…supposed to tease me? Is that what this is? Are you trying to issue a payback, Belle?"

"This is just what I wear to bed." Her shrug is weak and I can see right through it. I can't tell yet if this is a chink in her stunningly-crafted armor or if she's crazier than I ever anticipated.

"Oh come off it. You knew I was coming over." I rise up out of my chair and lean over the table. My voice is husky and hot against hers. "You wore that to throw me off and make me not think straight. Well, I'm seeing everything very clearly now, *Belle*." My eyes drop to her lips.

Her gaze lifts to mine and I watch her pupils dilate. "What is it you're seeing, oh brilliant, superstar, Tanner Harris?"

I pull away, breaking the cosmic crackle between us before I give in to what my body is begging for and what my dick is already pulsing with need to get inside of.

"I'm seeing that it was good I didn't shag you that night at Old George. That you're a head case with more issues than any man can handle."

I sit back down with a huff, exhausted by this exchange already.

She laughs. Full-blown belly laughs. The timbre of it makes me grimace because it reminds me of the sound of tyres screeching right before a mighty crash.

Through a scary, forced smile of gritted teeth, she replies, "I may be a head case, but your diseased dick is the one that's going to show up on a bad Google search."

This makes me laugh. "My cock is perfection, woman. Just like it is in your fantasies."

She sneers. "Yes, thank you for that, Tanner. You've made it crystal clear that your dick and all of *this*"—she stands, gesturing to her body—"have no place in your reality."

I growl like a madman and rake my hands through my hair at this total, utter hysteria. I meet her eyes with a cold and calculated stare. "The things I could do to your body are endless, Belle Ryan. You're fucking perfect and you know it. You're the kind of woman blokes marry, not fuck and leave!"

Silence stretches out before us as my words sink in. I revealed more than I meant to, but it's the truth. I'm hard just from fighting with her. But, no matter how badly I want to show her how fucking gorgeous she is, I have to be smart.

"So is that why you blew me off that night?" she asks with a haughty laugh.

I sigh. "That and I didn't want to cause problems with Indie or Cam when I buggered off afterwards."

"What kind of problems?"

"The kind that happen when a girl wants more than one night."

And now the truth comes to a head between us.

"Well, luckily for you, I'm not the marrying kind." She crosses her arms over her chest and her breasts push together, drawing my eyes to the beautiful valley of cleavage that rises and falls with her every breath. Her angry voice is shaky when she adds, "In fact, quick and casual is my preference."

My eyes snap back to hers to search for proof that she's telling the truth. Her teeth come down on her lush lower lip, practically laying it all out there for me to grab.

"So what are you saying?" I grind the words out like I'm a second away from losing my mind.

She exhales. "I'm saying neither of us are able to get it from anybody else, so why don't we get it from each other?"

When her voice abruptly halts and the only sound that's left in the room is our heavy breaths, I know exactly what's coming next. It's all there, plain as day. Her chin is dropped. Her eyes are nearly black. Her hands clutch the edges of the table like she's holding on by a tiny thread that's about to snap.

Sex.

Sex, sex, sex, sex, sex.

It's all I can see, smell, taste, and hear as soon as the demand tumbles out of her mouth.

There's no turning back now.

In a flash, I reach out and grab her hand, hauling her onto my lap. Our bodies snap together like two magnets that were once repelling each other and have now been flipped.

Her legs wrap around me and the heat of her centre warms my own as my dick jumps to life inside my trousers. The silk of her nightie bunches up around her thighs as she slices her hand roughly through my hair, catching on some tangles. She grabs hold of me like I'm her property and she's going to claim me. My hands cup the nape of her neck as I roughly pull her face down toward me and connect our lips.

She angers me so much. She's so loud and so brash and so fucking pushy!

I'm desperate to fuck this out with her.

How she can call herself fat is delusional. It's incomprehensible. Unimaginable. She has the most beautiful body. I've fantasised about defiling it in about eighty different positions.

"This won't be one night," she pants, her forehead pressed to mine, her lips raw from my beard. "We have weeks left together, Tanner. This will get complicated."

"Let's just enjoy it while it lasts," I murmur, hearing the faint tear of fabric as I rip the tiny spaghetti straps off her shoulders. "One night. Four weeks. What's the difference if we're both on the same page?"

She nods and shimmies her arms out of the straps, allowing the nightie to slip down off her chest and revealing the hottest set of cans I've ever seen. I'd never heard the word "cans" before when referring to tits, let alone used it in a sentence, until my American teammate said it one night at a club. For some reason unbeknownst to me, staring at Belle's bare breasts before me, "cans" seems like the perfect adjective.

"Fuck me," I curse and bury my face in her chest that's currently eye level. "Fuck me, I've died and gone to tit heaven."

"God, you're stupid," she groans, rolling her hips into my hard-on that just grew an inch bigger than it's ever been before. All because of these glorious cans.

"I want to live here," I hum against her flesh, cupping the sides of her breasts to increase the pressure of them around my face. "I want to open up a little shop where my everyday job is to rub myself on these glorious creatures all day long."

"Shut up and fuck me!" she demands, moving her hand down between us to touch herself.

No knickers. She was completely bare beneath this little scrap of fabric, completely content to taunt me mercilessly.

She leans back to give herself better access to her pussy, and I'm torn between enjoying her glorious performance or ploughing myself inside of her. I dry-hump her a few more times, my dick rubbing harshly on the zipper of my jeans. The pain is excruciatingly erotic. I attempt to rock her arse back and forth with my hands before my resolve cracks wide open.

Gripping her beneath her legs, I stand and set her on the glass table. She cries out, "It's freezing! Tanner, you fuck!"

"Fucking you is exactly what I'm going to do," I growl, plunging my fingers deep inside of her wet centre. God, she's soaked. Fighting with me turns her on, too. "Fucking hell, you're perfect."

She groans out loudly. I can tell she wants to yell at me some more, but she's too busy riding my fingers like a rollercoaster. I grab hold of her nipple with my free hand and squeeze the hardened bud between my fingers. So pert, so huge, so impeccable. Her body is on full display for me, with just a strip of the nightie covering a few inches of her torso. She has smooth sculpted arms, lush, big tits, and legs that belong around my face at some point this evening.

"God, you're fucking gorgeous," I grind. "Your body is so bloody hot."

"Tanner," she groans. "Stop."

"Stop what?" I ask, stalling my fingers. "Stop this?" I wiggle them again.

Her eyes fly wide and she looks up at me. "No, don't stop that!" She reaches down and grips my hand in hers, urging me to continue. "Stop talking about my body."

I lean over her and drop a wet kiss on her smooth abdomen. It's curvy and soft and welcoming to my very aroused state.

"Not until you tell me you're beautiful," I murmur against her flesh.

I don't know why this is bothering me so much but it is. Belle projects all the confidence in the world, but sometimes it's the loudest women that have the most to hide.

"Don't, Tanner," she begs, her voice softening to a whimper as I feel her climax coming and know that I hold all the power right now. I have a moment of regret for forcing this on her, but deep down I know she's strong enough to handle it.

"Please, Belle?" I ask, dropping several open-mouthed kisses on her breasts. "Just say it once."

Her heavy breathing slows and she bites her lip, her eyes crashing on mine. I see her throat move before she finally replies, "I'm beautiful."

The corner of my mouth tugs up. "Fuck yes you are. And I'm going to scream that when I empty my balls inside of you."

Devil's Advocate

Belle

WITHIN SECONDS, TANNER HAS A CONDOM ON. IN ANOTHER second, my legs are on his shoulders and he's buried so deep inside of me, I can feel him in my heart. Or perhaps that sensation in my chest is the words he sex-leveraged over me.

I'm beautiful.

What a smug bastard, thinking he can come into my flat and start barking orders at me.

But bark he did. And like a dog, I am lying here begging for more.

I didn't mean to get so fixated on my appearance. I like my body. I do think I'm beautiful. *Most days.* Sure, there are the odd jiggly parts I really wish didn't exist. And there are some things I can't get away with, like prints. If I wear certain prints, I come off looking like a sofa cushion instead of a fashion icon.

But if it's a choice between eliminating chocolate from my life or a softer landing on my arse, I'll pick a soft landing every day and twice on Sundays.

Perhaps I was searching too hard for a reason for Tanner to cast me away like he did. But if what's happening now is the result of enduring a couple months of suspense, I have three words to say.

Worth. The. Wait.

Tanner between my legs is hot in that knuckle-dragging cave-man sort of way. How he picked me up as if I weigh nothing and dropped me on the table like a feast he was desperate to devour... *Sign me up for seconds of that meal, please.*

I hate to admit it because I've chosen to loathe him from here to eternity, but the entire time his tight, firm body pounds into mine at a punishing, hateful pace, I can't help but think it's been forever since I was fucked this well. Perhaps it was all the pent-up aggression between the two of us. Or perhaps it's the fact that the last great shag I had was four years ago with my old med school fling. We used each other on a regular basis to relieve stress. There was absolutely no chemistry between us during the day, but at night we helped each other learn exactly what buttons needed pushing for maximum pleasure. We attacked our sex life the same way we attacked a surgery: with careful precision and textbook research.

Tanner is the opposite of that in every way.

He's wild and messy and dirty. Even the long stringy hair on his head makes me wet. His taut jaw is rugged as his eyes pin me with complete possession. He says and does whatever comes to his mind without any thought of holding back. I mean, for God's sake, we're fucking on my dining room table next to our half-eaten Chinese food. If Indie decided to come home right now, she'd probably pass out from germophobe shock.

Maybe I'll buy a new table tomorrow.

Regardless, I'm enjoying this ride more than I should. By the time Tanner gives me my second mind-shattering orgasm, my lungs ache from all the screaming and heavy breathing. He follows closely behind with his own guttural release, moaning out his promised words and confusing the hell out of my natural hatred for him.

But I won't get this twisted. It's fucking. Not sex, not love-making. It's just two people fulfiling each other's needs as they are required in order to work closely together. Like me and my med school partner.

Seconds later, he pulls out of me and flops back down on the chair he vacated earlier. Our breaths are loud and I can hear the sound of him pulling off the sticky condom.

"You weren't kidding about superior endurance," I murmur, my voice hoarse from the crazy adrenaline high.

A soft laugh rumbles from somewhere deep inside of him. "I'd never kid about that." He stands up. "I'm going to pop into the loo."

He walks over to the nearby bathroom while I manage to peel myself off the table and haphazardly put my nightie back in order. One of the straps is trashed and the other is hanging on by a thread. I knew wearing this would get a rise out of him, but I honestly didn't expect all of this.

I'm spraying down the table with disinfecting cleaner when he comes out and our eyes meet.

"Hungry?" I ask with a laugh and drop the surface cleaner bottle beside the Chinese.

"For more food or more you?"

His heated gaze pins me to my place. I wasn't sure if we'd go back to hating each other or if sex gave us a somewhat common ground. A peace treaty, so to speak. I watch him thoughtfully for a moment and we exchange a slough of silent questions. Questions I'm not sure either of us have answers to yet.

"Let's start with Chinese and go from there," I reply.

He simply smirks and a glimmer of a dimple forms on one side of his lips. *That mouth will be my ruin.*

We sit back down and begin eating as if nothing happened. It's quiet but not awkward. I'm trying to work this all out in my head but, to be frank, all I can think about is the delicious ache between my legs and how truly satisfied I am.

As I take a drink of my beer, I see Tanner's eyes flick to the spot where I was lain out moments ago. I assume his mind is where mine is until he turns to me with a grave expression.

"You don't think Cam and Indie have fucked on this table, do you?"

I spit liquid out everywhere, including on Tanner's face. He flinches, his eyes pinched tightly as he reacts to the onslaught. He wipes the dew from his eyes, slowly opening them.

"Is that a no? Or a yes?"

"It's a—"

"Wait," he reaches out, his warm hand gripping my arm firmly. "Just lie to me."

I laugh. Truly laugh. I can't believe this is the same man I was screaming at before, first in anger, then in pleasure.

"They've never touched this table."

He exhales with relief and it makes me giggle around another bite of food. Indie's told me how close she and Tanner have become, and his reaction just now secures that fact for me.

After we finish eating and clean up, I stride into the living room and flop myself on the sofa fully prepared to ignore the sexual elephant in the room.

"Shall we discuss that email?"

Tanner nods, joining me and pulling his mobile out of the pocket of his jeans. He looks delicious in worn jeans and a T-shirt, his black inked arms on display. Or perhaps he looks more delicious because I've had his cock inside of me.

"It's not quite as painful as I anticipated," Tanner says, scrolling through his mobile as he sits down beside me. I try not to take his comment personally, but I need to remember and hold on to the fact that, despite everything Tanner said before he shagged me senseless, he still has walls up when it comes to me. "We have to go on a London Eye double date with Cam and Indie. He wants us to do that next. Talk about cliché and touristy."

This is the one event I am actually looking forward to. "I've never done the London Eye."

"What?" Tanner exclaims. "You grew up in London. Didn't your parents ever take you, or wouldn't you go there for a school field trip?"

"No," I reply with a shrug. "Never. We had a nanny growing up, but the London Eye wasn't on our list of approved sites to visit."

He blows out some air. "That's a shame. Vi took us on a regular basis as kids. We even knew the best times to go to avoid the long queues."

Hearing about Tanner and Camden's family life is odd. They all seem so close despite losing their mother at a young age. Perhaps that tragedy only unified them more. I've never had that with my brother. We had completely different interests, and his constant need to please our father was so off-putting, I could hardly stand to be around him.

"Anyway, what else is there?"

"Bethnal Green has a home match in two weeks that they want us to attend as…spectators." He grinds the words out as if they are painful to say. "Then there are a couple of dinner things. Pretty typical stuff."

My brows lift. We actually won't have to see each other all that much, based on this list. I can't help but wonder how us sleeping together will change any of that. Regardless, I have to do my part in all of this and get back in good graces with Dr. Miller.

"I have one event I need to add to the list that might be a bit of a headache." He looks at me with curiosity. "My attending talked to me today…my boss. She wants me to get you and some of your footballer friends to come to a benefit the hospital puts on every year to raise money for research."

He looks surprised but not put off. "All right then. I'm sure I can get my brothers to go at the very least. What kind of research is it?"

"Baby saving stuff. To make what I do possible."

He turns, pulling one leg up on the sofa so he's angled toward me. His steely blue eyes look serious. "I don't think I realised what it is you do exactly until you told Sedgwick. It sounds…heavy."

I exhale through my nose. "It is heavy. It's hard and it's heartbreaking and it's awful, but the payoffs when it works are just…"

"Aces?" The corner of his mouth tugs up.

"Yeah." I smile. "My boss has thousands of baby pictures all over her office of the little patients she's saved. Little babies that probably would not have even made it to delivery if it wasn't for what she does."

"What made you want to go into that field?" he asks, looking at me with honest and genuine curiosity.

I prop my feet up on the coffee table. "Is this Tanner Harris Deep Talk again?"

"It is if you want it to be." He waits for my reply.

Perhaps it would do Tanner good to hear some real world, scary shit. My eyes narrow at this challenge. "You've heard Indie and me talk about our Tequila Sunrise outings, right?"

I look over at him and he nods. "But it honestly sounds like an excuse to get pissed," he replies, draping an arm on the back of the sofa. His fingers accidently brush my hair and the sensation makes my eyes close.

"It kind of is, but it's so much more." I shake off the warmth of his touch that's in the forefront of my mind. "The reason we started that tradition is the reason I selected this specialty. When we were interns at the hospital, the first death we witnessed was a little baby girl who died from SIDS."

He frowns. "What is SIDS?"

"Sudden infant death syndrome," I reply, letting the weighty words have a moment in reality before explaining further. "It's unexplained and doctors can't correlate it to any specific cause. It's just… random."

I look toward the window, needing to mentally pull myself away from Tanner before I can continue. I'm instantly transported back to that night. That cold, dark night when life slapped me right in my naïve face. Back when my biggest issue was dealing with my parents moaning at me for not going to law school like they wanted.

I saw the baby roll into the hospital, so small on that adult-sized stretcher. Her hands limp. Her face slack. All I could think about was the mother picking her up at home and trying to awaken her. I didn't even know what was wrong with her at that point, but I could tell by looking at her that she was dead. The familiar knot forms in my throat and I hurt inside all over again.

I look at Tanner. "I was so distraught when I saw her that I ended up sick in the toilet. It was like my body was trying to projectile vomit the pain out of me. I hated the feeling that little baby gave me. I was powerless, you know? That baby was so small and helpless, and I went to school and trained and studied and tried to make myself into the best doctor I could be. But in that moment, none of it mattered. I was completely ill-equipped."

"Christ, Belle." Tanner shakes his head, his face marred with a mixture of sympathy and horror.

I talk through the pain, though. "I couldn't believe that life could be so cruel. The baby was only four months old. She still had a soft spot on her head."

My fingers twitch at the memory of touching her in the exam room after the parents had been ushered away by the grief counsellor. I had to feel her. I had to know she was real. That it wasn't some horrid nightmare. I'd touched tons of cadavers in all of my various surgical trainings.

But no babies.

I look over at Tanner and his head is dropped. I instantly wish I hadn't unloaded all of that on him. "Sorry."

He shakes his head, his eyes rimmed red when they meet mine. I don't see the sadness I thought I would, though. I see...awe. His voice is thick when he says, "Don't be sorry."

I swallow, nervously shaking my head. "I took Deep Talk too deep I think. Must be the beer." I reach out and grab my bottle up off the coffee table.

"I wanted to know." He clears his throat loudly and looks at me with a furrow to his brow. "So that is how you chose your specialty."

"Pretty much. I thought I wanted paediatrics, but then seeing what Dr. Miller does, how she saves a baby when it's still inside of its mother…It feels almost as if you're taking an angel from heaven and demanding that God give them their own life first."

He smiles and gets a sort of glint in his eyes. Is it admiration?

"So what are you? Their immortal legal representation?"

I laugh at the notion and think it's an ironic choice of words considering what my family does for a living. "I'll leave the lawyering to my family." Then a dark thought crosses my mind. "I'd call myself something more like the devil's advocate."

I can feel his quizzical frown on me. "That seems like an odd choice of words when you just referred to them as angels."

My eyes sting as a flash of my childhood hits me out of nowhere. I was eleven years old and in a dazzling party dress. My mother and father welcomed people at the door of our home, one by one. There were loads of smiles, gushing conversations, and incredible food and drinks. Everything was glamorous and exciting to a young girl, but my spirit was low…because I had a word count. A specific number of words I could utter before I had to go to bed. Eleven, same as my age. As soon as I hit eleven words, I had to excuse myself and go to my room for the rest of the evening.

I look at Tanner, who's still eyeing me with curiosity, awaiting my reply. "In my family, children were supposed to be seen, not heard. So perhaps when I say devil's advocate, it's a bit of my upbringing leaking out." The sympathetic expression on Tanner's face pains me, so I quickly stammer, "It's not how I see children, though. Not at all. Doing this kind of work gives those voiceless tiny babes a way to be heard. I'm proud of that." I exhale a shaky breath, feeling like I've launched into complete verbal diarrhea and it needs to stop right the hell now. "You know, I've never spoken this deeply about any of this before, not even with Indie. Tanner Harris Deep Talk is pungent."

I look up at him with a forced smile and am mortified when a stray tear slips down my face. I didn't even feel it coming. But what surprises me more is the tenderness that washes over Tanner's face.

He reaches toward me and drags his knuckle along my cheek. "Stings the eyes." He winks and offers me a kind smile.

This is too much. Too intimate. Too much sharing. Time to get back to business.

"So," I bark out loudly, doing my best to shatter the moment. "You think your brothers would be willing to come to the event with their deep pockets?"

He huffs. "I think I can manage."

London Eye

TANNER

SPENDING THE NEXT FEW DAYS ALONE IN MY FLAT MAKES ME want to climb the walls. I work out in our home gym more than I should, fatiguing my muscles until I can barely sit up to grab the remote for the telly. I run around the neighbourhood, passing by a vacant Tower Park as my team is off playing somewhere else. *Without me.* I ache to be back in the stadium and on the pitch working out with my team instead of running out here like a lone wolf. Regardless, this is what I have to do. I may be suspended from the team but I refuse to let myself fall behind because of it. And when the time comes, I know my dad will make sure I earn my spot back on the pitch.

I was, however, allowed a brief visit inside the hallowed walls of Tower Park to talk to the stadium staffing manager and secure Sedgwick a job picking up garbage in the stands after matches. It's not what I wanted for him, but it was all they had available. When I told him the news, he did what he's been doing since the second I stepped on him in that phone box. He surprised me.

Sedgwick immediately sits down on the hotel bed, blinking and absorbing what I've just told him. He props his elbows on his knees and holds his head in his hands for several long, nerve-wracking minutes.

"I know it's not ideal, Sedg, but they say the best way to find a job is to have a job," I stammer. "And well, this is a job. I know you don't care for football, but the pay isn't bad. There's a hostel nearby you can stay at until you get some money saved. Though, I'd really appreciate it if you'd let me pay a deposit on a flat for you. It's something I really want to do."

My words are stopped short by a garbled cry. "I don't deserve this."

"It's an honest job. Of course you deserve it."

"But there are so many others out there..." His voice trails off as he looks out the window.

I run my hand through my hair, my brow furrowed with thought. I pin him with a serious look. "You take this job and I'll see what I can do for the others."

Sedg smiles. "You're a lot more than you seem, Tanner Harris."

"I could say the same thing."

By the time our London Eye double date with Camden and Indie comes, I'm more than ready to feast my eyes on the woman I had spread out naked on a table a few short days ago.

Belle strolls into my flat with Indie and there's a heaviness between us that feels...different than I expected.

After that night at her place, I did wonder if I handled my exit appropriately. I wasn't sure what to do. I'm not typically one to linger in a bird's flat after an epic fuck, so once we worked out our schedule, I left.

"Hi Tan, bye Tan," Indie says as she makes a mad dash for Camden's room. Christ, they've been apart for a few days and you'd think they were dying from separation anxiety.

I shift my gaze to see Belle still standing firm in the entryway. Her arms are crossed over her chest and her posture is decidedly stiff. I gesture to where I'm at in the living room. "You can come in, Ryan. It's not like you haven't been here before."

She rolls her eyes and leans her back against the wall beside the door, crossing one heeled foot over her ankle. "I'm fine right here."

I frown and point down the hallway toward where Indie just went. "Those two could be fucking in there for all I know. You may as well come in and get comfortable."

"I won't be getting comfortable at all, don't you worry. I'm ready to get this double date over with." The sneer on her face is unmistakable.

"Did I miss something here?" I ask, looking around me. "Did you take your icy bitch pill before you came over here tonight just for my pleasure?"

"Are you fucking kidding me?" she snaps, standing up straight and balling her hands at her sides like someone needs to come in and hold her back.

"Well, last time you greeted me in a saucy little nightie. Tonight it looks like you're dressed for battle."

I glance down at her all-black ensemble. Black ripped jeans, black top, large black knitted sweater, and camel boots with danger-ous-looking studded heels.

"Don't worry. There'll be no more of that." She spears me with a glare. "Everything is different now."

I smirk. "Is it because I've seen you naked?"

Her eyes fly wide and she looks down the hallway. "I haven't told Indie and I sure as fuck hope you haven't told Camden," she seethes.

"Tell Cam what? That you have a sexy nightie, or what we did together as a result of that sexy nightie?" I tweak my brows lascivi-ously at her.

"Both," she snaps, completely ignoring my boyish Harris charm that always serves me well. I'm offended.

"Why the bloody hell not? I thought we made a good team."

"So did I!" she exclaims.

"Then what the fuck is the problem?" I rake my hand through my hair, grateful that I left it down tonight for moments like this that seem so frequent with Belle Ryan.

"You're the problem! You didn't call, you didn't text. I had to get the time and details from Indie for tonight. What the fuck is that about?" She props her hands on her hips like a scolding mother. She reminds me of Vi right now.

My eyes are wide and confused. "What would you have me do?"

"Call! Text! You just fucked me and left. A text was literally the least you could do."

"I thought we were keeping things casual," I reply, feeling like I've entered the Twilight Zone. "You told me you preferred casual, and I know this might shock you but...I listened!"

She growls, literally growls. "These are extenuating circumstances."

"I agree."

"Well, what are we going to do about it then?" Her shoulders heave with heavy breaths.

"Well, I have an idea, but are you really asking? Because I'm happy to take the lead here, but you seem to have an issue letting go of control."

"Oh fuck off, Tanner," she baulks and crosses her arms as she turns away from me.

Darkness clouds my vision. Enough of this shit. I'm not letting her control me anymore. Not if it turns her into this owly, moody, stubborn arse. She used sexy pyjamas to gain power over me last time. Well, two can play at that game.

She turns when she hears my approach. I don't stop until she's backed up all the way against the wall. Her red painted lips are begging to be kissed and I can smell the fragrant shampoo of her hair that's hanging down loose over her shoulders. I cage her in with one hand on the wall beside her head and the other gripped firmly on her hip.

"How about this," I whisper in her ear and feel her tremble beneath my touch. "Tonight, after we put on this charade, I'm going to take you back to your place and I'm going to fuck you."

She opens her mouth to argue, but I cut her off. "Let me finish or I'll kiss those words right off your mouth. I don't give a shit if Indie and Cam come out."

She closes her mouth and swallows.

I tilt my head and eye her entire face thoughtfully, committing each tiny freckle to memory. "Then tomorrow, I'm going to text you to see when we might be able to fuck again because, believe me when I tell you, Belle, these past few days you were all I thought about. Naked. Panting. And so fucking wet." I pull her hip toward me and she greedily arches into my touch. "So if a call is all it takes to get you back in that position, baby, you better watch your mobile because I'm going to blow it the fuck up."

My lips are an inch away from hers, so I am able to taste her audible gasp at my sexy promise.

"You think I'll come to you just like that?"

I half smile. "With what I have planned for ya...Yes, Belle. Yes, I think you'll come. Just. Like. That."

I drop a soft kiss on her lips, and she breaks her façade completely with an amused laugh. She playfully shoves me away and I inhale deeply with a proud smile. I see something out of the corner of my eye and turn to find Indie and Cam staring at us from the hallway.

"Oh fuck," Belle murmurs behind me.

I look back at her with a sheepish smile. "I should have mentioned that you can't hide shit in my family."

Belle

"So you two slept together?" Indie's cheeks blush as her and Cam sit across from us in the back of a cab.

"Yes," I reply.

"So what does that mean then?" She glances between the two of us.

"It means we had sex," Tanner replies and I elbow him in the ribs. "But the really respectful kind."

Indie's eyes roll skyward. "I know what *that* means, but what does it really mean?" She looks at me.

"Nothing. It's no different than any other Tequila Sunrise fling." I say it in words I know she'll understand.

Tanner smiles proudly and drapes an arm on the back of the seat. "I'm a fling, bro. Are you proud? It's a step up from a one-night stand."

Camden shakes his head and pulls a confused Indie closer to him. Using his classic Queen of England voice, he replies, "These two turtle doves are beginning their journey toward finding their truest love."

Indie shoves Cam. "Well, if you're both happy, then I'm happy."

I exhale a deep breath as Indie frowns at the two of us as if we're the strangest pair in the world, which is probably accurate. She's seen nothing but fighting between Tanner and me for months. This is certainly a change of events, but I really hope she's not idealising this into something it's not.

Tanner leans forward and pats Indie on the knee. "Just don't overthink this, Indie. I'll be good. I promise. Let's focus on having fun tonight, all right?"

It's nearing eight o'clock by the time the cab drops us off in front of the London Eye. My eyes are wide and excited as I take in its grandeur and all the city lights twinkling around it. I can see why this is the perfect place to take a date.

We queue for tickets and Camden and Tanner buy out a whole pod so we don't have to share one with anyone else. Indie tries to argue that it's not worth the money, but neither of them give it a second thought.

I can feel people's eyes on us as we file in line for the ride. They might not be recognising Camden and Tanner straight away, but they can tell they are important. They're both so tall and muscular and striking. They look practically inhuman, like Greek gods walking amongst mortals. And with Tanner's extensive ink and long blonde hair, he stands out even more.

My parents must hate seeing me all over the news being romantically photographed with a tattooed footballer. I can't believe they agreed to all of this. They have to be getting something more out of this in the end. I just don't know what. I eye Tanner for a moment, trying to decide if he knows. He looks at me with a smile and I quickly shake the idea away.

As we wait in line, Indie and Camden are all over each other and it makes Tanner and me look like boring arseholes by comparison. We both stare at them for a bit and then look at each other. Exhaling in unison, we come together. His hands snake around my waist; mine reach up to hold onto his arms.

"Why are you smiling like a creep?" I ask.

"I thought I was doing a sexy smile."

"If by sexy you mean the kind of smile my Uncle Morty gives me then, by all means, continue."

His face falls, but he shakes it off and smiles again. "I'm just thinking about all the naughty things I'm going to do to you tonight."

My brows lift. "Do tell."

"I think I'd rather keep you in suspense."

He leans down and drops a kiss on my lips as if it's the most normal thing in the world. It's both surprising and pleasing.

"How was that?" he asks with a wink.

I frown. "How was what?"

He leans down to whisper in my ear. "There's a photographer at ten o'clock."

I feel my giddiness plummet. I want to pull away, but I know I need to stop being such a moping martyr. Instead, I decide to raise the stakes.

I reach up and pull him down to my lips and moan in satisfaction when I get a hold of his lower lip. I feel him chuckle against my mouth and then his tongue dives in, taking a commanding sweep of me. He pulls back and murmurs, "Trying to steal a sneak peek of what my tongue will be doing to you later?"

I smirk. "Oh God, I hope that's a promise, Harris."

"You know it is, Ryan."

I'm smiling happily as I turn around in his arms to move down the line. He continues holding me from behind as we approach the pod. When I see that the pods don't stop for us to board, I suddenly get nervous. I stop midstride and Tanner clobbers into me.

"What's wrong?"

"It doesn't stop," I answer, fear prickling my scalp. "I don't think I can do this. I'm scared of heights."

"Scared of heights? Why didn't you say anything?"

"I didn't know the bloody things don't stop for us to board! I thought I'd be okay!" This is so not the Tequila Sunrise moment I thought it would be.

He rakes a hand through his hair. "We've been in line ages."

"I'm sorry, all right. Just go without me." I try to shoo him away.

He scowls. "Don't be stupid."

"Don't be yourself!"

His nostrils flare at my snipe, but I don't care.

"Fucking hell, come here." He reaches his hand out toward me.

"No!"

"Just...trust me, all right? Come here."

His demand is firm but sincere, so I take his hand. We're ushered up to the pod while Indie and Cam are still too busy smiling like loons at each other to even notice that I'm in the middle of a full-blown panic attack.

"I don't know what your plan is, but I'm not going on that thing." My body is stiff as a board.

"Just keep quiet and trust me, woman," he growls.

"I don't think I like your tone."

"That's funny. I don't think I ever like your tone."

"You know, Tanner, this tone only comes out around you. In everyday life, I'm lovely."

I turn to see the pod coming closer when Tanner suddenly bends over and scoops me up like a baby.

"Don't you dare!" I pound a fist on his chest. "You're going to hurt yourself!"

"I'm going to hurt you if you don't shut up." He walks with purpose onto the pod, carrying me in his arms as if it's the simplest thing in the world. He sets me down just as quickly as he picked me up, and I'm shocked to see I made it on safely.

The pod is bigger than I expected, like the size of a small bedroom. It's a big round glass ball with a long bench down the middle.

I beam up at him. "I didn't die."

He fights a losing battle with his scowl. "You didn't die."

"You just hefted me in here like it was your job."

He rolls his eyes. "You're pretty much my only job for the next few weeks, so I figured it was up to me to make sure you've seen London properly while you have me."

I smile and stare at him for a moment. "Thank you."

His brow flashes into a frown. "It was nothing."

"Belle, look!" Indie says, tearing my gaze away from Tanner.

I look around to see us slowly rising up over the River Thames, the city lights casting a golden glow on all of us with slices of shadows moving over us from the pods above us as we climb. It's stunning. I slowly make my way to the edge and grab the railing, feeling a little unsteady but getting more comfortable with every passing second. I stare out at the city and marvel over how incredible London truly is from up above like this. Warm arms wrap around me, encasing me against the railing.

"You like it?" Tanner whispers in my ear, resting his head on my shoulder.

I nod. "I love it. Can we ride it twice?"

I feel his chest shake with laughter. "We'll come back another time."

I frown at the empty promise, but let it go because I don't want anything to ruin this experience.

"Is it this pretty during the day?"

He nods. "It's a different pretty. You can see farther out if it's not too overcast, so you get a sense of the grandness of London. At night, though, you get a sense of the magic of London."

His words make me smile. "Would you ever leave London?"

"What do you mean?"

"Like if you got an offer to play somewhere else?"

He exhales. "Footballers go where contracts are, especially if they aren't married with kids. I have nothing tying me down, so yeah, I guess I'd leave London."

His words hurt me because they speak some of my truth, too. I have Indie and we're incredibly close, but that's it. It's a rather lonely existence when you think about it.

I turn in his arms and thread my fingers through his hair. "Don't you forget I'm tying you down for the next month."

He stares at my lips and tweaks his eyebrows. "I hope that means to your bedpost."

I laugh and drop my face to his chest. "I would love nothing more."

He kisses the top of my head and I hear the sound of a camera shutter go off. I turn my head to see Indie holding her mobile up and capturing a picture. That simple sound effect brings me right back to reality.

My Face Is Your Chair

TANNER

"**S**IT ON MY FACE," I COMMAND, SEATED AT THE FOOT OF BELLE'S bed with my bare feet on the ground, naked as the night she picked me up.

"What?" Belle's brows crinkle as she steps out of her attached bath, unabashedly mirroring my nakedness. *God, she's sexy.*

We've been at it like rabbits since the second we left Cam and Indie. I'd like to say I was able to hold out until we made it upstairs to her bedroom, but I'm afraid her staircase suited us just fine for round one. I can still picture her perfectly sculpted arm reaching out and gripping the iron railing as I pounded into her as fast as my footballer legs would allow.

Round two took place on her bed where she fulfilled her promise and tied me down with scarves, going as far as blindfolding me and dominating me like the wild temptress she is.

"Sit on my face," I repeat.

She crosses her arms and leans against the doorframe. "Tanner, this is stupid. I appreciate that you want to have 'dinner beneath the bridge,' but why can't I lie down on the bed like a normal human?"

"Because I've wanted to taste you since forever, but I can't seem to stop myself from fucking you. So I want your sweet little pussy to

120

use my face as a chair until I beg for air."

"God, you're a sick fuck," she scoffs.

"Stop acting like it's not turning you on." I crack her bare arse with my hand as she walks by me and stretches herself out on the bed.

As far as coming back for seconds of sex, Camden was right. This isn't bad so far.

Belle's hands are stretched out above her head, and I smirk at the bite mark I left on the inside of her bicep. "Is it weird I like my mark on you?"

She looks at her arm and rolls her eyes. "Of the list of creep-factors you've wowed me with this evening, this seems rather adolescent in comparison."

I climb back up onto her bed, hovering over the top of her. Her cheeks are flushed red from our exertions, but I'm pleased to see she's abandoned any self-conscious ideas she had about her body. Every inch of her is stunning, even down to her smart mouth.

I bite down on her nipple until she screams. "Your fucking mouth gets you into a lot of trouble, doesn't it?"

She grabs my hair and yanks my head up so I'm looking at her. "Probably not as much as your dick gets you into trouble."

Touché, Belle Ryan. Touché.

I drop all pretenses. "Now, climb on my face already before I decide to tie you down this time."

I spent the night with a woman for the first time in my entire life and I didn't die.

I woke up with all my faculties still about me and my limbs all intact. Though, my dick is a bit on the raw side so I can't imagine how Belle is feeling, the insatiable minx she is.

After our epic fuckathon last night, I intended to go home. I really did. But screwing Belle Ryan most of the night was more exhausting than two-a-day workouts for Bethnal Green. Believe me, I'm not complaining.

When I finally muster up the strength to sit up, I see Belle stride out of her bathroom in green scrubs. Her eyes are bright and alert, her black hair is pulled back into a high bun, and she's got a bag over her shoulder. She looks intimidating.

"Morning," she says with a small smile.

"Off to work already?" I ask, feeling like a lazy sod.

She nods and bites her lip. "I have a special patient coming in this morning so I'm heading in early to prepare."

"Are you…erm…operating?" I suddenly feel very weird about fucking her like an animal last night when she's about to go and save a baby's life or something.

"No, it's actually just an ultrasound appointment, so no surgeries scheduled."

I nod. "That's good. I erm…feel kind of bad keeping you up late like that. I forget that you're not suspended from your job."

She baulks, "If I needed to go to bed, I would have said. Have you ever known me to hold back on you?"

This makes me smirk. "No, certainly not."

"I'll be fine." She begins rummaging in her bag and pulls out a set of keys. "But can you maybe lock up after you leave? I mean, you don't have to hurry out or anything. I just erm…There's no other way for me to lock my flat. Or if you want, I can give you a lift home."

"I'll get dressed." I move to get out of the bed.

"I didn't mean to rush you."

"No, it's fine. I need to work out anyway." I stand and stretch, my morning wood still at an honourable salute. I tweak my brows right at Belle.

"Hurry the fuck up, Tan," she grumbles and strides out the door.

I laugh. There's my girl.

Triple Threat

Belle

I'M NOT SURE WHAT I EXPECTED DR. MILLER'S DAUGHTER TO LOOK like, but I'm certain I never would have envisioned the woman sitting on the exam table before me.

Reyna is a short, curvy, brunette vision with deep, soulful eyes that haunt you if you stare into them for too long. As if her face wasn't striking enough, her artfully inked arms peek out from beneath the sleeves of her pale blue hospital gown. I've never seen body art so…suiting. Without knowing anything about her, I can tell that this ink is the story of her life, from the pocket watch to the sunflower bouquet and everything in between.

Her husband sitting beside her is a much more traditional sort of bloke. Liam is handsome but has a cleaner, more prep school sort of appearance with no alternative edge to him whatsoever. But the way his eyes stay trained on Reyna, even as I introduce myself, makes me weak in the knees. It's a look of complete and utter devotion.

"So you're eleven weeks, two days?" I ask, pulling out the transducer and covering it with a condom. Reyna nods, swallowing nervously as she watches my actions. I reach out and touch her arm. "Take some deep breaths and try to relax."

"Easier said than done," she mumbles, and Liam leans down and whispers something in her ear. Whatever it was seems to comfort her. He kisses her temple and she looks at me with a wobbly smile. "I'll try."

I return the smile as I squirt some gel on the tip of the probe. "Your last ultrasound was vaginal, correct?"

She nods and lies back, propping her feet in the stirrups and shimmying down to the end of the table. "I know exactly where you'll be shoving that long thing."

This makes Liam and me both chuckle.

"All right then," I reply. "This gets us the best pictures this early in the pregnancy." I position the probe between her legs. "All set?"

Reyna gives me a tight nod and I insert slowly. The screen is a mess of blotches until I twist and focus in on the three tiny figures. Reyna and Liam press their foreheads together, their eyes shut tightly, almost as if they are bracing themselves for bad news. I let them have their moment as I confirm what I hoped to see right away.

"Have you guys heard their heartbeats yet?" I bite my lip as Reyna looks at me with a shake of her head, tears slipping down her cheeks.

"They said it was too early before," Liam adds. His eyes are wide and grave as they flick between me and the screen.

I quickly move my free hand from the keyboard to the audio monitor and twist the knob until a sound erupts in the room.

A sound similar to that of a galloping horse.

"Those are your babies." I beam and then add, "Well, one of them right now, but I can see all their hearts drumming away." I turn the screen so they can see it better and point to the tiny spots contracting and expanding at high speed. "Right there, there, and there. Three babies, three heartbeats."

"All three are still there?" Reyna's voice croaks.

My heart falls at the desperation in her tone, but I inhale deeply and give her all the confidence I can muster. "Yes, all three are there. I still have to take measurements, but at a glance, they all look to be about the same size, which is a good sign."

Liam looks at me with concern. "Are the heartbeats supposed to be that fast?"

I nod. "Foetal heart rates usually peak around ten weeks and then slow as you go into the second trimester."

"They're all still there." Reyna's voice is breathy as her chin begins to wobble. She looks up at Liam and tears fall down her face one after another. Her belly shakes with a small cry. "I know we still have so far to go, but they're all still there. I can hardly believe it."

Liam kisses her hard on the lips, cupping her face reverently and stroking his thumbs down the lines of her tears. He sniffs through his own tears and murmurs, "I believe it."

I feel inappropriate as I watch them, but I can't look away. She smiles in a way that only a woman accepting the role of a mother could. It's inspiring. My eyes begin to sting and I'm a bit mortified when Reyna turns to look at me.

"Would you mind doing me a favour?" Reyna's voice sounds urgent. "Can you page my mother to come in here?"

I smile around my emotions. "I'd love to."

As I leave the hospital, I'm on a high I haven't been on in months. The images I captured for Dr. Miller's daughter and son-in-law were some of the best 4D images I've ever seen, let alone produced myself. The pride that Dr. Miller had in her eyes when she thanked me and the look on Reyna and Liam's faces...It just gave me *life*!

I grab my mobile and call Indie.

"Hello, Belle," she answers on the second ring.

"Indie, darling. I had the absolute best day. We need to celebrate. Tequila Sunrise style."

"Oh...erm...yeah. I think I could do that! Don't you have to work tomorrow, though?"

I sense her hesitation has something to do with Camden, but I'm glad she's willing to put him aside for the night and be my wing-woman.

"I was able to secure a personal day for tomorrow. I miss our girl time."

She sighs. "Me, too. Great then, I'm looking forward to it."

"See you at home?" I ask.

"See you at home."

I stop at the store to pick up the necessary items for our drinks. It's a recipe the paediatric doctor on call gave us the night the baby came into the hospital DOA.

Tequila Sunrise:
1 part Grenadine
3 parts Tequila
6 parts Orange Juice
Do not mix.

The recipe was a metaphor for life that changed my outlook on everything. The simple words that doctor uttered to Indie and me still ring so true in my soul. *"There's always sunshine above the chaos, ladies. Celebrate it."*

I hope that even in our old age, Indie and I are still celebrating life together because it can be so rewarding sometimes.

Reyna, Liam, and their three little babies are on my mind the entire time I get myself ready for the night. The hope and possibility I saw in their eyes...the transformation from complete and utter fear to total blissed-out acceptance was magic.

"Is this good enough?" Indie asks, her mouth sucking down a gulp of her colourful drink as she materialises in my bathroom doorway.

I'm seated crisscross on the counter as close to the mirror as I can get, wearing nothing but my black bra and knickers. I pause my mascara application to appraise my best friend. Her hair is down and in a riot of untamed red curls that only she can pull off. She's dressed in a black jumpsuit that plunges deeply to her cleavage.

"That's fucking hot. Put on my Stuart Weitzman's and you're all set."

"Oh! The strappy ones!" Indie turns to rush over to my closet and I hurry up to finish my makeup.

Once complete, I hop off my counter and grab my simple black jersey dress that I have laid out on a towel warmer. It's long sleeve and venturing on too short, but when I pair it with my lambskin Chanel, over-the-knee boots, it's the kind of outfit that gets me noticed by both males and females.

"Yes!" Indie croons as I stride out with my drink in hand, ready and raring to go.

"It's the boots," I reply knowingly. Shoes are an indulgence that I can't seem to kick. "Ready for Club Taint?" I ask.

"So ready."

It's eleven before we arrive at Club Taint, and Indie and I are already feeling fucking fantastic as we push our way through the crowd to find the dancefloor. The beat of the music calls to me like a drug. A drug that wants me to lose myself with it for hours.

I pull Indie out with me and we dance and dance and dance, throwing ourselves into movements that feel so good I never want them to stop. Hours tick by, drinks get drunk, laughs get had, dance partners come and go, all while I allow the synthetic melody breathe energy into me. All of it helps me forget everything horrid in the world. All the crap, all the sadness, lives lost, vacant parents, arsehole brothers, babies dying…all of it, gone. Evaporated with the swirling pink fog of the club.

Indie smiles, locking eyes with me, a look of exhilaration and sublime happiness spreading over her features. She pulls me in for a hug. "I miss you, Belle."

My eyes sting at her words. "I miss you, too, darling."

"I miss working with you."

I pull back and look into her eyes. "I miss working with you!"

"I hate not seeing you in the on call room."

"I hate not seeing *you* in the on call room."

"I know we live together now."

"We do." I nod, my vision blurring so I widen my eyes to focus more fully on her.

"But it's different now."

"It is so different." My face falls with sadness.

"I love Cam."

I smile sadly and nod. "You love Cam."

"But I still love you."

"Me, too!"

"Let's do this more often."

"Abso-fucking-lutely! Tequila Sunrise!" I cheers my beer with hers and chug the rest down. I drop the bottle and begin swirling Indie around in a childish spin that sends us both flying in different directions and crashing to the ground. Hot, sweaty hands wrap around me and pull me to my feet.

"Thank you, Good Samaritan," I slur, turning to face my gallant saviour.

When my eyes glance up and focus, I'm stunned by the bearded vision before me. "You look like a guy I know!"

He clutches his hands firmly around my waist and holds me to him. "You look like a girl I want to know."

I laugh half-heartedly and try to pull away.

"Are you trying to leave me, lass?" he slurs into my ear.

I frown and my head bobbles. "How could I leave you, Jesus?

You're God's son…You're everywhere." I throw my hands out wide to punctuate my "everywhere" and attempt to stumble away.

He grabs me again, this time his hands dipping lower to my arse. My good mood evaporates instantly. "Hey!" I shout. "Watch your fucking hands!"

I attempt to shove him away, but he feels like one of those doors that you push when you're supposed to pull. He doesn't budge. He leans in close and whispers in my ear, "I'd like to put my hands on your tight little—"

Right when I'm about ready to punch the wank stain in his vile mouth, I nearly fall over as a strange momentum spins me away. The man's hands are no longer groping me. They are now pinned deftly behind his back by no other than—

"Tanner?" I utter with a gasp, my hands covering my mouth at the shock of the scene before me.

"Shove the fuck off, you disgusting prat, before I turn your wrist into a pretzel." Tanner pushes him into a nearby table, and the man almost topples over but catches himself before scurrying away without a look back.

Blue, angry eyes swerve to me. "Ryan," Tanner growls, slicing a hand through his hair to get it off of his face. "I've texted you like twenty times."

"I…I…I haven't looked at my mobile in a while."

"No fucking shit." His bearded jaw is taut with anger. "I'm taking you home."

He reaches out for my arm but I yank it away from him.

"No, you're not."

His shoulders rise and fall with a deep breath. "I'm taking you home. You're completely pissed."

My eyes narrow. "Of course I am. It's Tequila Sunrise night."

"I don't give a fuck," he snaps. "Let's go."

I shoot him a murderous look when a voice interrupts us. "I've got mine. You got yours?" I turn to see Camden holding a sleepy-looking Indie against his body.

Determination slices through Tanner's voice. "I've got her."

I turn to face him, stumbling a bit as I wag my finger in his face. "Hey, I am *not* yours!" Suddenly, Tanner bends over and I'm airborne for a second, landing heavily on top of Tanner's shoulder. "Are you fucking kidding me, Harris?" I begin pounding on his back but it's to no avail. "I'm in a dress. My arse is hanging out for all of England!"

"Your arse was hanging out when you spread out on the floor a minute ago. I'm taking you home, Ryan. Even if you're kicking and screaming."

"You're such an arrogant arsehole!" My hands stop their assault on Tanner's backside in favour of covering my rump. This is mortifying. I hang my head and let my hair cover my face, praying like fuck I don't see anyone I know. "I can't believe this is happening."

"Believe it, woman." Tanner pauses at the door and turns his body so my head is facing a different direction. "Now, tell this nice man I'm not a rapist."

A bouncer-looking bloke turns his head upside down to make eye contact with me. I mumble, "He's not a rapist. Just a walking dead man." I straighten a bit with my crescendoed scream. The bouncer lets out a hearty laugh that dumps hot coals into the pit of my belly. So *not* the reaction I was looking for.

He moves to let us pass and then Tanner drops me down in front of a cab. I ball up my fists and wallop him a few times. "I'm not a petulant child, you animal."

He doesn't even flinch.

I exhale in concession and fold myself in behind Indie and Camden. When we're all in the cab and it begins moving, Tanner breaks the silence with a surprisingly jovial tone. "Well, did you all have a fun night?"

Pukes McGee

TANNER

BY THE TIME WE PULL UP TO BELLE'S FLAT, SHE LOOKS A LOT LESS angry and a lot more green around the gills.

"I'm going to take Indie back to our flat," Camden murmurs, looking down at Indie asleep on his shoulder. "I leave for Manchester at the end of the week, so…"

His voice trails off and my stomach drops at his mention of Manchester. In all the craziness of the past week, I completely forgot this weekend is when Arsenal plays at Man U. My two brothers will be facing off. Not only is it a pretty sticky rival, but Gareth is a starting defender and Camden is a striker. This is a huge weekend for my family.

Belle nods and hiccups. "Take good care of her. Make sure she has aspirin before she passes out. Tequila Sunrises give Indie a massive headache."

She moves to get out of the cab and I don't like how she's looking. In a split decision, I decide that my family stuff can wait and I get out after her.

"What are you doing?" she croaks, trying to shove me back in.

"I'm coming inside." I bat her hands away from me. They remind me of fluttering moths.

"No, you're not." She stomps her foot and tries to push me again.

"Yes, I am. You're pissed and I don't trust you to take care of yourself."

"Bloody hell, you're so overbearing!" she exclaims and then her eyes go wide as I move closer to her. She covers her mouth with her hand for a split second before bending over and retching all over the pavement. She cries out pathetically, "I got puke on my hand."

I grimace, stepping away from the splatter. "Like I said, I'm coming inside."

I help Belle up to her flat and unlock the door for her. She trudges straight for the stairs, not even bothering to take off the knockout boots she's wearing. I tell her I'll be right up and pop into her kitchen to get her a glass of water.

As I stand at the sink, I pull my mobile out to reread the twenty texts I fired off to Belle in a blind panic earlier this evening. Indie had texted Camden over two hours ago saying she and Belle were completely pissed and she wanted him to come dance with her so she didn't have to dance with anyone else. Camden's a bit of a possessive sod, so he texted her back immediately, asking where she was.

Then she never replied. So he made me text Belle to find out where they were. Not wanting to come off too clingy, I kept my texts light at first.

Tanner: What are you wearing? Want me to come check it out?
Tanner: Need a dance partner? You know I have great moves.

After an hour of nothing, they got less cute…

Tanner: Where are you guys?
Tanner: Camden is worried about Indie. Text me back.

Closing in on hour two of *Operation Find Belle and Indie*, my texts were a little more like:

Tanner: You ask me to text you and then you blow me off. Real mature.
Tanner: Belle, I am your fucking boyfriend. Fake or not, the least you can do is text me back.
Tanner: TELL ME WHERE YOU ARE. NOW.

Thankfully, Camden had an idea of where to start our search and we lucked out at Club Taint. Though, seeing that loser with his hands on Belle did not please me. She was clearly pissed and he was clearly taking advantage. Say what you want about my history with women, but I would *never* take advantage of a situation like Belle's. Thank fuck I showed up when I did. And then she had the cheek to fight me when I told her we were leaving. I am not pleased.

Ready to rip her a new one, I pause before I leave her kitchen, turning around and grabbing her a couple of chocolates out of her cubby. I may be angry, but I'm not a monster.

When I come upstairs to give her a piece of my mind, I find her hunched over the toilet with her head resting on her arms. Her long, booted legs are tucked up under her butt and her dress is riding so high I can see her arse hanging out of her thong. It would be hot…if it weren't for the whole vomit/toilet conundrum.

"Why are you still here?" she groans and begins dry-heaving, her hair slipping out of her feeble grasp.

I set the glass of water down and grab a hair tie off the counter.

"Because I'd like to make sure you live through the night."

She rolls her mascara-smeared eyes. "I'm drunk Tanner, not dying."

I shake off her argument and bend over to scrape her hair back away from the toilet bowl.

"Stop messing with my hair," she groans. "You don't know what you're doing."

"Hush," I chastise. "Haven't you seen my awesome mane? I'm an expert." I ball her inky hair up into a messy bun and tighten it just as she begins puking again.

I kneel down behind her, rubbing her back in small circles, feeling the heave of every breath she takes. I hear her weeping a bit between retches, so I bring my other hand up as well.

God, puking is the worst. Self-inflicted puking is double worse.

After a while with no more upchucking, she inhales deeply and flushes the toilet again. I move with her as she drops off to her side, sidling up next to me against the wall. I stretch my arm over her shoulders and she tucks into me with a tremble.

"My breath stinks."

"No it doesn't," I murmur and pull a chocolate out of my pocket.

"You're a liar and a thief," she mumbles, deftly unwrapping the dark bar.

My chest rumbles with silent laughter. "Don't get your knickers in a twist. I grabbed them for you."

"You have no power over my knickers, Tan."

She looks up at me, nibbling on the sweet. Her lips are close, and it's a strange sensation to want to kiss her right now after she's been puking for the last twenty minutes. I kiss her forehead instead.

She tucks her head back against my chest. "Thanks for taking care of me."

"It's no big deal," I reply, realising I kind of like taking care of her.

"And sorry for fighting with you like that. You were just trying to help."

My brows lift, surprised by her apology coming so easily. I thought for sure she'd make me fight for it. "I needed to make sure you were safe. You weren't safe tonight."

"I know," she moans. "I just...I miss Indie and I got carried away I think."

A sympathetic look creases my brow. "She misses you, too. She talks about you all the time you know?"

She looks up with a childlike smile. "She does?"

I nod. "We're on the road together a lot, so there's plenty of time for talking. She's incessantly singing your praises. At work, as a friend, whatever. It's completely mental because you two are bloody flatmates and you act like you've got countries separating you."

She sighs. "We're best friends."

I nod. "I get it."

"Is Camden your best friend? You two seem to have a rather natural bromance about you."

I huff. "I suppose so. But it's different for brothers I think. And with him at Arsenal and me at Bethnal…we're changing."

Belle giggles. "God, we're a couple of pathetic mopes, aren't we? Moaning over people we miss in our lives and we can't even have sex with them."

This makes me laugh. "I wouldn't mind seeing you and Indie have a go at it."

"Gross!" she exclaims. "Better, you and Camden get busy. I can just see *Twin Brother Dearest* blowing up as the next hot new romance novel."

"God, you're disgusting," I chuckle.

"You like it."

I squeeze her to me and trail my hand down her back in smooth, comforting motions. We settle into a natural, comfortable sort of silence on the bathroom floor next to the toilet. It's peculiar but something that feels right in some ways.

"I think I'm good to go to bed now." Belle's voice interrupts my brooding.

I nod and stand to help her up. I watch her as she brushes her teeth, eyeing her handbag on the floor in the bathroom as we walk out. She slips into her closet and changes into a long cotton T-shirt. I strip down to my boxer briefs and tell her I'm going to go use the loo one last time before we go to bed.

Closing myself in the bathroom, I riffle through her bag until I find her mobile. Swiping the screen, I'm grateful to see there's no lock on it as I pull my text messages up and delete all the crazy-sounding ones. After that, I tuck it away and ignore the fact that I'm trying way too hard to look cool.

When I slip into bed, she curls up next to me like it's the most natural thing ever. I guess I just let it be because, all in all, this hasn't been the worst night of my life.

Rivals

Belle

THE NEXT MORNING, I WAKE TO FIND TANNER PERUSING THE shelves of my built-in bookcase. He's standing in the morning light, wearing nothing but his underwear like an inky, muscly, mussed-up wet dream. The sight does wonders for a hangover, I'll tell you that.

He picks up one of the several small drawings that I have stacked one right after another, similar to my books. I have so many drawings. I've been making them since I was five. It was a hobby my mother and father both pushed on me adamantly. I think mostly because it was something I was quiet while doing, and a quiet Belle made for a happy mummy and daddy.

A smirk plays on Tanner's lips as he stares at one longer than normal.

"Which one is it?" I croak, my voice hoarse.

He jumps and his eyes snap to mine. With a sheepish shrug, he turns it around to face me. It's a self-portrait I drew when I was four-teen, but I defiled it by adding devil horns, a pitch fork, and a curly mustache.

"That's my parent's favourite one."

He chuckles. "I hardly believe that. You were quite cute, metal mouth and all. Are those dungarees you're wearing?"

"Hey, they were in style back then!" I screech, feeling my headache a bit more now.

Tanner points to the bedside table. "There's water and aspirin right there."

I turn and snatch them up quicker than I thought humanly possible with this kind of hangover. "You just making yourself at home now? Digging around my medicine cabinet?"

His brows lift. "I didn't hear you complaining when you swallowed the pills."

"All right, all right, keep your shirt on. It's not even nine."

"Speaking of, don't you have to work?" he asks.

"Took a personal day."

"Nice. What are you going to do with it?"

My eyes trail down Tanner's body. "After a shower to wash the stink off, I'm sure I can think of a couple of things."

Tanner shoots me a mock-surprised look. "Why, Dr. Ryan, are you hitting on me?"

A ring stops me from responding. Tanner strides over to his jeans in a heap on the floor and pulls out his mobile.

"Hiya, Vi," he says, walking back over to the bookcase to replace the drawing. "Yes, I did realise that was the match this weekend...No, I haven't talked to him about it yet...I don't know. He seemed fine last night I guess...No, Gareth hasn't called. Gareth never calls...I agree with Hayden. You shouldn't go, it's too far...Sure, I'll stop by later...Okay, bye."

"Family problems?" I ask.

He shakes his head from side to side. "Sort of. Camden and our older brother, Gareth, are playing each other on Saturday."

"Oh, that's right! Arsenal and Man U rivalry is pretty epic."

His brows lift. "Yeah, Vi's concerned. She wants to go, but she's way too pregnant to travel that far. She's just mother-henning like she always does."

Tanner sighs and flops down on the bed beside me, staring up at the ceiling, obviously deep in thought.

Not sure how to help, I say the first thing that comes to mind. "Would it help if you went?"

He frowns and side-eyes me. "I don't need to go."

"Why not? You're off. It sounds like your brothers could use some support. It's the perfect time to go."

"I'd have to see if Gareth has dumped his tickets yet, then find a hotel. I bet the trains are all full. Everybody and their dog will be at this match."

"Can't you stay with your brother?"

"Yeah." He shrugs sullenly. "I guess."

"Then it's settled. I'll drive."

He turns to look at me. "You want to go to the match?"

"An Arsenal and Man U game? Hell yes. I'm a Devils fan through and through. I thought you knew!"

He gives me a look like I've just committed treason, but then glances down at my breasts and redirects his thoughts. "Let's get you in that shower."

Praying Mantis

TANNER

"I'M DRIVING," I SAY TO BELLE, WALKING UP TO HER CAR AS SHE parks along the side of the road by my flat. Her window is down and she looks at me like I'm deranged as I toss my suitcase in the backseat and move to open her door.

Her jaw is dropped. "It's my bloody car. You're not driving!" She closes the door.

"I'm not going to have you driving in the dark for five hours, woman. End of." I open it again.

"Well, you're the one who changed the plans from leaving tomorrow morning to tonight instead. I was perfectly fine with leaving early tomorrow."

I exhale. Everything with Belle is a confrontation. She can't just follow the simplest instructions.

"I want to beat the traffic and have a lie in tomorrow. You haven't seen Gareth's house. Trust me, you'll thank me for this." I head nod for her to get out.

"Well, I can still drive! I'm not some meek female who can't handle the treacherous motorways without my girdle. Fuck off. I'm driving." She closes the door.

Shaking my head, I rip it open again, unbuckle her seatbelt, and pull her out. I do my best to ignore the hateful words spewing out of her mouth as I walk her over to the passenger side. When she's still moaning on and on about what an arrogant prat I am, I spin on my heel and shove her hips back until her arse is pressed up against the door. My fingers bite into the arc of her hip bone, pinning her to the vehicle. I drop my mouth into the same breathing space as hers and she still won't stop.

With a frustrated growl, I mesh my lips with hers. She lets out a whimper of surprise but catches up quickly and returns my kiss with vigour. My tongue swirls deeply between her lips, aching to taste more than just her mouth but knowing this will have to do for now. She pulls me to her so our bodies are flush together. I swear our pulses synchronise because the whir of traffic around us goes silent and all I can hear is the pounding of my heart inside my chest.

A smile teases the corner of my mouth when a pleasant hum rumbles from somewhere deep inside of her. She practically thrusts her groin against me when my hands slide up to the sides of her breasts. I smooth my thumbs over her nipples and nearly fall apart when I feel them bead beneath my touch.

No. Fucking. Bra.

And in a blink of an eye, she's topping from the bottom again.

I like to think I've got Belle all figured out by now. Her day off from work consisted of us spending the majority of our time in her bed. In her shower. Even in her kitchen at one point. So to say I'm familiar with how to stimulate Belle Ryan's body would be a gross understatement. But somehow, she still finds a way to make things interesting. To stir the pot. To get me going. To surprise me. And something simple like not wearing a bra is a perfect example of the control she manages to maintain.

I'm becoming addicted.

Thankfully, she had a big surgery at the end of the week that she needed to focus on so we were forced to part ways until this evening. My mind and my cock needed a break. It also gave me a chance to call Santino yesterday to check in and see how we're doing. He said he'd been talking to Belle's father and they were pleased with the coverage thus far. I let him know we would need some addendums to our scheduled dates for this weekend, and he seemed chuffed that we were headed on a mini holiday to Manchester. He said he'd spin that to the press and they'd lap it up like dogs, especially with it being such a high-profile game.

So far this fake dating hasn't been hard at all. Belle's a bit of a head case from time to time, but it's nothing a good swizzle stick can't fix. I think a fair amount of dickin' keeps us both in better spirits.

But apparently I haven't had enough because the bulge pressed up against her stomach seems to have a strong muscle memory.

"Fine, you can drive." Belle gasps against my lips as she pulls away. She's breathless as her eyes glance down between us. "But only because that thing can't take care of itself."

Belle's Mercedes isn't the most masculine of vehicles, but it's been a while since I've driven and it feels good to be behind the wheel again. The drive to Manchester is congested, dark, and bland, but Belle's nattering on beside me makes time pass rather quickly. She's a funny storyteller. Her eyes get so big in the blue dashboard lights as she animates her story. She likes to ask a lot of questions, too, like, "And then do you know what happened?" It's kind of adorable.

Her enthusiasm tonight is because of a set of twins they separated inside the womb earlier today. She tells me how hands-on she got to be during the surgery, and how Dr. Miller is finally starting to trust her more. It blows my mind that she spent her day inside a woman's pregnant stomach, saving babies who weigh no more than a pound each. Most people sit in front of computers at a dull office. She touches the untouchable. She plays God.

The passion she has for her job radiates off of her and it makes me miss my own. Being a career athlete is incredible but it's hard at times, too. The physical and mental stress is exhausting. You're not just paid to play football. You're paid to win. And your fans feel like they own a piece of you. Your victory is their victory. Your loss is their loss. When you don't perform up to their standards, they turn on you rather quickly.

However, when you're on top of your game—when the crowd chants your name and their cheers are for you and you alone—it's the stuff gods are made of.

"All right then," Belle states, interrupting my thoughts and propping a bare foot on the dashboard. "I shared some Deep Talk, now it's your turn." She breaks the shell off a pistachio nut and hands it to me. "Are you worried that watching the match tomorrow will be hard?"

I frown at her and pop the nut into my mouth, chewing on it thoughtfully. "Why would you think it'd be hard?"

Her brows lift. "I imagine you're itching to get back on the pitch. Seeing your two brothers play on their dream teams while you're stuck with me sounds a bit brutal."

I think about that for a minute. I'd love to play again but, for some reason, I don't feel ready. As hard as this break I've had has been, it feels like it came at a good time. Maybe some time away from the pitch is exactly what I needed to get myself sorted.

"First of all, now that I can be stuck *inside* of you, this fake dating isn't so bad." I shoot her a lewd smirk.

"Oh, aren't you such a romantic." She winks and hands me another nut.

"Second of all, watching my brothers play tomorrow will be a bit of a luxury that I don't get to partake in much. Our football schedules are always conflicting, so I'm excited to be able to just sit and cheer for them."

"Won't it be hard seeing Camden on another team, though? You guys have played closely together for so long."

A tenseness forms in my shoulders, but I shake it away and reply through clenched teeth, "Harris family support is unwavering."

I can feel her watching me as she pries, "But surely things have changed since he started playing for Arsenal?"

"They have," I reply, feeling an annoying prickle on the back of my neck. "But I don't think it will matter in the long run. My siblings are top priority…always."

"But what about when they all start their own families? Your sister is having a baby. Camden and Indie are all over each other. I mean, everyone's kind of moving on, right? Even though in the end, we all end up alone."

Her last words are murmured to the window and they shock me more than anything else she said. "You save families from despair every day. Surely you're not that cynical."

"I save them from medical circumstances," she corrects. "I have no idea what their lives are like when they go home."

"Well, I don't go a day without speaking to one of my siblings. My dad has managed my entire career. Vi supports everything we do. We're thick as thieves. We may be one tent away from a full-blown circus, but we're woven into each other's everyday decisions and I don't see that ever changing."

I see her brow furrow in the dark as she mulls over what I've just said like she's warring with something. Belle's eyes are so expressive, you'd have to be blind not to notice.

"What are you thinking about?" I push and her gaze snaps over at me like she forgot I was there.

"Nothing." She smiles but it looks odd. "I think we've had enough Deep Talk. Let's do something fun." She sets the bag of pistachios on the dashboard.

"Did you have something in mind?"

She shoots me a sly, secretive smile. "I was thinking more along the lines of *deep throat*."

My eyes swerve to her and she's tweaking her brows at me, her gaze dropping down to my trousers. When she sucks her lower lip into her mouth and her teeth bite down on the spongy flesh, I forget all about what we were talking about. Truthfully, I think I forget my own name.

"You better not be giving me that look unless you intend to put it to action," I warn.

Her smile grows. "What kind of action specifically?"

My hips pulse with need and I take a cleansing breath when my dick presses against my zipper. "The kind that involves very different nuts."

She giggles and leans across the seat to whisper in my ear, "Good, I'm still hungry."

She reaches out and takes my hand in hers, bringing it up to her mouth for a chaste kiss before pulling my pointer finger between her lips. She sucks hard and bites down softly. I have to mentally scream at myself to keep my eyes on the road.

Her voice is the epitome of sexy when she utters, "You taste good to me, Harris." She releases my hand and reaches over to palm my denim clad groin. Her fingers tighten around the shape of my erection stamped through my trousers, like a snake under a blanket. She lets out a breathy moan as she firmly strokes me. "You feel good, too."

I drop my head back on the headrest and focus my eyes on the road. "For fuck's sake, Ryan."

"Call me Belle when I'm sucking you off," she demands.

I nod without looking at her. I'll call her whatever she bloody well wants me to call her right now.

She undoes the button of my jeans, then slides my zipper down. The erotic noise in the car is deafening.

"The first time I saw your cock when I picked you up in my car," she says, working to pull me free, "I wanted to suck you off."

I moan when air touches my crown. "You did? I thought you wanted to kill me."

Her hand wraps tightly around my shaft. "I did. But not before I tasted you." Her head drops to my lap.

Warmth.

Warm, heated, wet-sucking perfection encases my hard-on. *I think I've died and gone to heaven.* My vision clouds for a second before I shake my head and watch the road more carefully.

She pulls her mouth off of me while her hand works me up and down. "Maybe I'm like a praying mantis," she murmurs, watching her action on my dick. "Maybe I wanted to fuck you before I killed you."

As she drops her mouth down on me again, I let out a nervous laugh. "God, you're crazy."

She sucks hard for a minute and releases, stroking the slippery skin with her hand. "You like crazy."

My brows lift as I reach down and grip her hair in my hand, riding the motions of her head bobbing on my cock. "Yes, I fucking do."

She pauses, the cool breath of her voice teasing my sanity. "But did you know that not all female mantises bite the heads off their mates? There are studies that show some of them let their lovers live."

She drops down and swirls her tongue around the pre-come I can feel beading out, lapping at it like it's her last meal. Her lips wrap tighter around me this time as she deep throats me over and over and over. My dick hits the back of her throat, bringing me right to the edge. Right to the brink. Right to the—

"Belle, I'm going to come."

"Good," she growls. "I have you right where I want you."

She sucks so hard I lose all control and topple over the edge in a painful, aching orgasm. Her hands are splayed out on my thighs and she continues sucking, swallowing every drop of me down her throat.

When I'm finished, she lets go of me. Her cheeks are red as she wipes the bottom of her lip with her hand.

I fight to catch my breath. The car suddenly too warm. The air suddenly too moist. The urge I have to pull over and fuck her until neither of us can see straight is so strong, I'm not sure I'll be able to resist. I grab her by the jaw and pull her lips to mine for a quick, chaste kiss of thanks. With my hungry eyes back on the road, I murmur, "You're going to be the death of me."

Belle

Despite my little joyride on Tanner, we make good time. Gareth's house is in Astbury—a village right outside of Manchester—and when we drive down his long, private gravel lane, it feels a bit like coming home.

However, when his detached house finally comes into view, I'm pleased to see it's much more contemporary than what I grew up in. I don't think I could stand walking into another dusty, old, Victorian mansion.

Tanner grabs our bags and we walk up the steps toward the front porch. I see some movement through the large plate glass windows surrounding the oak door before it opens.

"Tanner!" Gareth's deep voice exclaims as he steps out onto the brick porch. He looks a bit dishevelled. His dark hair is unruly on top of his head, and his hazel eyes dart between Tanner and whatever is behind him inside the house. He looks as if he didn't know we were coming. His voice is tight when he adds, "Surprised to see you tonight."

I frown up at Tanner. "Didn't you tell him you decided to come early?"

Tanner shrugs at me. "Didn't occur to me."

I look at Gareth, ready to voice my apologies, but a woman steps out into the doorway behind him. She's simply dressed in all black, and her chestnut hair is tied back into a ponytail at the nape of her neck.

"It's fine. We're all done here." Her American accent is smooth and confident as she throws a garment bag over her shoulder.

"Who's this?" Tanner leers, a look of shock and curiosity on his face.

"This is no one," Gareth snaps. "I mean, she's someone, but… Sloan is my personal shopper."

"Personal shopper?" Tanner's voice is unconvinced.

"I prefer celebrity fashion stylist," Sloan states, her voice crisp and unforgiving as she moves past us. I watch Gareth's eyes drink her in with a pained look on his face. "And I really need to be going. I only did this late call as a favour. Good luck at your event tomorrow, Mr. Harris."

Without a glance back, Sloan strides down the drive toward her car parked in front of the garage. I frown when I see her ponytail is mussed into a bit of a nest down her back.

"Who the fuck was that really?" Tanner asks, placing a hand on Gareth's shoulder. "Cam and I thought you were fucking celibate!"

Gareth shakes him off. "Don't be daft. She's no one." He looks at me. "I'm sorry you're saddled up with my twat of a brother. Vi's told me the particulars of what you guys are going through and, knowing Tanner here, I'm sure you're about ready to kill someone. I'm Gareth. It's nice to meet you, officially. Cam and Indie speak very highly of you."

He reaches out and shakes my hand. I see a tiny bit of resemblance between him and Tanner in the shape of their eyes, but that's where the similarities end. Gareth is more the tall, dark, and handsome variety, whereas Tanner is more the dirty, blonde, and sexy category. However, they both tower over me and ooze that athletic sort of posture. The kind that makes walking through a foyer look artful.

We follow Gareth through the living room and into a bright,

modern kitchen where he grabs us both a bottle of water from the fridge.

"Sorry, no booze in the house. I don't drink during the season."

I roll the bottle in my hands. "It's no problem."

Tanner throws a lazy arm around my shoulders. "Yeah, this one got rat-arsed the other night and is probably still feeling the effects."

I scoff, "I am not. And would you kindly shut the fuck up?"

Gareth booms with a deep laugh. "Yes! Finally! A woman not afraid to put you in your place."

Tanner's eyes narrow as he prepares to take a sip. "I put her in places, too."

My jaw drops. "You better watch it, or the only place you'll end up tonight is a cold shower."

This silences him and Gareth's shoulders shake with a silent laugh.

"So why did you guys come down tonight? I thought you weren't coming until tomorrow?"

Tanner gives me a random cheeky arse squeeze and says, "I just needed to get the fuck out of London. It feels like a bloody fishbowl lately."

I nod feeling similarly. I didn't even have the heart to tell Tanner that our little snog outside his flat before we left was photographed. "The vultures are everywhere."

Gareth shakes his head. "I don't envy you guys. That's why I like it out here. It's private. It's quiet. The London nightlife is not for me. Manchester is bad enough at times."

"I'm beginning to see the appeal." Tanner looks around the kitchen as if considering it from a different perspective.

"Well, I hate to rush off but I need sleep. Match day tomorrow and all." He turns to Tanner. "All the guestrooms are ready so take whichever you'd like. I'll be heading in early, so I probably won't see you until after the match. We can grab a quick drink, but then I have an event I need to attend."

"No problem. I think Cam was hoping to catch up with us."

He half smiles. "Yes, Camden." A look of amazement casts over his features and he shakes his head. "I still can't get over the fact that I'll be defending him tomorrow. It's been years since we've played on the same pitch."

"I didn't realise you ever played for Bethnal Green," I state.

"Yeah, for two years and then I got a Man U offer I couldn't refuse."

"Wouldn't refuse is more like it," Tanner adds. "You were desperate to get away from Dad."

"I wouldn't say desperate." Gareth shifts on his feet.

"I would. And not very wise considering you signed with his old team."

A dark look crosses Gareth's face. "I had my reasons."

Tanner holds his hands back in surrender. "I'm not saying you didn't. It's just got to be weird living in his shadow at Man U. Seems like every time you're interviewed after a match, they bring up his glory days."

Gareth scoffs, "The media are looking for a story. Something to sensationalise and make viral. Hopefully tomorrow you two are the focus instead of me."

I roll my eyes. "Looking forward to it!"

Gareth smiles. "Well, you're a trooper for doing this. Tanner is going to owe you a major favour when this is all over."

"Oh yes," I reply with a smirk. "Tanner will pay me back for many things."

Tanner's tone is warning when he says, "Belle, your crazy is showing."

"That's because I want it to," I whisper and wink.

Gareth chuckles. "I've never seen Tanner squirm like this. You're bloody perfect for him."

His comment knocks me down a peg. "That's what we're trying to make everyone believe."

When Gareth leaves, Tanner takes me upstairs to the guestroom farthest from Gareth's room. He's about as subtle as a flying brick. It's a huge, lush room with a gorgeous bed and en-suite bath. It immediately makes me glad we came down tonight instead of tomorrow. The bed looks like heaven and it's been ages since I've had a good night's sleep.

"Did you pack your bathing suit?" Tanner asks, setting my suitcase on the dresser and opening it up.

"Yes." I stride over and attempt to shoo him away from my personal effects. "Get out of my stuff."

"Never," he replies, grabbing a pair of my knickers and tucking them into his pocket.

"God, you're mental."

"Put your suit on." Tanner winks and disappears into the loo.

By the time he comes out, I'm already covered up with a cotton sundress. Tanner holds my hand as he walks us down the stairs and to the other wing of the house. After passing through an impressive media room and a fully kitted professional gym, it's then that I see the gorgeous indoor poolroom glowing blue in the darkness. It's completely flanked in glass, the pool lights reflecting off the surfaces like a shimmering oasis. Outside there are loads of overgrown trees giving the sense of seclusion and privacy.

Tanner smirks at me and wastes no time pulling his T-shirt over his head. I have to pause and admire the beauty before me. He looks like a beach bum as he tucks his long blonde locks behind his ears. His tan skin is smooth and bumpy in all the right places. His trimmed beard and ink add a masculine edge to him that is utterly mouth-watering.

He tweaks his eyebrows, sucking me back to reality. His eyes dip. "I showed you mine, now show me yours."

His cheek makes me feel a bit brazen. I glance at the door. "Is there any chance your brother will come down here?"

He frowns. "Tired of me already, Ryan?"

151

I laugh and shake my head. "Not even close, Harris." I frown as I realise just how truly I meant that.

He narrows his eyes. "Gareth is a devoted footballer. Nothing will stop him from getting his eight hours of sleep. We should be safe."

Biting my lip, I reach under my dress and slide my black bikini bottoms down and toss them to him. He catches them deftly with one hand and brings them right to his face, inhaling deeply.

I laugh and shake my head. "Animal."

"Tease," he replies, his eyes turning positively feral.

I do the same with my top and, before I lose my nerve, I slide my dress down, letting it pool around my feet. I'm now standing before him in nothing at all. The look he gives me makes my knees tremble. It's one of complete and total animalistic attraction. He drinks in every bare inch of me—not at all shy, not at all polite. He ogles me as if I was made for him.

And I let him.

I resist all my previous insecurities about my body.

I've never felt such instant comfort with a man before. Perhaps it has to do with our first time together. Or perhaps it's the fact that we've had sex more than a dozen times in a short burst of time. That much intimacy and that much exploration can certainly help a person find comfort. Or perhaps it's the fact that every time I'm naked with him, he has this look of tunnel vision as if nothing else exists in the world besides me and him and what he wants to do to me.

I move to walk past him and over to the water, but he captures my wrist in his hand, stopping me in my tracks. He jerks once and I fall into him, my hands coming to his arms and my breasts brushing against his chest.

"You're fucking gorgeous." He states it with a deep growl and seizes my lips in a surprising and possessive kiss. His hands slide down my backside and he pulls me against his erection.

I pull back with a sharp intake of air and whisper, "Ditch the trunks. We're skinny dipping."

He lets me slip out of his grasp, and I quickly dive into the water, expecting it to cool down the raging inferno swirling in my belly. I'm shocked to find it's warm, like a glorious bath. I pop my head up out of the water with a smile.

"It's a warm water pool!" I exclaim. "Oh my God, it's wonderful. Get in here."

He shakes off the heated look in his eyes and moves to pull his trunks down, his package standing at a full salute. "What you do to me, woman." Shaking his head, he drops down into the water right next to me.

His hands immediately reach, pulling me to him. We tread water in the deep end, our legs tangling together as we swap giggles and kisses and brush up against all our overly sensitive wobbly bits. There's something delicious about skinny dipping that makes me feel like a sex goddess. And skinny dipping in a warm pool is downright erotic, especially when Tanner looks at me the way he's looking at me now. His blue eyes are stunning next to the water. It makes me nervous.

"Tell me something, Belle Ryan," he says, his breath uneven as he swims over to the shallow end by the steps. "Why don't you have a boyfriend?"

His question makes me frown. "Why don't you have a girlfriend?"

He sits down on a step so the water is chest high on him. With a shrug, he leans back and props his elbows on the step behind him. "That's easy. Don't want one."

"Same," I repeat, swimming over next to him. I rest my arms on the edge of the pool, my bare breasts touching the smooth tile.

He scrubs his hand over his wet face. "Well, why don't you want one?"

I think about that for a moment. "I suppose I'm focusing all my energy on my job."

He raises his brows. "Well, you've managed to balance a fake relationship with me okay."

"That's different," I reply.

"How?"

"Because I don't have to give you anything emotional. I just have to give you some time…and my body." I grin.

His eyes narrow thoughtfully at my response. "What if you did have to give me something emotional? What would change?"

"Well, everything." I wipe away some water streaking down from my hair and onto my face. "You say I'm crazy now. Wait until you see me when I actually care about someone. If I *feel* too much, I turn into a life-ruiner. Indie's the only friend I've ever managed to keep, and I think that's because we're cut from the same cloth."

His brow furrows. "How do you mean?"

"Her parents want nothing to do with her. Mine want nothing to do with me."

"Surely that's not true. You're a doctor. They must be proud of you. Hell, I'm proud of you."

His comment shoots through me like a lightning bolt trying to heat my frozen heart. "Thanks, but it's different. Imagine if you didn't play football. What do you think your dad would have done?"

He frowns. "I honestly don't know. I'd like to think he'd support me."

"Well, my parents aren't like that. They have expectations. I chose to go to med school instead of law school and, to my parents, that was the equivalent of spitting on the family crest."

"Christ," he scoffs, but I continue because I'm on a roll now.

"You get along with your family because you're all wild and outspoken and say how you feel and love each other no matter what. Well, mine isn't like that. They love the box my birth checked. But the second I stepped out of that box of the dutiful child, I did more harm than good. And well, you've seen a glimpse of my crazy. Imagine getting that full force."

He frowns. "You don't scare me, Belle."

"Then you are in the minority. I'm just being realistic." I turn around and press my back to the wall. "My family lives the society life. They are political and social climbers. Constant parties, constant dinners, constant charities, schmoozing, boozing. And it's always for a selfish goal. My brother is perfectly suited for that life. He does what he's told. He says the right things. To them, I'm like…a live wire they are terrified of tripping. I'm better off not existing. Being invisible."

Silence stretches out between us and I worry that I shared too much. Got too personal. I just admitted I don't get emotional with blokes and here I am, gushing like a bloody water fountain.

Tanner reaches over and pulls me into his space, dropping his knees so I slide up his body and straddle his lap. My arms wrap around his neck as I try to hide the raw vulnerability that creeps up from a dark place inside of me that I don't often visit. Ever since I met Indie and we started our Tequila Sunrise tradition, I don't let my family hurt me anymore. I know life is so much bigger than the pretentious expectations they'd like me to uphold to help them get ahead. Saving lives, helping babies…That's a way to really live life.

Tanner pushes a wet strand of hair off my face. "If your parents don't see the incredible work you do, they are knobheads."

I huff out a pathetic laugh and pin my eyes to his with determination, not wanting to come off weak. "I don't need their approval anymore. I gave up on that a long time ago."

He looks down, pondering that comment. "Still sucks, though."

It does. In my heart of hearts, it actually really does hurt. I look outside, into the darkness all around us, staring up through the skylight for any sign of stars, anything to remind me that the world is bigger than my drama.

My words are quiet when I give voice to them again. "It was a relief when they quit expecting me to attend their events. To stop participating in the charade. I could never fit the mould they expected of me. Honestly, what I'm doing for you is the first time in years they've asked anything of me. It's partly why I didn't fight it more." I look straight into Tanner's eyes. "But do you know the worst part of it all?"

"What?" he asks, a seriousness to his face that lets me know he's really listening.

"Even though I never want to attend another one of their parties for as long as I live, I still want to be invited."

A tenderness washes over his face, and I hope to God he can't tell that the drip falling down my cheek is a tear. I'm mortified by how much I've babbled and immediately wish I could reverse time and just shut the fuck up.

I wait for Tanner to crack some rude joke, make some snarky comment, or do something silly to lighten the mood. Instead, he grabs my face in his hands and strokes his thumbs down my cheeks. He tenderly tucks my dark tendrils behind my ears and angles his head to skim his mouth over mine.

His lips are soft and comforting at first. A light touch to show support and understanding. But his hands move slowly from my face to my back and neck as he wraps both of his arms around me into a hug so tight, my breath has to synchronise with his.

Our bodies are completely flush, not a sliver of space to be found while our lips never stop moving. He continues hugging me and kissing me, his tongue warm and lyrical as he maintains a complete hold over me. It's as if he's trying to squeeze the ache out of me and pass it from me to him.

We're both panting when we break apart, overwhelmed by the emotional exchange of our embrace. Tanner's eyes stay on mine as his hands dip under the water and he positions me over his erection. He quirks a brow in silent question. I grant permission, trusting that he wouldn't ask if he didn't think it was safe. He pulls me down over top of him. The water makes for a rough entry but once he's in, I quiver with need. The intensity in his eyes and the raw, carnal ache he's showing me is too much. I work myself against him, my breath heavy as he tucks further and further inside of me. I moan and throw my head back as my need becomes nearly unbearable.

"No, Belle. Eyes on me." He pulls my face down to him. "I see you."

I drop my chin and nod. Our gazes lock. We hold each other hostage as our bodies tense, our grip on each other biting as we become lost in some sort of alternate universe where our eyes turn into windows to our souls and reveal absolutely everything. I swear if his dick wasn't inside me, the look in his eyes alone would be enough to send me over the edge.

We continue grinding against each other, his hips thrusting upward as he holds me in place above him. Warm waves lap between us with each pulse. My cries of pleasure echo off the walls like the riot of reflecting lights. When my climax nears, desperation takes over and I have to look away while I come or I might never survive this. I scream out his name and he drops his face to my chest, rolling his forehead over my heart. I clutch him to me, ringing my hands through his hair, riding the aftershocks of my intense orgasm. One so strong I swear I could be splitting in two.

"Belle." Tanner's voice is guttural, and I immediately feel the wet heat of him explode inside of me. I grab his face and look into his eyes. They are vacant with shock at first, then slam closed as he presses his forehead to mine. "Oh my God, Belle." His voice is hoarse and disbelieving as he fights to catch his breath.

We hold each other, naked and panting, both coming back down from whatever universe we disappeared into for that brief moment in time. When he pulls back from me, I think he's going to apologise, but all he does is kiss me. He kisses me and I think I hear him whisper "thank you."

For what, I'm not really sure.

Old Trafford

TANNER

THE HOUR GLASS SHAPE OF A WOMAN WAS MADE FOR ONE THING and one thing only. Spooning.

It's nearly ten o'clock the next morning and I've been tucked in bed, holding onto Belle Ryan all night. I don't think a woman's body has ever felt this good pressed up against me. Maybe it's because I've fucked her so many times now and it's a completely new experience for me. Regardless, I'm enjoying it while it lasts.

I feel Belle begin to stir in my arms and I reflexively tighten my grip on her, my morning erection pressed up against her supple arse.

"If you're going for accidental anal, I'm going to throat punch you." Belle's morning voice is deep and throaty.

I shake with laughter. "I'm not going for accidental anal, I promise. Actually, I was just lying here realising I had no idea how fantastic spooning was. I've been converted. The way your arse rests perfectly on my dick and how the dip of your waist is like a nice resting spot for my arm…The warmth of you against the warmth of me. Fuck me, it's utter heaven. People should talk about spooning more. It feeds the soul or some shit."

"How long have you been awake?"

158

"An hour maybe?"

"Did you mean to speak all of that out loud just now?"

"Yes, why?"

"Okay, well, maybe just...don't." She chuckles in disbelief. "Who are you and what have you done with Tanner Harris?"

Ignoring her snipe, I nuzzle into her neck. "He's still here, woman. Want to play hide the sausage?" I flex my hips into her back.

"Bloody hell, I've just woken up to you moaning on and on about how spooning feeds your soul. What more could you possibly ask of life?"

"I need you to feed the beast." I nibble her ear and add, "The beast is my cock."

Her laugh is the only sound uttered until I'm balls deep in her and her giggles turn to cries of sexual perfection.

As I dress for the match, I can't help but wonder what life was like for my mum and dad when they used to live here in Manchester with all of us. Dad was a star defender for Man U. Mum was home raising the five of us. They had a posh flat here where we all lived for most of the season, and then they had a big brick mansion in Chigwell just outside of London. Gareth once told me that our mum preferred life in London so she refused to make Manchester our year-round home. Truthfully, it's one of the very few things I've ever got Gareth to reveal about our mother. Neither he nor Dad like to talk about her. Vi knows a bit because she found boxes of her old poems and pored through them, gifting us several of them right around the time she started up with Hayden. It helped give us a window into who she was, but I still have a million questions about her.

I was three years old when she got sick. I don't remember a lot of what happened. The only thing I know is that our dad immediately broke his contract with Man U, sold our Manchester flat, and took us all back to Chigwell. It was a big to-do with the press because it was such a huge loss for United.

Gareth was eight years old when we moved. Booker was one and Vi was four. The time around our mum's death was ugly. Our dad did not do well for many years, refusing help from pretty much everyone. He was content to stow us away in that mansion, only letting us out for school and nothing more.

But somehow, Bethnal Green F.C. got through the door, and that's when things began to turn around for our family. Needless to say, an appreciation for the sport of football is highly coveted in my world. It brought our family back together and made us who we are today. Lord knows what might have happened to us otherwise.

Belle comes out of the loo wearing a tight, faded red Man U tee. It shows off her large tits, but she still looks comfortable enough to do some serious cheering.

I give her jean clad arse a hardy smack. "You look good."

"You're going neutral I see," she states, eyeing my dark grey T-shirt and jeans.

"It's good business. I can't show favouritism. A footballing family feud ends in bloodshed."

"Am I okay in this? I didn't even think about the photos we might be in today."

I nod. "If you're a United fan, you're a United fan. No need to hide it for your fake boyfriend."

Her eyes tighten imperceptibly and I wonder if I misspoke. Or maybe she's getting tired of the circus our lives have become.

"Have I said thank you recently for doing all of this?"

She rolls her eyes. "It's not just for you, Tanner. I need it, too."

"Right," I reply with a frown. "I keep forgetting that part. Shall we be off then?"

Old Trafford is an imposing stadium with a rich, historical ambience to it. It's no Tower Park, but Mancunians practically piss themselves once they get inside. Seventy-five thousand fans all mash together drunk, loud, and proud, setting the tone for the whole day.

Belle and I find our seats in one of the sponsored upper level sections with several of the other WAGs—the wives and girlfriends of the players. It's not where I would have preferred to sit, but it's a sold out match and these are the seats Gareth had for us.

"Tanner Harris?" A woman says my name like it's a song. I turn to see a blonde, big-titted WAG sitting behind me with several like-faced ladies. "Hi! I'm Sasha, Benny's wife. Ladies, this is another one of those Harris Brothers. The one I told you about."

"Oh my God, one's hotter than the next. How is that possible?" a woman beside Sasha croons. "I'm Billy's girlfriend. We live near Gareth's house."

Another woman pipes in, "Gareth said you were coming with your little friend to the match. So nice you could make it." The woman reaches out and touches my shoulder for no apparent reason other than to squeeze the girth of it.

I hear Belle huff beside me and immediately wrap an arm around her, inserting her between me and the ladies. "This is my girlfriend, Dr. Belle Ryan. She saves babies."

The women all look down at Belle, inspecting her attire. She's kitted out like a proper football fan. Her dark hair is in a high ponytail and she has a Devils tattoo on one cheek that she bought at a stand outside. The WAGs look like they were dressed by Gareth's personal shopper, designer money dripping all over them.

Belle chuckles next to me and murmurs in my ear, "Real subtle, Harris."

"You can call me Belle." She smiles politely, but the women

barely look at her.

"But Dr. Ryan is more respectful," I add. "Enjoy the match."

I turn around and pull Belle down into her seat, encasing her in my protective arm.

"Bitchy WAGs, can't handle any fresh meat stepping in?" she asks.

"They look at you like a wannabe WAG," I reply. "It's my fault. My reputation puts a target on your back."

She cuts her dark eyes at me. "And what will you be like when this is all over?"

"What do you mean?" I ask.

"I mean when you and I are done. Will you go back to how you were before?"

I frown, not having given it much thought. "I suppose a version of that, yes. Not as bad as before, of course. My contract won't allow it."

Her brows lift. "I see." She turns toward the field and stands as the team song begins playing.

"You all right?" I ask in her ear.

She nods and sings loudly with a bright, toothy smile on her face the whole time.

Frowning, I turn my attention to the pitch and listen closely as both of my brothers' names are announced. Goosebumps prickle my skin when I hear the crowd chanting the Harris name at a deafening volume. This is Gareth's home turf and he's served this team well as a defender for quite some time now. He deserves this.

Cam and Gareth find each other on the pitch before the kick-off. Camden says something in Gareth's ear, and Gareth laughs and socks him in the stomach. The two part ways with big smiles. Cam's a striker; Gareth's a defender. The odds are certainly in their favour for colliding again before the end of the match, but nothing can tear away the immense sense of pride I have watching them down there right now.

A cameraman shows up in our section, no doubt having been tipped off by Santino that Belle and I are up here. When he makes it completely obvious he's shooting us, I throw an arm around Belle's shoulders and chant right along with her even though our section is a bit sedate.

Belle seems clueless about the cameraman as she screams something vile at the ref. I laugh heartily, feeling like I could just as easily be sitting next to Vi. Vi's voice carries more than my dad's at our Tower Park matches. It's like my ears are hardwired to the tone of her voice.

After watching Belle's enthusiasm for several minutes, I lean into her ear. "I need to make you a Bethnal fan before this is all said and done."

She frowns at me like I'm speaking a different language. "I already am! I've been to several of your matches. My love for football is multi levelled." She laughs and trains her eyes back on the pitch.

"So you've seen me play?" I ask, not ready to let this go.

"Of course! I live in Bethnal Green. How could I have not been to Tower Park?"

This shocks me. "So what did you think?" I ask, needing some level of approval from her before I can allow us to enjoy the match.

She keeps her eyes focused on the pitch but they narrow, seemingly deep in thought. After a few seconds, she leans over toward me to shout out the side of her mouth, "I think it's a fucking travesty your brother left. You two danced out there on that pitch together. You were more than strikers. You were goal scorers working in tandem, and both two-footed to boot. It was like nothing I've ever seen. But if you suck it up and find your balls again, you can get that stride with DeWalt. He's not as good as Camden, but he's deceptively quick and practically surgical with his passing. You can use that. You're the best goal scorer Bethnal has ever seen. You're better than Camden, but I'll chop your balls off if you ever tell him I said so."

I'm speechless. Utterly speechless. I didn't have a clue she was even remotely invested in football until now. She gave me no indication except for saying she was a United fan. But hearing her speak so fluently about not only the sport I love, but the team that is my pride and joy, makes me want to drop down on one knee and marry her on the spot.

I grab her arm until she turns to look at me. "You're not at all what I expected, Belle Ryan."

She shoots me a sneaky smirk. "The crazy ones are always the most surprising."

She winks and I can't help myself. I grab her face and plant my lips on her in an inappropriate for public kiss.

She pulls away laughing. "Good grief, Harris! Control yourself."

"Never," I yell and pull her under my arm, dropping a kiss on the top of her head and looking back down at the pitch. "Come on, Harrises! Get your pansy arses moving and stop prancing around like fucking ballerinas!"

Belle laughs and high fives me, and we get back to the task at hand.

The pre-match talk had Man U topping Arsenal three goals to one. They were spot-on. Camden scored a long, thunderous strike into the top-left corner up against Man U's left defender only three minutes into the match. It had the Red Devils all shook up, but I smiled with pride when I saw Gareth give Cam a pat on the back as they jogged past each other. As beautiful as that moment was between them, I was disheartened not to be out there myself.

I can close my eyes and think of at least twenty different times when Camden and I embraced after a goal. If it was my goal, Cam would always ruffle my hair and fuck up my sweatband. I would shove him away and we'd push each other back and forth until it turned into a cheesy brotherly hug. If he scored, I usually tried to smack his arse or pinch his nipple, anything to embarrass him as only a twin brother can.

But this match was different. This was two brothers playing

against each other. Two rival teams. The stakes were high. So seeing them congratulate each other in any small fashion proved that they put the Harris family pride above football, and that was a thing of beauty.

The Arsenal high from Cam's goal was short-lived. Man U shook up the Gunners' defence by popping in two goals within forty-four seconds of each other. They came out looking better after the break with some big stops from their keeper, but a final midfielder belt from United left Arsenal two down by the end of the match.

It was a sharp, clean game. Beautiful football through and through, which made me happy. No matter how frustrating a loss is, it's never more maddening than when there's dirty play and shoddy calls. I didn't want that stress for my brothers. Not for their first face off.

We head to the South Stand entrance where the players come out so we can meet up with Camden and Gareth. Our plan is to grab a quick pint before Gareth has to leave. The press are swarming the area and I end up being pulled into three interviews, asking how I thought my brothers did. Just when I thought I was going to get out of there scot-free, a female reporter with way too white of teeth calls me her way.

"Tanner, did you and Belle Ryan enjoy the match?"

Belle is standing near the barricades, but her head perks up when she hears her name.

"We did. It was a great, clean game of football."

"I see Belle is a Man U fan. How do you feel about that?"

I smile knowingly. "She's a fan of football. That's good enough for me."

"So you two are spending a lot of time together it seems. Now a mini holiday away. Sightings of you are popping up all over. Does this mean it's getting serious?"

The question makes me laugh, but I'm used to pushy reporters by now. This is no worse than when they grill me after a loss.

"I seriously think Dr. Ryan is lovely." I wink at the reporter, trying to charm her a bit as I walk away.

"Is it true her father is planning to use connections within the Bethnal Green football club to get elected into the Supreme Court?"

This gives me pause. "What?"

"There's speculation that a member of the selection commission is a season ticket holder at Tower Park, and Lord Ryan is first in line to take the next open spot on the court. Can you confirm that?"

"No, I can't confirm that. But there are loads of people who like football in England, so I'm not surprised. I have to go."

I stride over to Belle, who's frowning at me in confusion. I grab her gently by the crook of her arm and usher her away from the crowd and into a quieter area.

"Any clue what that was all about?"

"No, what did she say exactly?"

"That your father is using some connections at Bethnal to get into the Supreme Court. What the fuck does the law and football have to do with one another?"

"I haven't the faintest idea," she replies with a scoff. "But knowing my father, he's working an angle any way he can."

I roll my eyes and drop a kiss on her lips. "Let's not let him muck up our night."

After Cam and Gareth are done with their interviews, the four of us head over to Sam Platt's Pub for a quick pint. They have a VIP section for players to help them avoid the mobs of fans who are packing into the establishment. Manchester is out of this world with energy after a United victory.

We order a round of beers, and Belle has Cam and Gareth in rapture as she discusses highlights with them, referencing several different players and old matches the guys know all too well. Both of them give me a look several times like they can't believe she is for real. I have to agree with them.

"Isn't she great?" Gareth directs his question to Camden, who looks straight at Belle.

"I've known for a while." Camden winks at Belle and it irritates me.

"Mind filling me in on what your cheeky wink is about?" I bark, annoyed at this little exchange and feeling a tightness in my neck that I don't all together care for.

Belle laughs. "Easy boy, they are just impressed by my wicked football knowledge. Camden is always too busy snogging Indie to ever have a proper conversation with me."

"Had I known all of this, I would have made time! Indie must be trying to keep you all to herself," Camden cajoles.

"Well, you're doing a proper job of keeping her all to yourself, which I fully approve of. You make Indie happy and that's what's most important."

Camden gets a faraway look in his eyes when Belle mentions Indie, but Gareth doesn't seem to notice. He elbows him and adds, "But I mean, isn't Belle great for Tanner? I've never seen a girl bust his balls like this. It's really impressive."

"Tan the Man's balls are made of mush anyway." Belle wrinkles her nose and Camden and Gareth erupt into laughs. Again.

This is all really starting to make me uncomfortable. Before, when it was just Belle and me alone at the pool last night and at the match today, was manageable. I could let myself enjoy it. Now, seeing her invade my family life so easily and fit in with my brothers, I feel completely disarmed.

A few minutes later, Gareth mumbles something about needing to head home. He stands up and surprises all of us by pulling Belle into a hug. "Belle, it's been a pleasure. You rival the likes of Vi and that's a feat not easily achieved. I hope to see more of you."

Belle flushes in surprise. My face heats as well. The compliment goes down my throat like broken glass. This is probably the highest form of praise a Harris Brother could ever bestow and it's all too much.

It brings a heavy feeling to the pit of my stomach. A feeling I don't welcome. I miss knowing myself. I miss having my routine: Football and family. That's it. Between the suspension and losing Camden on my team, everything has been thrown out of whack for me. It's forced me to look inside and see myself…see that it's just me, not one of the Harris twins.

I need to get back to being the Tanner Harris I used to be. Light. Carefree. The Tanner Harris that makes sense to me. Whatever is happening around me right now doesn't make sense.

Camden excuses himself shortly after Gareth leaves, so Belle and I make our way back to Gareth's. I can feel her questioning gaze on me as we crawl into bed but, for whatever reason, she doesn't push it. It's the first time Belle Ryan actually holds back.

It was a long day and since we'll be leaving early in the morning, we go right to sleep. It's the first time in my life I sleep with a woman and do just that. Sleep.

Not Invited

Belle

"HI!" INDIE'S VOICE IS HIGH-PITCHED AND EXCITED AS SHE comes clumping into our flat late on Sunday afternoon with three big bags in tow.

"Indie! I've missed you, darling!" I get up and run to hug her, knowing I'm being dramatic but practically bursting to talk to her.

I dropped Tanner off at his flat over three hours ago and I haven't sat down once. I even popped in a workout DVD and lasted ten whole minutes before bailing ship and grabbing a chocolate. The bitch in the video kept saying, "I'm going to make you earn this!"

I showed her when I stuffed three chocolates into my mouth. But hell, I needed something to try to distract my thoughts until Indie got home.

Indie drops all her stuff at the bottom of the stairs while I pop into the kitchen for a couple of waters. I hand one to her as she tucks up on the sofa.

"How was the Bethnal match? I saw they lost."

"Yeah, it was awful. Mendes twisted his ankle. He heard it pop and the X-ray showed torn cartilage. He's probably out for a few weeks."

"Oh, fuck me." I wince. "Did you do the exam?"

169

"Yes, Dr. Nabours was tending to DeWalt."

"Did he get hurt, too?"

"No, they think he was dehydrated. He's a bit of a party boy. You could look at him and know why. He looks like Shemar Moore and has moves like Beckham. He's in the muck with Vaughn big time."

"Oh, that still sucks."

"Yeah, but enough about me and my work. I'm dying to hear about you. Tell me everything. I can't believe you went to Manchester with Tanner! How did it go?"

I exhale heavily. "It went!" I force a toothy grin. Her brown eyes are wide and waiting. "I don't know, Indie. It was bloody perfect. It was fun. I got to hang out with Gareth and Cam for a bit and they were so great. Tanner was surprising, yet still so…Tanner. And… ugh!" I throw my head back in frustration and cover my face with my arm.

"Why are you ughing?" Indie pries.

"Because it's Tanner! And he's Tanner and he's a pig and he's a whore, and one second he makes me so happy and then the next second he makes me so furious!"

"What did he do to piss you off?"

"He got all awkward at the end! Things were so great. Friday night was incredible. Saturday was amazing, but then Saturday night he just…flipped a switch. He wouldn't even pick a fight with me like he normally does. He did a complete one-eighty."

"Did something happen?"

I shrug. "He was with me the whole time. Nothing happened. I think I'm maybe…confusing drama with happiness maybe."

"Oh, don't say that," Indie chastises. "Drama is passion, and passion in a footballer is second nature!"

"But why the change in script? I mean, I know what we're doing is fake, but I thought we were both sort of enjoying this ride together." I take a big drink of my water, attempting to cool down the anxiety pooling in my belly.

"What do you want to happen with you guys?" she asks, eyeing me thoughtfully.

"I don't know. I guess I want to keep doing what we're doing. The sex is incredible. I laugh so much. Yeah we quarrel, but it doesn't seem to bother either of us. I don't want serious, and I don't think that's what Tanner wants either. I just thought we could keep having fun and see what happens."

Out of nowhere, tears prick the backs of my eyes and fall down my cheeks like they are operating on their own free will. I point to my face, a look of complete and utter horror. "Look at this shit! I'm ridiculous. Tanner Harris has made me utterly ridiculous."

Indie giggles, "You're not ridiculous."

"My mother would say, 'Come now, Belle, don't turn the taps on again.'" I sniff once and swipe at my cheeks.

"Your mother is a cold, unfeeling cow," Indie states deadpan.

"Bravo!" I exclaim with a smile. Indie being riled up is exactly what I need.

She baulks, "Well, since when did we start living our lives by her standards?"

"Since never." I hold my bottle of water out to Indie for a cheers. She returns it with a bit of a scowl, still brooding over everything I've said.

She looks deeply into my eyes. "Belle, you're a strong, confident doctor. You have the world by the balls. Don't let Tanner's stupidity make you crumble. He's probably just sorting things out in his head. I'm sure he's feeling the same way you are. You're fabulous."

I sigh. "I feel very unfabulous today. Perhaps it's those three chocolates I ate while watching Jillian Michaels scream at me to move." I prop my feet on the coffee table and ask, "What are you doing tonight? Maybe we can go see a film or rent something stupid and order in?"

Her face falls. "Well, I'm erm...heading out to Chigwell for Sunday dinner as soon as Camden gets here to pick me up."

"What's Sunday dinner?"

"Vi cooks at Vaughn's house. All the boys come home for it. Even Gareth when he can manage."

Hot shards of irritation course through me.

"Do you want to come?" Indie asks, looking horribly uncomfortable.

"Are you kidding?" I exclaim. "To a family dinner at the Harris' house? That sounds about as fun as a dead vibrator."

Indie eyes me with concern. "You look hurt."

"I'm not hurt!" I snap, standing up and suppressing my grimace. "I'm just going to grab a bottle of wine and have a nice long bath. It'll be the perfect night."

"I'd really love it if you'd come with me."

"Indie, will you just go?" My voice is harsher than I intended. "I have a big surgery this week I need to study for anyway."

"Okay, but I really—"

"Go!"

And after hearing the slow click of the door to our flat, I let my faucets run.

TANNER

"You're an idiot," Indie snipes, waltzing into Dad's kitchen and whacking me upside the head.

"Ouch! What the bloody hell for this time?" I rub the spot where she cracked me, smarting over how such a tiny person can hit so hard.

"You couldn't think to invite Belle to dinner tonight?" She throws her hands on her hips, looking scarily like Vi.

"Tanner!" Vi exclaims, pulling a roasted chicken out of the oven and setting it down. She rubs her belly in small circles like she's trying to soothe the baby inside of her. "What's wrong with you?"

My eyes fly wide as I look back and forth between the two of them. "Why would I invite her?"

"Because you two are dating!" Indie replies.

"Fake dating!" I exclaim, my voice raising to a strange pitch in response to the urgency in her face.

"But you knew I'd come with Camden and she'd be home alone. It's mean, Tanner." Indie's face is softer now, which only makes me feel worse.

"So mean," Vi punctuates.

They are like a couple of footballers practicing their passing game.

I slide a hand through my hair. "How is it mean? I've just spent the whole weekend with her."

"So what's another meal?" Indie asks.

"She doesn't need to come witness all of this." I gesture out through the patio door to the garden where Gareth, Booker, and Hayden are standing.

Gareth actually made better time getting to London than Belle and I did today. Taking the train with him would have been a lot easier than the awkward silence in Belle's car during our journey back, that's for sure.

"Just look at them!" I exclaim. Gareth currently has Booker's shirt pulled over his head and has him gripped in a headlock. Hayden is standing off to the side laughing his arse off and tossing a stick for Vi's dog, Bruce.

Indie's eyes fill with disappointment and it guts me almost as badly as Vi's. She turns to walk away.

"Indie…" I move to stand up, but she waves her hand like she can't hear another word and goes to join the guys outside.

Camden shifts awkwardly in the doorway.

"You had nothing to say there?" I ask.

His eyes fly wide. "What was I going to do?"

"Defend me! Tell your woman what this is between Belle and me. I told Indie not to get any bright ideas. She's so bloody soft."

Cam shakes his head. "Belle's awesome. You're an arse." And then he leaves me, too.

Vi frowns at me and, without another word, walks outside to join everyone else.

"Well, what the fuck?" I mumble to myself.

Dad comes striding in next from somewhere outside. "What did you do this time, Tanner? Indie looks like she's about to release the red-headed kraken." He laughs at his stupid joke.

"Dad, I did nothing! Literally nothing! I didn't invite Belle out here for dinner and now that makes me the worst kind of human. What the bloody hell? This is a fake relationship. It's not real. Everybody needs to get that through their stubborn skulls."

I reach out and pluck an apple from the fruit basket on the counter, shoving a frustrated finger into it until it bruises. It makes me feel better.

He looks at me and shakes his head. "Who are you trying to convince, Tan?"

I pound the apple on the counter. "What do you mean?"

His eyes grow wide. "I've seen the coverage of you two. Santino sends me everything. It doesn't look fake. It looks...natural. It reminds me of..." He pauses and swallows hard. "It reminds me of how I looked at your mother when we first started dating. And well, you see how that turned out." He looks out at Gareth like he has "whoopsie child" printed on his forehead.

The words strike me straight through the heart. Dad rarely talks about Mum and the one time he does, he compares her to Belle? I can't take it. I'm going to explode.

"Would everyone just give me some space?" I mumble and stand to head upstairs to the room I lived in when things were simple...

when Booker, Camden, and I all played on the same team and football was all that mattered.

As I walk in, everything suddenly feels different. The bed looks smaller. The area seems tighter. Even my furniture seems to have aged tremendously. I glance down inside my trousers to ensure that my fucking cock hasn't shrunk back into the prepubescent stage. I exhale a sigh of relief to see it's still at its adult glory.

However, that realisation doesn't bring me peace. It just makes the fact that I've changed all the more obvious. I'm no longer the person I used to be. I can see that now. And the guilt that Vi and Indie were projecting on me hits me like a ton of bricks.

I didn't invite Belle here because I thought nothing had changed between us. But, looking around right now, I realise that everything has changed. Even my bloody bedroom.

It wasn't long ago that I still lived here. Camden was in his room across from me. Booker was down the hall. We all stayed here for longer than normal as grown men because football and family was all we allowed into our lives. It consumed us so much that we became codependent on it and each other, not allowing anything else to penetrate that force field.

Well, Belle's penetrated it. Hard. And no matter how much I enjoy penetration, this is a different kind of balls deep than I'm used to.

As much as that thought scares me...as much as I want to fight it, the idea of losing her scares me, too.

One in Four Thousand Chance

Belle

STANDING IN A DARK SURGERY THEATRE WITH DR. MILLER, TWO other fellows, and several surgical support staff, my eyes are razor focused on a bright screen and the control panel beside it.

Today we are working to correct a fatal abnormality called congenital diaphragmatic hernia with a procedure that is currently undergoing randomised trials. CDH happens to about one in four thousand unborn babies. It is when a hole develops in their diaphragm. If left untreated, it can leave their lungs underdeveloped, making a healthy delivery impossible.

Dr. Miller's voice is loud and clear as she speaks to the viewers in the gallery window above us. "Today we are attempting to perform foetoscopic tracheal occlusion. This is the surgery that your donor funds will go toward this year as we continue to expand on this highly treatable condition." She pauses to touch the mother's shoulder who's lying on her back wide awake as we wait for the epidural anaesthesia to take effect.

The mother looks at me with wide, glossy eyes, so I give her a nod of encouragement that she seems to appreciate.

Dr. Miller continues, "I will insert a miniature latex balloon through the uterine wall and down through the mouth of our tiny patient. Positioned in the windpipe, I will then inflate. The balloon will operate as a little cork until it needs to come out when our mother reaches full term pregnancy. This will help the baby's lungs to develop and increase the survival rate by thirty-five percent. Any questions?"

I have a million but I'm biting my tongue, doing my best to take it all in.

"Then let's begin."

I can feel Dr. Miller's eyes on me as I look back at the screen. "Dr. Ryan, I was very impressed with you last week when we worked on those TTTS twins."

My mask covers my jaw dropping. "Thank you, Dr. Miller," I stammer.

"I'd like you to feed in the foetoscope." Her eyes narrow and look down at the side of the mother's belly where the camera will be inserted into the uterus.

"Yes, Dr. Miller," I reply, wishing I could thank her for the opportunity, but knowing confidence is all that I need to project when we have a conscious mother on the table.

My hands are rock steady as I move to take Dr. Miller's place and begin a once-in-a-lifetime experience. This is what I appreciate about this specialty. I get to touch something that is untouchable. I have the chance to save something that someone deemed unsavable. It makes everything outside of this room disappear. These moments of clarity I receive when I'm operating fill my veins with meaning and purpose. This is where I belong.

This is what real life is about. Nothing else will ever feel so big when I'm able to save something so small.

As I drive home after a long day in surgery, I feel desperate for a drink and to lie down. My mind is whirling with all that happened today, not only for the family that got a second chance with their baby, but with my career. It was an incredible day.

It's not until I park in front of my flat that I finally pull out my mobile and see I have several texts. I slide out of my car and begin to open the first one when I hear someone clear their throat.

I practically jump out of my trainers when I see Tanner seated on the concrete steps leading up to my building.

"Tanner, you scared me half to death! What are you doing, perving in the dark like a creeper?"

"I'm not perving, I'm just...waiting," he stammers, a sheepish look on his face as he stands up and shoves his hands in his pockets. "I've been texting you."

I sigh, taking in his tall, large frame, his stupid, messy man bun, and his nappy beard. It all makes me sad.

"I literally just looked at my mobile for the first time all day."

"What about yesterday?" His brow is furrowed as he awaits my reply. He looks so much younger than twenty-six right now.

"I was busy prepping for the surgery I had today," I lie.

"How'd it go?" He looks genuinely interested.

My smile is tired but undisputable. "Amazing. It was...amazing." I drop down onto the place he vacated on the steps. My legs feel as if they're going to give out from all the standing I did in surgery today. "I've turned a corner with Dr. Miller. She told me that if I keep it up, she'll be offering me a full-time position next year."

"That's incredible." He huffs a laugh of admiration. "Seriously, I'm really happy for ya."

"Thanks," I reply, suddenly feeling very tired. "So what are your texts about? I haven't read them yet."

His happiness falls fractionally. "Our next date."

A hopeful raise of his eyebrows has me nodding stiffly. "Ah yes, we need another public appearance I suppose. It's been a few days.

What will people think?" I bob my head, adding a touch of flare to the end but he doesn't seem amused.

Tanner scratches the back of his neck. "There's this thing going on at Welly's Pub on Friday night with the Bethnal team. They don't have a game until Wednesday, so they want a team night out. Bonding and all that. Indie will be there, too. I haven't seen any of them since the last game and I'd like it if you would go with me. The guys have booked the place, so there won't be any press inside."

This confuses me. "Well, what's the point if we're not being photographed?" I ask.

He shrugs and speaks slowly. "It'd just be for fun."

I watch him for a moment, trying to get a read on him. Tanner Harris is standing before me, asking me to hang out and not making a sexual pass at me. This throws so many red flags.

"Did Indie say something to you?"

"No." He looks guilty and I scoff with annoyance. "Maybe," he adds.

I ruffle my messy ponytail. "Bloody Indie."

"Don't go skinning her," he defends, making a move closer to me. So close I get a whiff of his scent and it brings back unwelcome memories.

"Well, I should," I snipe. "That was private girl talk shit. Not something you needed to know."

"If I hurt you, I should know. So I can apologise and grovel and…I don't know…do whatever it is blokes do when they fuck up. I'm sorry, Belle. I just thought…I just thought—"

"You didn't think at all!" I exclaim, standing up and losing control of my emotions. I begin pacing the sidewalk, a renewed sense of energy coursing through my hot, angry veins. "I had literally *just* opened up to you about how much my parents hurt me by not inviting me to stuff. Then you turned around and did it the very first chance you got."

"Christ, Belle, I didn't think of it like that." He makes a move to touch me, so I spin away from him, holding my hands out to block him.

"Don't, all right? I don't want to go crazy over this, Tanner! I don't want to lose my shit on you right now."

"You should!" he exclaims, his eyes panicky. "Hit me with your full on crazy. I deserve it. I was a jerk. Talk to me about that."

"No, I'm not going to do it. Because for one silly moment, I thought you were actually human. And I thought that we had become friends. I forgot that you're being forced into all of this. How ridiculous of me!"

"We have become friends," he booms, his jaw taut with anger. "Fuck me, Belle, I care about you!"

"Then you have to know that how you handled the end of our weekend in Manchester is not the way you treat a friend! You're not that stupid. You might look it, but I know better."

"It's more complicated than that, Ryan," he growls and kicks at the pavement with his foot.

"See? Why'd you call me Ryan there?" I challenge him with a sadistic little smile because I already know the answer.

"What do you mean?" He rolls his eyes. "I call you Ryan all the time."

"Not all the time. Only when you're trying to distance yourself."

"Don't be mental. I don't need to be psychoanalysed right now," he snaps.

I have to laugh. It's all I can do at this point. "I haven't even got started with all the other shit I could mention. I could Deep Talk you so hard right now, you wouldn't know what hit you."

"Just save it, all right?" he shouts, vibrating with rage. "You don't want to come on Friday? Don't. You don't want to be in this with me anymore? Then don't. I'm not going to sit here and let you make me feel like an arse for sticking to an agreement that *you* signed up for."

"Did the agreement include you fucking me bareback in your brother's pool?" I scream and his face contorts with something along the lines of horrified realisation. My eyes turn to slits. "Didn't think so."

I could push him so hard right now. I could send him right over the edge and tell him everything he's not saying. But what's the point? None of this is real. And he's not evolved enough to even admit the truth to himself, let alone to me. Deep Talk is a joke.

"Just go home, Tanner," I add with a huff and turn to make my way up the steps.

"Belle," he croaks and rushes up behind me, folding his arms around my waist.

I fight his hold for a while, trying to push him off of me. I pinch his arms like a child and he growls in pain but refuses to let go, only squeezing me tighter.

I stop for a moment, shivering against his warm breath on my shoulder. All I would have to do is turn my head into him and I know what would happen. He would kiss me. He would consume me. He'd make me forget. We'd trip over each other as we walk backwards into my flat, never releasing the others lips. We'd go to bed. We'd fuck or maybe even make love. He'd bring me so much pleasure that I'd forget everything that hurts me about him.

Instead, I drop my arms to my sides, willing them to stop fighting…Turning them into lifeless noodles, no longer resisting him but not embracing him either. I want to cry from the ache of no action. It feels so bloody wrong. Fighting Tanner is more my style, but everything is different now. Acknowledging that is what gives me the strength to say no when he asks the next question.

"Can I come up?"

My eyes sting as I reply, "No, Tanner. You can't."

With a huff, he releases me.

I don't look back as I walk into my flat, close the door behind me, and lean my back against the wall to catch my breath. A masochist through and through, I pull out my mobile and read a text he sent me earlier.

Tanner: I miss you.

Well, Well, Well

TANNER

I'VE SPENT THE LAST WEEK ACTING LIKE A GIRLIE FUCKING BASKET case because of Belle Ryan and her painfully icy shoulder. I know I got weird after Manchester, but I needed some time to think. I don't know what the fuck I'm doing with this woman and it's making me completely bloody mental.

After she refused my invite to Welly's, I texted her to see if we were still finishing out our arrangement or if she wanted out full stop. She responded that she would attend the events mapped out in the email and that she hoped I'd still honour my part by attending the hospital charity function coming up.

It felt like she nut-punched me.

How we went from fucking like animals, arguing like an old married couple, and laughing like mates to this clipped, formal, stranger-like texting is infuriating. It made me want to hole up in my flat and hide until this entire suspension was over.

But then I found a note from my mum in a keepsake box Vi gave me last year. When I read it, something clicked. The note made me realise that sitting still is getting me nowhere fast.

Belle goes to work and saves babies. She's bigger than life. I play football, but I intend to be more than just football. I intend to find my own way to change lives, which starts with going to Welly's to-night and rebuilding my team's trust in me, owly mood or not.

"Hey, Tan, you ready?" Booker crows, letting himself into my flat and striding down the hallway toward where I'm sitting in my room. "We're going to be late for Welly's if we don't leave now. I would have come here to fetch you earlier, but you told me you weren't coming."

I just finish pushing my foot into my boot when he comes to stand in my doorway. "I'm ready," I reply and grab the finger of whiskey off my bedside table and polish it off like a shot.

He eyes the glass in my hand. "Couldn't wait until the pub?"

I breathe against the burn in my throat. "Nope."

His brows rise as I wipe my mouth with the back of my hand. "What made you change your mind and decide to come?"

I glare at him. "It's still my team, isn't it?"

His eyes fly wide. "Christ, you're a moody sod. Want to talk about it?"

"Nope," I growl as I stand up, grabbing my jacket and putting it on. "It's just…" I start but then stop. "Nope, I'm not doing it."

I brush past Booker and make my way down the hallway toward the door, stopping in my tracks before walking out. The whiskey burning in my throat is doing nothing to damper the inferno boiling in my body. It's just stoking it. Giving it life.

My grip on the doorknob turns lethal as I snap, "You know, I didn't ask for *her*." I glance over my shoulder at Booker. He's watching me all meek and nervous from the hallway, like I'm some sort of wild animal and he's not sure what I'll do next. "I didn't ask for Belle Ryan to pick me up that night. I sure as fuck didn't want to have to fake date her. I did it to be a bloody gentleman. To try to help her find a way out of this mess so her family would get off her arse."

Booker moves to open his mouth but I cut him off. "Her family is fucked, too," I continue as I turn and prop myself against the door. "They are nothing like us, which makes her a God damned anomaly to figure out. One minute she's funny and light and making my dick hard with all her sexy football talk. The next, she's dark and broody and her temper…Christ, Belle's temper is a hair-trigger. Set it off and she's got a razor-sharp tongue that will send your testicles back inside your body."

I open the door and storm over to the lift, pushing the button over and over and over. The damn thing never stays on the fourth level. I turn back to see Booker closing the door behind him, so I continue, "You know what she's like, Book? She is like a drug. When I look at her from the outside, she seems crazy and out of control. I'm best to stay away. But when I'm inside her, with her, breathing her in, it's like there is no other reality in the world that matters." I slam my fist against the button and it feels good.

"Tanner, get a hold of yourself," Booker deadpans. "I'm worried about you."

"I'm trying!" I roar, ramming my hands through my hair. "But if she's not making me feel like shit, it's Vi. And if it's not Vi, now I've got bloody Indie up my arse. These women are ruining my life."

Booker laughs openly and it makes me want to tackle him to the ground. How dare he mock my pain. "Do you have a death wish?"

"No," he laughs again. "I just think it's funny. You're blaming your problems on the women in your life, but the truth of the matter is you've been a prat for a long time and your conscience finally isn't letting you get away with it anymore. It's revolted against you and turned you into"—he pauses, looking me up and down like I'm a bloody alien—"a human."

"Sod off," I growl and step into the lift. I immaturely try to close the doors before he gets in and he looks at me like I'm a moron.

I feel it.

He props himself on the railing as we begin our decent. "You only have what, two more times you have to see her? The match on Wednesday and then that fundraiser we're all going to, right?"

"And the stupid magazine interview," I mumble through clenched teeth.

"All right then. Three times and then you're home free. Just focus on the prize. Tonight is important. You need to reconnect with the team. We miss you. You're our captain and we've not had you around for three weeks now. You need to sober up, man up, and be a leader. Let them know you're ready to come back, boots swinging."

I sniff and nod. "You're right. Thanks, Book."

"Don't mention it." He looks at me one more time as the lift doors open. He turns and begins walking backwards away from me. "And hey, whatever happens, I think if football doesn't work out, you could find work in a theatre. That little rant up there was an epic fucking performance. I'm thinking... *Vagina Monologues*."

He makes a peace sign around his lips and his tongue darts out between his fingers. His laugh turns to a girlie squeal as I lunge toward him, tearing through the lobby after him.

Fuck me. For a keeper, he's bloody fast.

Belle

"You don't have a choice!" Indie exclaims as she darts back and forth between my closet and my bed, laying out options of clothing. "I'm never here on the weekends anymore. We haven't had a proper make up session since you screamed at me for telling Tanner he was an arse, even though he was. You're coming with me to Welly's."

"No, I'm not," I groan.

"Yes, you are!" She stamps her foot. "Belle, we haven't even had a chance to celebrate your small victory with Dr. Miller. This isn't like us. We celebrate our successes in this family."

I shake my head at her. "Well, sis, I don't feel like going to a pub with a bunch of bloody footballers. I'm tapped out on footballers at the moment. Tanner will probably think I've come for him, and I'll have to play the part of the dutiful girlfriend."

"No, you won't. Booker said Tanner's not coming."

My head snaps to attention. "He's not?"

She shakes her head. "Nope. I don't know why, but he won't be there."

"Interesting," I mumble, chewing on my lip.

"We won't stay for long." She tosses some shoes on the bed and adjusts her glasses to look back at me. "I just want to introduce you to a couple of my favourite guys and then we can go have a laugh somewhere else."

I moan.

"Pretty please?" she whines.

"Fine. Damn you and your cherubic face. If you and Camden ever have children, you're fucked."

She laughs and gets a daydreamy twinkle in her eyes that makes me sick.

Indie selects my hottest pair of black leather skinnies that have double zippers on each side. She grabs a light knitted sweater that hangs dramatically off one shoulder and yells at me when I try to wear a bra with it.

"You have gorgeous, big, perky breasts. Enjoy them while you can."

I roll my eyes and finish it off with a pair of nude heels and super dark purple lipstick, feeling about as good as I possibly can considering I'll be walking into the lion's den.

We head out, but I make Indie stop at a wine bar for a couple glasses before we make our way to Welly's in Brick Lane. I couldn't stomach the thought of going in there completely sober and being around loads of men who act like Tanner Harris.

Thankfully, Indie brightens my mood immensely with stories about athlete's foot on dicks. Apparently, it's a thing. Why she thinks she wants a career in sports medicine is beyond me.

By the time the cab drops us in front of Welly's Pub, I'm in marginally better spirits than I was before. Welly's is a standard English pub. I've been here before because they do a good fish and chips. It has the standard dim lighting, worn carpet, and red, distressed leather booths. It also usually has good music playing and the staff is decent. It's a well-known Harris hangout but, considering Booker will be the only one in attendance, I think I can handle it.

We waltz in, completely unnoticed and I think it's God's way of easing me into this whole charade. I know the Harrises have kept Tanner and my fake dating scheme quiet, but I can't help but wonder if everyone here knows who I am and what the bloody hell a guy like Tanner is doing with a girl like me.

All of my old insecurities are back, and they are fucking ugly and in need of a stiff drink.

My eyes do a cursory scan for Tanner and come up empty, so I can finally exhale. All I see are footballers, wannabe WAGs, and maybe a few actual WAGs.

"Let's sit at the bar and grab a drink first," Indie croons, waving to one of the players who's in the middle of a conversation with another player.

"Hiya, Doc," another guy says from down the bar.

"Hello, James!" Indie beams and then looks at the guy next to him. "Hey, Tau, how's the knee?"

"Better," he replies. "I'm icing it, don't worry."

"Good," she approves.

I shake my head as we drop down onto two stools and order our drinks.

"God, no wonder Camden is a jealous sod," I murmur.

Indie frowns and takes a sip of her white wine as soon as the bartender sets it down in front of us. "Why do you say that?"

"You're a fantasy for these guys. An untouchable carrot with your big doe eyes, your red, luscious hair, and genius, fuck-me-sideways brain. You know half of them wank off to you, right?"

"Stop!" Indie bellows with a horrified look behind her cheetah-print specs.

I laugh. "It's true. I guarantee it." I glance over at a guy who's watching us. "He does." Another guy right beside him looks at us. "He does, too." Two more guys eye us as they walk in. "You know those two jackals are jerking their meat and picturing their sexy team doctor."

"I'm going to murder you," Indie grinds through clenched teeth. "Drink your wine and shut up."

My shoulders shake with silent laughter as I take a sip and look around the pub. When my eyes land on someone, I stop mid-drink and lower my glass.

Tanner comes walking around the corner from where the loos are and has a girl on his arm. She's nattering away to him as if he's the best thing since sliced bread. Her blonde hair, inches of exposed cleavage, and fake nails scream Harris Ho.

I could kill her with one hand.

The weight of a thousand footballers begins pressing down on my shoulders. I spin on my chair and look at the wall of liquor bottles behind the bar. "Can we get a couple of shots here?" I bark none too kindly.

Indie looks at me with a frown. "Shots?"

"Yeah, tequila please," I add when the bartender waits for me to clarify.

"Maybe we should switch to Tequila Sunrises instead. Those are easier to pace ourselves with."

"I'm not feeling very sunny right now, darling." I jerk my head over in Tanner's direction while taking another gulp of my wine.

Indie's eyes follow the trail and I know instantly when she sees him.

"Oh no—" Her voice is deep and halts mid-sentence as her eyes zero in more closely. "Oh no, no, no. That just won't do."

She moves to get up from her stool, but I grab her arm, yanking her down next to me. "He didn't know I was coming."

"I don't bloody care!" she hisses. "And since when do you stay silent?"

"Since now." I grab the shot from the bartender and knock it back in one swig. I hand Indie hers and gesture for two more.

Indie shoots hers, refusing to tear her eyes off of Tanner, who's now surrounded by more girls and a few teammates.

Tonight was a bad idea.

"Hello, ladies," a low voice utters from the other side of my stool, breaking through my cone of hell.

I turn and am surprised to see Tanner's fellow striker, Roan DeWalt, commandeering the spot right beside me. I've only seen him play once since he joined Bethnal, but he's one of those footballers you can't not know. He looks like a movie star with his caramel skin and super light brown eyes that suck you in.

He smiles kindly right at me. "How are we this evening?"

"Hi, Roan," Indie practically growls over her shoulder, still watching Tanner like a creepy Peeping Tom while chugging down her wine like water.

"Hey, Doc." He gestures to the guy standing next to him. "This is my mate, Adam. He's a friend visiting from back home."

"Hello, Adam," I say, reaching out to shake both their hands because Indie seems to have lost all common courtesy.

Roan holds my grip for longer than necessary, his eyes dropping down to my bare shoulder and drinking in every beauty mark speckling my flesh.

He finally releases my hand and furrows his brow at Indie, who's still horribly distracted. "Everything all right, Doc?"

She swerves her slanted eyes to him. "I'm thinking it might not be, Roan."

"Anything I can do to help?" He looks at me.

My eyes snap to his with fierce intensity. I reach out and grab his shoulders. "I'm good with a scalpel. How are you with a shovel?"

"What?" He looks completely confused, his perfect skin forming a single crease between his brows.

"Oh never mind." I turn away from him, grab my next shot that's been kindly delivered, and down it like a champ.

"So you're friends with our lovely doc here?" Roan asks, his voice far too low and smooth, reaching places inside of me that haven't been touched since Tanner.

My answer is short and clipped, trying to quiet the beast inside. "Yep, since med school."

"So you're a doctor, too?"

"She saves babies," Indie adds, grabbing her shot, drinking it, and training her eyes back on Tanner, whom I can't bring myself to look at again.

"I really wish people would stop saying it like that." Indie should know better.

"Is that what you do?" I can feel Roan's eyes on me. They are the same eyes that all men get when they first discover my profession and all their fantasies pop into the forefront of their minds.

I turn my drooping eyes to Roan who's blatantly checking me out. I smile coyly. "Let me guess, you're envisioning a naughty nurse scenario right now?"

He nearly chokes on his lager. "How did you guess?"

I shrug. "Call it female intuition."

"I'm good with naughty doctor, too." He waggles his brows right at me.

This feels right. This exchange. This pithy banter. It's what I excel at. Indie and I spent our Tequila Sunrise nights dancing at clubs and I never had a problem pulling guys. It was as easy as breathing for me. This is exactly what I need in order to forget about Tanner and the Harris Hoes he's currently talking his stupid, ape-like drivel to.

I bite my lip and then ask quietly, "Would you be a bad patient?"

His smirk is pure sex. "I'd be whatever you want, babe."

I roll my eyes, hating his answer.

"Belle!" Indie shouts my name as if she's been saying it for a while. I swerve my head to look at her and nearly fall off my stool when I find a seething Tanner standing three feet away from me, nose to nose with a small but fearsome Indie. Well, more like chest to nose.

"What do you need, Tanner?" Indie asks, crossing her tiny arms over her chest like she's a seven-foot-tall bodyguard.

"I was just coming to say hello." Tanner's voice is deep and threatening as he cuts his eyes past me to Roan and then back to me again. "Surprised to see you here, Ryan."

Roan looks at me. "You're Belle Ryan?" I nod and watch realisation dawn on him. His hands go up as if to say he didn't touch me. He looks at Tanner and says, "I didn't know." He rises and slinks away with his friend on his tail, repeating once more, "I really didn't know."

I roll my eyes and turn around on my stool, fully facing Tanner and noting his fists gripped tightly by his sides. The tension radiating in his shoulders is palpable.

He makes a move to get past Indie, but she jumps over to stop him. "You can stay right where you are or go back to your mates. We're just fine over here."

Tanner's eyes narrow as he tilts his head at Indie. "Et tu Brute?"

She huffs at his Julius Caesar reference and then shakes her head. "Well, you looked rather busy over there!" Her attempt at catty comes out more plucky, like a cute bird, but I know she's pulling out the big guns for me. She's probably on her way to full on pissed after our hasty wine and shot consumption.

The bartender drops a third set of shots in front of me, and I hear Tanner growl as I throw it back.

"Belle, we need to talk. Call off your guard and come with me."

191

I turn to pin him with my dark gaze. The anger and desperation pouring off of him makes my voice tremble. "Indie is operating of her own free will, Tanner. Unlike you."

He rolls his eyes. "A word. Now." A muscle ticks beneath his bearded jaw, and I can feel my dramatic side calling to me like a drug in response. I want to take my wine and throw it in his face for thinking he can bark orders at me. But last time I did that, he ended up snogging me senseless. So instead of crazy, perhaps I'll try mature and logical.

I exhale and stand, moving past Indie and feeling a bit more wobbly on my feet than I did when we first arrived. Indie doesn't look much better as she gives me a drunken nod of solidarity.

"I'll be right here," she says, taking a big gulp of her wine as Tanner grabs me around the waist like some Neanderthal.

"I'm perfectly capable of walking without your paws on me," I hiss quietly in his ear, not wanting to give the spectators the satisfaction of a scene.

"I'm about ready to fucking spank you in front of everyone, so just shut up and keep walking," he growls, ushering us in the direction of the loos.

The nerve of him! "You better not be taking me to the same place you took that other girl," I seethe, my hand biting into his forearm so hard my knuckles turn white. "Great snag by the way. She looks like a walking Tesco. Cheap, cheerful, and open all hours."

A grumble comes from deep in his chest as we round the corner and he continues us past the loos and to the rear exit. He slams his hand hard on the door, shoving it open into a small, dimly lit alley where a couple of vehicles are parked. The cool autumn air is cleansing on my tequila-soaked brain cells.

Tanner shuffles me backwards until my back is pressed against a brick wall. The yellow bulb sconce casts just enough light for me to see him lick his lips. Without a word, he cups my face and slams his mouth to mine.

Shock and pain are the first reactions my body has. Then need and want come rolling in like fog in the night. The taste of him is familiar, even with the spicy whiskey on his tongue. It's all heady and strong, and I feel the ache in my body to get completely lost in it.

But I won't. I'm stronger than that. I shove him away with a well-deserved slap across his face that he doesn't even react to.

"What the fuck, Tanner?" I touch the tender spot on my lip where his teeth bit in to. "What do you think you're doing?"

He shakes his head and moves closer to me again, sliding his hands down my body and gripping my waist firmly. He exhales heavily as he looks down at the space between our chests. His voice is like sandpaper when he utters, "There's a lot I want to do and say, but first we need to get one thing straight." His steely eyes bore into me. "You are mine, Belle. In whatever fucked up way we're doing this right now, you are *mine*."

His words stun me and his close proximity brings a heaviness to my chest.

"You know this is all a lie!"

That is apparently not the response he was looking for. His eyes turn to slits and he rips himself away from me. He begins aggressively pacing the alley, looking a whole lot like a gorilla pounding the ground in front of its cave. Grateful for the space, I drag in a huge breath and attempt to slow my heart rate before it pops out of my chest.

"So that's why you're here flirting with DeWalt?" He shoots me a venomous look, pushing his hair back behind his ears. "Because this is all a lie and you're looking for the real deal to fuck?"

"No!" I answer with a haughty bark. "DeWalt is nothing."

"Well then, what do you want?" he roars.

"I don't know."

"I think you do."

"Oh, then by all means, enlighten me," I snarl.

Suddenly, he moves close to me again, towering over me. One

hand is pressed on the wall by my head while the other grazes all over my body but never actually touches me. Every deep inhale of breath I take brings me closer to his hand, but he continually adjusts his location so he never actually lays a finger on me.

"You want *me*, Belle."

I scoff and look away. "How could I? You're acting like a bloody maniac."

"*For you.*" His voice is guttural and I can't help but meet his eyes. They are so blue and probing I can hardly breathe. "I act like a maniac for you. We have issues, but past all of them is the fact that I want you and you want me."

My jaw juts out defiantly, shaking my silent refusal but feeling an alarming tickling sensation on my shoulder blade.

"Say the words, Belle," he pleads, dropping his face down closer to mine.

I can smell him. I can taste him. His lips are only a centimetre from mine, so close I could stick my tongue out and touch them if I wanted.

His breath trembles when he adds, "Just tell me you want me."

I sniff, unable to find my words with his aching eyes on me.

He moves his mouth to my ear and whispers, "That's all you have to do." He breathes in deeply. "Because *I'm already yours.*"

He pulls back and looks into my eyes with total and complete dire need. Like a ship in the night, his presence is the swirling light, drawing me in from the dark sea. His vulnerability is too much. His need is too heady. My gaze waters as my body arches into him.

Of course I want him. I've wanted him since he rejected me. I've wanted him since he hurt me. I've wanted him even when I hated him. And I know I can't hold out a second longer. My endurance has crumbled.

So I feed the beast.

"I want you," I whisper and a strange noise rises from my throat as I brush my quivering lips against his. A feather-light touch of our mouths that I feel all over my body.

He pulls back and closes his eyes, exhaling the weight of the world out of his lungs. His eyes crack open for a split second before he angles his face and drops a hard, claiming kiss on my lips. It's wet and sloppy and possessive, and it's turning into so much more but nowhere near enough.

We shift into a mess of groping, squeezing limbs, crushing our bodies together completely and giving in to the beast of need roaring between us. My chest heaves with longing against his. My breasts yearn to be touched. My body aches to be filled. This kiss isn't suffi-cient. The desperation to reconnect in the most carnal way possible is urgent.

Tanner moves us away from the wall and farther into the dark-ness of the alley. My back collides with something hard and cold, and I break our kiss to see I'm pressed up against a truck.

His voice is deep and throaty as he presses his hard-on into me. "I'm fucking you right here, right now. I can't wait."

He starts frantically digging in his pocket and I hear the most glorious sound ever. The beep of a key fob.

He opens the door and lifts me into the driver's side, crawling in behind me and pushing me across the bench. I give the alley a cur-sory glance, knowing it is nuts to fuck in an alley outside a pub with his entire team inside.

But that's us. We're crazy.

Once he's past the gear stick, I fly toward him and frantically fumble with his jeans, opening the zipper and grabbing his hardened shaft in my hands. I squeeze the silky skin with all the anger I have still coursing through my veins. Rage and frustration fuelling this crazy act of sex.

Tanner unceremoniously tosses my heels and rips me out of my skinnies and knickers. He leaves my long sweater on as he manhan-dles me astride him. His eyes are dark on me as the head of his cock nudges my opening. I use the roof to brace myself and moan loudly, already soaked with a wanton ache to be filled.

As if my cry was a shotgun at a starting gate, he yanks down on my hips and meets me with a hard thrust upward, impaling me with a ferocity that has me seeing spots.

A garbled cry of relief escapes his throat, like being inside me stopped something from completely breaking inside of him. His hold on my thighs is bruising as I grind down on him, begging him to move.

He drops his head to my chest and groans, "I don't like you flirting with other guys."

His hips resume pumping up into me again, and my arousal is only intensified by the possessive tone of his voice. I bite my lip and slide up and down on his dick. "I wasn't flirting," I breathlessly snipe, realising sex isn't going to fix all of our problems.

"Oh really? Then tell me, do you like it when I flirt with other girls?" His voice is moany as he power drives into me over and over, my arse bouncing on top of his balls.

"I couldn't give a fuck," I lie as he yanks down my top and pulls a hard nipple into his mouth. When he bites down, my hands drop from the roof and I claw my nails into his shoulders so hard, I'm sure they've ripped the fabric of his shirt.

The pain drives my arousal higher.

"Bullshit," he growls, his eyes wild on mine with determination. "I know you, Belle."

He twists his hips in a way that hits a spot so deep, I'm not sure it's ever been touched before. Recognising how I respond, he begins rapidly thrusting up inside me, punching that spot over and over and over. I claw and scratch at anything I can find. His hair. His face. I even bite down on his shoulder at one point, desperate to find control over this painful climb.

Right when I think I'm going to blast into the universe, he stops all movement and says, "Admit it."

I growl, my fiery eyes snapping to his. "Fine, I care! I want to tear that girl's eyes out. Are you fucking happy?"

He yanks my face down to him and I feel his triumphant smile as he captures my lips. Pulling back, he murmurs, "That girl I was talking to in there…those women…All I spoke about was you and how incredible I think you are and how amazing your job is. I even told them about your fucking hospital charity."

My breath is heavy as I process his words, but I don't even have a chance to respond before he suddenly quickens his pace inside of me. My hands grapple for purchase, but they are reaching for the unknown, flailing in the dark shadows and trusting that Tanner will continue to never let me go.

My hard and fast climax takes me completely off guard in all its Tannerific glory. I could sing at the electric tingle all over my body that I so desperately needed after all the wrath and anger I felt moments ago.

Tanner follows seconds after. We're both slick with sweat and panting for a while before I roll off of him. Then he moves to pull his jeans up, which only made it down to his thighs.

I feel his come dripping out from between my legs. "You don't have a tissue in here, do you?"

He winces and eyes my legs. "I don't…but…here." He reaches into his pocket and pulls out a pair of my knickers. Not the ones I was wearing tonight, but the ones he nicked out of my suitcase in Manchester.

He shoots me a lewd smirk. One that brings me right back to how we were before. A little nuts, but happy. He shrugs and I laugh, sounding a bit insane but not giving a shit.

I use them to clean up and then toss them out the window toward the dumpster. Tanner side-eyes me.

"Oh, did you want to keep those?"

"Not as long as there are more where they came from." He winks.

I sigh and slide back into my clothes, smoothing down my hair so it's not glaringly obvious to the rest of the world that I was just angry-fucked in an alley.

"So what now?" I ask.

"We're doing this." He says it so simply as he throws his arm on the back of the seat behind me and plays with a tendril of my hair. His eyes are perfectly serious. His breath is smooth and steady. The angry, maniacal glint in his gaze from before is gone. He brushes the back of his finger along my cheek with one hand and says, "No more fake dating. No more bullshit. You're mine. I'm yours. We walk back in there and we act like it. But this time, it's not an act."

My heart skips a beat, so I decide deflection is the best response. "Stop barking orders at me, you fiend."

He leans across the seat and kisses me with a tenderness that feels as if it was reserved specifically for this moment. "Woman, say you're mine."

I sigh against his lips. "Why do you need to hear it so badly?"

"Because I fucked up once and I won't do it again." He pulls back and his hands begin to tremble as he runs a nervous hand through his hair.

"What's wrong?" I ask, feeling the sudden shift in him. I slide across the bench and hold onto his arm.

He swallows hard and stares out the windscreen while he speaks. "My mum died when I was three and I didn't know much about her, other than what she left behind." He turns and pierces me with a serious look. "There was this one note from her that I've always con-nected with. I had all but forgotten about it until earlier today when I came across it again."

"What did it say?" I ask, searching his eyes and finding a vulner-ability he has never revealed to me before.

"It said, 'When you don't know what to do, sit still.'" He sighs heavily with realisation dawning on his features. "I was sitting still before, Belle, but I'm done with that now. This is new territory for me, but I'm asking you to move…with me."

I smile at his sincerity and take his hand in mine, dropping a kiss on the back of it before answering, "Let's get our arses in gear then."

TANNER

Possessive pride courses through my veins as I hold Belle's hand and walk back into Welly's Pub. I wanted her here with me before I knew that I wanted to be with her. Officially. It's simple. Having her near me, breathing the same air as me, makes me happy.

And fuck if I could use some happiness right now.

The idea of introducing her to some of my teammates tonight gives me a thrill. They'd all been winding me up most of the night for "wifing up" as they say. I've done the same to Cam, truthfully.

The girls I was talking to earlier were some of the nicer WAGs of my teammates who were genuinely curious about Belle and what she does at the hospital. They've never seen me serious with anyone, and their eyes were wide with amazement when I told them about the one surgery Belle described to me in great detail. It made me proud of her even though she wasn't mine to be proud of.

Yet.

Now everything's changed. No more fake dating. No more charade. Belle and I can just be what we are, which is pretty much what we've been doing as it stands.

When we round the corner past the loos, I hear loud, riotous singing with one voice piercing above them all.

"Indie!" Belle gasps. Her free hand moves to cover her shocked expression as the noisy scene comes into full sight.

Indie is standing up on the bar, leading the entire team and some of the WAGs in the Bethnal Green Pride song. Her curly red hair is in a huge messy bun on top of her head, her jeans are wet from an apparent spill, and her glasses are crooked on her face.

But her grin is larger than life.

"Belle!" Indie crows as we step into her line of vision. She looks down at our hands encased in one another. "You guys made up!" The dopey smile on her face grows, making me laugh.

A hand reaches up toward Indie, but she swats it away and then tries a ninja swizzle kick. The bartender steps behind her with his hands up like he's ready to catch her, but she corrects herself. Once both feet are stable again, she thrusts her arms up in victory.

The team all cheers along with her.

A desperate-looking Booker is the owner of the reaching hand. He looks over his shoulder at Belle and me. "A little help here!"

Belle and I do everything we can to stifle our laughs as we talk Indie down from the bar. She falls into Booker's arms but won't stop beaming back and forth between Belle and me.

"This is really happening, isn't it?" she slurs.

I grin and push her glasses up on her nose. "Are you happy, Indie?"

Her dilated eyes widen. "Tanner, I couldn't be happier than if you guys were getting married."

We all laugh. Then Booker and Belle both help Indie out to the alley toward our truck. The four of us squeeze side by side in the cab as Booker drives us to Belle and Indie's flat.

Booker offers to help carry a now sleeping Indie inside, but I wave him off, telling him to go back to the pub and have some fun. He gives me a nod and a smile—a simple exchange of words happening without a sound.

Once I get Indie tucked into her bed and Belle puts water and aspirin on her nightstand, we both stare down at her for a minute.

"Think she'll remember any of this tomorrow?" I ask.

"Doubtful," Belle replies.

"I'll be happy to tell her again," I murmur, tucking my head into

Belle's neck and slinking my hands around her waist.

She lets out a throaty sound, and I walk her backwards out of Indie's room. My lips travel the length from her bare shoulder to her ear as we shuffle down the hallway and into her room, kicking the door closed behind us. When the back of her legs hit the bed, I pause.

Slowly, I peel her sweater over her head and trail my hands down her sides until her nipples pebble into little buds. I take my time unbuttoning her trousers, pausing to dip my hands into her knickers. She reaches up and grabs hold of my head for support. Her fingers grip my locks as I cup and knead her, relishing in her obvious desire for me.

"I'll never tire of this body," I husk, staring at her nakedness as I slide her trousers off and lay her back on the bed. "Every curve is fucking perfection." I eye her for a minute, marvelling in the fact that she's really mine.

"Stop staring at me like that," she croaks, pulling her legs up as a self-conscious shield. "You're making it weird."

I refuse to let her turn this into a joke. I pull my shirt over my head and crawl toward her on the bed. Positioning myself between her thighs, I pin her wrists by her head so she has nothing to do but look into my eyes. "Belle. I see you now and I can't look away." She blinks slowly, a softness in her eyes that consumes me. "You make other women look tame and boring. You're fucking incredible." I kiss her deeply, inhaling her gasp.

"My beautiful." *Kiss.* "Crazy." *Kiss.* "Wild." *Kiss.* "Woman."

She moans loudly, bucking her hips up into mine. "I need you inside of me, Tanner. Now."

I nod and free her hands to do what they must, knowing deep down that I need a whole lot more than this. But this will do. For now.

Harris Heart

TANNER

"**W**ELL, THIS IS IT," I SAY, LOOKING AT BELLE AS WE WALK through the bright yellow front door of my dad's home in Chigwell, charged and ready for Sunday night dinner.

After Welly's, we spent the rest of our weekend together doing normal, ordinary things. Shopping, brunching, laughing, screwing. Even fighting over the film we were going to rent.

She won.

However, bringing her to my dad's today feels like anything but ordinary. It feels important. Things with Belle and me are happening crazy fast, but it feels right. Truthfully, I've always been this way. Once I decide on something, I go full steam ahead and I don't let anything get in my way. What happened to me after Manchester was a bit of temporary blindness. I thought the heart couldn't miss what it can't see, but that was bollocks. I missed Belle. Our time at Gareth's was special and real and probably something I'll never forget. So her being here today is me opening myself up to more with her. This isn't a game anymore.

"So this is where the infamous Harris Brothers grew up?" Belle asks, taking a turn around the foyer, stopping at the large wooden staircase that leads to the bedrooms. She grins. "I bet you got up to

202

naughty things up there, didn't you?"

I lift my brows as a random neighbour girl pops in my brain like a camera flash. She wasn't anyone important, but she existed.

"I'd rather not talk about it," I mumble, grabbing Belle's hand and pulling her away from the stairs.

"No need to be awkward, Tanner," she states, her heels clacking along the white marble floor as I lead her down the hallway. "I know you've been with other women. I've been with other men! It's fine. We both have a past."

"That we don't need to discuss," I grumble, my face twisting in disgust as I contemplate how hard it would be to kill every other man who's ever touched Belle Ryan.

She stops abruptly and yanks me to her. Her hands reach up to cup my jaw as she says, "We'll just have to make some new memories. Dirty ones maybe."

She kisses me with a nip on my lip and I exhale. Caring about someone this much is a strange, uncomfortable sort of feeling. Only a month ago, shagging women was a sport to me. It's all my teammates and I thought about besides football. But once you have someone that you don't want to let go, it makes you wish you never would have taken hold of anyone else.

I give her arse a cheeky squeeze and pull her the rest of the way toward the kitchen. Turning my back to the door, I cock a brow at her. "Contrary to what you might believe about how much time I spent in my bedroom, this is where we spent most of our time."

I back up through the double doors and turn to find Dad and Booker propped at the high-top island that sits parallel to the chef-style kitchen. Vi is at the sink, her apron dangling over top of the football that's invaded her stomach.

"Hello there," Dad states, standing up and pushing the condiment bottles off to the side. He reaches out and shakes Belle's hand, bowing his head awkwardly. "You must be Belle."

"I am. It's nice to meet you, Mr. Harris."

"Please, call me Vaughn."

I eye the playbook. "Going over tactics?"

He frowns and flicks his hand. "Just some manoeuvres I want Booker to be aware of for Wednesday. Middlesbrough has crazy attacking runs, so we want to be on the lookout. It's nothing we can't handle." He looks at Belle and a tightness forms around his eyes. "I erm…know this whole thing between you and Tanner hasn't been ideal these last few weeks, but I really appreciate you doing this for the team."

Belle turns to me with a sexy glint in her eyes. "It hasn't been so bad."

"Hi, Belle," Vi beams, walking over to her and giving her an awkward arse-out hug. "Welcome to the madhouse."

Belle laughs. "I'm sure I'll fit right in."

"Cam and Indie are out back," Booker says, gesturing toward the French doors that lead out to the patio. "They're fighting about Indie's bartop performance in front of the whole team on Friday."

My brows lift. "Oh, shiiiiit. Is Gareth refereeing?"

"No, he's on the road," Booker answers. "Hayden is out there."

"I still can't believe Indie danced on top of a bar!" Dad cajoles with a twinkle of chagrin. "She's so professional at practice and matches. And she's quiet when she comes over here."

"That's because it's hard to get a word in edgewise around here," Vi interjects, striding back into the kitchen just as Hayden comes through the door laughing. He covers his mouth with his hand and Vi's face drops. "How bad is it?"

"It's more comical than bad." Hayden grips his side, his eyes crinkled with amusement. "They've officially challenged each other to a footie match. I'm here to recruit."

I laugh and look at Belle. "You up for it?"

"Of course!" she exclaims. "I was there to witness it after all. It was a lot more Kristen Wiig comedy than it was Coyote Ugly provocative. Camden needs to lighten up."

Vi laughs. "Too right! God, I wish I could have seen it."

"Trust me, you don't," Booker mumbles, a disturbed look on his face.

"Oh, but I'm in heels." Belle looks down at her feet regretfully.

"Try on my garden shoes by the door. I'm obviously in no condition to play." Vi points to her stomach.

Hayden waltzes over to her and kisses her temple, his hand cupping her belly like it's the most natural resting place for it. "I'll stay here with you," he murmurs, pinching a piece of cheese from the counter.

"No!" Vi exclaims. "Go play, really." He frowns but she's not having it. "Tanner can stay inside with me. Too many Harrises out there will surely result in an injury. You take Belle and make sure they all play clean. Camden can be a cheating wanker."

I check with Belle to see if she's good with this. Going against Vi wouldn't be easy, but I'd fight the cause if Belle wants me out there. She assures me she's good, though, so I do as my sister says and hang back.

I sidle up at the island and watch Vi grab a block of cheese out of the fridge. "Aren't you exhausted?" I ask, watching her lumber around in the kitchen. She's petite and this baby looks like it's taking over.

"I was completely shattered for the longest time, but the last couple of weeks I've felt great!" She reaches in the drawer and pulls out a cheese grater. "I can't believe I'm only two weeks away from my due date."

"You guys decide on a name yet? Tanner for a girl has a nice ring to it."

She pauses to stroke her belly, ignoring my suggestion completely. "We'll know it when we see her." The twinkle in her eyes is like a Disney movie.

"You seem happy," I state, unable to hide my smile. Her aura is infectious.

"I am, Tan." Her chin wobbles and she scoffs like she's being ridiculous. She resumes her activity. "So you and Belle?"

I roll my eyes. "Did Booker fill you in?"

She cuts her eyes to me. "Of course. You know you can't hide anything in this family."

"I wasn't hiding it," I exhale, fiddling with the label on the mustard. "I just thought I might be able to tell you myself for once. Silly me."

She begins grating the cheese. "So that didn't take long." She shoots her prying eyes straight at me.

My brows lift. "Felt like it took ages. Last week was murder after I left here."

"Well, can you blame us?"

I frown. "No, but I do prefer to come to things on my own."

She ponders that thought. "That's very true. Even when you struggled in school, you never really struggled. You were just on your own timeframe."

"See? I get there eventually."

"So you really like her? I mean, you must. This is the first girl you've ever brought around here that you weren't sneaking in through the conservatory to shag."

My jaw drops. "You knew about that? I thought I was being sly."

She purses her lips. "Mission failed. The whole village of Chigwell knew about that." She looks down again. "Belle must be different."

"She's certainly that." I drag in a large breath and grab a bottle of tomato sauce and spin it on its side in front of me. The mindless task helps clear my thoughts. "She's funny and wild and a bit crazy, which is kind of hot because I never know what to expect. And she's so fucking smart, Vi. She's acing it at her job, and she's so passionate about it that it makes me want to do *more*. I don't know." My voice trails off.

Vi props a hand on her hip. "What kind of more?"

I shrug. "Like, maybe start my own charity or something."

I wince having now spoken the words aloud. Normally in my family, I'm the joke, the punchline, the comedic laugh charged and ready for when things get too serious. Now I'm putting something very serious into the universe for judgement. It makes my butthole pucker.

I look up to see Vi's glossy eyes locked on mine. "Are you serious?"

"Yeah, I think so. There was a homeless bloke who helped me out the night I was caught on camera in Belle's car, and I sort of re-paid the favour to him. But it didn't feel like enough to just give him a warm bed and a shower, so I ended up securing him a job with the grounds crew at Tower Park."

"You did?" Vi's jaw is slack.

"Yeah. It's not a big deal. Dad lined up most of it. But the guy's name is Sedgwick and he keeps talking about these friends of his on the street. I can't help but feel like I can do more for them."

I look up and Vi is staring at me in watery-eyed wonder. "You absolutely can do more, Tan. You can do anything you set your mind to! Belle inspired all of this?"

I shrug. "I just want to be good enough for her, you know?"

She reaches across the counter and grabs my hand. "You were good enough for her before all of this." I half smile and she pulls back, resuming her cheese grating process. "I'm proud of you, Tanner."

"Thanks," I murmur, feeling like a child all over again because I still crave Vi's approval.

We've all changed so much as we've grown up, yet we're all still the same. Still five siblings roughing out life together one story at a time. Vi's engaged and having a baby. Camden is in love with Indie. I'm with Belle. Maybe Booker or Gareth will be next. Even Dad seems to be in better spirits these days. I'm still floored that he brought up Mum to me last week. He never would have done that before.

A random question on the tip of my tongue falls out. "How did you know you were in love with Hayden?"

Vi looks up at me with a grin and glances out the window to watch the action in the back garden for a moment before answering. "I don't know. I mean, it wasn't love at first sight by any means. We had an immediate connection I suppose. But I don't think it was until he told me all the dark corners of his past that I completely fell for him."

I frown, recalling the little bit Vi told me about Hayden attempting to take his own life after the death of his sister. Suicide is never the answer, but if something ever happened to Vi, I don't know what I'd do with myself.

"Do you ever worry that he would try again?" My eyes slant with sympathy, but she immediately shakes her head.

"Not a drop." She sets down the cheese grater and braces her hands on the worktop, inhaling and exhaling deeply. She closes her eyes, and I'm surprised when two tears slip out from beneath her lashes.

"Vi, I'm so sorry." I make a move to get up, but she lifts her hand to stop me.

"It's all right," she says, smiling and clutching her belly. "I cry about everything these days. It's the hormones. But to answer your question, no, I'm not worried about Hayden anymore. This baby is tethering us together so much, our hearts are one right now. Deep down, I *know* no matter what happens to us, we'll get through it together."

I look down at my clasped hands because it's hard to look at her face when she's so open like this. My chest burns with an ache at her blatant display of raw love and vulnerability. My sister and Hayden have laid everything bare with each other. They've played all their cards and they hold nothing back. And rather than feeling exposed and susceptible to attack, they feel...safe.

I clear my throat, snapping myself out of my inner thoughts and find Vi staring at me with a curious look on her face.

I let out a laugh. "What?"

She shakes her head and swallows, shooting me a wobbly smile. "Nothing. I...erm...Why don't you tell everyone that dinner is ready."

Bethnal, Baby!

Belle

D R. MILLER AGREED TO LET ME OUT EARLY ON WEDNESDAY FOR the big Bethnal Green match. She was especially amenable when I told her that Tanner had recruited several of his team members and WAGs to attend our charity event next weekend, which I'm actually looking forward to now.

The last couple of days, Tanner has been staying at my place, saying that he preferred it because it put him farther away from Tower Park. He said the way dark chocolate calls to me in the night is the way Tower Park calls to him. He's worried that watching the match this evening and not being allowed on the sidelines with his team might crush his soul.

He's a bit dramatic.

Hoping to brighten his spirits, I pop out of work early to go pick up a gift I ordered for him. It's just something silly that I hoped might take his mind off the fact that he's not putting on his kit today.

Right before I walk into the store, my mobile alights with a call from my father. Aside from our short, clipped emails, I haven't spoken to him since the day I screamed at him in my flat.

"Hello?" I answer, looking around suspiciously as if he's watching me from somewhere.

"Belle, this is your father."

"Hello, Father. How are you?" My voice sounds different, reverting back to that proper tone I only ever use around my family.

"I'm well. And yourself?"

"I can't complain."

"Good. I wanted to let you know you've done a very proper job with that Harris boy these past few weeks."

"I have?"

"Yes, aside from those first couple of photos, things have looked, well, appropriate for someone like you. So well done."

"Someone like me," I repeat slowly.

"Yes, young, social, carefree."

Wild, unpredictable, embarrassing.

My jaw tightens "Thank you." As halfcocked as his compliment may be, I can't remember a time when my father has ever told me "well done."

"Listen, darling. I know we haven't always seen eye-to-eye. And I know you chose a different path for your life, but it was good to know that when the time came, you could do what was right for the family."

I shake my head even though he can't see me. "I've always wanted what's right for the family, Father. I just couldn't deliver it the way you wanted me to and our relationship suffered for it."

"Yes, well, you resisted generations of tradition, Belle. Arguably, we were going to be upset when you walked away."

"I walked away to become a doctor. *A doctor.* I'm not scrubbing bedpans. Although, if I were, you should be proud of that, too, because it's an honest living and I'm your daughter."

"We had a plan," he barks. "Becoming a lawyer was all laid out for you. You and your brother were to take over my practice so I could focus on rising to the Supreme Court. The money was there. The status. The connections. You can't have achieved half of that all on your own in *medicine.*"

His voice is laced with disdain.

"I save babies, Father! I'm a surgical fellow for a world-renowned high-risk foetal surgeon. I operate inside expecting mothers' uteruses. Who cares about money!"

"Only people who have money say such things. And you, my darling, have money. It may not be in paper form in your pocket, but that bohemian flat you live in is paid for. Your car. My profession and connections provided those luxuries you take for granted every day."

"I'd give up those simple luxuries if it meant you'd respect what I'm doing!" I exclaim, a knot forming in my throat.

"Don't get emotional," he scoffs. "I called for a reason. There will be an important man at the match tonight whom I need you to say hello to."

"Who?"

"Do you recall Lord Sanbury? He and his wife had a daughter about your age."

"Juliet Sanbury?"

"Yes, well, her father has a rather large investment in the Bethnal Green football club, so I need you to say hello. If you could bring that Harris boy with you, even better."

"Why do I need to say hello?"

He sighs heavily, most likely because I had the nerve to ask questions instead of simply following orders. "Because a vacancy arose on the Supreme Court two months ago and Lord Sanbury is on the selection committee. The vote is next week, and a good, polite visit from you and that boy might be just what I need to secure his vote."

I smile and shake my head. "So this is what you get out of this."

"What do you mean?"

"I've been wondering this entire time what could possibly motivate you to push me into the arms of a footballer." I laugh as realisation dawns on me. "You said you didn't want me to be perceived as a common whore, but what you fail to recognise, Father, is that you pimped me out like a whore for your own selfish gain."

"I never—"

"You did!" I shout, boiling over with anger. "And I won't go talk to your Lord Sausage boujie friend. And I won't put on a show for you any longer. Because, guess what, Father? I'm not faking it with Tanner anymore. We're in a relationship now and making a proper go of it."

"Don't be ridiculous. That boy can't possibly intend to keep it in his pants for you. He's a footballer, Belle. He can have any woman he wants. A different girl every night if he'd like, which from the looks of it, he does. If you think you have a chance with this man, you're dumber than I thought."

His words pierce right through me. They make little slits in my soul and shed light on the scary parts of my heart that I'm constantly trying to hide.

"Well, thankfully, I'm not your problem."

I hang up on him and inhale quickly, emotion bubbling deep inside of me.

I can't let his words hurt me. I can't give them life. Giving them life means letting him win, and I'm stronger than that. Tanner does care for me. He won't cheat on me. He knows I'll fucking kill him if he does. *We can make this work.*

I set my jaw and raise my shoulders, striding into the shop with a newfound strength that I almost believe.

"Is it stupid?" I ask, perched on the edge of my sofa and watching Tanner's reaction to my gift. "It's stupid. We don't have to wear them. I thought they'd be funny for the media pictures and that they might help take your mind off the fact that you're not wearing your kit. Maybe have a laugh. But don't worry, we don't have to wear these. They were just a gag."

I snatch the T-shirt gift out of Tanner's hands, along with the gift bag the set came in. I stand to go upstairs, but before I get even two steps away, I'm yanked backwards onto his lap.

"Why are you taking away my present?" he murmurs in my ear.

"Because it was just a joke." I lie, heat rising in my cheeks.

"There's one for you, too, right?" he asks, nibbling my ear and burrowing his furry chin into my neck.

"Yes," I reply weakly.

"Let's fucking do it. I love them." He nips my ear playfully, and I giggle with delight that he fucking gets me.

Moments later, we're standing in front of my bathroom mirror, staring at each other in our matching shamrock green T-shirts—the official colour for Bethnal.

"We look ridiculous," I croak.

"We look amazing!" he exclaims.

I turn my eyes to him, examining his whole body with purpose. His jeans are artfully faded and hugging his gloriously thick thighs. His blonde man bun and lush beard are properly groomed. And his sculpted pecs are showcased perfectly below the thin fabric with the text "BIG SPOON" scrawled across the top.

"You really want to waltz into Tower Park wearing a shirt that says big spoon on it?" I ask, propping a hand on my hip.

The merriment on his face is infectious.

"Only if you wear your little spoon shirt. Otherwise, I'd look ridiculous!" he scoffs with a serious tone that has me nearly crying with laughter.

He glances at his watch. "Shit, we have to go. Come on, Little Spoon."

We arrive at Tower Park and Tanner gets stopped nearly twenty times outside the stadium to talk to fans and various people he knows. This is his home turf and he doesn't have the protection of the players' entrance today. He's like a king amongst his people, charming them left and right, signing T-shirts and snapping selfies. I even get asked to pop into a few shots.

The best part of the whole scene is that *everybody* is laughing at our shirts. Even the security guys. Tanner's smile is genuine the entire time as he laughs along with everybody, pointing to the "BIG SPOON" text on his chest. I can't help but feel good about how well my little gag gift is going over. It's the perfect distraction for him, and he's crazy enough to have gone for it.

When we finally get past the ticket counter, Tanner is on a mission, and it's not to our seats located in the first row on the sideline right behind the team. He's moving through the concrete halls of Tower Park as if he knows exactly where he's headed. It isn't until I see a familiar face that realisation dawns on me.

"Sedgwick!" I exclaim, noting his official Tower Park staff clothing and the large roller bin of rubbish he's emptying into a dumpster.

"Dr. Ryan, what a treat." He takes off his gloves and offers me his hand, which I gladly shake.

"How are you?" I ask, amazed that he's standing here before me.

"I'm doing very well thanks to him." He smiles proudly up at Tanner. "This job suits me perfectly. No stuffy uniforms. Fresh air to breathe. I can't complain a bit."

My eyes are wide and watery as they swerve to Tanner, asking the silent question, "Did you do this?"

He has that knowing half-smile on his face. The one that swirls deep in my belly and makes it hard for me to think.

I shake my head and look back at Sedgwick. "I'm so happy for you."

He nods enthusiastically. "Who would have thought the funny circumstances of that night would end up helping more than just me?"

"More than you?" I ask, frowning at Tanner for clarification.

"Well, for the charity we're working on, of course," Sedgwick answers, but his face falls as his eyes meet Tanner's. "Was I not supposed to say?"

"I was going to tell you about it," Tanner replies smoothly, a quiet confidence in his tone that comforts me. "It's all just come about the last couple of days. Sedgwick and I only came up with a name for it yesterday."

"What kind of charity?"

Sedgwick answers. "It's called Shirt Off My Back. It's a nonprofit Tanner is starting to help feed those in need and find them shelters, clothing, and jobs." He gestures to himself as if he's the prime example. "Tower Park is partnering with us."

You could knock me over with a feather right now. My throat closes up and I nod woodenly, overwhelmed by this new information. Finally, I croak out, "Well, that is exciting indeed. You must let me help somehow."

I glance at Tanner, who smiles and kisses my temple. "I would love that."

Sedgwick's eyes sparkle. "Well, go on. The match is about to start. I'll be seeing more of you two very soon, I'm sure."

We say our goodbyes to Sedgwick and begin our journey to our seats, swerving through the crowds of people drinking beers and eating food. The longer we walk, the more I become overwhelmed. I'm in awe of how much Tanner has achieved in the short amount of time I've known him. He went from a slutty, self-sabotaging footballer to a grown man in a relationship and starting up a charity. It's...humbling.

I halt our movements and Tanner turns to face me, concern marring his beautiful features.

"Belle, are you all right?"

I nod. Smile. And kiss him like I've never kissed him before. Right in the middle of people buzzing around us. Right in our dopey T-shirts.

I pull away after feeling satisfied and murmur against his lips, "You're crazy cool, Big Spoon."

He chuckles against my cheek. "You're crazy cool, too, Little Spoon. Now control yourself, woman. We're in public for Christ's sake."

I look out to see several people's mobiles pointed at us and I don't even care.

When we find our seats, I'm stunned by the familiar couple I see sitting in the two chairs beside ours.

"Vi?" Tanner exclaims, cutting a serious look at Hayden. "What are you doing here? You shouldn't be here. You should be at home with your feet up."

Tanner ushers me next to Vi and the two men bookend us.

Vi's blonde ponytail bounces as she rolls her eyes and rubs her belly. "Oh stop. I couldn't miss this match."

"Wouldn't miss this match is more like it. I tried to stop her," Hayden defends, his eyes strained from obvious stress over having her here. "I all but laid down in front of the cab. It was either go with her to the match or die. I can't die, man. We have a baby coming."

I stifle my giggle because Tanner's face is still so serious. "Vi, this isn't smart," he says, shaking his head.

She smiles softly at him. "I needed to be here for you. I know today is hard."

My heart lunges at her sweet words, and I can see the manipulation tactics she's pulling over on Tanner right before me. His face turns soft and he half smiles his gratitude. Oh, she is good. This is how she has those Harris Brothers wrapped around her finger. I must have her teach me all the things.

Vi's pretty blue eyes fall to our shirts, taking them in for the first time. "Man! Had I known you were wearing those I would have had a T-shirt made, too!"

I frown and ask, "What would yours have said?"

She looks at me as if I'm stupid. "Baby spoon, of course!"

We all laugh. Even stressed-out Hayden's eyes alight with amusement.

He puts an arm around her. "Remember, no screaming at the refs or the players, or I'll be carrying you out of here like a baby. I mean it."

Vi nods solemnly and puckers her lips up to Hayden until he leans over and kisses her. They are so cute, I could die.

And here Tanner and I are in our stupid fucking T-shirts.

Tanner tweaks my sides excitedly when the Bethnal Green Pride song begins and the team comes running out onto the pitch with the energy of a thousand galloping horses. The crowd goes wild as our men in green and white line up on the sidelines for player announcements.

When Booker Harris is announced over the PA system, he jogs out in his brightly coloured keeper's shirt and waves a gloved hand to the crowd. His eyes search the stands until finds us. Grinning sheepishly, he makes a beeline our way. Everyone watches with curiosity as he hops over a couple of barricades and comes to stand right below our row. He raises his fist to us and Tanner leans over the rail and knuckle bumps him. Pride and sincere happiness drip from every part of his body.

The crowd erupts even louder as Booker blows a kiss to Vi who's full on bawling her eyes out at the tender exchange between the two brothers. Two teammates. A family bonded together through football.

He turns and runs back out to join his team as the crowd begins to chant, *"Harris, Harris, Harris."*

Goosebumps tingle all the way from my head to my toes at this incredible moment happening here at Tower Park.

Tanner's chin wobbles as he turns and offers a quick wave to the crowd, further stoking their cheers. When he faces the pitch again, I watch his jaw tick as he struggles to control his emotions. Vi utters a choked sob as Tanner pulls me under his arm and presses his forehead to my hair, clearly overwhelmed by everything as well.

Suddenly, we see Vaughn Harris emerge in front of us on the sidelines, clipboard in hand, and a small smile on his lips. He cups his hand to the side of his mouth and mouths, "We'll see you next week."

Tanner nods, narrowing his eyes with focused determination. And with that single, solitary look, I know he's ready to get back to work and find his stride again.

The commentator continues with the visiting team announcements when, out of nowhere, I see Vi hunch over in her seat.

I bend down next to her. "Vi, are you all right?"

Her eyes are pinched as she nods. "Yeah, just a weird cramp. Braxton Hicks, I'm sure. I've been getting those a lot."

"Are you sure?" Hayden's voice is laced with concern as he squats down beside her. "Damnit, Vi, I don't like this."

"I'm fine!" she crows, standing up straight and then freezing. She reaches out and grips mine and Hayden's forearms.

"Belle, can you do me a favour and tell me if I'm bleeding?" Her voice is trembling with fear and anxiety as her grip tightens on me.

Hayden's eyes find mine and I school my features to look calm, cool, and collected. I quickly bend down and see a wetness all over the crotch of her jeans. Thankfully her jeans are light.

"It's clear, Vi." I glance up at her and add, "Your water just broke."

"Oh fuck!" Hayden and Tanner say in unison, Tanner just now catching on to what's happening before us.

"Bugger, bugger, bugger!" Vi crows. "I'm going to miss the match."

"Stuff the match, Vi. You're having our baby!" Hayden roars.

She nods, schooling her features into crisis mode. "All right, we're going to go." She makes a move to get past us and says, "You guys have fun. We'll see you after."

"After?" Tanner barks. "What do you mean? I'm coming with you!"

"Oh stop! You don't have to do that, Tan. It could take hours. Right, Belle?"

I shrug unhelpfully because I have no clue where her contractions are to even guess. This is a standard issue when you're a doctor. People look to you for answers as if you have them, even without a proper examination.

"I don't give a fuck," Tanner barks. "You're not taking a bloody cab to the hospital, Vi."

"Well, you don't have a car!" she argues.

Tanner digs into his pocket and pulls out a key fob. "I have the spare set to my truck. Booker drove here, so it's in the players' lot. We'll take that."

"Great!" Vi winces from what I can only assume is a contraction. "One big happy family."

Hayden and Tanner usher Vi up the stone steps until we're out the door.

"You stay with Vi while I run and get the truck." Tanner passes Vi's arm to me and jogs off down the sidewalk at lightning speed.

"Can you believe the odds?" Vi croaks, dropping down onto a bench and cupping her round belly. "I mean, bloody hell, I walk Bruce almost every day and nothing. One tearful moment with my brothers and BAM! Baby's coming!"

I laugh. "Are you feeling all right?"

She exhales. "These cramps are coming and going a lot, but I'm okay."

"How often are they coming?" I ask, pulling my mobile out so we can time them.

"I don't know," she croaks. "It's too intense to tell."

My eyes widen and lock on Hayden, who looks equally concerned.

Tanner pulls up right when another contraction hits. We file into the truck—me next to Tanner, then Hayden next to me. Vi is sitting by the passenger door, holding the "oh shit" handle on the roof of the vehicle.

I lean over to whisper in Tanner's ear, "I don't want to alarm your sister, but her contractions are only two minutes apart. You need to step on it."

Tanner's eyes fly wide and he punches the gas, driving like a bat out of hell. Thankfully, The Royal London Hospital is right up the street. I only quit working there a few months ago and know it better than any other hospital. I pull out my mobile and call to let them know we're coming in and it'll likely be a quick delivery.

"Christ, Tanner!" Vi bellows as he slams the brakes in front of the accident and emergency entrance. "You're driving like a complete moron."

"Excuse me for not being well-versed on driving my sister to the hospital while she's in fucking labour," he roars, and I place my hand on his thigh to calm him.

"So dramatic," Vi mumbles as she opens the door and inches her way out of the vehicle.

A familiar nurse comes striding outside with a wheelchair as I round the truck. "Hello, Dr. Ryan! Nice to see you again. We miss you around here!"

"Oh, hi, Liz." I offer her a wave as Hayden and Tanner help Vi into the wheelchair. She moans softly with another contraction. "I'm so glad it's you working OB today. I think she's going to go quickly. Take good care of these guys. They're…important."

Liz gives me a jolly thumbs up and begins pushing the wheelchair inside. Hayden freezes beside Tanner and me, a look of sheer terror on his face.

"You've got this, Hayden," I state, grabbing his arm in

encouragement. "You love her. She loves you. That's all you need to do this."

He swallows hard and nods. Before running in after her, he turns and falls into Tanner and me with an awkward, strangled hug.

"Thanks, guys," he croaks and then he's off to start his family.

TANNER

I stare across the sterile tile floor over at Booker's boots that have bits of the pitch wedged between the studs. He's still in his kit, his keeper gloves off and moving them from one hand to the other as we sit in the waiting room of the hospital.

Beside him sits Dad, still in his official Bethnal Green polo. Next to Dad is Gareth, just having arrived five minutes ago by train. Camden and Indie are seated next to Belle and me. And perpendicular to us is Hayden's family, the Clarkes. They consist of his mum, his dad, his younger sister, and his older brother whose wife and one-year-old child are fast asleep in a chair beside him.

We first met the Clarkes at Vi and Hayden's engagement party. It was the same night Vi found out she was pregnant. She ended up telling all of us—Cam, Gareth, Booker, and me—in her bathroom. We might have forced it out of her a bit, but she was having a meltdown and needed to be talked off the ledge.

I know Vi and Hayden weren't planning on this baby at this time in their lives, but watching them embrace this adventure together and become stronger for it has been inspiring. Family goals.

All of us are unified again, filling a large waiting room, silent and anxious to hear any shred of news.

Booker scoffs, "Christ, you'd think Hayden would have texted by now. Something!" Frustration radiates off his shoulders as he looks toward the double doors that lead to the delivery rooms.

Camden's voice pipes up next. "What could be happening in there, Indie? It's after eleven and it's been hours."

Indie and Belle look nervously at each other, and I can feel the Clarkes all staring at them expectantly.

"What aren't you girls saying?" Dad's voice booms with authority.

"Dad, calm down," I snap, not liking the tone he's taking with Belle and Indie.

"I will not calm down!" He stands up and begins pacing the floor. "Christ, how has Hayden not texted someone something? Anything. This is ridiculous." He cuts his eyes to Belle. "You said she was close when she arrived almost five hours ago. I'm going to get answers."

Gareth stands up, stopping him in his tracks. "I'll go, Dad."

Just as he moves to make his way to the nurses station, the double doors open and Hayden comes striding out, completely swathed in blue scrubs and a surgical cap.

We all stand, our breaths held high in our shoulders as he pulls the mask off his face. Breathlessly, he confirms, "Everyone is okay. Vi and the baby are wonderful. They're—" His voice cracks, his eyes dumping unexpected tears down his face. "They're so beautiful."

Gareth's closest to Hayden, so he places a firm hand on his back and pulls him into a hug. Hayden all but loses it. He was obviously holding on by a thread before. Now that he's had time to think, it's all hitting him at once.

Hayden's brother, Theo, pushes past everybody to stand beside him. When he claps his back, Hayden lets go of Gareth and clears his throat loudly, nodding to his brother that he's okay. We wait as he chokes back his emotions and regains control of himself.

"The baby's heart rate kept dipping every time Vi started to push, so they did an ultrasound and discovered that somehow she had turned around in there and was breech."

I turn when I hear Belle intake a sharp breath.

"They rushed her in for an emergency C-section. It all happened crazy fast. Then, when they pulled the baby out, her colour was off. It was terrifying, but there were doctors right there and they rushed her off to the NICU straight away. I wanted to stay with Vi, but she screamed at me to go with the baby, so I did." Hayden's face crumples with more tears, and Belle begins trembling beside me. I take her hand and clutch it firmly against my chest.

"They got the baby's oxygen levels up rather quickly and said she was looking really good. That the NICU was only a precaution and she could go meet her mummy. But then—" He clears his scratchy throat. "Then a nurse came in and told me there was a tear in Vi's uterine wall and she was losing too much blood. They had to put her under in order to repair it. But she's okay now."

Hayden's mum releases a quiet sob as Hayden covers his face with his hand, his entire body racked with cries. "I'm sorry. Everyone's all right. Everyone's fine now. Vi's awake and has just properly met the baby for the first time. They're moving them both to a patient room now."

Hayden finally looks up, his eyes wide and tearful. He looks at his brother and adds, "I can't believe how close I was to losing them both in one fell swoop."

Dad steps in front of all of us and grabs Hayden by the shoulders. "You didn't lose them. They're okay, son."

Hayden wipes his face and sniffs. "But to think that Vi was bleeding like that and I left her. She had to have been so frightened."

"You took care of my granddaughter. You did what a good father should. You did what Vi wanted. Everyone is okay now." Dad's voice is choked with just as much emotion, but his words seem to help.

Hayden nods woodenly and pulls the scrub cap off his head. "They put us up in a big room, but I'll have to take you back in shifts."

Hayden's mum speaks up, looking straight at Dad. "You all go first. Go see your daughter."

Your Crazy Is Showing

Belle

FOR AS LONG AS I'VE BEEN A SURGEON, THERE'S THIS LITTLE tickle I get on the back of my shoulder blade whenever a patient is about to go downhill. It's like a small electric pulse that tingles with a sense of foreboding. I don't know if it's some sort of mental intuition or just a fluke, but it almost always occurs right before things take a turn.

So whenever I get that tingle, I've learned to stop what I'm doing and wait.

Wait.

Wait.

Wait.

And then it happens. Monitors start going off, a bleeder sprays, pressure drops. Then it's the rush of problem-solving in order to right what went wrong, push the correct meds, stop the bleed, and send them into emergency surgery.

Sadly, it doesn't always end in my favour. I remember all of the patients I've lost. And with foetal surgery, I don't just remember the baby, but the mother as well. Mostly because if the baby dies in surgery, then the mother has to subsequently deliver them afterwards.

Stillborn.

It's the worst part of my job.

But without surgery, the baby has little to no chance of survival. So the rewards of a healthy baby outweigh the risks of a dangerous surgery. That's how I get myself through the bad cases. Through the losses.

We give the doomed a chance at salvation.

With Vi, I felt the tickle as soon as we were outside of Tower Park. Everything happened too quickly. Her contractions were coupling, coming out of nowhere, one on top of the other. And then to hear nothing for hours was alarming. Indie and I kept exchanging worried looks but couldn't say anything. We were on the wrong side of the doors.

But it all could have turned out so much worse. What if we hadn't got them to the hospital in time? Would there still be a baby? Would there still be a Vi? Suddenly, I wonder if the rewards are worth the risks. When you're talking about a person you know and care about, and not just a name on a chart, everything feels different.

I feel my guard coming up as I file through the hallway with the Harris clan. It's rising up over the knots in my stomach, that tickle on my back, and the heaviness in my chest. It's climbing to numb my mind and push me back to a safe distance.

I'm an outsider in this group. I've been amongst them for barely a month, and they have no idea that I'm nothing like them. I never speak to my brother. My mother is a vapid, emotionless ice queen who shames emotion. My father all but told me there's no reality in this world where Tanner Harris could ever commit to me, let alone love me.

The Harrises all lean on each other and talk to each other and have silent conversations by giving each other a simple look. They do public displays of affection and have a waiting room bursting with loved ones.

That's not me. Those aren't my people. My people are like Indie, who understands crazy eyes and side-eyes and emotional outbursts.

We're exactly alike. Or we used to be before she found Camden.

We're different in the sense that she grew up in boarding schools and never knew her parents, whereas I had a home life with mine. But our pasts are one in the same. She was two plus two; I was three plus one. Our equations were different, but we both resulted in the same sum.

Our families don't sit in waiting rooms.

And now I have something different right on the tips of my fingers like Indie does with Camden. A different life. A different equation. A different sum.

Yet all I'm feeling is that bloody tickle on my shoulder blade again.

We reach the door to Vi's patient suite. I hesitate in the hallway while everyone else moves their way inside like they belong, including Indie.

Tanner pauses when he realises I'm no longer beside him. "What's wrong?"

I smile brightly at him. Too bright. "I'm…not going in," I stammer. "You go ahead."

He moves closer to me. "Why don't you want to come in?"

I scoff awkwardly. "I think it's inappropriate. Your family barely knows me. Vi just had surgery. They don't need an outsider in there."

He frowns. "They know you're important to me. What else is there to know?"

"I know, but I'm not, you know, a part of the family."

"So what? Neither is Indie and she's in there."

I roll my eyes. "Indie and Camden are different."

"Different than what?" he asks, a serious look in his eyes. "Different than you and me?"

My jaw drops at the shock registering all over his face, as if what I'm saying is ludicrous. "Don't be daft, Tanner. You know they are. I'm just going to grab a cab home. Call me tomorrow."

I move to kiss his cheek, but he jerks away from me as if I slapped him.

"No," he barks.

"No, what?" I hiss, frustrated that he's being so dramatic.

"No, I don't want you to leave. No, I don't think we're different than Cam and Indie. No, I don't want you to believe that you're not a part of this."

His words are spoken, but I don't hear them. I chew on my lip, protective rage crescendoing inside of me like a tea kettle whistle.

"Tanner, don't push this," I whisper. "I'm barely keeping it together right now. Don't go poking the bear."

"Keeping what together?"

"My mind!" I exclaim and then lower my voice as I step closer to him, looking up into his eyes. "Hayden almost lost Vi and his baby girl. Just like that. And they love each other, Tanner. Like, truly love each other. If I stay here with you, I'm going to go nuts. I'm not used to relationships and families. I feel too much. My emotions are too strong. I have no barrier with you and it's all just...crushing me. I don't do relationships because of this very reason. I go crazy. I get jealous and become irrational, all because my emotions allow me to get invested. Then I think of the future and I go *completely off the rails* with happily ever after thoughts, and you don't want that mess! You don't need that crazy shit coming at you in the night!"

Tanner opens his mouth to speak but then closes it again, the brow of his forehead crinkled deep in thought.

"See!" I exclaim, tears welling in my eyes. His silence is enough confirmation for me. "This is why I told you not to poke the bear." I turn to walk away, mortified that I've shown all my true colours like an ugly, paint-splattered mural.

He catches hold of my arm, swirling me to a halt against the wall. His fierce eyes pin me to my place. "Don't do this, Belle. Don't start pulling away," he begs, cupping my face in his hands. "I adore the ground you walk on. You have to see that!"

I shake my head, my voice trembling as I reply, "Is that enough? Is that enough for you to want a future with me? Your whole family bleeds for each other! I'm never going to be like them. I'm not built that way! Do you honestly and truly want someone who can't give you all of that?" I point to the hospital door. "If your answer isn't a resounding yes, we should cut our losses because, if we push this, it's only going to make it that much harder when it all implodes."

Air gusts out of my mouth. My shoulders rise and fall in rapid succession as I've officially dropped the gauntlet and left it all on him.

"For fuck's sake, Belle!" Tanner jams a hand through his hair, his eyes flooded with desperation and confusion. "My sister just had a baby and emergency surgery, and you're throwing all of this at me on top of it. I can barely see straight, let alone think straight. Isn't it enough for me to just want you to stay with me?"

I drag in a deep, cleansing breath. "I wish it was."

TANNER

She walks away. She turns and walks away after unloading what felt like a fucking mountain of baggage onto me. I want to grab her and kiss her. I want to toss her arse into a utility room and fuck her until she admits what we have.

But there's one thing anchoring me in place that's bigger than our crazy.

My family.

My sister could have died today. My niece almost didn't make it. Whatever Belle needs from me pales in comparison to that. I'm a Harris. That name and my family has been my identity for twenty-six years. Our lives haven't been easy. The loss of our mother left us in a dark hole where the only light we had was each other. I can't discredit that.

I steel myself to walk into the hospital room, sticking my hand under the antibacterial machine by the door as I go in. All I see are backs huddled around a bed. I can't even see a glimpse of Vi, Hayden, or the baby, so I pause, resting my hand on the nearby bassinet. It has clear walls and looks clinical and sterile, but inside is a tiny pink hat. I reach in and pick it up, rubbing my fingers over the knitted ridges. It's so small. So innocent. So—

"Come over and see why we don't have the heart to put it on her head." Vi's voice cuts into my internal reverie.

I look over and see a sliver of her between my dad and Booker. They separate so she can see me better, and I feel my knees wobble when her tired, tear-soaked blue eyes find mine. "Hiya, Tan," she smiles.

I swallow. "Hiya, Vi."

"Would you like to meet your niece?" I nod and move closer to the bed, the baby entering my eye line as I approach. My breath is pulled from my body. "Now you can see why she's not wearing the hat."

I gaze down at the tiny bundle resting against Vi's chest and note the huge mass of golden blonde hair sticking straight out all over her head. It's shiny, bone straight, and thicker than any baby's hair I've ever seen in movies or in real life.

Vi's hospital gown is split open across her chest and there they lie together. Skin to skin, heart to heart. A soft baby cheek pressing against Vi's collarbone. A pink blanket covers the baby's back and Vi's exposed chest.

"That hair." I reach out and brush my fingertips along the feathery soft ends.

Vi sniffles. "I know. The nurse said they usually wait to do their first baths, but with everything that happened…" She pauses and looks at Hayden for reassurance. His grey eyes are already locked on her in silent devotion. "They thought I'd like to wake up to her all clean and ready to be loved on." She drops a soft kiss to the fluff. "They want us to do skin to skin like this for a while since I didn't get to bond with her when she came out." Her chin trembles as tears fall freely down her cheeks.

"You've got her now," I reassure her. "And she's perfect, Vi."

She laughs with a garbled cry mixed in. "That she is, even if she did scare the shit out of us."

Everybody chuckles awkwardly except for Hayden. He lowers his head to Vi and kisses her temple, breathing her in for a moment before he repeats the gesture to the baby.

"What's her name?" I ask, looking between the two of them.

Vi swallows around a smile. "Well, none of our choices suited her. Then Hayden suggested Adrienne from Rocky because she had a bit of a rocky entrance, and well..." Her lips crumple with the on-slaught of more tears and my eyes fill right along with hers.

I reach out and grab Vi's hand, squeezing hard and ignoring the IV and medical bracelets littering her small wrists. Suddenly, my sister who has always been bigger than life to me, seems so small, so young, so tired, yet magically stronger than I've ever seen her look.

I move my hand from Vi's to the baby's, picking up her tiny clenched fist and testing the weight of it. "Well, it's nice to meet you, Rocky." I smile and Vi laughs, the sadness in her eyes depleting fractionally.

"Where's Belle?" she asks, looking around the room like she must be standing in a corner somewhere.

I swallow and divert my attention back to the baby. "She wanted to give you guys some privacy."

Vi tilts her head. "Privacy? What the bloody hell is that? She was seconds away from delivering the baby herself."

"I know." My gaze lifts to hers and I silently will her to leave it be.

Gareth's voice rescues me from a Vi interrogation. "You never mentioned what her middle name is."

Vi nods and looks past me to Dad. "It's Vilma." A sad smile breaks across her face as she utters our mother's name aloud. Vi's given birth name, actually, even though she's always just been our Vi.

I turn and see Dad's eyes are red-rimmed as the presence of our mum's memory grows in the room. He nods stiffly, turning away to hide the pain and regret shimmering deep in his eyes.

Gareth's voice breaks the heavy silence. "She'd be very proud, Vi." He clears his throat and pulls himself up tall. "You're going to make a wonderful mum, just like her."

Dad and Gareth exchange a look that's equal parts emotional and tense. What they experienced together—caring for Mum when she was sick at the end—is such an unspoken territory to the rest of us. There's a pain between them that none of us can ever truly know. Camden places a hand on Gareth's shoulder, which causes him to blink and a single tear slips down his cheek.

"Gareth's right," Dad says, his brow furrowed in determination. "It will be nice to continue her name in the family."

I hear a shaky intake of air come from Vi as she clutches Adrienne to her chest, eyes closed, tears flowing. Hayden folds over on her, rubbing the baby's back and pulling Vi's attention to him. The three of them finding strength in their own little family.

They gaze into each other's eyes, saying things that none of us could ever understand. Only them.

I watch them in amazement. Hayden almost lost everything tonight, yet I've never seen him look happier or more proud. He's suffered great loss before. His grief over his sister's death almost killed him, yet here he is, taking risks, because the reward of the climb surpasses the risk of the fall.

And it always will.

As soon as we're out of the hospital, I turn to Booker. "I need to take the truck."

He frowns and nods at me. "Okay, I can ride home with Dad. Everything all right?"

Camden and Indie walk up on our conversation as he asks. I glance at Indie and reply, "I hope so."

Indie fishes into her purse and hands me her keys. "For the flat, although"—she pauses and looks at her watch—"she might not be home yet."

My brows knit. "Why wouldn't she be home?"

Indie looks uncomfortable. "She might have walked home."

"Walked?" I exclaim. "At this time of night?"

She cringes and shrugs. "Yeah, it's about a twenty minute stretch. She walked it all the time when we worked here."

Camden scoffs Indie's name, but I don't stay to listen to them quarrel. I'm already jogging for the truck. I was desperate to see Belle before. Now, thinking of her out here by herself makes me vibrate with urgency.

I drive down the road I think she would have taken. It's a relatively straight shot to her building from here and the area doesn't look too dangerous, but I'm still not comforted. My eyes swerve everywhere the entire trip, searching for her and regretting that I let her leave at all.

When I see someone wearing a bright green shirt walking in a dark corner off in the distance, I exhale in relief. I punch the gas and turn onto the road she's preparing to cross, forcing her to jump back from the curb. I park with a hefty screech of the tyres and fly out of the vehicle, not even bothering to close the door as I march straight toward her.

"Are you bloody kidding me, Ryan?" I growl. "It's after midnight and you decide to walk your arse home? Do you not have any sense?"

Her dark eyes shift from shock to annoyance. "I've walked this road a million times. I worked at that hospital for years, Tanner."

"Oh, so you're psychic now? You can predict whether a rapist is going to come driving down this road or not?"

"Maybe I am psychic!" she snaps. "You don't know me."

"The fuck I don't," I roar, my voice reaching high octaves that probably make the residents wonder if *I'm* a rapist.

When she moves to turn away from me, the yellow streetlight catches her face, illuminating her features more clearly. Her eyes are puffy and her skin is blotchy.

"Have you been crying?" I ask, circling around her to see her face.

She continues avoiding my gaze. "No, all right. Just…leave it, Tanner."

"I will not bloody leave it, and I will not leave you. We're following a pattern here, Belle. Don't you see it?"

She scoffs, "What are you going on about?"

"Fighting and making up. Fighting and making up. You flip out on me, I chase after you. I hurt you, you make me pay for it. And I'm okay with it. I'll endure these ups and downs with you. But eventually, you're going to have to stop thinking it's the end every time we fight."

"Well, maybe you should just end it and save us both such an emotional rollercoaster!" she retorts.

"I like the ride!" I explode, shoving a hand through my hair. "I like that frightening twinkle you get in your eyes when you go off the rails."

"Christ, I can't understand why. I'm a fucking mess," she dejects.

"So your crazy is showing. Who gives a fuck!" I bark, grabbing the crook of her arm to twist her until she has to look into my eyes. "It's not scaring me off, Belle. Don't you see? It's pulling me in. It's wrapping it's way around me and binding me to you in a way that makes me want to protect you…indefinitely."

I pause, shocking myself with the last word and how right it feels falling out of my mouth. It's like the words I just spoke open some vault deep inside me because I'm suddenly seeing everything so much clearer.

Belle looks at my face like she's seeing something brand new. Like she's seeing and feeling the shift. Her voice is quiet when she asks, "Why do you want me? Seriously, Tanner. You're going to want someone better than me. You will. I know it."

I reach out and brush my thumb down her cheek. Her dark eyes swim with emotion. Her freckles like a canvas I could have painted myself. "Belle, my soul has grown with you. So much so, I wonder if it would have shrunk into nothing if I'd never met you."

Her jaw drops as she huffs out a self-deprecating sort of laugh. Shaking her head, she replies, "I could have never seen you coming, Tanner."

"I hope that's a good thing," I reply with a small smile.

She slow blinks and her face softens into my beautiful, warm Belle. Then she giggles, a look of disbelief twinkling in her eyes. "I can't believe you're the same man who told me women called you the thigh tickler!"

This makes me laugh. Hard. She joins in, too, and the sound of it mixed with mine soothes my troubled soul. Aching to feel her again, I lean down and crush her body to mine, encasing her with one arm behind her neck and the other around her ribcage. I use my lips to turn her smile into a kiss as I tip her back and breathe in the wildfire that is so quintessentially Belle.

Belle Ryan is unpredictable and the exact opposite of easy. But her spirit calls to me on some deep level that I cannot stay away from.

I straighten her back up and press my forehead to hers. "You inspire poetry, woman."

She hugs me, rubbing her hands down my back. "I'm sorry for freaking out back there. I'll apologise to your sister tomorrow."

"Don't even worry about it," I reply, looking down at her. "Vi is in her own little bubble right now. I've never seen a happier family."

Her brows lift. "You Harrises seem to have happiness figured out rather well."

I frown. "We aren't perfect. Far from it. You've got your family issues, I've got mine. If you share yours with me, I'll share mine with you. Maybe then we can figure out the meaning of life." I waggle my brows at her playfully.

"The meaning of life, you say?" She bites her lip around a sexy half-smile that makes my dick jolt. Her eyes narrow conspiratorially. "Let's go ponder that over some chocolate."

My brows climb. "As long as the chocolate is drizzled on your body, this thigh tickler is definitely in."

Belle

Tanner and I visit Vi and Hayden at the hospital the next day. I was warned by Tanner that the baby was beautiful, but nothing could have prepared me for her hair. Adrienne, or Rocky, as all the Harris Brothers have apparently taken to calling her, is simply magic. I couldn't stop touching her feathery hair as I held her for nearly an hour in their hospital suite.

When Tanner held her, however, it was less dreamlike. I could hardly stop laughing as he awkwardly tried to find a position to rest his arm. I kept picking at him to adjust her so her head wasn't sagging back, and he just snapped back at me like he knew how to figure it out because he wasn't a moron. So I asked him if he was sure about that because I seem to remember him naked on a street corner only a month ago. That escalated into a quarrel of epic proportions.

Since he had Rocky in his arms, we weren't flat out screaming at each other like we wanted to. We were talking in slow, saccharinely sweet voices and smiling bright white teeth as we calmly called each other a knobhead spunk bubble and a nagging know-it-all cow.

Vi and Hayden didn't know what to say, except for, "Thank God Adrienne can't understand words yet."

Afterwards, in the hospital parking lot, Tanner leaned across the console of my car, grabbed my face in his hands, and kissed me with an aggression that revved more than my car engine. When he pulled away and said, "You looked absolutely beautiful holding my niece," I think I died a thousand deaths.

Indie had warned me about on-season footballers and off-season footballers being so different, but what I witnessed the next week with Tanner is not at all what I expected.

Originally, I thought he might pull away once he started attending practices again, requiring some space to help get back into his routine and focus. I couldn't have been more wrong.

After his first practice back, he showed up at my door, smelly kit and all, and asked me if I wanted a shower, a forking, and then a spooning. We ended up spending every night together after that.

But things aren't exactly like they were before. Tanner is still goofy and he's still *Tanner*, crude jokes and all, but he's more…intense. More focused. Even in the bedroom.

We no longer just have sex. We create movement. We connect on a different level that's so much more…soulful. The way he looks at me and the things he says while inside of me have given me the most powerful orgasms of my entire life.

So I have to say, I'm a *massive* fan of On-Season Tanner.

A few days into practice, after a particularly incredible session of love-making, Tanner spoons me and begins opening up as if the words have been aching to come out.

"Did you know Camden and I had our own secret language

growing up?" he asks, his voice husky as he adjusts me so his left arm is tucked under me like a pillow. His right arm snakes around the dip of my waist and he pulls the back of my naked body flush against the front of his.

"Like cryptophasia?" I ask.

"Crypto what?" he asks, his breath puffing against the hair on my head.

"Cryptophasia is a language developed by twins that only they can understand," I answer.

"Well, yeah then, I guess that's what we had. Didn't know there was a medical fucking term for it."

I smile and bite my lip. A heavy silence stretches out and I can tell he wants to say more so I add, "I'm sure that meant you two were very close."

He exhales and drops a soft kiss to my hair. "We were, *are* I mean. We still are, but we're not. It's…different now that he's not on the pitch with me anymore."

My brows knit as he continues.

"I think being twins put us at a huge advantage in a match. Communication was instinctual. Effortless, like breathing. Have you ever noticed how we always stand on the same side of each other?"

"No," I reply, a bit fascinated.

"Yeah, not just on the pitch either. It's everywhere we go. Cam is always on my right side. It's bizarre. We don't even mean to do it, but we have a constant awareness of each other."

"That's incredible."

"So we've had this our whole lives. Then when he left for Arsenal and I went to Tower Park without him…it felt like…one of my lungs was missing."

My heart clenches at the vulnerability in his words. "I'm sure you miss him."

"But I'm also so fucking proud of him I could burst. He's acing it with Arsenal, and watching him out there is incredible." He pauses for a beat before adding, "But is it completely selfish of me to want him back by my side?"

"Not at all," I answer and scrunch into him while dropping a kiss on his forearm. "I understand it. I felt similar when Indie left The Royal London Hospital."

Indie and I had been beside each other since med school, but as our interests became more focused, it pulled us further apart professionally. Then she started getting serious with Camden and things continued to change. We probably had an easier time of it than Tanner and Camden because we're used to being on our own more than they are. We didn't grow up like the Harris family and we certainly never shared a womb. But she's still my version of family.

"If I wouldn't have had my fellowship with Dr. Miller coming up, I think I would have been completely gutted to lose Indie."

His grip on me tightens. "It's like having a security blanket taken away."

I half smile. "Exactly."

He kisses me and sighs, "I'm finally starting to see myself without Cam. I need my team to see that, too."

"They will," I reply. "You're a hard one to miss, Tanner Harris. And you may have lost a teammate, but you haven't lost Cam. You're biological brothers. Nothing will ever change that."

He pulls in a large breath and I feel his chest rise against my back. When he exhales, his muscles soften and his body relaxes into me as if he's unloaded the world off his shoulders. He nuzzles his chin into my hair and whispers, "I..." He pauses as he searches for his words. "I need to be inside you again."

My brows lift. "Oh, I suppose I could withstand another mind-shattering orgasm."

He kisses my giggles away and makes love to me like I never knew he could.

Jump or Fall

Belle

"**WHAT DO YOU THINK OF THIS ONE?**" INDIE ASKS, STEPPING out of the dressing room at a secondhand boutique she insisted we go to.

I squint at the strapless red dress. "It's good but I liked the black one better, darling," I answer from the purple chaise lounge that I'm currently stretched out on like a cat in heat. It's the only perk to this godforsaken shop.

I don't consider myself a snob, but Indie is the cheapest person I've ever met. She constantly looks at the price tags everywhere we go. Even on a menu. And it's not to differentiate the steak price from the burger. It's to save two pounds by getting a tuna sandwich instead of salmon. I know her job shadowing at Bethnal Green F.C. pays practically nothing but still. Her defiant independence is maddening. I could have easily ordered her a new dress and we could be drinking wine right now instead of rifling through used clothing in Shoreditch, but she's a willful little thing.

"Black it is," Indie says, disappearing behind the curtain. "How much time do we have?"

"About an hour before the guys said to be back."

"Okay, perfect. I'm just about done here."

Indie and I are out last minute shopping in preparation for the big hospital fundraiser tomorrow night. We've both been in Loversville with our hot Harris men all week, so we were in dire need of some girl time. However, it will be short-lived because Tanner and Camden are making dinner for the four of us tonight. It's likely going to be chicken and rice or some derivative of that because that's apparently all footballers eat during the season.

"I'm so done with this shopping nonsense," Indie adds. "I hate trying on dresses. You have to take all of your clothes off and think about what undergarments you're wearing. It's a pain in the arse."

"But you look gorgeous in them." I laugh at her tiny fit.

"So do you. Your dress for tomorrow night is wicked."

I exhale, relieved that I've got mine sorted already. It's a Badgley Mischka gown that looks as if it was custom made for me. It hugs all the good spots and minimises all the problem areas. Although, if you asked Tanner, he would say there are no bad areas on my body. He would know since we experimented with that chocolate drizzle, meaning of life talk he promised.

"I'm really looking forward to this fundraiser."

Indie's comment makes me smile. I can't believe the big night is already here. Both Bethnal and Arsenal are playing neighbouring teams, so Indie, Camden, Booker, and of course Tanner are all planning to come to the event after their matches finish, along with several other Bethnal players and WAGs. They bought a large sponsor table and everything.

Tomorrow is also Tanner's first match back with Bethnal Green, so he's been vibrating with nerves the last couple of days. Sadly, I'm not able to attend. Dr. Miller asked me to welcome the charity's honoured family at the Shangri-La Hotel at The Shard. The event is taking place in the ballroom that evening, but I'm to have high tea with them in the Westminster Suite when they arrive. The upside is that I get to keep the room for the night.

And, win or lose, Tanner has made serious promises for how

we'll take advantage of that.

But tonight we're doing ordinary things that couples do.

Indie steps out of her dressing room, back in her athletic pants and Bethnal T-shirt. I shake my head at her. "I forgot what you even look like in scrubs."

She frowns at her clothing. "I just came from practice, thank you very much."

I put my hands up in defence. "You look great. I'm just curious if you miss surgery at all."

She adjusts her yellow eyewear and slings her black gown over her shoulder. "I certainly don't miss the anxiety of life or death, nor do I miss the politics and the networking I always had to do. Football has its fair share, too, but, I don't know…The energy of the match and the athletes excites me so much more than a stuffy surgical theatre ever did."

"More like the energy of Camden Harris," I jeer and tweak my eyebrows at her.

She smiles and drops down by my feet on the lounger. She has a starry-eyed look about her that makes me smile.

"I'm kind of crazy in love with that man."

My brows lift. "Well done, you." She rolls her eyes but I don't relent. "There was a time when you never thought you'd have sex, let alone fall in love."

She sets her toffee eyes on me. "And now look at me…A big pile of mushy, pun-loving goo."

My smile falters a little. "Are you really that secure in your love, Indie?"

"Of course I am!" she exclaims. "What do you mean?"

I swallow hard. "I mean, look. You and I understand each other. We're the perfect roommates because we're cut from the same cloth. Our families might appear night and day different from the outside, but there are some definite parallels I can draw that make us so alike it's scary."

"Yes, I would agree with that," Indie states with a pragmatic nod of the head.

"Don't you find it hard to let go completely? I mean, you are the first real sense of family I've ever had and that took us years to build. How did you get past your issues with Camden?"

She eyes me thoughtfully. "Well, I think my friendship with you helped me learn how to open up a bit."

I quirk a brow as I ponder my takeaway from our friendship. "I'd say you helped me not turn into a completely cynical arsehole."

Indie beams. "That's the sweetest thing you've ever said to me."

I huff out a self-deprecating laugh. "But really, how do you ever trust that your love with someone is genuine?"

She looks embarrassed. "So I'm going to tell you something, but promise not to take the piss out of me."

"What?" I ask, frowning.

"I sort of...have a philosophy on love."

My eyes twinkle with mirth. God, Indie is such a nerd sometimes. I'm betting she's read a few books on love and formed her own theory. Always the researcher.

"Please, Indie Porter, Doctor of Love, tell me all that you've learned since you've been in love for a hot five months."

She rolls her eyes and continues as if I didn't just make some smart arse remark. "I think truly loving someone is a three-tier system." She holds up three fingers and slowly ticks each number off as she goes. "First, and most important, is how they make you feel about yourself. Are they good to you? Do they accept you for your flaws? See the best in you? The second is how they feel about themselves. Do they take pride in what they do? Do they strive to become more? Do they love themselves? And the third tier is..." She pauses and pushes her glasses up on her nose. Then she pins me to the chaise lounge with her eyes, showing me she's one hundred percent serious. "Do you inspire each other?"

A simple nod of the head and a sigh is indication that she's done. She looks down and adjusts the dress on her lap, allowing silence to fill the room all around us.

Finally, I let out a chortle. "So that's all?"

She shoots me a determined frown. "Yes."

"I erm…don't even have a proper snarky comment to respond to that right now."

"Good," she replies. "Now, since we're sharing so much, can I ask you a question?"

"Of course," I reply, skeptically.

"What made you take a chance with Tanner? I've known you since med school, Belle, and you've never let a guy get this close before."

"Is it not enough that he's hot as fuck?" I shoot her a salacious grin and I can tell she is in no way satisfied. So I go for a novel approach. Honesty.

"Well, I think it's a lot of what you said about tier one. He made me feel beautiful and he never shamed me for my outbursts. He just…embraces me as I am. Because of that, Tanner is my favourite person to be around. After you, of course."

"Naturally," she giggles.

"And even though we bicker at each other constantly, I've learned that it's how we show affection. If we're not arguing, we're not caring."

"And tiers two and three?" Indie asks, a knowing gleam in her eyes.

I look down, feeling my cheeks heat but still not ready to admit the truth aloud. I shrug my shoulders. "Stay tuned."

TANNER

"Why didn't Vi give us an easier recipe?" I growl as I pull the chicken out of the oven and look at the travesty before me. I slam the oven door. "We totally fucked this up."

Camden pops up over my shoulder to get a closer look. "Sod it, I'll eat it."

My eyes fly wide. "What about the girls?"

He shrugs. "I got them a bottle of wine. After a glass or two, they won't even notice."

I toss the pot holder on the counter. "I'm going to call Vi. You might be content with mediocrity in your relationship, but I'm still trying to impress my woman."

Camden chokes on the drink of water he's just taken. "Good grief, keep your shirt on, broseph! It's only dinner. We don't need to be bothering Vi. She has her own family to worry about."

His remark brings me up short. "We're still her family, too! Rocky is just an extension of all of us. Hayden, too, for that matter."

Camden jerks back. "Christ, you're a moody bugger today."

I scowl and move over to the rice cooker on the counter and give it a cursory check. Vi says a rice slow cooker is something apes could operate, so luckily it doesn't look like we fucked that up.

Grabbing the leaf lettuce and veggies out of the fridge, I bring them over to the counter peninsula. I toss a cucumber to Camden. "Make yourself useful."

He exhales and begins carefully slicing while I work on the carrots. I haven't been in my flat very much as of late, opting for the sanctuary of Belle's body, I mean bedroom, over my own. Though, if I'm being honest, I don't just go over there for the shag. I simply prefer to be around her. And with her big event coming up tomorrow, I wanted to do something special here at our flat to help her relax and take her mind off the stress of that.

I can feel Camden's eyes on me as I chop.

"You all right, Tanner? You seem...tense. Is it the match tomorrow? That magazine interview next week?"

I exhale heavily. "No, I mean, I'm dreading the magazine interview, especially because Santino said they converted it into a video feature or some bullshit."

"Oh, what a sensation!" Camden peals in his imitation of the Queen's voice. "You and Belle are going to be positively scrumptious on camera!"

I roll my eyes and reply flatly, "You're one to talk."

He drops the joke. "Indie and I had our moment in the spotlight, but now you and Belle are the shiny new object everyone cares about. But if it's not that, what's your deal? Is it the game?"

My brows knit together. "I'm anxious but like...hyped, mostly. Practice this week has been solid. DeWalt and I are finally getting a rhythm out there. It feels right. I think we have a shot at winning if we can get everything to go our way."

Cam's brows lift. "That's brilliant. So what is it then?"

"I don't know," I mumble, sliding the chopped carrots into the bowl of lettuce.

"Are things bad between you and Belle?"

"No, she's fucking fantastic," I answer quickly because it's the truth. This week with Belle has been perfect. This month with Belle has been perfect. The ups and downs included in all of that because it just made me want her more.

What started as the worst month of my life with a suspension morphed into something extraordinary. But I can't shake the feeling that I'm on the precipice of something major, and I'm either going to jump or I'm going to fall.

"Then out with it already, what is your problem?" he snaps.

Pursing my lips, I brush my hands off on my jeans and decide to answer his question with another question. "How do you handle the balance between football and Indie?" I turn and toss the utensils in the sink and hoist myself up on the counter next to it. "I find myself completely engulfed in all things Belle and it seems a bit insane."

Camden mulls over his answer for a minute. "Well, Indie and I both travel a lot, so our breaks apart are self-inflicted. It gives her the space she requires to feel human, and it gives me the chance to miss the fuck out of her. It makes our time together even more special when we return."

"Are you consumed by her when you return?" I ask, dreading the answer a bit because it's Indie we're talking about and she's like a sister to me. But I need advice, so I have to suck it up and put my big boy pants on.

"Yes. Yes, I completely am," he smiles knowingly and I have to look away because I can practically hear his dirty thoughts. "When you know, you know, broseph. And if your game isn't being affected negatively, why fight it?"

I pause, searching for the right words. "I have this…urgency to make Belle mine, like permanently. Do you have that with Indie?"

Cam's eyes narrow like I just sussed something out. "I mean, yeah. That was actually something I was wanting to talk to you about."

"Talk to me about what?"

"I erm…want to get a place for Indie and me. Maybe a house, I don't know. But something that's ours. I want to surprise her with it because I know if I include her in the process, she'll get awkward about the money and I don't want that. I thought I'd get Belle to help me so I don't pick something she'll hate."

I smile, genuinely pleased for him. "That sounds brilliant, Cam. Really. I'm chuffed for ya."

"Yeah," he murmurs, looking down and fumbling with the cucumber slices. "It would just mean that I, uh…wouldn't be living here anymore."

Then it hits me why he's being so awkward. Of course a new home with Indie would mean that he would move out of here permanently. How could I be so stupid? The pang of disappointment is heavy, but not unbearable. Nodding, I reply, "I understand."

"Well, it's just…I know you and I haven't been spending as much time together lately," he stammers but I cut him off.

"Camden, don't get soft on me. Your vagina is showing again."

He rolls his eyes.

"I'll be fine," I confirm.

He nods stoically and a darkness casts over his face. "Can I ask you a serious question?"

I shrug. "Of course."

"Do you miss playing with me as much as I miss playing with you?"

A thickness forms in my throat as I lock my matching blue eyes with his. There's no humour in his expression. He's not taking a piss. He's being sincere and honest with me right now. We're saying a thousand words a minute with our eyes, but out loud, I simply reply, "Every day."

He looks down and murmurs, "Me, too."

I half smile. "We had to grow up some time I guess."

He lets out a haughty laugh. "I never saw this for us. I thought we'd be single until we were old and grey. And even then, we'd be shagging birds half our age and talking about our old glory days on the pitch."

This makes me laugh.

Then he adds, "But now that you've been with Belle for a bit, can you honestly tell me you'd go back to that?"

"Fuck no." I smirk to myself. "Being tied down has its perks."

This makes him smile triumphantly. "Now, if we could just get you over to Arsenal, life would be fucking perfect."

"I don't know," I reply, looking off into the distance. "I wouldn't mind bleeding green and white until the day I die."

He shakes his head. "So you'd be okay with it then? Me moving out?"

I nod, knowing deep down that while Camden and I will no longer share a flat and a pitch, he'll always be my brother. "I'll be fine.

248

I'm happy for ya, pussy."

"Thanks, Vagina Face."

The sound of keys breaks our tender bro moment, and I hear giggles wafting down the hallway.

"Hello?" Indie calls.

"We're in here," Camden replies.

Belle and Indie come shuffling into the kitchen, and I do this weird frowny smile when I see her. The smile is because I'm happy to see her. I always am. The frown is because I think she's—

"We're pissed!" Indie peals with a smile, her glasses a bit topsy-turvy. "We were just going to have a cheeky glass of wine, but it escalated rather quickly into a proper Tequila Sunrise Happy Hour." She hiccups.

Belle covers her lips as she attempts to stifle a giggle. Her hooded eyes lock on mine and I get that possessive feeling about me again. That urge to take her back to my bedroom and engulf her with my scent, like an animal.

"I know you're going to blame me, Camden, but Indie was the instigator this time," Belle says over her shoulder as she strides toward me. Her dark hair is hanging long and loose around her face. Her mouth is upturned into a dopey but happy smirk. She looks at the food as she reaches up and clasps her hands around my neck. "It looks lovely."

"It looks like crap," I grumble, pulling her flush against me for comfort. "We fucked it up."

"No," she shakes her head. "It's going to be great."

"Careful on that subject, Belle," Camden's voice cuts in. "He's a wee bit sensitive about the food. Apparently, he's still trying to woo you."

Her long lashes flutter up as her eyes find mine in silent question.

Indie's voice says from somewhere in the distance, "You're not trying to woo me?"

Camden replies, "No, I've already got you, Specs."

"Well, what if I want to be wooed?"

"Then you better prepare yourself because…" Camden's voice trails off as Belle speaks softly to me.

"You were trying to impress me?" Her voice is warm, like a heated blanket wrapped all around me.

"I'm always trying to impress you," I reply, twirling her and trapping her against the worktop. I lift her up so her arse is resting on the counter and her jean clad legs wrap around my hips. I press myself against her, having her right where I want her. "Can't you tell?"

I expect her to say something snarky, scathing, and rude. Something that will make me laugh. Instead, she strokes my hair and replies, "Yes, it's easy to see."

I quirk a brow. "So does that mean it's working?"

"It might be." She laughs softly and I nuzzle into her neck, licking a path up to her ear and tasting what's rightfully mine.

Indie's voice chirps from behind us with the clatter of dishes. "Let's eat, love birds!"

Wishing them away, I close my eyes and inhale Belle's scent. My heart is aching with need to say something to her right now, but my mind compels me to hold back. I whisper in her ear, "How about I take you to bed instead?"

"No!" she exclaims with a laugh and pushes me away. "You've made me dinner and I intend to enjoy it."

I sag. "And so another dream dies."

For years, the first thing I thought about when I woke up in the morning was football. Not just on match days but every day. I'd wake up thinking about the last goal I scored and when I'd score the next one. How practice went that week. A manoeuvre I wanted to run by Dad. How we were going to push our team to the next level. The politics, the players, the passion. The struggle. Football always consumed me.

So when I crack my eyes open to the light of day on the morning of my first match after my suspension and the first thing that crosses my mind is Belle, I know that everything has changed.

The pitch is wet and spongey from this morning's rain, like a baptism, cleansing the area for my readmission into the sport. The air is heavy with cool moisture and the faint smell of stale beer and Pukka Pies permeates my nose. All of it feels like home.

I stand here, awaiting the kickoff, practically coming out of my skin with an urgency to turn this vibrating focus coursing through my veins into a fucking win to relegate all other wins. My team feels it, too. DeWalt, Booker, Dad. They all look at me and feed off the energy I'm pushing out.

I'm determined to honour this coloured armband with the word "CAPTAIN" scrawled on it. I'm determined to prove that Bethnal Green isn't the beleaguered team it once was. I'm determined to show them that Tanner Harris is not half a striker. Not anymore.

I'm determined to show them that I've been reborn a new man.

The whistle blows...and it's exactly what I do.

Victory and Consolation Prize

Belle

AS SOON AS THE PARKERS WALK OUT OF THE WESTMINSTER Suite of the Shangri-La Hotel, I tear into my handbag for my mobile.

I've been dying to know how Tanner's match went, but it was important to give due respect to the Parker family who travelled here all the way from America. We had a lovely afternoon of high tea thirty-eight levels up in Europe's tallest building, The Shard. The suite is decadently kitted out in soft creams and under-stated Asian interior design. But let's face it, you don't notice much of the room when you have floor-to-ceiling windows with stunning views of the River Thames and Tower Bridge.

The Parkers were blown away. Their daughter, twelve-year-old, Nevaeh, was one of Dr. Miller's first spina bifida success stories from a clinical trial she did at her former hospital in Indiana.

Spina bifida is when the spine doesn't close properly in-utero and can cause severe nerve damage over time. Nevaeh's lesion was located at the top of her spinal cord, so the prognosis for foetuses like her is not good. Most are unable to even breathe on their own.

The Parker's OB advised them to abort, as do many doctors, but then they found out about the clinical trial. Dr. Miller operated on Nevaeh when she was a twenty-five-week foetus. Now she's a healthy, vibrant girl who recently became captain of her debate team. It's the stuff miracles are made of.

Miracle or not, it doesn't take away from the fact that I need to know how Tanner did today. He may not be saving the lives of tiny patients, but people depend on him. His teammates look up to him; his fans root for him. Football breathes life into an often times dreary world. Watching him give it his all and commit to the match one hundred percent is miraculous in and of itself.

And when I left his flat this morning, I saw a graveness in his eyes that frightened me. I don't know if it was because of the game or because of something with us, but I've been worried about him all day.

I scroll through my mobile and pull up football highlights for the day. When a headline catches my eye, I nearly squeal with joy.

"A carnival performance," is what the media will be calling the *Bethnal Green F.C. win today. Bethnal inflicted humiliation on their opponents with a seven to one powerhouse victory when the ninety minutes was up.*

"Yes!" I shriek and throw my hands up into the air before I continue reading.

A massive comeback for striker Tanner Harris, who captured his third career hat-trick after a month-long suspension. There are a million different ways a ball can enter the net, and Tanner showed us some of the best. But his reign didn't stop there. He proved beautiful leadership on the pitch with two stunning passes to fellow striker and South African transport, Roan DeWalt, resulting in two more balls between the posts.

I sigh with relief as I read more gushing specifics about every one of Tanner's impressive goals. Needing to connect with him, I pull up my text box to send him a message. Suddenly, his face lights up on my screen with a call.

I'm smiling ear to ear when I answer. "You fucking hotshot, you did it."

His deep laugh warms my nether regions. "We did. It was a match I'll never forget. God, I wish you could have been here."

"Me, too," I groan. "You're going to demand a blowie tonight as retribution, aren't you?"

He coughs out a surprised laugh. "I certainly would never say no. They say the way to a man's heart is through his stomach, but that's because they've never had Belle Ryan's mouth wrapped around their cock."

I giggle and shake my head. "You better not have people around you."

"Oh, I'm in the changing room talking into the megaphone. It's fine. The guys are really happy for me."

"Tanner, you knob!" I can't hide my laugh. I don't want to hide my laugh. Need creeps between my thighs. A great afternoon for me; an incredible win for him. I'm all by myself in a lush room. He needs to be here. "When are you getting here?"

"The team is going out for a pint to celebrate and then I'll head back to the flat to change. I can be there by a quarter to eight to pick you up from the room if you'd like."

I exhale. "That works I suppose."

"Did you have something else in mind?" he asks.

"We both had good days. I wanted to…celebrate." My tone leaves nothing to the imagination.

A low growl vibrates through the line. "Woman, I'm going to celebrate with you so much tonight you're going to need me to carry you home tomorrow."

"Promises, promises." I smile when he huffs out a laugh. "I'll see you in a couple of hours."

We hang up and I hop in the shower, willing my hand not to touch myself like I so desperately want it to.

Tanner Harris deserves all the wrath of this sexual tension.

TANNER

Charcoal slim suit, deep purple tie, brown leather boots, and belt. I'm looking fine and feeling on top of the world.

I ride the lift up to the thirty-eighth level, utilising the mirrored walls to flatten my blonde mane that I actually styled tonight. Well, styled in the sense that I blow-dried it and ran a brush through it more than a few strokes. That's about the extent of my mane taming. I smooth down my freshly trimmed beard and my mouth curves into a half-smirk. *Tonight's going to be a great fucking night.*

It feels like a celebration for so many things. It's mine and Belle's last fake date, even though we dropped the fake label; we're celebrating Belle's achievements at her new job; we're helping a great cause; and lastly, the huge Bethnal Green win that included me back on the pitch. So many great things have happened. I hope that tonight is just the start of more to come.

I rap on her room door and am looking down to adjust my cufflinks when it opens up.

Belle's voice croaks, "I'm nearly finished. Just struggling with this stupid earring..."

My eyes start a slow crawl up her body as her voice trails off into some faraway land where sound disappears to when you're busy trying not to blow it in your trousers like a pubescent teenager.

Her   curves—her   perfect,   beautiful,   ripe-like-a-peach curves—are swathed in a floor-length champagne sequined gown. She glitters with every breath she takes and is the epitome of elegance.

She's too good for me.

"What?" Belle asks, catching me gawking and smoothing down her dress self-consciously.

"You look like a bride." The words fall out of my mouth.

She smirks. "I think brides wear white."

I shake my head, mesmerised. "You're fucking beautiful."

Her dramatic, smoky eyes meet mine, accepting my crass phrasing as truth because that's me and she knows it. Her dark hair is curled into soft tendrils down one side of her neck, making me want to reach out and run my fingers through it. I coincidentally know that that thought makes my vagina show a bit, so the fact that I'm standing here half-mast reassures me that I'm still a proper bloke.

She props a hand on her hip and her gaze drops down my body. "You clean up rather nicely yourself, Striker." She winks up at me through her thick lashes with a disbelieving shake of the head. "But I would have loved to have seen how you looked on that pitch today. God!" She squeals and tightens her fists in excited frustration as she falls into my arms. I swear the world stops moving as she adds, "I'm gutted I couldn't be there. I'm so proud of you."

I snake my hands around her waist and pull her to me, overwhelmed by her adoration. I've never had someone like her to share football with. Sure, I've shared it with my family, but this feels different. This feels…extraordinary.

I connect our lips in a needful kiss, desperate to feel her words against my skin. To test the weight of them and commit them to memory. She tastes so good. Like a victory and a consolation prize all at once. I'd lose a thousand matches if it meant I got to continue kissing her like this.

I pull away, breathing harder than I'd like, my eyes wide and grave as they lock on hers. Her brow furrows with a silent question and I can't find my voice to answer it. To answer her. To tell her what

I need to tell her. I swallow hard. "Fancy a shag?"

She laughs and it feels so right. Licking her dark lips, she turns to grab her clutch on the side table. As she brushes past me, she replies, "Patience, beast. Good things come to those who wait."

I follow while murmuring under my breath, "I've never been good at patience."

We arrive at the ballroom located on the fourth level of the Shangri-La Hotel. It's got a midnight starry sky sort of theme about it. Navy tablecloths, silver, glittery centrepieces, and sparkling accents decorate the room. Belle has to stop and say hello to several people as we make our way to our table. It's a lot of white-haired, laboratory-looking blokes whose tuxes look like they were bought in the 90s and they've since outgrown them. Belle doesn't seem the least bit nervous. She's calm, cool, collected, and completely brilliant.

I do my best to not behave like the stupid footballer I'm sure the entire world assumes I am. There are several guests who congratulate me on my game. Many are probably not Bethnal fans but did their research before tonight since they knew so many of us would be in attendance.

When Belle gets pulled away by the caterer, I make my way over to the Bethnal Green sponsored table to find my people. In a sea of stiff upper-lipped, crusty old geezers, our group looks like it just finished a photoshoot for *The Great Gatsby*. Booker is kitted out in a suit and is engrossed in conversation with his date—some blonde who grew up down the street from us in Chigwell. I've seen her around before, but he's never dated her officially like this. Camden and Indie are here as well, dressed to the nines and quietly looking down at their mobiles.

"Why are you two so distracted? Did something bad happen?"

I ask, mostly serious because these days you can't joke about horrid world events.

Indie's head snaps up. "No! They have a silent auction going and you have to text in your bid. I've been really fighting to win this trip to Spain."

Camden's head pops up next. "I've been fighting to win a trip to Spain!"

Booker hoots with laughter, draping an arm around the blonde. "You guys have been bidding against each other this entire time!"

Indie deflates. "How sad. I thought I was doing so well."

"You were, Specs," Camden coos, stroking her arms. "I'll stop bidding and let you win."

Her lip sticks out. "That's not nearly as fun." She crosses her arms to pout but then brightens as she sees something behind me. "Belle! I'm winning!"

"Yay!" Belle exclaims reflexively as she moves to stand next to where I'm seated. She assesses the table. "You all look gorgeous."

Indie eyes Belle appreciatively. "So do you."

"Thank you all for coming tonight," Belle states, addressing the table full of my family, fellow teammates, and WAGs. "Be sure to go have your picture taken in the huge photo booth over there." She gestures to the large, white, tent-like structure positioned along the side of the ballroom. "It's unlimited photos, so have at it. Oh, they also will be live-auctioning some really cool things after a little speech that I have to give, so don't go far!"

My brows lift. "I didn't know you have to give a speech."

She baulks like it's nothing. "It's just an introduction for Dr. Miller."

I nod as DeWalt pipes up from the other side of the table with a question about something on his mobile for the silent auction. She moves over to help him, so I head to the bar and grab us a couple of champagnes. When I return, she's still talking to him, laughing and looking gorgeous beside him. My jaw clenches as I try not to get my hackles up. DeWalt and I played a great match today, but I've still got my eye on him after that night at Welly's.

I overhear her congratulate him on his goals from today, and I have to restrain myself from marching over there and pissing on her to mark my territory. When she rejoins me and he's off at the bar, well out of earshot, I whisper in her ear, "Do you remember what happened last time you flirted with DeWalt?"

She cuts her black-rimmed eyes at me. "I'm not flirting. I'm being a polite hostess."

I arch a brow. "You don't need to stroke his ego about the goals he scored. I'm the only one really scoring here, woman." I look down at her body with complete possession rioting through me. I lean in and my lips tickle her ear as I add, "And if you want to get fucked in my truck again, all you have to do is ask."

She pulls back, biting her tongue to silence a retort that I can see growing to life in her eyes. Checking around us to see the coast is clear, she licks her lips and purrs into my ear, "I'd like to get fucked in a lot of places, Tanner Harris, but let's get creative and move from your truck to say…Tower Park pitch?" Her voice rises in sexy question, and a satisfied grin breaks across my face as she nuzzles my jawline. "I want you to reenact all those goals you scored today. But instead of using a ball and a net, you're using your cock and me."

My dick jolts inside my trousers. It can't be helped. I close my eyes to steel myself to be proper right now and not reveal the horny manboy my cock believes I am. *This woman*, I think to myself. She bewitches me. Belle Ryan is both light and dark, and all I want is to spend hours getting lost in her shadows.

Suddenly, Belle's heated eyes turn bright as she looks behind me. "Oh, Dr. Miller, hello!" Her voice is high-pitched as she stands and reaches out to shake someone's hand.

I remain seated for a second to try and shake the sexual stupor off of my face. I turn around in my chair just as Belle begins to introduce me.

"This is my boyfriend, Tanner Harris."

On cue, I rise out of my chair, my dirty thoughts all but vanished after her "boyfriend" label. It seems trivial compared to everything I feel inside of me. Not an accurate representation of how I see us. Regardless, I turn and find myself towering over a small, robust woman in a matronly evening gown. I'm surprised to see that this is the woman Belle calls a baby-saving genius.

We shake hands and I detect a lilt in her American accent. "Nice to meet you, Mr. Harris. I really appreciate you and your team supporting us this evening."

I wave her off as she head nods to everyone at the table behind me. I reply, "It's our pleasure. I'm very proud of the work Belle does with you. She was telling me about your honoured guest this evening on our ride in the lift. What you all manage to accomplish is incredible."

Dr. Miller smiles at Belle. "Well, we need strong, motivated doctors like Dr. Ryan to keep our work going. I have high hopes for her."

Belle blushes and murmurs a thank you, but then her eyes fly wide toward someone off in the distance. "Is that your daughter, Reyna? And Liam?"

My gaze shifts to the couple approaching us, and I immediately zero in on the woman's extensively inked arms. A full sleeve decorates one; a half decorates the other. While appreciating the artistry, I can't help but notice the vast disparity between her and Dr. Miller. They aren't your typical mother/daughter combination. It would be unusual to grow up with a mother like Dr. Miller and possess that much ink and *not* have a story to tell.

"Dr. Ryan, I thought it was you my mother was talking to. I just wanted to come say hello."

The woman removes her grasp from her small bump and reaches out to shake Belle's hand. The man does the same.

"Tanner, this is Dr. Miller's daughter, Reyna, and her husband, Liam. This is my boyfriend, Tanner Harris." We exchange more handshakes, and I do my best to hide the furrow in my brow over that annoying word again.

"How are you…all?" Belle asks, gesturing to Reyna's stomach.

"We're brilliant," Liam answers. "We just had another scan this week and all three babies are looking excellent."

"That's wonderful!" Belle exclaims. "Oh, I'm so happy for you all. Dr. Miller will make the best grandmother."

Reyna laughs. "She'll let them get away with murder, I'm sure." She looks at her mother. "I can't wait."

Dr. Miller and Reyna watch each other for a moment, exchanging some sort of silent communication that feels important. A pang hits me as I realise I'll never know what it would be like to have a mum be a grandmother to my child. Truthfully, I've never thought about children much before, but the idea doesn't terrify me like it once did.

"Great match today, mate," Liam says, cutting into my thoughts and reaching out to shake my hand again. "You Harrises make football fun to watch."

I nod and shake his hand. "Cheers, that's really kind of you to say."

Dr. Miller clears her throat, interrupting our conversation. "I was wondering if I might steal Dr. Ryan for a moment. We have a guest at the door that I sort of need her to chat with."

"Of course," I reply and step back to let her pass.

I can hardly believe my eyes when they land on my father standing in the foyer of the ballroom. He's tall and overly slim as usual. But his grey hair is a bit dishevelled and his classic navy suit is wrinkled in the back.

As we approach, Dr. Miller murmurs in my ear, "He said he didn't know he needed a ticket to get in. I thought it would be best for you to decide how we handle it. I'm perfectly happy to do whatever you'd like. I trust you completely."

I nod as she departs, leaving me with the man who raised me.

"Father, what are you doing here?"

He spins on his heel at the sound of my voice, stumbling backwards a bit. "Belle, darling. Don't you look regal."

I frown. "I'm surprised to see you here."

His eyes are glossy and I can smell the scotch on his breath. "Well, you say I don't support what you do, so here I am. Regrettably, I wasn't aware that an RSVP was in order. Do you think it would be okay for me to pop in?"

I look around nervously. "It's a fundraiser. Plates are a thousand quid a piece."

He pulls his chequebook out of his back pocket. "Who do I make it to? You? The hospital? The paunchy bird who brought you over here?"

My eyes fly wide. "That is Dr. Miller, a world-renowned surgeon and the only reason I even exist in this profession," I seethe, feeling the constraints of my ball gown as I suck in a large breath of air. "You *will* show her some respect."

He lifts his hands up in defence. "No need to get so *upset.*" He says the last word in the exact tone he said it to me as a child. He rips his cheque out. "Make it to whomever. Now then, point me in the direction of the bar and I'll be just fine."

"Maybe you should go home, Father. Does Mother know where you are?"

This makes him scowl. "Of course she does."

"Then why aren't you with her?"

"She didn't want to come. She has no desire to see all of this, but

I do." He jams a finger into his chest. "Now, are you going to find a seat for your father or not?"

What he's asking me to do feels wrong. However, a sick, deep, dark part of me wants to play this out. To have him here and allow him to witness what I do. To force him to hear the words Dr. Miller and I will be saying shortly. Perhaps this is a Tequila Sunrise opportunity to prove myself to my father once and for all.

I pull myself up tall. "I do have an open seat, but I will only give it to you with conditions."

He smirks a disgusting sneer that makes me want to punch him in his long, sloped nose that he's doing so well looking down on me from. "That's my girl."

The reply haunts me, but I step in and steel myself to appear intimidating. "You don't talk to Tanner. You don't look at Tanner. You don't introduce yourself to Tanner, or Dr. Miller for that matter. I mean it, Father. Nothing, or I won't bring you in."

"Scout's honour." He holds up a peace sign.

I move to walk away, mumbling, "You'll be in the back with some medical staff from Denmark, so talking will be a struggle."

"I know how to speak to people, Belle. Even foreigners. It's all I do for a living."

I roll my eyes as he follows me through the ballroom. Trust is not something I have with my father, and after the horrid things he said about Tanner on the phone the other day, I refuse to put Tanner in the firing range.

I find him a table with two open seats that were booked by the Danes' chief of surgery and his wife, neither of which could make it.

Before I leave, I pin my father with a death stare. "I've got to go give a little speech here shortly. Maybe…have some coffee or tea, and I'll come see you afterwards."

His drooped eyes slow blink as he nods, so I turn and walk away on shaky legs. This is the first time in my life I've ever seen my father pissed like this. Openly intoxicated. He's not falling over drunk, but he's definitely not acting the way I'm used to. It's…unnerving.

After a couple glasses of champagne, some food in my stomach, and some laughs over photos Indie and Camden have taken in the booth, I've all but forgotten about my father.

My palms are sweaty as I pull out the piece of paper with the words I'll be speaking tonight. I repeat them in my head over and over until the event coordinator finally pulls me aside and says it's time to take the stage.

Tanner gives me a kiss and squeezes my side as I leave. When I walk up the stairs to the stage, I'm suddenly very aware of all five hundred people here tonight.

The master of ceremonies introduces me and I stride up to the podium, my dress shooting out blasts of sparkles underneath the stage lights.

I clear my throat and dig deep for all my confidence. "Thank you all for joining us this evening. The Foetal Medicine Foundation is a charity that aims to improve the health of pregnant women and their unborn babies through research and training in foetal medicine."

I pause and exhale a shaky breath. My eyes find Tanner's and he nods in encouragement.

"With the support of people like you here tonight, the foundation has raised more than fifteen million pounds in the past ten years it has been in operation.

"With your help, we are able to maintain our educational programme so that doctors like myself can have the opportunity to train with some of the most brilliant minds in this field.

"The work we do here tonight helps us save little girls, like Nevaeh Parker from Indiana, whose mother was advised by her obstetrician to have an abortion at only sixteen weeks pregnant when they realised she had spina bifida. Because of Dr. Miller's efforts, Nevaeh is now a thriving twelve-year-old little girl with an excellent quality of life. So excellent, in fact, that she informed me at tea today that she was sent to the principal's office at her school last week for splashing mud in gym class."

I pause as the room breaks into pleasant laughter.

"As I sat beside Nevaeh and watched her fall in love with clotted cream, I marvelled over the fact that Dr. Miller touched her when no one else could. She healed her when everyone else was certain all was lost. As doctors, we like to think we play God. But looking at Nevaeh now, whose name spelled backwards is Heaven, I think it's she who has touched us. I think it's her who inspires our healing hands because there is nothing more godlike than being in the presence of a miracle."

I pause and blink away my tears. The room is so still and so silent, you could hear a pin drop. Smiling, I compose myself to say the last line. "So, without further ado, please welcome the protector of our tiny patients, Dr. Elizabeth Miller."

Say Cheese

TANNER

PRIDE.
Heaping mounds of pride erupt in my chest, causing the ache that I've been feeling for days to break apart and crumble into the reality of what is. Reality being that I love Belle Ryan. I love her more than I've ever loved anything in this world.

Belle steps back and shakes Dr. Miller's hand as she takes the microphone and thanks Belle for the kind words. Belle stands up there, a golden goddess of radiant light, beaming with pride and joy for what she does and all that she is. She's breathtaking and inspiring and everything I never knew existed in a partner. And I love her.

A man sits down in her vacant chair beside me, interrupting my life-changing realisation. I instinctively shuffle away when a heady scent of scotch wafts off of him.

After a minute or two of listening to Dr. Miller speak about Nevaeh Parker, the man's voice husks into my ear, "So you're the in-famous Tanner Harris."

I turn to look at him. He's an older bloke, likely in his sixties. Pissed to be sure. But just looking at him, I can tell he comes from money based on his expensive suit and watch. Plus, there's some-thing about the way he holds himself—nose slightly upturned, eyes narrowed in judgement—that makes him seem superior.

My response is short and curt. "Yes, I'm Tanner." I look back up at the stage, trying to be polite and listen to Dr. Miller's words.

He huffs out a laugh beside me and adds, "You don't know who I am, do you?"

I eye him curiously, shaking my head.

"I'm Lord Ryan, of course. Belle Ryan's father." His response stuns me into silence. When my brows lift, he smiles knowingly and confirms, "Now you're getting it."

We both train our eyes on the stage again, confusion and tension passing back and forth between us like a heat wave. I didn't know he was going to be here tonight. Surely Belle would have mentioned it.

He leans into me. "I shouldn't be surprised you don't know who I am. We don't exactly run in similar social circles."

Out of the corner of my eye, I see him glance around our table at everyone. No one seems to be curious about who the strange man is who's plonked himself in amongst us, but I sure as hell am.

After another minute or two of silence, he asks, "Did you hear the news then?"

I find my voice and whisper, "What news?"

His brows lift. "That hotshot lawyer of yours didn't tell you? Santino?" He lengthens all the vowels in a patronising tone. I shake my head. "I lost the vote for the Supreme Court today."

A heaviness settles in the air, weighing down the ambience of the room. His slanted eyes are locked on me as he gauges my reaction.

"I wasn't aware."

"Surely you knew I was in line for the Supreme Court?" I shrug and tension radiates off his high shoulders. "Well, I was. And that was the whole point of this *sham*. To help secure my seat. So your little *performance* with my daughter didn't work."

I clear my throat, shifting nervously in my seat. "I don't know what you want me to say."

He huffs out a laugh. "How about you just listen? You may have won a match today, but you lost the cup. So you can pack it in and go back to your pedestrian life where you fuck anything that walks and spread your future illegitimate seed to someone else."

The bone in my jaw ticks with barely contained fury. I lean into him so that no one else can overhear. "I don't know what your problem is with me, but maybe you should keep your voice down."

"Why?" he barks, sitting back in his chair like he's the King of England and everyone around him are peasants. The people at our table turn to look at him, catching on to the unfolding scene. "What's the point of keeping quiet? The reason you were dating my daughter at all was for me to rise to the Court. And that's all gone now, so none of this matters."

Shaking my head, I reply through clenched teeth, "That wasn't the only reason I dated Belle. There were many factors."

He jeers, "Maybe for you, but not for my Belle."

Possessiveness heats my blood as he attempts to claim her. The Ryans have never seen Belle the way I see her. She's confirmed it on more than one occasion. His tone, his demeanour, his lack of respect for the doctor speaking on stage right now is all proof of that.

I practically growl my reply. "You know nothing about Belle."

He drops his elbows on the table so we're nose to nose and his drunken gaze locks with mine. "I know that when the chips are down, she'll do what she must to help our family. No matter what. That is the only reason she'd ever give you the time of day, other than for a one off shag. Something to sow that wild streak of hers that she can't ever *fucking* control."

I blink away the rage clouding my vision. The man deserves to have his face smashed in. A lethal smack right to that pompous nose. How does he think it's okay to speak of his own daughter this way? Why does he have it in his head that she cares about her family? She has nothing to do with them. She never sees them. Not that I know of at least.

"You're wrong. Belle and I aren't a sham. Not anymore." I state, running nervous hands down my thighs and trying to quiet the paranoia creeping in around me.

He barks out a haughty laugh, and Booker and Camden's eyes narrow with caution. "Well, she didn't want me to talk to you this evening. You think someone in a relationship would want to hide you from her family? Please," he scoffs. "This is all a lie."

"It's not."

"Maybe not for you, but Belle knows exactly what she's doing. Look at her up there." I turn my gaze and see her watching us with the look of an ice princess. Hard and emotionless, but powerful, nonetheless. "Like father, like daughter. She's climbing her way to the top, manipulating people the same way I do. She's using you to get her contract with the clinic extended, nothing more. She doesn't care about you." He picks up a silk flower from the middle of the table. "The whole scenario is pathetic."

Just when I think I might lunge at him, applause from the audience erupts all around me. In the same beat, Booker launches out of his seat and grabs Lord Ryan by the shoulder. "Let's get some fresh air, shall we?"

Camden stands up and grabs the other arm. "That sounds divine, Booker. What a great idea."

Lord Ryan argues, swerving his head back and forth as my brothers effortlessly escort him away from me and my clenched fist. The rest of the ballroom gets noisy as people begin milling about now that the speeches are over. I turn just as Belle comes marching toward me.

"What are they doing?" she asks with wide, questioning eyes and pointing to Camden and Booker, who are nearly out the door. "They need to get their hands off of him...He'll sue."

"Don't worry about your fucking father," I growl, shoving my hands through my hair.

She frowns. "What's happened? What did he say?"

The guilty look in her eyes makes me even more paranoid. I

know Belle, but I don't know much about her home life. Not first-hand anyway. How could she not tell me he was coming here to-night? How could she intend to keep him away from me? And why? I've submerged her completely in the Harris family, yet she thinks she can shield me from hers?

"Is this still an act to you?" I ask, squeezing my hands into hard fists at my sides.

She frowns and looks around nervously. "What are you going on about?"

"You. Me. Are you just fucking with me?" I seethe. "Using me to climb your way to the top?"

"What on earth has happened out here?" she cries, her eyes wide with disbelief that I'm speaking so openly.

"Your father, that's what. He's unloaded a lifetime's worth of shit that sounds scarily close to the truth. So tell me the truth, Ryan. Are you just like him?"

This hits a nerve. A big one. Her dark eyes alight with fire and she grabs my arm, shuffling me off to the side of the ballroom. She push-es on a random side exit door, and when she discovers it's locked, I think she might scream. Her gaze lands on the empty photo booth. Yanking the curtain back, she shoves me inside and tucks in behind me and closes the drape. She pulls me down onto the long bench opposite the camera. The colour changing LED lights in the booth shift, turning us both from blue to purple to red in rapid succession.

"Did you just compare me to my fucking father?" She spits the words out with a deep, throaty voice like Satan.

The camera flashes.

Not the least bit intimidated by her rage, I retort, "Well, he just told me a load of bollocks about how you're still faking it with me. That you're trying to get your fellowship extended into a full-time contract."

"I am!" she exclaims. "You know this!"

"So you are faking it?"

"No! Christ, you can't be this thick!" She clenches her hands in front of her chest like she wants to punch something. Probably me.

"Well, fuck!" I bark, the music cranking up out on the dance-floor, thankfully drowning out our voices. "What am I supposed to think? You seem rather in your element tonight, Belle, rubbing shoulders with these doctors. And you never once mentioned your father would be here. How am I to know if you're actually in this with me or just playing me as a stupid footballer?"

"You're not a stupid footballer, Tanner. Not even bloody close!"

FLASH.

"Then why are you hiding me from your family?"

She exhales a heavy breath and hunches over, resting her elbows on her knees, the position completely at odds with her formal dress. "Because I'm great with patients but crap with real life."

This gives me pause. "What's that supposed to mean?"

"I don't know if I have the emotional capacity to do this with you, Tanner. You saw my father, he's a monster. He's a self-serving arsehole. That's what runs in my veins. I didn't have a Vi or a Camden to lean on growing up. I grew up around that." She points outside the booth.

"Well, so what?"

She sits up again, her shoulders sagged in defeat. "You're going to hit a wall with me and you're going to tire of climbing. You'll want someone normal. Someone less," she sighs. "Crazy."

That bloody word again! I'm so fucking tired of her calling herself crazy.

"Woman!" I exclaim, grabbing her face in my hands and staring so deeply into her eyes I swear I can feel her soul touch mine. "You're my kind of crazy, and I am crazy in *love* with you!"

FLASH.

Her gaze flicks back and forth between my eyes in utter disbelief. "How can you possibly feel that? We haven't been together that long."

"It's been coming on for a while now." I lighten my grip on her face and drag the backs of my fingers down her cheeks. I pull a leg up between us and throw it over the bench so I'm straddling it now. I move closer to her so she's completely encased in my arms and legs. I need her space to be my space and my breath to be her breath. I need to own her in this moment.

"I don't care what you came from or who you didn't have to lean on. Lean on me. Love me. Because I fucking love you, Belle. Your free spirit is what draws me to you. Your soul matches mine." I grab her hand and place it over my chest so she can feel my heart racing. Her hands tremble and her breath is shaky as she inhales and exhales.

"Belle, on the pitch, my endurance isn't matched. With you, I'm exhausted and I'm weak and I'm desperate to keep you. You keep me on my toes and I fucking love that about you."

She rolls her eyes with a half-smile. "Of course you'd bring this all back to football."

I smile back. "Football is all I know…but it comes in second to you," I murmur, dragging in a deep breath and preparing to set everything else in my heart free. "I don't just want to love you, Belle. *I want to marry you.*"

FLASH.

She blinks rapidly for what feels like ages. Her voice is a mere whisper when she asks, "What did you just say?"

The words didn't surprise me like I thought they would. They didn't scare me or bring me anxiety. They brought me peace.

I clear my throat. "I said I want to marry you."

"I heard what you said. Stop shouting!" she exclaims, her crazy eyes glossing over.

I give her the side-eye and mumble, "I'm not shouting."

Her watery gaze turns accusatory. "You know, Tanner, that's a really fucking awful thing to say. Those aren't casual words! When you say those words to a woman, you should mean them because she's going to remember them forever. You just ruined them for me because you're completely talking out of your arse right now!"

FLASH.

"I'm not talking out of my arse, Belle," I reply slowly, cupping the nape of her neck and pressing my forehead to hers. "When you don't know what to do, you should sit still. I know exactly what I want to do…I want to marry you. Soon. I don't want to wait. I want to embrace our fucking crazy and do what feels right. Love is an action. You either jump or fall. Jump with me, Belle. Marry me."

"I can't believe you." Her eyes are wide and searching my face, her disbelief morphing into shock. "I really can't believe you. You're actually serious?"

"Completely serious." I pause, licking my lips and pinning her gaze with mine. "Say yes."

The motion of her cheekbones turning up into a smile forces tears to fall down her face. She covers her eyes and laughs maniacally before replying, "Yes."

My jaw drops. "Yes?"

"Yes!"

FLASH.

She laughs as I crash into her like a wrecking ball, brushing my lips all over her face. "I love you," I mutter. "God, I love you."

She giggles and tugs on my hair so she can look me in the eyes and reply, "I love you, too."

Belle

We step out of the photo booth to find Indie, Camden, Booker, and several of the Bethnal team members hovering around the display screen that shows the pictures in progress. I glance over and see a shot of Tanner and me kissing and wince.

"Shiiiiit," I groan, realising they all witnessed the entire exchange that just happened.

Tanner takes in the screen and then waggles his brows at me. "That one's a keeper. We could make porn I think."

His sexy half-smirk makes me chortle as he continues pulling me by the hand past everyone, desperate to get us out of this fishbowl and up to our hotel room. Indie notices us and steps in front of me.

"Everything okay?" she asks.

Her concerned face tells me she has no idea what's truly happened inside that crazy box. And perhaps that's okay for now. Perhaps for now, Tanner and I live in this crazy moment and enjoy it. Bask in it and not let anyone else in quite yet.

Tanner and I look at each other and communicate without words.

"We're great," I answer. "Really great. I'm going to go talk to Dr. Miller quickly and see if I can leave. I'll call you tomorrow?"

She nods and half smiles, unease tensing in her shoulders. Tanner begins dragging me away again, but I slip out from his grasp and move back to Indie for a hug.

A hug.

Indie and I aren't huggers. I can probably count on one hand the number of times we've actually hugged and over half were because we were pissed.

She giggles at my unexpected attack and I pull back, smiling down on her. "I love you."

She shoots me a confused sort of grin. "I love you, too."

"Talk later!" I brush a kiss on her cheek and run to catch up with Tanner, like a newlywed couple rushing off to their honeymoon suite.

Because that's exactly what it feels like we're doing.

The London city lights cast an erotic glow into the Shangri-La hotel suite, bathing both Tanner and me in a luscious blue hue. My breath is heavy as I stand in front of the window, looking out at the River Thames and a city full of life.

But all I can focus on is the man behind me.

Need pools in my belly as I feel the heat of his bare chest skim along the back of my dress. I was only able to get his shirt off before he took over and demanded to let him undress me.

He draws the exposed zipper of my dress down my back, dragging his warm fingers along the wake of my flesh. He pauses to drop a soft kiss on my shoulder.

"You're so beautiful," he murmurs against my flesh, his coarse beard sending goosebumps down my spine as my legs begin to tremble. He slides the fabric down my arms and I shimmy it off my rear, carefully stepping out of it in my nude heels.

"Fucking love these curves," he husks into my ear as he splays his hands out on my hips and presses his trouser-covered erection against the small of my back. "I've loved them for a long time."

He skims his grasp forward, mirroring each hand as they slide down my lower belly to cup my pussy. He massages me over the top of my knickers, eliciting a soft moan from somewhere deep inside of me.

"Do you remember when we first met?" he murmurs, his breath hot in my ear.

I swallow and frown, trying to tell my brain to think instead of feel. "At the hospital?"

I feel the huff of his smirk on my earlobe. "Yes, in the cafeteria. You had an apple stuck in your mouth because you were stunned by my bearded beauty."

A lazy laugh shakes my shoulders. "You were a cocky sod then, and you're a cocky sod now."

He bites down on my lobe and growls, slipping one hand beneath the fabric of my knickers. When his rough finger swipes over my sensitive nub, I gasp, to which he responds, "I'm going to be *your* cocky sod forever."

This notion brings a smile to my lips as his fingers roll over me and I ride his hand, my hips pumping against his touch. My expression is a pure, unadulterated happiness as I let the idea of his words truly sink in.

This is madness. A completely impulsive life choice that we made on a whim. All of it has the potential to turn into utter chaos. But it feels…right. I have no barriers with Tanner anymore. He's erased every line between us and has embraced all of me…bare… open.

When I think about spending every day with him, it makes me giddy. He found the part of me that wanted to be loved and appreciated. He fucking gets me. I want to be his in every way because he accepts me for me and I accept him for him. Every beautiful, pervy, funny, deep, charismatic part of him. I know there's a laundry list of things we have to discuss, but right now, I want to dream with this man.

My head falls back on his shoulder as he kneads my breast, all while continuing his noble work between my legs. When he speaks this time, his voice is thick with arousal. "People will say we're crazy for wanting to get married, but I know you, Belle. Those months that I avoided you, I always saw you."

I gasp as his thick fingers plunge inside of me, crooking and working at a spot that I feel in my throat. I reach back and grip the sides of his head, twining my fingers through his thick hair. "God, yes. I saw you, too," I utter.

Our voyeuristic words and his relentless touch have me so close to my climax, I can hardly stay on my feet. I croak out the only thing my heart wants me to say. "Tanner, I…I love you."

Suddenly, his hands leave me. He spins me on my heel and presses my back against the cold window. The look in his smouldering, silent expression speaks directly to my soul.

"I love you, Belle."

He slams his desperate lips on mine, deftly unclasping my bra and flinging it away in the process. Our flesh against flesh feels perfect as he reaches down and grabs my legs, pulling me up so I'm wrapped around his hips.

He walks us over to the bed and falls down on top of me, kissing me and smashing his erection into the place I need him most. I begin fumbling with his trousers, but he pulls back, stopping my motion. With a quirked brow, he crooks his fingers into the sides of my knickers and slides them off over my heels. He tucks them in his pocket.

I shake my head. "You're lucky I brought another pair."

"You'll be lucky if I let you keep them," he growls, and I giggle as he hurriedly kicks out of the rest of his clothes.

When he's gloriously naked, he angles his head, eyeing every inch of me and trailing the tips of his fingers down the peak of my breast, across my belly, and between my legs. "I can't believe you'll be mine forever."

I smile at the utter devotion in his gaze as he climbs on top of me and situates himself between my legs. His skin is like silk against the bareness of me as he consumes me. This man holds every part of my body and soul in his hands.

"We'll never be bored," I joke but am deathly serious.

Tanner Harris and I are like oil and water in so many ways. But if you shake us up really hard, we bubble and swirl and mix and mingle. *We dance.*

His face grows grave. "I'll make you happy, Belle."

My eyes sting at his words. They are so simple, but they hold so much promise. I cradle his face in my hands, smoothing my fingers over the furrow in his brow. "I know you will."

I close my eyes when he pushes inside me, hitting a spot so deep and filling me so full, not just physically but emotionally.

He drops a soft kiss on each of my closed eyelids and whispers, "Eyes on me."

My lashes flutter open as he stares into my eyes and makes love to me, repeating his promises the entire time.

36
Goals

Belle

TANNER HARRIS HAS MADE AN ART OF SPOONING.

So much so, I can't even bring myself to get out of bed the next morning to go pee like I desperately need to.

He stirs next to me, nuzzling his jaw into my hair and sleepily pumping his hips against my arse.

"Are you awake?" I ask, already knowing the answer.

"No," he croaks. "My penis is just cold and seeking the warm blanket of your vagina."

I roll my eyes. "I'm going to wet the bed."

He tightens his grip on me. "You can't leave me."

"Seriously, your penis will be plenty warm with my pee in seconds if you don't let me go."

His hand flies straight up into the air, making me smile. I slide out of the covers and pad across our sun-filled hotel suite, butt-arse naked and thanking the Lord I don't have to go to work. After last night, my mind is buzzing with a million different grown-up thoughts. Doctoring today would probably make me implode.

After I do my business, I scamper back into the room and swan dive into the bed. Tanner's warm arms wrap around me, holding me to him as if he's been doing it his entire life.

"I don't want to leave this bed," I murmur into his chest as we lie face to face.

He hums and drops a soft kiss to my hair, his eyes still closed. "Me neither."

"When I leave this bed, my mind starts racing," I add.

"Then we shall stay here all day."

"But—" I start.

"Butt," Tanner replies, sliding his hand down and palming my cheek, pulling it against his growing erection.

It'd be so easy to get lost in him again. It'd be so nice to reach under the covers and grip him in my hand, and to climb on top and ride him until I have no more coherent thoughts.

But.

"We need to talk," I say, my voice more firm than before.

He sighs heavily and, with a bit of effort, I manage to get him propped up against the cream upholstered headboard. His abs and inky arms call to me, but I remain seated by his feet, facing him. I wrap a sheet around my chest so we'll have no more distractions.

"How do you feel this morning?" I ask, ready to attack this situation with a bit of business sense about me.

He quirks a playful brow. "I'd feel better if I was balls deep in you, but I can't complain." His smirk makes me smile.

"I mean…after last night. Do you…" My voice trails off as I adjust the sheet around my breasts.

"Regret what I said?" he asks, losing his playful smile.

I nod.

"No, not at all." He leans forward and grips my ankle in his hand, pinning his blue eyes on mine. "I want to marry you, Belle, and if you need to hear that in the light of day, then hear this. I would go to the Register Office right now if you gave me the green light."

My eyes fly wide. "You're crazy!"

"Pot, meet kettle," he retorts.

"We need to figure *a lot* of things out before we do this, Tanner," I stammer.

"Like what?" he asks, genuine curiosity painted all over his face.

"Like, life plans. Goals!" I gesticulate with my hand.

"Well, fire away." He sits back against the headboard again, crossing his thick, veined arms over his chest expectantly.

I roll my eyes and reply, "All right, where do we plan to live?"

He shrugs. "Probably your place. Camden thinks he'll be moving out soon and our lease is up for renewal, so I can come to yours. Or we can go flat-hunting and get our own."

"I would like to get our own. My father bought my flat and I'm completely over being under his thumb."

He nods. "I couldn't agree more."

"All right. What about jobs? You could get traded or lent out or accept a contract from somewhere far away. I can't be a doctor in South America, Tanner. It doesn't work like that for me."

He frowns. "I know when we first talked about my career, I said I had nothing tying me down, but that's all changed. You are a game changer, Belle. Truthfully, I've never had the Premiership aspirations that Camden did. Tower Park is my home. It always has been. I'd love to grow old and die in that stadium. I think I could be a good manager there if my dad ever heaves off. Or hell, maybe Shirt Off My Back will be something I can focus my efforts on. I'm up for anything. And I love and respect that you're a doctor. I fully recognise that you need to stay near Dr. Miller. That works for me. I have no desire to leave London. Ever."

I frown, taken aback by his detailed answer, so I fire a tougher one at him. "Kids?"

This gives him pause. He turns and looks out the window, his jaw firm and strong. "Truthfully, I never thought I'd want kids, but after seeing you hold Rocky the other day, I have to admit that's changed, too." He leans forward and grabs my hand, kissing it softly. "I like the idea of having a family with you…down the road. We don't need a baker's dozen or anything. But I quite think one or two would be nice."

I think I ovulate on the spot.

"What about you?" he asks, concern creeping up in his eyes.

I swallow and pull my lips in between my teeth before responding. "I hated my upbringing. It was cold and unfeeling. I was around nannies and staff more than my parents. I worry that I could be like that."

His eyes slant with sympathy. "You could never be cold and unfeeling." He kisses my hand again and shifts closer to caress my cheek, tucking messy, dark tendrils of hair behind my ear. "You are fireworks, Belle. You are warm and full of feelings. You'd make a wonderful mum."

His words force my eyes to close against the stinging of tears. I clear my throat. "Religion?"

My lashes flutter open and he pulls back with a shrug. "I'm Christian but not actively. I'd consider going more if that was important to you."

"It would be something I'd enjoy doing as a...family I think." The word *family* coming out of my mouth feels terrifyingly incredible.

A half-smirk slides up on his face as if he can tell he's acing this test with flying colours.

"Okay then, what else?"

So I go for a bit more abstract. "What kind of wife do you want me to be? If we have children, will you want me to stay at home with them?"

"Christ, no!" he exclaims. "You're a fucking incredible doctor, Belle. You can't just stop doing that."

I raise a brow. "So a nanny then?"

He shrugs. "I wouldn't be opposed to having a nanny, but I'd rather see if we can have a go at it ourselves first. I see us with a fifty-fifty partnership. I don't expect you to do everything. I don't want a wife who mothers me or acts like a housekeeper. I want a wife who lets me stick it in her on a regular basis, so if that means I need to do the dishes or Hoover the floor, I will."

Now I feel like he's lying. "Tanner, how is it possible that we went through a huge list of life goals and agreed on everything. That is not possible."

His face crumples in horror. "No…it's not. And to be honest, it's creeping me out."

"Me, too."

"Quick, pick a fight with me about something," he says hurriedly.

"What do you mean?" I ask, totally confused.

"This isn't normal. I want to make sure we're still us. Do that thing you do where you pick a fight with me about nothing."

"I do not do that," I bite back, crossing my arms in a proper pout. "Everything I say is perfectly logical. You're the crazy one."

"Just pick a fight with me and I'll feel better," he moans.

I roll my eyes and glance around the room for inspiration. When I see one of his feet sticking out of the covers, I say in clipped notes, "I hate your pinkie toe."

"What?" He looks down at his offensive foot.

"It sticks out to the side…It looks like a birth defect."

His face drops in dismay. "That's rather specific."

"It makes me sick," I sputter.

"Well, I'm not asking you to suck it!" His eyes are accusatory and annoyed, our glorious and agreeable bubble well and popped now.

"The minute you do, we'll be divorced faster than you can—"

He dives across the bed and tackles me, silencing my words with a kiss. "I fucking love you, future wife."

I giggle and look up at him. "I fucking love you, future husband."

TANNER

Standing outside of my dad's gated entry in Chigwell, I pull Belle by the waist, attempting to pry her off the wrought iron fence.

"Stop being so dramatic."

"Says the future Queen of England," she snipes and then lets go, falling against my chest. She looks up at me through thick lashes. "You're sure we can't keep this from your family for like…one week?"

I shake my head. "There's no fucking way. Secrets like this don't survive the Harris household. Believe me, they are like drug dogs. They sniff that shit out. Besides, you won't be able to keep this from Indie anyway."

She groans. "I'm scared of Indie. She's small, but she has that ginger blood in her and that shit is unpredictable."

I chuckle and kiss her forehead.

"Fine, let's do this." She pulls away and jogs in place, shaking her head side to side like a fighter preparing for a battle.

I shake my head as she hustles past me. "There's my future wife I know and love." I run to catch up and crack her on the arse as we make our way up the front step.

When we walk into Dad's kitchen, everything looks different. Normally, Vi is busy cooking, Dad is at the table going over manoeuvres, and an old football game is on in the background. It's noisy and bustling. But today, all I see is Dad, Vi, Hayden, Booker, Gareth, Camden, and Indie all huddled around the table, peering down at something in stony silence.

"Well, hello, hello, family," I bellow. They all turn and hiss at me to be quiet. "What's going on?" I ask, eyeing them curiously and pulling Belle along with me to see where they are standing.

I peer over Gareth's shoulder and see Adrienne, or Rocky, lying in her car seat. Her wild spray of blonde hair has a big pink bow clipped in it, and her big blue eyes are drooping slowly, like she's starting to nod off but fighting it every step of the way.

"This is what we're watching?" I whisper.

Everyone cuts menacing glowers at me, except Vi. She answers me from the other side of the table. "They find it fascinating." She shrugs. "They are just getting a glimpse of my day-to-day life. How are you guys?"

She looks at Belle with a big, warm smile and must see something she doesn't like. Her face falls. "What is it? What's the matter? Has something horrid happened?"

I frown and look at Belle, who's swiping at tears on her face. *Bloody hell!* "What is it?" I ask, moving to cup her cheeks, concern rioting through my body.

"Nothing, I'm fine. Just tell them quickly," she says with a weepy smile that doesn't look sad but happy. "I'm going to lose it."

I laugh, drop a kiss on her lips, and then tuck her under my arm. I turn to face everyone who've now diverted their attention from the almost sleeping Rocky to us.

"I've asked Belle to marry me," I declare proudly, holding back none of my gusto.

We're met with silence and some blinking.

"I proposed to her," I clarify, thinking that'll help spark some sort of reaction.

Silence.

"Last night," I add.

Nothing.

"In…erm…the photo booth thing at her charity event. It was rather romantic." Still nothing so I add, "She said yes."

Vi is the first to break the silence.

"She did?" Her eyes blink wide with disbelief.

"Yes!" I exclaim defensively. "Is that so hard to believe?"

"I'd say," Gareth's deep voice booms. "Are you sure you know what you're doing, Belle?"

"Thanks a lot," I grumble.

"You can't blame him, Tan. This is just a bit of a shock," Booker adds helpfully. "You have a reputation of being…ridiculous."

"Well, I love her and she loves me, so we're getting married. Sod all of you. You're not invited."

I shove a hand through my hair, turning my back on them, agitated that their shock isn't over the fact that I proposed, but that she said yes.

"I know it's fast," Belle adds, tension high and tight in her shoulders. "But as insane as this is, it's real. I love Tanner."

Her words sooth my soul just as Camden speaks next. "I can't believe you didn't tell me."

I turn to look at him. "I didn't plan it."

"So it was spontaneous?" Booker asks.

I nod.

"Well, I'm happy for you," Indie peals—the only bloody voice of reason in this God forsaken room. She adjusts her yellow glasses and adds, "You guys are crazy, but I think you're meant to be."

Hayden pipes in his rosy opinion next. "Tanner marrying a doctor. I never in a million years would have guessed that."

They all break out into laughter, and I'm two seconds away from launching into a proper pout. Belle's hand creeps up my arm and she nudges me with encouragement.

Vi moves toward us, her hands outstretched to Belle. "You are perfect for Tanner. I'm thrilled for you both."

"So am I," Camden confirms.

I look over at Dad, whose stoic face is marred with apprehension. We lock eyes as Indie and Vi begin hugging and asking Belle about wedding plans already.

I walk around them to approach Dad. "You okay with this?" I ask him cautiously.

"You just got your game back, Tan," he replies, his brow furrowed with concern. "Are you sure this is a good idea?"

I purse my lips. "I think Belle helps me play well. I feel grounded with her. Focused."

"Well, surely you didn't propose because of football." His concerned eyes turn grave.

"Never," I defend, pushing my hair out of my face and trying to find the right words to prove this to him. "Dad, I love her. It was like…it felt like…" I stammer. "Like…marry her or quit breathing, and I chose to marry her. Football wasn't even a factor."

His eyes soften. "You really love her."

I huff. "More than I even knew I could."

A glossiness shimmers in his gaze and he frowns, clearing his throat.

"What is it?" I ask.

He shakes his head. "I proposed to your mother after only two weeks. Seeing your face today is bringing back memories."

Memories. Memories he's never shared. I know the logistics. I know that Mum was pregnant with Gareth when they married. However, all the warm and fuzzy stuff about how Dad fell for Mum has been hidden for so long that I actually forgot to keep asking.

"I'd like to hear more about that sometime," I add.

He nods and looks around at everyone. "Another time. For now, I'd like to go congratulate your fiancé."

That label brings a smile to my face.

Belle continues fielding hugs from everyone. Even Gareth, who's saying something to her about how she could do a lot better.

I don't care.

She said yes.

Put A Ring On It

TANNER

THE DAY OF THE MAGAZINE INTERVIEW IS UPON US. IT'S BEEN A few days since Belle's charity event, and the only people we've told about our engagement is my family and Indie. I thought she'd want to go home and tell her parents, introduce me to them properly, but she refused. She said she didn't matter to them unmarried so she won't matter to them married. It's sad, but I'm relieved I won't have to see her prick of a father again. He deserves a knock to the jaw.

However, someday she may want them in our lives again. And when that day comes, I'll endure him…for her.

Speaking of wedding bells, Belle says she wants to wait to get married. Apparently there's some archaic twenty-eight day notice we have to give the Register Office before we can make it legal. Now she wants to finish her fellowship and me finish out my season, then take a long holiday. She's wanting to get married on a beach, just the two of us, which in girl talk means Indie and Cam can come, too.

So, for the past few days, Belle and I have been keeping our engagement quiet. She seemed slightly bothered when I told her I didn't want to mention it in the interview either. I hated planting that seed of insecurity in her but…

I have plans.

288

The interview is at Tower Park after the team finishes practice, so Belle plans to meet me here when she gets off work. It's a small crew. Two cameras, two camera operators, and the interviewer, who's a short, little, Irish spitfire that introduces herself as Georgina. They set up near the east side goal post so their shots can get both the pitch and the stands in the background.

When Belle arrives, my nerves set in. I'd been so calm and cool and collected before. Now that I see her, that's all gone.

The London sun is beginning to set, bathing the lush grass of the pitch in a warm, heavenly sort of glow. Belle's dressed in a simple pair of black leggings, hot black boots, and a green plaid button down, subconsciously representing Bethnal Green through and through. She looks perfect.

Her dark hair is long and straight, blowing in the wind as she strolls onto the pitch toward me. I meet her halfway, pulling her in for a kiss that I need to breathe some life back into me.

"Hiya," I husk against her lips.

"Hiya," she smiles back.

"How was your day?"

"It was great. Yours?"

"Just another day at the office." I tweak my brows around the stadium.

"Sedgwick let me in." She shoots a sneaky smirk at me. "Feels kind of cool to be down here, actually on the pitch."

My eyes heat. "I have plans for afterwards." I wink and she bites her lip, a crimson blush colouring her cheeks.

We walk over to join the crew.

"Hello, guys, I'm Georgina. Thanks for chatting with me today." She gestures to the two director's chairs seated next to each other as she takes one facing opposite ours. There's one camera angled at us and another angled at her. "This is going to feel like friends talking, so please be candid, be colourful, have fun. Your fans will love it."

"Fans," Belle huffs. "His fans you mean. I have no fans."

"Oh, you have fans, dearie," Georgina corrects, her heavily mascara-covered lashes batting excitedly. "You're a high-risk foetal surgeon dating a famous footballer. Together you two are a power couple and an inspiration to women and men everywhere."

This brings both Belle and me up short. It's sometimes hard to realise that people look up to us. I can see how they would admire Belle. She saves lives. But me? I just play football. It makes me even more determined to make my Shirt Off My Back charity event as successful as it can possibly be.

The interview starts off easily. Questions about how we met. What we enjoy doing together. Truthfully, it's a thousand times easier to answer them now that we're the real deal. If we would have still been fake dating, this could have been a nightmare.

"So, Tanner," Georgina asks, her Irish lilt smooth and confident. "Tell me a funny tidbit about Belle. Something that made you fall for her maybe."

I narrow my eyes as I ponder this for a minute and then start laughing. "Whenever Belle eats out at restaurants, she doesn't select her own food. She either goes along with what her guest thinks she should eat or has the server choose for her. At first glance, you would think she's indecisive. But she's not."

"No?" Georgina asks, her eyes alight with curiosity.

I turn to look at Belle. "It's because she likes the adventure of the meal, not just the taste. It's a very trusting quality that I admire about her."

Belle's eyes are locked on mine in shock like she had no idea I ever noticed that. I wink at her and she reaches out to hold my hand.

"Belle, how about Tanner? What is it that made you fancy him?"

Belle smiles to herself like she has an inside joke none of us know. "Tanner looks like this cool and tough footballer with his man bun and perfectly trimmed beard, so you would assume he's a pretentious sod. Most athletes think they have to keep up this persona of prestige and perfection, but Tanner doesn't. He is the exact opposite of conceited. He puts it all out there. No filter, the good with the bad. The cool with the emotional. He goes from pig to pussy in seconds because he has no ego. He is who he is, goofiness and all. He's a softy and that…is hot."

Her eyes are still locked on mine and express an intensity that winds me. I can't believe all that she sees in me sometimes.

Georgina clears her throat, her own cheeks red from witnessing the chemistry sizzling between us. "Tanner, when did you first realise you loved Belle?"

Belle

Tanner answers Georgina instantly. "I tried to hide it from her for a while."

This makes me frown because it's not the answer I expected. "You did?"

The interviewer asks, "How so?"

He laughs. "Well, one night Belle got a little tipsy out at a club with her mate. I was trying to find her to get her home safely, but she wasn't answering my texts or my calls."

My eyes fill with realisation over the night at Club Taint that he's recalling. That was so long ago. We were still faking it back then. Surely he didn't love me then. What is he talking about?

He adds, "I was decidedly worried, so I called and texted an embarrassing number of times."

"It wasn't that many!" I chime in, calling his bluff. "There were only a couple."

He quirks a brow. "Because I deleted them from your mobile."

My eyes widen. "You did?"

He confirms, "While you were in bed."

I shake my head, stunned. "I had no idea."

The interviewer laughs with us. "So was that when you realised you were falling for Dr. Ryan?"

This gives him pause as he answers, "As she said, I'm not a man who holds back. So when I realised I had something to hide from her, I knew it was already too late."

His answer floors me. His words are so simple, so basic and ordinary. But suddenly, everything about him is even more extraordinary. I don't have time to ponder it before he rises from his chair.

Georgina frowns. "I just have a couple more questions and then you can be off."

Tanner digs into his jeans pocket. "I have a more important question, if you don't mind."

He turns on his heel to face me and my eyes lock on a small, black velvet box in his hands. "Tanner, no. Not here," I argue feeling the cameras and Georgina's gasp of breath.

"We started this on camera and we're going to finish it on camera, Ryan." He winks and licks his lips. "Belle, when I first asked you to marry me a few days ago, it was rushed and quick and I wasn't fully prepared. Now I want to put a ring on it."

I giggle and cover my mouth, my head shaking in wonder at him as he drops down to one knee and opens a ring box, revealing a disgustingly large emerald cut diamond. My hands slice through my hair in utter shock. I can't believe he's doing this right here.

He leans in and whispers, "This is how you propose to someone." He winks and gestures out around him at Tower Park. I take in its grandeur, its splendour, its magical ambience. It's the place he calls home and the place I fell in love with him wearing a T-shirt that said "BIG SPOON." It's utterly perfect.

Clearing his throat, he says, "Belle Ryan, I'm officially inviting you to come to Harris Sunday dinners with me from now until forever, or until you can no longer stand my family because they're horribly obnoxious."

"Shut up," I cry through tears. "I love your family."

"And I love you," he echoes. "I thought all there was in life was football and family, but it was only because I hadn't met you yet. Every step of the way, you have tested the endurance of my heart. But now I want to go the distance with you. I want to do life with you for so long that I won't be able to remember what it was like before you." He pauses. "Will you marry me?"

I laugh, sniffing back my tears. "Yes…again!" I jump out of my chair and launch myself into his arms as he stands. He holds me as I wrap my legs around his waist and squeeze every part of him against me as hard as I can.

Here we stand, on the pitch next to the goal post, confirming our life goals to each other.

"I don't want to get married on a beach. I want to get married here," I state and kiss him fiercely.

He laughs against my mouth. "I think that can be arranged."

I gaze into his eyes. "I'm crazy in love with you, Big Spoon."

"I'm crazy in love with you, Little Spoon."

EPILOGUE
Shirt Off My Back

TANNER
Eight Months Later

MARRIAGE IS A LOT LIKE FOOTBALL. IT'S A GAME OF TRUST. YOU support your team and you help them take risks. Sometimes it pays off. And sometimes it doesn't. You celebrate every victory and you grieve every loss. But then you get back up and you do it again. Because the end result is a family you only ever dreamed of.

Watching my wife sit behind a table with Sedgwick, registering the masses of professional athletes that showed up for my first annual celebrity 5k run, is the most beautiful dream of all.

Today is a big day for us. Almost as big as our wedding day a month ago at Tower Park. Today is the first annual Shirt Off My Back Celebrity 5k Walk and Run.

Groups of London's homeless are currently filing into a large white tent we have set up in Hyde Park. We're serving food and drinks and have a table with donated clothing that they can grab from to help with job interviews. There's also a job fair area where grounds managers from various London stadiums are doing on the spot interviews. It was Sedgwick's idea to extend the job outreach programme

294

beyond Tower Park, and I was stunned when other stadiums quickly jumped on board. There are no promises that anybody will be hired today, but getting face to face time with people in position is an opportunity that many on the street would have never had otherwise.

My entire family is here, dressed and ready to run. Even Hayden's family and friends are out here to show support. Vi brought Rocky in a pram, and she's all suited up in a little track suit and sweat band, just like her Uncle Tanner. Gareth and Camden were able to secure several of their teammates to join in on the run, and they're all mingling with the homeless, eating and learning about their backgrounds. It's inspiring.

We've raised over one hundred thousand pounds so far between donations and entry tickets. It's only half of my goal, which is disappointing. But Belle continues to reassure me that for a first annual, it's a great start.

At nine o'clock, I'll say a few words and then a gun will sound for the official race to start.

I stride over to Belle at the table. She's just finished registering DeWalt, who gives me a polite nod. The prat wasn't invited to the wedding.

"Hello, wife," I say proudly. "How are things over here?"

She looks up at me with a smile, her dark eyes glittering with pride. "It's going great, isn't it Sedgwick?"

"It really is," Sedg beams from beside her. "And you just missed it, but I got to hold Rocky." His eyes twinkle with delight. "Your sister thrust her into my hands, not afraid at all. She's just heavenly, Tanner."

I smile and agree completely. It's nice to have my family all meet Sedgwick today. I don't know what I would have done without him these last few months. He's practically become the unofficial vice president of our operation here.

Our hope is to turn Shirt Off My Back into a nonprofit with a location that would allow the homeless to shower and wash their

clothes. We've brainstormed ideas, like an onsite clothing closet for job interviews and whatever else people might need to gain
back some dignity. I'd love to give Sedgwick a new job as operations
manager. Though, he's still more than happy working the grounds at
Tower Park.

"Oh! I have to talk to you," Belle says, standing up from her chair.
"Are you good here, Sedg?"

He looks around. "I think we've got everyone registered. I'm just
going to grab a quick bite before they put the food away."

"Excellent." Belle picks up a bag from the ground and swerves
around to grab me by the arm. "Let's go somewhere a bit more
private."

Her voice sounds funny. I don't like it when her voice sounds
funny.

"The media tent is empty," I offer.

"Brilliant."

We walk over there and when she turns to face me, she has a
frightening twinkle in her eyes. It's that same dangerous one she gets
when she's getting ready to go down on me. Where I can't quite tell
if she's going to suck me like a champion or bite it off and dance on
my grave.

I grab her and pull her toward me.

"I'm not here for that." She pulls away from my lips.

"What?" I murmur against her neck. "You said you wanted privacy and you have that look in your eyes. You know where my mind
goes."

"Tanner, be serious," she states as I run my finger over the scrawling text on her forearm.

On the night of our wedding, Belle and I got matching tattoos.
Mine is scrawling text perfectly entwined in my sleeve that says,
"Love her but leave her wild."

Belle had her ink cherry popped with, "Love him but leave him
wild."

It's the perfect mantra to our marriage. We fight and we push each other to our breaking points, but we've learned that fighting is our foreplay. *And I do so enjoy playing with Belle.*

"Tanner, we need to have Deep Talk right now," she states, pulling my mind out of the gutter.

"Yes, my wife?" I half smirk at her, removing my hands from her arse.

She licks her lips. "What if I told you that I found a donor to double all of the funds we raised today with one simple stipulation?"

"I'd tell you I love you and ask you where we can go for a victory shag," I rush out, grabbing her around the waist.

She gives me a look. "We're not shagging, Tanner."

I sigh heavily. "So another dream dies."

"Do you know a Frank McElroy?"

I frown. "A mate of Hayden's, right? Yeah, I met him at Vi and Hayden's engagement party. He's a funny bloke. Not exactly your type seeing how he bats for the other side."

She rolls her eyes. "Well, apparently he comes from loads of money. I've heard the McElroy name in my father's circle, but he's not a prat like them and he had an idea to make today an even bigger splash."

"Okay…" I say, my curiosity more than piqued.

"If you and your brothers do this, he'll match all the proceeds raised today."

"I'm listening!" I exclaim. This is incredible.

"And remember that time I picked you up naked on a street corner and you said you'd owe me one?"

"Yes…"

"Attending my hospital fundraiser wasn't nearly enough, so…" She giggles and bends over to pick up the bag. She pulls out a bright neon green strip of fabric.

"What's that?"

Belle smiles. "A mankini."

"A what?" I ask, completely confused.

She holds it up more clearly. It's a tiny strip of underwear with straps that go up over your shoulders. The back is—

"Belle, the back is a thong!" I say incredulously. "What on earth are you going to do with that thing?"

She gets that look in her eyes again. Pure fucking evil.

"If you and your brothers wear a mankini to start off the 5k, we've officially made our goal for the charity."

My jaw drops. "You want me and my brothers to wear that thing and run a 5k?"

She nods. "It's for a *great* cause."

"I'm out. This is ridiculous. I quit being a Harris." Booker groans, pulling on the tight fabric beneath his sweats, awkwardly adjusting his package.

"I don't even fit in mine," Gareth says, tweaking his athletic shorts and pulling his T-shirt down over his head. "We need an addendum to this clause. We have to wear shorts or something."

"Yeah, same problem here, bro," Camden states, striding out from behind the makeshift changing room we created in the vacated media tent.

He's not covering anything up. Literally. I wince at the sight of his nut sack spilling out the sides. At least he shaved I guess.

Okay, I'll admit, this idea is ridiculous. But first of all, I would do just about anything for my wife. And second of all, when Belle told me the amount of money we could make with a viral YouTube video, I suddenly became a lot less embarrassed.

I pin my three brothers with a serious look. More serious than I feel, standing here in a pair of joggers with two neon straps over my shoulders that cover my nipples. "Look. I know this is crazy. I know that we're going to look like a bunch of wankers out there. But we're Harrises. We rise above it. We're not too proud to do something a little outside the box. Those people are out there on the street with a lot less, and we would give the shirt off our backs to anyone who needed it and that's what this represents."

I snap the neon fabric on my chest and Gareth's shoulders shake with silent laughter. Camden and Booker are less concealed in their blatant amusement.

I continue, "It's a hundred thousand pounds with major potential for so much more."

"But we could pay the difference," Gareth states.

I sigh and shake my head. "It's not just about the money. It's about making a splash. Going big. This ridiculous idea will set up the charity for life. It's going to go viral, and that will enable us to help even more people."

"Or scare people away," Booker grumbles.

"Not if we do it right. Not if we do it loud and proud as only Harrises can."

Camden leans over to Gareth's ear. "Is it just me or are you getting a Braveheart freedom speech vibe right now?"

"It's for a great cause!" I roar. "Now let's go out there, bro up, cup our nutty buddies, and do this!"

We cover up the rest of ourselves and make our way out of the tent to the makeshift stage where crowds of people are gathered to watch the start of the race. If I was nervous before, now I'm completely cool as a cucumber. There's something kind of empowering about wearing this mankini. I might have to make this a thing.

My whole family is standing in front of the crowd of several hundred people. Hayden has Rocky in his arms; Indie and Vi are talking quietly to Dad; and Booker, Gareth, and Camden walk up to join them, looking awkward as fuck.

My eyes land on a bright red mane of hair, recognising the man immediately.

Frank.

He tips his head to me with a sneaky smirk, and I shake my own back at him. He might be the most brilliant pervert I've ever met.

I clear my throat to speak into the mic. "I don't have a lot to say, but I do have some people I want to thank. First of all, thank you all for coming, either as athletes participating in the run, friends and family here to show support, or all of you who donated today. We've raised a lot of money and it makes me incredibly proud because I know it's only the beginning.

"Shirt Off My Back started because a man helped me who didn't have a shirt to spare. He literally had nothing but was willing to give me everything. And it made me realise that, as a professional athlete, I wasn't giving enough. So I hope to make a big impact here today."

I pause and exhale, anxiety spiraling inside of me over what I'm about to do. I look at my brothers, who look like they're about ready to vomit or cry. I can relate. A nervous smile breaks across my face. "And to throw a wrench in the mix, my brothers and I have a little surprise for everyone to make today…extra memorable."

I can see everyone looking around like they are expecting some big pop star to come running in to bring the house down or something. We'll be bringing the house down all right.

Belle smiles bigger than I think I've ever seen, Vi frowns with confusion, and I swear I hear Frank's cackle from somewhere in the distance.

"Let's have a good race!" I shout and hop down off of the stage, heading straight for Belle. Her face is the picture of amazement as I grab her and plant a sloppy kiss on her lips. "Just remember, you asked for this."

She giggles and looks me up and down. One would have thought she'd be disgusted by what I'm about to do, totally turned off by the strips of neon lycra peeking out beneath my clothes. But the fire I see in the dark pools of her eyes forces me to look away before I grow right out of this getup.

She stands on her tiptoes to whisper in my ear, "Is it completely mad that I'm turned on thinking about what you're wearing under your clothes right now?"

I lick my lips and side-eye her. "Completely. But I would expect nothing less from you."

She giggles and moves in closer. "The worst part of all of this is that Frank would have donated the money regardless."

"He what?" I exclaim, rearing back, my shock so great I think my heart stopped.

She yanks me down by the shirt and murmurs against my lips, "But you doing this only made me fall in love with you even more."

Despite my shock, I kiss her, completely powerless to my attraction when she's like this. When we break apart, we're both laughing.

"Wife," I husk. "You really are crazy."

"Husband, you love my crazy." Her smile is bigger than life.

I growl and kiss her chastely one last time, then jog over to join the runners waiting at the starting line. *No going back now.*

Belle's laugh echoes in my ears as my brothers stand beside me. There are at least sixty athletes stacked up behind us—big names that only Harris connections could pull in. They are about to have a view of their lifetime right now.

The man with the starting gun looks at me, and I hold up a finger to him and swerve my gaze to Vi and Hayden located at the other end of the line. Hayden is holding Rocky and waving her cute chubby little hands at me.

"I'm not proud, boys," Camden groans.

"I immediately regret this decision," Booker states.

"Fucking Tanner," Gareth growls.

"Vi," I yell and wait for her gaze to find mine. "Cover Rocky's eyes."

"What?" she screams.

Thankfully Hayden's action is immediate and he shields my poor niece's innocent sight.

And then…we strip.

But it's nothing like the Magic Mike body roll, head-snapping strip show that you see on the telly or in the Las Vegas shows. It's more like overly muscled men fighting the foetal position.

Laughter erupts all around us as we wrench our shirts off over our heads and quickly slip out of our sweats. We begin kicking everything off to the side with our feet because our hands are all busy cupping our twigs and berries.

"What the fuck?" I hear a random voice shout amongst the laughter.

I see a few other parents turn their kids away from the scene. The god awful scene.

"Boys!" Vi admonishes.

I can't even bring myself to look at my dad. I don't know if I'll ever be able to look him in the eyes again.

But I see my wife laughing so hard with Indie that she has tears streaming down her face.

God, I love seeing her laugh.

The sight of her like that turns my insides to pudding and, despite my current get-up, all I can think about is how wonderful it is to see her so happy.

Eyes locked on her, I lean over and murmur to Camden, "I can't wait to get her pregnant."

"What?" Camden exclaims, but I don't bother looking at him.

"We're ready!" I yell.

Before Camden has a chance to ask another question, the gun sounds.

Then, we—the four Harris Brothers—lead the pack, proving to

everyone that there is absolutely nothing we wouldn't do for each other.

However, what I would do for Belle tops even them. And that is something I never realised was a possibility in my life.

I think it was Oscar Wilde who said life imitates art. Well, to the Harris family, football imitates life. My brothers and I developed into our prospective roles in life by mirroring our spots on the pitch.

Camden and I are strikers, both always poised and ready to attack. We create the rhythm of the pitch, a dance of giving and taking, passing and shooting. We control the highs. We gift the biggest moments. Together, we shoot for the glory, but it's always in service to the greater goal.

Booker is the gate keeper. He has blinders on to anything outside of the poles because nothing matters more than protecting what's inside his web. He's not intimidating at first glance, but when you look beneath his soft, quiet demeanour, there's a ferocity to him that would kill for what's his.

Gareth is a defender. He's a proud, solid guard, rugged in his style of play but strong in his attack. He shields what's behind him with stoicism and grace, never buckling to even the most intense pressure. It's all because what he hides from people is what he holds most dear.

Above all of us is our sister, Vi, and our dad, Vaughn. They are the tactical manoeuvres. One battles for personal praise, the other, for professional excellence. Both immersed in the game, a tangled web of behaviours. Both fighting a slightly different goal, but each picking up where the other left off.

But the women in our lives. The women who break us Harris men…They are the fiercest of all. Because it is *they* who inspire our Happily Ever Afters.

Now, we wait to see what's in store for Gareth and Booker. Hell, maybe even Dad someday.

The End

There's more Harris Brothers Love coming!
Sign up for my newsletter to be notified of the next release date.
www.AmyDawsAuthor.com

Or check out some of the secondary characters available now.
Camden and Indie: *Challenge*

Hayden and Vi: *That One Moment*
Reyna and Liam: *Not The One*

Read on for the full list of my work.

More Books by Amy Daws

The London Lovers Serie:
Becoming Us: Finley's Story Part 1
A Broken Us: Finley's Story Part 2
London Bound: Leslie's Story
Not the One: Reyna's Story

A London Lovers/Harris Brothers Crossover Novel:
Strength: Vi Harris & Hayden's Story

The Harris Brothers Series:
Challenge: Camden's Story
Endurance: Tanner's Story
Keeper: Booker's Story
Surrender & Dominate: Gareth's Duet

Payback: A Harris Brother Spin-off Standalone
Blindsided: A Harris Brother Spin-off Standalone
Replay: A Harris Brother Spin-off Standalone
Sweeper: A Secret Harris Brother Standalone

The Wait With Me Series:
Wait With Me: A Tire Shop Rom-Com
Next in Line: A Bait Shop Rom-Com
One Moment Please: A Hospital Cafeteria Rom-Com
Take A Number: A Bakery Rom-Com

Pointe of Breaking: A College Dance Standalone by Amy Daws &
Sarah J. Pepper

Chasing Hope: A Mother's *True* Story of Loss, Heartbreak,
and the Miracle of Hope

For all retailer purchase links, visit:
www.amydawsauthor.com

Acknowledgements

Oh my goodness! What FUN I had with Tanner and Belle! A mankini ending was an idea I had early on in the book. I knew it was a risky, wild, and wacky sort of finale to an love story, but if you're a member of the Amy Daws London Lovers Fan Group on Facebook, then you know how hilarious I find mankinis. And if ever there was a couple to do something that crazy, it would be Tanner and Belle. I hope you loved my crazy.

I have so many people to thank for helping me with this book.

First, my alpha readers Jaci, Julia, Bethy, and Belinda. I like a lot of hand-holding with the Harris Brothers because they stress me out! Having you read as I write made this process so much more fun. I love that you become just as invested in these characters as I do, and I love that you push me! Thank you for dealing with my crazy author neuroses. Your endurance for me is astounding!

My British sounding board, Lynsey! Thank you for replying to my copious amounts of British lingo inquiries. It's not easy being an American author writing English characters, but having you on my team makes it miles more fun. I freaking love you, Bruv!

To all my killer betas and proofers that read quickly and give me thoughtful feedback, thank you! You push me and I appreciate you helping me make my books the best they can be. I loved having you on my beardy Harris rollercoaster. (That almost sounds like mustache ride.)

My editor, Stephanie! Thank you for knowing my characters inside and out and helping me stay true to them for every book. I owe you a new notebook for the awesome notes you keep of my work. You're the best. Never quit me!

My London Lovers reading group. This book was dedicated to you. You guys make writing fun. Thank you for allowing me to torture you with Mankini Mondays and embracing my crazy. Your love for the Harris family is unwavering and I am enjoying the hell out of this ride with you all.

To my hubby. Thank you for accepting the times I need to be absent from life to get the words out. These characters consume me, but it's your support that drives me. I'll try not to release another book during tax season! (That's probably a lie, but at least the thought is there.)

To my Lolo girl. You get more like me every day and that both thrills and terrifies me. I will always embrace your crazy and I will always dance with you like no one is watching.

To my sky babies. It's crazy that there was a time in my life when I lost six babies. For how happy I am today and how wonderful I see life now, I know that I wouldn't be where I am without having gone through all of that. You six are my life barometer. You help me see the beauty in the mundane because losing all of you was anything but ordinary. Thank you for making my life extraordinary.

More about the Author

Number 1 Amazon Bestselling author Amy Daws writes spicy love stories that take place in America, as well as across the pond. She's most known for her footy-playing Harris Brothers and writing in a tire shop waiting room. When Amy is not writing, she's likely making charcuterie boards from her home in South Dakota where she lives with her daughter and husband.

Follow Amy on all social media channels, including Tik Tok under @amydawsauthor

For more of Amy's work, visit: www.amydawsauthor.com

Made in the USA
Las Vegas, NV
19 December 2022

63479513R00182